I0672274

Flight of Destiny

Francis H. Powell

Savant Books and Publications
Honolulu, HI, USA
2015

Published in the USA by Savant Books and Publications
2630 Kapiolani Blvd #1601
Honolulu, HI 96826
http://www.savantbooksandpublications.com

Printed in the USA

Edited by Doris Chu/Daniel S. Janik
Cover by Francis H. Powell; Cover Artwork by Francis H. Powell

Copyright 2015 Francis H. Powell. All rights reserved. No part of this
work may be reproduced without the prior written permission of the
author.

13 digit ISBN: 978-0-9886640-9-8
10-digit ISBN: 0988664097

All names, characters, places and incidents are fictitious or used
fictitiously. Any resemblance to actual persons, living or dead, and any
places or events is purely coincidental.

Dedication

To Stéphanie Prost: It took us a long time to meet, but I'm eternally happy we did, being now not only my wife, but mother to our wonderful little boy, Robin.

To Alan Clark, for his continual encouragement and for setting me on the short story trail with *Rat Mort*.

To Nina Zivancevic, for introducing me to her world of creativity and her ensemble of creative friends.

To Rupert Thompson: a long lost friend, great writer, and a big inspiration.

To Andrew Tyler: a great artist.

To Brook Fischer, formerly Bacon, from Orange County, a bundle of positive energy.

And, to my mother, an inspiration throughout my life.

Table of Contents

Forward

Arrival...1

Snatched..15

Opium...29

Bug-eyes...41

Seed..57

Mutant..77

Maggot..89

Little Mite...105

Gomford...117

Blind Shot..143

Black Widow..163

The Duke..179

Bitch...193

Slashed...203

Visitors...221

The Pact...237

Flawless..249

Two Sides of the Truth..261

Body Parts..269

Branded..283

Fire and Brimstone..301

Cast from Hell...317

About the Author...345

Other Works by this Publisher....................................346

Flight of Destiny

Forward

As publisher and editor of this unique collection of short stories, I am generally disinclined to take up pen and also provide a forward. In this case, however, I had no choice. Francis' short stories, both individually and collectively beg for such.

I'm not entirely sure that "short stories" is the best name for these highly atypical works. While they are short stories in general presentation and length, they seem to me more like long reflections in that newest of genres, flash fiction. Each seems to have that new genre's gutsy "he was born, he lived, and died" feeling about it. In addition, many of the stories, sometimes under the guise of rambling storytelling, cut incisively to the quick and include an unexpected, sometimes totally bizarre ending. One is left with a sense of twisted justice bordering on amorality, causing a Kafkaesque series of slaps to the reader's face, awakening him or her to what is a completely new world more surreal than just.

In the tradition of Rod Sterling's *Twilight Zone*, things in *Flight of Destiny* typically aren't what they seem. They are rather reflections of a parallel, but darker, often fatalistic *noir* world that proceeds quite independently by it's own machinations to grind away at the grist of humanity for what appears no apparent purpose.

And yet…

While this parallel world may seem indifferent to us, one can't afford to be indifferent to it. Mortal creatures, of need, assign meaning to everything, whether pleasant, untoward, or serendipitous, in spite of whether the person, place or event indeed has any. We do it because we must to survive the otherwise insanity of it all. It is, I suspect, these oddly assigned meanings that humans associate with life during that brief interlude on earth from eternity that is used in turn to define the very eternity from which we originally come, and ultimately prepare us for what, if anything, awaits us.

- Daniel S. Janik, 2014

Francis H. Powell

Flight of Destiny

Not everyone is destined to have a life that runs smoothly. Often we are the victims of cruel fate. Yet, sometimes the downtrodden and oppressed rise up against all odds and take revenge!

- Francis H. Powell

Flight of Destiny

Arrival

"*Mr. Weisler* is coming! Mr. Weisler is *coming*! *Mr. Weisler is coming!*" The words swirled around in his head like a rampant tornado, scooping up all his thoughts, amplifying them until the mixture seemed ready to devour him. Yet, what was most vexing was that he could neither connect to nor put a face to the name.

He understood the imperative, "Mr. Weisler is coming!" but who exactly this Mr. Weisler was, when exactly he would be coming, and why he should personally be concerned with his coming were questions that loomed like vast vortices in the maelstrom of his mind. For a man with a normally tidy mind, perplexities like this tormented him. Maybe he and this Weisler had crossed paths somewhere in the past, but if so, the details of their encounter were hidden deep in the chasms of his memory. The name echoing in his mind smothered, crushed, then absorbed him, as if he were a field mouse caught in the coils of a ravenous snake, and no matter how hard he tried to shake it, the feeling would not let go.

Neither impulsive or fractious, Branden Jay Houseman, a man in his mid-thirties, rough-skinned, dark-haired, doe-eyed, was a meticulous man who, at the end of every workday, serially lotioned his hands, slicked back what remained of his thinning hair, and splashed his face with cold water before slipping into evening clothes. Normally, he was a man with a retentive memory, and could pinpoint places, names and faces effortlessly, even recall events stretching back over the years. But whatever way Branden looked at it, he simply couldn't place Weisler and this left him feeling desperate. Leafing through his neatly kept address book proved fruitless. There were some "W's, "namely, "Watson," "Williams," several "Weston's" (long time friends of the family) and even an errant "Wildebeast" and a "Wurst," but no Weisler.

He searched next through the local telephone directory for the name, but there was no name listed that was even close.

He began making mental lists to jog his memory. There was the list of his ex-bosses, and several lists of ex-lovers with previous and present partners. There was the list of relatives, both close and distant, but scouring the lists, even the remotest branches of the family tree, there was no inkling of a Weisler.

Frustrated, Branden directed his mind to wander wider and deeper into both past and present: television broadcasts he'd watched, radio shows he'd recently listened to, business contacts from overseas, friend's who'd had guests staying with them. Nothing. Branden rolled the name across his tongue. Perhaps the *sound* of the name would reveal something about its owner? Weisler sounded German, but in all probability he could equally be American or Canadian with Germanic roots. Was the man a Muslim, Christian, or Jew, or of some other religious bent? Was he heterosexual, homosexual, bisexual, or perhaps something even more exotic? Was he a "somebody," or, perhaps by intent, a complete nobody?

Branden resorted to scouring recent newspapers. Maybe "Mr. Weisler is coming" had been a barely noticed headline? Finding nothing of the kind in any of the several newspapers to which he customarily subscribed, he imagined himself walking down a street, perhaps noting the troublesome statement on the front page of a magazine at a paper stand, or on a piece of a discarded paper lying on the street that flickered momentarily into his frame of vision. But no, try as he might, he could recall no references of any kind to Weisler. Weisler, to be blunt, simply wasn't newsworthy. Nonetheless, "Mr. Weisler is coming" kept roiling incessantly in his mind, like a radio broadcaster shouting an urgent warning in advance of an impending disaster.

While still reeling from the weight of the mantra echoing inside his head, his live-in partner of five years returned home from her secretarial job, and he decided to broach the subject with her. Perhaps she could shed some light on the confusion. Perhaps *she* could place the name Weisler.

"Darling, I'm back," she called out, lazily shaking off the dusting of rain that had accumulated on her umbrella during her walk home.

Branden tried to act normally, to contain his suffering, suppress it, cast it away, as best he could. "Hi, darling. Did you have a good day at work?" he mumbled, spreading out on the sofa to create an impression of normality.

"Not so bad," she replied in the same voice she normally applied to such a mundane question, not wishing to elaborate further.

"Great," he replied. A labored conversation followed, during which he chose his moment to ask in a hushed voice, "Darling?"

"Yes," she answered, her eyes widening, her voice quivering ever so slightly with anticipation, as if perhaps he were at last about to ask her to marry him.

He returned her quizzical stare with one of precision and intensity, his eyes bearing on hers like those of an interrogator about to pry out a last, most important piece of information. "Do you know a man named Weisler?"

The question hung in the air like a lover's accusation, carrying with it an unknown weight and pertinence. He and Melissa were a good match despite their age gap, she being in her late twenties. Shedding her raincoat, she busied herself in tidying up. She was always tidying up herself or the apartment even though both were always spotless. "Um, no, should I?" she finally answered nonchalantly, the furrow between her raised eyebrows making her look vaguely puzzled by the question.

He suddenly felt foolish and wished he had kept the name to himself. He wanted to drop the subject, but, of course, once broached, Melissa would not let this happen, he having effectively opened the vault of her curiosity.

"Who is this Weisler?" she demanded softly, a frown now accompanying the furrow between her eyebrows.

"Well, you see, that's the problem," he lamented. "I simply don't know."

Melissa brushed a stray strand of chestnut brown hair back into place and feigned a laugh. "So, why ask me about a man called Weisler?" she demanded with a fraught expression, wondering what had possessed him to inquire of her so directly. There had never been room for outsiders between them. Their world was too tight, too insular.

"I don't really know," he offered, shrugging his shoulders and drawing in a sharp breath. "The name just popped into my head, like a pesky jingle, and I simply couldn't place it. It's been nagging at me ever since."

"Perhaps he was one of your university friends?" she offered pragmatically, shrugging her shoulders. "Someone you've forgotten over the years. It happens, you know."

"Yes, you're probably right," he responded, nodding gently in accord.

While talking, she had slipped from her work clothes into a showy red skirt and matching top she had placed on a chair next to the sofa before going to work.

She was obviously going out.

He watched her as she replaced her work stockings with a pair of flamboyant orchid-pink ones, kneading them deliciously up her shapely legs.

"Are you going somewhere, darling?" he asked, glancing at her from the sofa, having already surmised that she was.

"I'm going out for the evening," she called back to him casually. "I thought I told you this morning."

"I don't recall your saying you were going out tonight," he said, reflecting.

"A little gathering with some of the girls from work." Her face seemed to light up with the thought of the night ahead. "There's some food in the 'fridge, if you're hungry," she suggested before carefully applying lipstick with a lip brush. With some reticence, he reminded

5

himself it was just like her to forget failing to inform him and then suddenly springing it on him at the last minute. *With "the girls,"* he reminded himself, letting out a sigh of relief.

"You don't mind, do you?" she asked while hitching up her skirt.

"No, no," he replied, disguising his disappointment. "You go and have fun."

Before he knew it, she'd given him a cursory kiss on the cheek, and was closing the door behind her. He listened bleakly to her hurried footsteps trailing away. He was once again alone and prisoner to his nagging thoughts.

Drawing in a breath of the strong musky perfume she had sprayed liberally about her before her hasty departure, he sighed again. The scent reminded him of the glaring void left by her absence.

The words "Weisler is coming" abruptly and rudely re-entered his mind, this time louder and even more unrelenting. "Weisler" had taken on the demeanor of an uninvited guest, outstaying any welcome, the type of guest who drinks the last drop of one's prized cognac, and smokes the last of one's fine cigars—the rare ones bought with difficulty from Cuba and saved for a special occasion. Such detestable manners! Such vulgarity! The impertinence of the intrusion alone was impropriety stretched to its limit.

It wasn't long before terrible thoughts began to infest his mind. *A gathering of her coworkers. At night!* a voice in his head began whispering, then shouting. The words jarred him, their earlier honesty now sounded hollow, their implication ominous. Why would she come back from work, dress up, and then go out to meet the same girls she'd been talking with all day at work—girls with whom she'd often said she never had much affinity? There was this, allied to the fact he was now almost certain she had not mentioned the gathering earlier that morning. In fact, now that he thought about it, she'd never gone out "with the girls" at night before, so why now?

He'd always trusted and never questioned her, despite the fact that she was younger, high-spirited, and clearly enjoyed the attentions of younger men. He'd realized from the start that men naturally lusted after her, but up to this critical moment, he'd had had no reason to believe she would be unfaithful. He'd seen her enjoy, then fend off attention, stating clearly that she was "in a relationship" and unavailable.

When he'd asked her about Weisler, her replies *seemed* innocent. But what if that was all a big act? What if she knew the man, or, worse still, she was involved with him? It wasn't beyond the realm of possibility. This Weisler was quickly becoming a real threat, in effect, stealing from him the love of his life with impunity.

On the other hand, perhaps the weight of "Weisler is coming" was actually a self-premonition, a warning for him to be more attentive to his lover, to keep a more watchful eye on her. Yet, if it was, what really could he do? His mind was split, one part urging him to run and catch up with her, the other directing him to silently follow her…but that was absurd! What if she spotted him in the process? Worse still, what if she led him to Weisler? Then the mystery would be over, to be replaced by a long and painful truth, like the stitches of an old wound bursting open.

The more rational part of his mind insisted his thoughts were being egged on by pure paranoia emanating from this new obsession with Weisler. Weisler was playing mind games with him. Wreaking havoc, as if on some kind of cruel personal crusade.

Melissa's night out was surely just that: an innocent night out with some workmates, an evening of much-needed female bonding.

Some drinks, light banter, a few stories about men and jibes about their bosses, and she would return home satisfied. No harm done.

When she returned, they would discuss her night out over a nightcap. Yes, that's what he'd do: wait for her on the couch. Once settled home, she would doubtlessly curl up on the sofa beside him, flash that mesmeric smile of hers, and slip invitingly out of her clothes in that alluring way of hers. They would soon be wrapped in each other's arms. Perhaps they would make love, and the name Weisler would be jettisoned, all but forgotten, dispatched once and for all, the demon finally off his back, the name turning out to be no more than a folly of his over-active mind.

He decided to eat, even though he wasn't really hungry. The chicken scraps he found in the refrigerator were dry and tasteless, and he picked at them slowly, as if each mouthful was a duty. A half-bottle of wine embellished the otherwise prosaic meal.

As he downed the last of the wine, he thought he heard footsteps outside. They sounded, however, too solid to be Melissa's. Could they be Weisler's? The footsteps stopped, then resumed approaching the door. Had Weisler arrived at last? Was this to be the final unveiling?

The footsteps faltered, then reversed and when they continued past his apartment, Branden let out a sigh of relief. It was probably a man who had had too much to drink, or a person of absent-minded disposition, who couldn't place his rightful abode. The error discovered, the man had continued on his way. Either way, it wasn't Weisler.

The food he'd eaten began to feel heavy in his stomach, and in time, the discomfort progressed to cramps. Perhaps the chicken had been off a bit. The malevolent voice of Weisler inside him laughed sardonically at the thought, projecting an even darker one: Perhaps

Melissa, in her singular haste to rush into Weisler's arms, had poisoned the chicken? The very thought of poison made the cramps stronger and more unbearable. The knot in his stomach continued to worsen, so he got up, shuffled to the bathroom and rifled through their medicine cabinet. To both his surprise and disappointment there was nothing to aid him. Bent over, grasping his excruciatingly painful belly, he staggered to the bedroom and threw himself on the bed. He felt an inexplicable pressure building inside him, as if an entity which had somehow embedded itself in his stomach was now slowly but methodically clawing its way out.

Writhing on the bed, screaming in agony, the buttons of his shirt popping as his stomach continued distending, his last cohesive thought was that the force inside him was seemingly poised to make a decisive thrust to exit his belly. Something jostled inside him and he watched with horror, the seam of his belly split open like a ripe watermelon. Blood, the deep red of mature geraniums, began pouring out, soaking the bedsheets and dripping onto the floor.

As he watched in stunned astonishment, a pair of wrinkled, baby-sized hands appeared from within the opening, followed by a grapefruit-sized, shiny bald head. The two hands grasped tightly onto either side of the ragged incision and began stretching the cleft wider until the head popped out. The head to Branden's surprise was fully developed, like a man in his twilight years, replete with age-lines, wrinkles, and sagging features. The eyes turned and stared back at him blankly, without recognition, as if awakening from a long deep sleep.

The entity pushed the rest of its body from Branden, fell limply onto the bed, then dropped with a thud onto the floor, where it began a process of stretching and enlarging itself to that of a full-sized fully-formed man. Branden heard the man groaning and panting, and, as he continued to unfold, saw him become more animated. The last thing Branden saw before he slipped from consciousness, was the triumphant look of a being who had accomplished its sortie.

When Branden came around, though his head throbbed terribly, his aching lower body was, to his relief, visually back to normal without scar or blemish. There was no sign of blood anywhere. The sheets, which he vaguely recalled gripping tightly about him, were unsullied. But to his dismay, *he was also not alone.*

Branden tried to focus on the other person in the room, attempting to ascertain if it was a neighbor who, hearing his discomfort, had come to his aid, or perhaps his partner, returned from her night out. There was, of course, the far more unpalatable prospect that it was the man who had burst from within him like some aberrant newborn.

It soon became apparent that it was indeed the despicable man who'd so contemptuously exited his belly. The man by now was fully clothed in a somber, dark-gray suit, flamboyant yellow tie, and shoes polished to dazzling perfection. He had a thick head of black hair, obviously dyed, which he was meticulously styling in front of Brandon's bedroom mirror, making sure every hair was in place. He had an aristocratic *panache*, which, in other circumstances, Brandon would have admired.

"Do I know you?" inquired the intruder casually, talking with a strong Germanic accent and a decidedly feminine lilt to Branden's reflection in the mirror while he continued preening, his eyes searching for any last imperfections.

An agonizing silence ensued.

"Well, you don't have to..." the visitor began, shrugging his shoulders.

He was interrupted by Branden, who cleared his throat to ascertain if he could talk. "I don't think so," Branden responded at last, still dazed and confused.

Satisfied with his appearance, the stylish narcissist turned gracefully about and offered a faint smile. "Well," he replied calmly, "I suppose I should present myself. My name is Weisler," he said, smiling broadly and extending a hand. The two men awkwardly but politely shook hands like businessmen concluding an important transaction.

During the time his hand was in contact with Weisler's, Brandon felt two conflicting feelings: An unyieldingly strong sense of hatred towards Weisler (the man had, after all, violently taken possession of his mind and then abused his body), and, in stark contrast, an overwhelming sense of awe and affection for the man before him. After all, he and the man were connected. Weisler had come from out of his body, and the physical connection, like a mother might feel, though technically severed, remained embedded in his memory.

Weisler drew in a sharp breath. "I must excuse myself," he said, taking a quick glance at the mirror to check his appearance one final time. "I have another engagement, you see." He walked, though it would be more correct to say he glided out of the room, like a swan moving on a still pond. Weisler afforded no explanation as to what had happened, and appeared to have no further concern for the man from whose abdomen he had exited. Branden, at the same time, felt rendered helpless by Weisler, who seemed in total control of the situation.

Branden listened to Weisler's delicate steps diminish. Firmly rooted to his bed, Branden couldn't yet conceptionalize what had happened. His body, though no longer tender nor showing any signs of the abuse, had, nonetheless been violated. He had, he decided, been

11

somehow used as a vehicle by Weisler to insert himself into Brandon's world.

Feeling helpless, with all sense of reality blurred, Branden drifted in and out of consciousness. After an undefined period of time, he re-awoke to the sound of footsteps once again approaching his house from outside. This time, he heard a key inserting into the door lock, the metallic click of the lock releasing, and the creak of the door as it yielded. A person entered.

"Had a nice evening, darling?" he heard his partner call to him from downstairs.

A moment later, she was in the bedroom sitting beside him on the corner of the bed, pealing off her skirt and stockings. He nodded, but, try as he might, he could force no words from his open lips. He didn't want to take the chance of destabilizing their relationship with an insane story of a man called Weisler crawling out of him. He had never before withheld vital information from her, but, then, there had never been a man like Weisler, to his best recollection, meddling so overtly in his life. In fact, he was not even sure *he* believed what he'd experienced. Perhaps he'd conjured Weisler from some dark chasm of his mind. There was, after all, no longer any physical evidence that the man had ever been present.

"How was your evening?" he inquired, surprised to suddenly be able to speak.

"It was great," his lover cooed. She fixed herself a nightcap from the bedroom liquor cabinet, and looked like she was bursting to divulge some fantastic news. "I have something I simply can't wait to tell you," she finally blurted out, placing the emptied nightcap glass down on top of the cabinet.

"Oh?" he half-asked, half-stated.

"You mentioned a man named Weisler earlier, and guess what? I met him! He appeared out of nowhere and introduced himself just as we girls were about to go our separate ways. He said you two had recently met. It's not like you, Branden, to forget a name, especially after just meeting the person."

"Yes, that's right," Branden agreed unconvincingly, a haunted look passing over his face. "It, ah, must have somehow slipped my mind. Now that I recall, it was an exceedingly brief encounter."

As Melissa loosened her hair and began combing it out, her eyes lit with wonder. "He was a most delightful man. All the girls fell instantly for him," she responded, then stopped as if pondering, only to resume a moment later. "So charming. So unlike the usual types who hang around the bar we went to," she concluded.

"I see," Branden mumbled, unsure where the conversation was going. He curled up nervously on his side, facing Melissa, holding his stomach defensively like a beating victim fearing a renewal of blows.

"He seemed the perfect dinner guest, so I invited him for dinner tomorrow night. I hope you don't mind."

"Did he accept? " asked Branden with the greatest of urgency.

"Why, yes, he did," Melissa trilled. "Mr. Weisler is coming for dinner!"

Flight of Destiny

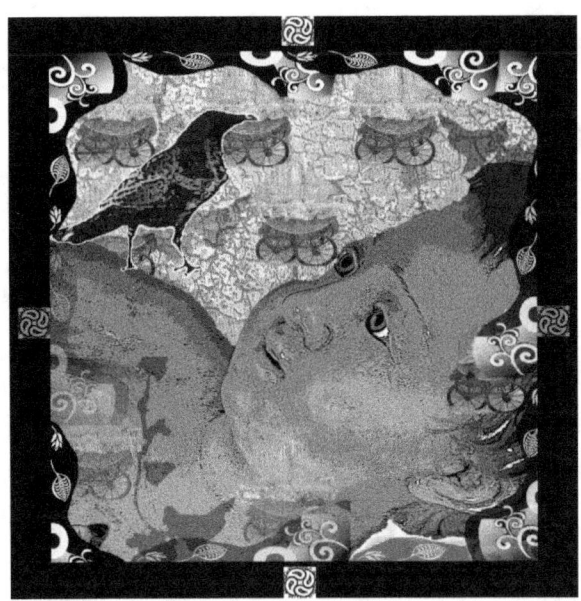

Snatched

Renton Graverson arrived home with a pram which should have had a baby in it. Instead it contained a gaping void, which he should have noticed long before his hysterical wife pointed it out.

"Where's Baby?" Nancy, his wife, shrieked.

Renton couldn't answer her. He hadn't the faintest idea. He had presumed the baby was in the pram, fast asleep, though upon further inspection, it clearly wasn't. He raced out of the house and retraced his steps, repeating in his head the same words over and over like a dark mantra: *Baby's been snatched! Our baby's been snatched!*

He ran along the path, stopping to interrogate every person in the vicinity. The most he got for his efforts were looks of concern, frowns of disbelief, and shakes of heads. How could anyone lose a baby on a walk through a park?

Frustrated, he ran faster, dodging people, gasping, struggling for both breath and words.

Half an hour before, he had been lazily pushing the pram along, his mind admittedly flittering from one subject to another. When it had begun drizzling, he had pulled down the hood. Unfortunately, he couldn't recall noticing Baby. Perhaps sometime while he was distracted—he *was* easily distracted he had to admit—someone had reached in and grabbed Baby, leaving him to carry on pushing an empty pram oblivious to what had happened.

On further thought, he remembered sitting on a bench for a while; there had been some street performers he'd decided to watch. It had turned out to be a lackluster performance, and he wondered if he might have actually dozed a short while. The night before he'd slept restlessly, the baby having cried relentlessly throughout the night. Teething problems, his wife had said.

That morning, he and his wife had had an intense argument, and this, among other things, had also weighed heavily on his mind during the walk. The argument, like many before, flared up out of nowhere. She just went at him, calling him a useless husband and an inadequate father, both of which he'd been constantly labeled ever since the baby had been born, but neither of which he acquiesced to. The day had gotten off to a bad start, but ended immeasurably worse.

When he'd retraced his route forwards and backwards several times with no result, he returned home to the sound of his overwrought wife weeping and calling out repeatedly their missing infant's name. "Jerome! Jerome! Where are you my little one? My lost angel?" When he entered the room, she peppered him with a barrage of new insults, each one with greater intensity.

The police arrived soon after, and, though they had many

questions for him, he didn't have many answers. He could only recount where he had been at each approximate time. As the questioning progressed, Renton did, however, develop a vague recollection of a hooded man, possibly elderly, who seemed to have been following him some of the way. He hadn't got a look at the man's face, so he didn't bring the matter up with the police, thinking it was more wishful thinking than fact. Even if a man had been following him, it was more likely coincidence than anything else.

Renton quickly came to wish he'd never suggested taking the baby for a walk to give his wife a "breather." As a result of his magnanimous gesture he was now facing the biggest calamity of his life, and, furthermore, this latest crisis was putting further strain on what was already an unstable marriage. Her constant outcries that she would hold this blunder against him forever, unless, of course, their baby was soon found, didn't help.

The evening, childless, was unbearable. His wife sat at the dinner table opposite him and stared, wordless, red-eyed, with a bitterness he'd never imagined possible.

There was no word from the police that night or next morning. At noon, a national appeal went out on the radio, which he and his wife listened to with heavy hearts. In the afternoon, the authorities escorted him to a television studio, where he was to make a personal entreaty for their baby's safe return, his wife being too distraught for words. While he fumbled through the appeal, his wife sobbed loudly in the background, her face a picture of abject misery. She was falling apart before his and the nation's eyes, and he was increasingly feeling the culprit. For the public at large, it was one thing to lose a wallet, suitcase, or even one's car, but to lose a baby was another matter entirely. Cruel whispers soon began circulating. Might *he* not have killed the baby and disposed of its body?

Days passed to weeks and weeks to months, and still no clue surfaced as to the baby's whereabouts. The couple's hopes and those of countless others following the drama sank into a bottomless pit of despair. Eventually, the police gave up on the case, saying it was simply taking up to much time and resources. In the meantime, Renton's wife slipped further into depression. She started acting strangely, getting up in the middle of the night like she used to when checking on the baby. It was as if she wouldn't or couldn't break the old routine. Renton decided, not unreasonably, that perhaps they should try for another.

"*Replace* Baby?" she snapped. "Never!" and shook her head vehemently, adding indigently, "How could you be so cruel!"

He immediately dropped the subject.

One evening, Renton arrived home from work, expecting his wife, Nancy, to be in one of what had become her "normal" dark, angry, spiteful moods, only to find her humming contently. It was as if the all-encompassing tension that had gripped their household for so many months had evaporated into thin air. Renton couldn't wait to find out the root of this change.

"Shush," she said quietly. "He's back."

Renton looked at his wife in total astonishment, inquiring in a whisper, "Who's back?"

"Baby, of course," she said, smiling up at him blissfully.

"That's wonderful! Simply wonderful! Can I see him?" he rejoiced.

His wife's mood changed in an instant without any forewarning. Her body tensed, her defenses came up, and an insane anger seemed to well up from inside her. Renton had never seen her in such a state, and trembled just watching her.

"You are *never* to see him!" she screamed wild-eyed. "Never! Not now! Not ever!"

"Come now, dearest. You're being most unreasonable," he protested, thinking, in fact, she had gone totally insane. He shrugged his shoulders in desperation, letting out a pained sigh.

"I've made my decision," she said, calming down at last and presenting him with a sour face. "I don't want you near him. Ever."

"But, darling, he's my child, too," Renton protested, adding defiantly, "I have rights."

"You lost all your rights the day you lost Baby," she said in an angry but hushed voice, as if fearful of waking the baby.

Renton tried one more time. "Alright, but please let me see him just this once, just to check out how he is," he pleaded.

She drew in a sharp breath and looked at him full in the face. "No!"

Renton heard wailing from somewhere upstairs.

"Now look what you've done!" she said accusingly, leaving the room. "Stay right where you are, and don't follow me."

Left on his own while she attended Baby, Renton had little else to do but to reflect. Had he really heard a baby's wail, or was he being caught up in her insanity? Was she able to care for a baby in her condition? And how long would she continue blaming and excluding him? Either way, he'd have to have to call for a psychiatric evaluation —not an easy choice as it would probably result in her piling more animosity on his head. Still, he had do it, if for no other reason than to protect his own sanity.

About eleven o'clock that night, Nancy returned to the living room looking happy, almost beautific. Baby had finally calmed down, she said, and was asleep. Renton looked askance at his wife, and carefully pressed her for details on how the baby had returned.

All she said was, "The doorbell rang, and there was Baby, asleep on the door mat."

This he found as hard to believe as her abrupt changes in personality. After more fraught exchanges, his wife announced that she would retire to their bedroom and that he was to sleep on the couch. Renton decided to do as instructed to avoid any return to the malignancy of their earlier conversation.

The next morning, he dressed in the previous day's clothes, washed and shaved in the kitchen, and went to work, sticking as closely as possible to his normal routine. When he arrived back from work that evening, his wife was waiting for him in the living room. She eyed him suspiciously. Upstairs he could hear vague noises, as if a baby were trying to say words, Renton concluding that "Daddy" would never be one of them. His wife, he noted, had made changes to the house. She had transferred his belongings to the living room, and had placed locks on all the upstairs rooms. When asked about it, she reminded him firmly that he was never to go near the baby. If he attempted such, she warned, he should remember that the house was in her name, her father having originally bought it for her, and she would throw him and all his possessions out onto the street.

Upon hearing this latest condition, Renton felt bound to act. The situation was spiraling totally out of control. "We need to talk, dearest. This simply can't go on," he said in his most earnest voice.

"Hush," she replied. "You'll wake the baby."

He let out a pained sigh of exasperation. "This has gone too far," he said forcibly. "I think you need to see a psychiatrist. This whole thing is absurd. I'm not going to put up with this lunacy."

To his surprise, his wife sat on the sofa, beckoned him to sit beside her, and congenially explained that she had that day taken Baby to the police station to show them he was alive and well.

Renton, imagining this an opening to once again enforce his parental rights, demanded, "I, too, should like to see our baby, and if not..."

She shook her head from side-to-side. "As I told you before, it's out of the question. And a psychiatrist, you say? Why do I need to see a psychiatrist? I see no reason why either Baby or I have need of a psychiatrist; however, a man who loses a baby surely might."

During her reply, his wife stood and began pacing up and down the room. If it was possible, she seemed more agitated than ever before. Then she stopped pacing and looked him directly in the eyes. "Baby and I don't like being threatened," she said in a troubled voice. "And if you do anything to upset either of us, you will not live to regret it."

"Good Lord, woman! I think we need to bring the police back to resolve this issue! Now!" Renton stood and crossed his arms in front of his chest.

His wife's sneer softened to an ironic smile. "As I recall, Renton, the police thought you a suspect the last time you dealt with them. And I could add some pretty incriminating things, should I chose to, like, for instance, that you are proving a menace to Baby and me right now." She jabbed a finger at Renton and warned, "The authorities take a pretty dim view of intimidating fathers."

A sound emanated from upstairs as if in concurrence.

"Now, stop your ridiculous talk about contacting the authorities, and go and warm some milk. Get a move on. We have a baby to look after." The determination in her voice should have comforted him, but instead it chilled him to the bone. He did as she said, mechanically, increasingly fearful of her next move.

Over the next few days, she took care of all of the tasks that directly involved Baby: changing his diapers, washing him, feeding him, rocking and singing to him. Renton was relegated to doing menial supportive tasks, downstairs, completely removed from Baby. Nancy, in fact, spent most of her time upstairs, leaving Renton to buy the family's provisions. His wife called the situation their "new regime," and, while it clearly suited her (she was the happiest he had ever seen her), it didn't suit him at all. He couldn't have been more miserable or felt more oppressed.

Then, unexplainable things started to happen.

One morning he woke to find the refrigerator door open and a chicken lying on the floor, stripped to the bone, as if a wild animal had gotten to it. When questioned about the bones, she declared that she had experienced a sudden pang of hunger during the night. When he cast doubt on her claim, she became viciously sarcastic. "Well, it certainly wasn't Baby, now was it?"

In the coming days, Renton came upon other inexplicable things: a pile of bones that looked like they had been mauled, then a heap of empty jars of baby food piled against a wall. He also noted the food bill rising. Mother and Baby, it seemed, were consuming food at an alarming rate, to the point that Renton began wondering if she might be harboring a flock of babies upstairs. He began dreaming of many babies, each one taking a turn clamping onto one to his wife's breasts and sucking her dry, only to move on to huge quantities of meat when she could provide no more milk.

Things were also being moved around. He discovered, for instance, a family photograph album that included pictures of Baby, just after his birth, some scribbled on, some torn to shreds. It was as if an unseen entity had come to live with them in the house.

One evening his wife came out of Baby's room, displaying a black eye and looking tormented. When he interrogated her, she claimed she had slipped on an errant toy.

Sitting together later that evening, his wife said calmly, "Baby's still mad at you."

He looked at her with astonishment. "What do you mean? I can't imagine he could convey such thoughts at his age," Renton said, shaking his head in disbelief.

She looked at him angrily. "Are you saying Baby is stupid? You haven't shown the slightest interest in his development."

"How can I?" he protested. "You won't let me near him!"

"True," she conceded, "but that doesn't hide the fact that Baby is most displeased with you. I don't suppose you will ever be free from his ire."

"Is there any way I can appease Baby?" he ventured.

"You're simply going to have to live with the fact he can't be appeased, and will probably hate you until your dying day."

"That's not much of a father-son relationship," mumbled Renton dryly.

His wife didn't hear him. It was bath time for Baby, a sacrosanct nightly ritual. Nancy left her husband, as usual, in the living room, and trudged upstairs, where, after a few minutes, Renton heard her gently singing to Baby. He thought or imagined he could hear Baby singing along, and suddenly had an idea.

He knew his wife's evening routine, but because he worked, her daytime routine was largely uncharted. If he could take time off work and surreptitiously return home, perhaps he could catch a glimpse of

Baby and the overwhelming intrigue that was consuming him would be satisfied. Maybe she unlocked Baby's door in his absence; maybe she took Baby out for a stroll during the day. It wouldn't surprise him if she took Baby to see her parents. Perhaps her whole family was in secret collusion, keeping him away from Baby after what he'd done. He was surprised he hadn't thought of this before.

One morning, while out searching for a client's home, he approached a road not far from his house, and saw his wife driving off alone in her car. Feeling like he was stalking his own wife, he decided instead of following her to check an hour later to see if his wife's car had returned. It hadn't. An second hour later, when the car finally returned, she climbed out without the baby, which suggested she'd left Baby alone in the house while she was away. This presented an opportunity. If this was a daily occurrence, he would have plenty of time while she was away to satisfy his curiosity without having to resort to more exotic arrangements.

At work the next day, he approached his boss and apologized, explaining his doctor had called early this morning to remind him of his annual physical examination appointment tomorrow. After discretely checking to make certain his wife was out, Renton entered the house and climbed the stairs, only to find entry to Baby's room inhibited by a sturdy combination lock requiring four numbers to open.

The next thirty frustrating minutes, he tried every combination code he could imagine his wife using. He tried her year and day of birth, and *vice versa*. Nothing. He tried Baby's date of birth. The lock remained resolute. Desperation started to creep in. What if his wife suddenly returned? She was unpredictable enough to do just that. He resorted to random numbers and was at point of giving up, when, on a whim, he substituted numbers for the letters in "Biff," the name his wife had given the teddy bear Baby always went to sleep with. The shackle lock abruptly opened. A palpable sense of relief washed over him as he quietly opened the door.

Baby's room wasn't at all as he remembered it. The room still had the same wallpaper, but in one area the wallpaper had been torn, scratched by what could have been talons of a bird of prey. The familiar cute pictures were still in place on the walls, but the crib had been replaced by a bed big enough for an adult. The floor was littered with chicken and animal bones, and the room had a disgustingly fetid odor to it. An adult-sized portable potty filled with stale urine rested in one corner. He could hear flies tapping lightly against a nearby closed and curtained window. The cabinet next to the bed was draped with a food-splattered straitjacket.

Renton approached the bed, in the process disturbing the body sleeping there. The occupant was not a baby but a fully-grown adult male, a seemingly grotesquely caricature of Baby as Renton remembered him. Around the room were speakers attached to a sophisticated sound system, issuing faint baby noises. It was obviously part of an elaborate and clever deception, but to what purpose, he hadn't a clue.

The man on the bed had his wrists and ankles restrained with metal chains to the corners of the bed. Aware of Renton's presence, the spine figure abruptly bolted upright. "Wha...Wha...what you want?" he asked in a childlike voice filled with innocent wonder. It was a voice Renton had heard before, but couldn't quite place given its high register.

Before Renton could reply, the man's mood shifted from childlike innocence to whirling rage. The man, began muttering wild obscenities and bellowing like a cow that had just been branded, attempting to rise from the bed only to be thwarted by his restraints.

Renton drew back, totally aghast at what he was seeing, his heart pounding.

While the man continued screeching and bawling, it dawned on him that the voice was like that of his wife's father!

Just then, his wife entered the room and stopped, staring first with surprise at Renton, then with horror at the howling abnormality thrashing about in the bed.

"So now you know," was all she could say.

Renton's mind was still grappling with everything. "But…why?" he finally managed to mutter.

She shrugged. "I did it for Baby. To protect him," she answered. A tear formed and rolled down the side of her face.

At first, her statement made no sense to him. Then, it came to him: His wife had more than once mentioned a rare psychological disorder that had struck down several members of her family, changing their behavior into that of a part-child, part-monster. Clearly, the disorder was afflicting her father.

Thinking back, Renton suddenly realized that the hooded figure who had followed Renton that fateful day must have been her father! It was he who had snatched Baby! Nancy's mother must be looking after their real baby at this very moment, while his wife, attempting to save her father from the ignominy of institutionalization, had brought him into their house.

"I did it to protect Baby," she stated.

"Protect Baby from who?" Renton finally asked, attempting to confirm which of the permutations racing through his mind might be correct.

"From *him*, of course," she said, pointing at her demented father, who was now slobbering and muttering infantile nonsense. Hearing his daughter's voice, the man looked meekly up at her and began cooing.

"Good boy," she replied, in the same manner she used with Baby.

A wave of satisfaction course coursed through Renton. When the real truth came to light, he could once again walk the local streets without guilt. Still, that left the observation that his wife, too, seemed to be slipping into the familial madness. With all this insanity, would he ever be able to publicly clear his name and experience real fatherhood? *Perhaps*, he thought, *if I were to snatch the real baby back...*

Flight of Destiny

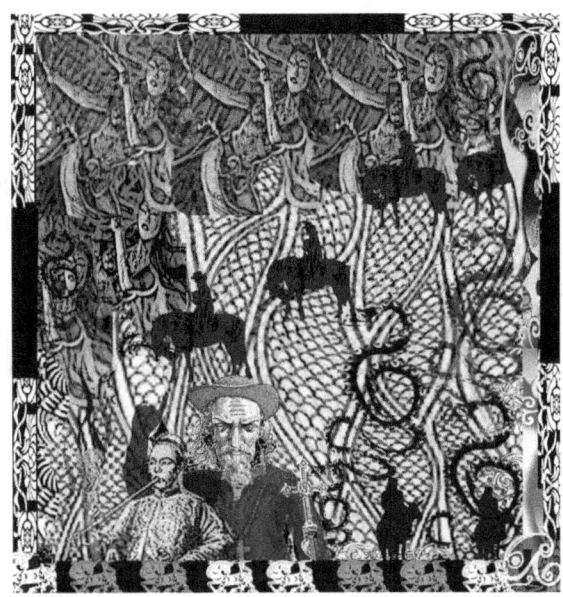

Opium

A time of unparalleled opportunity finally opened after the end of the long and painful Civil War. Southern scalawags and northern carpetbaggers alike were busy creating boomtowns along the newly proposed intercontinental railroad line, and following right behind them was Chinese labor.

Local whites had a passel of showy but pejorative names for them: "koolees," "bamboo coons," "chinks," "chonkies," "choo-choos," "coolies," "pigtails," "'rail hoppers," and just plain "the heathen." As cultures collided, problems mounted. Despite earnest warnings from the local church pulpits, saloons, bordellos and opium dens soon outnumbered homes in the new rail towns. Wages for imported Chinese laborers were so low, and working conditions so poor, there could be little surprise that some of their own would take to managing the increasing numbers of more lucrative forms of employment. Yet, of all these affectations of the times, it was "Mother Opium," who, once she sunk her talons into a man or woman, never let go, leaving these post-war rail towns overrun with sallow-complexioned denizens whose sole reason for existence was drug-induced pleasure. Jacksonville, was, all its citizens would agree, one such town on a decidedly downward trajectory to total moral collapse.

A town council meeting was called by the church elders. A new force was needed to counteract this seemingly unstoppable slide into iniquity, and, at their behest, that force arrived the next day on a spavined, overworked, mangy-looking brute of a horse, scarcely able to navigate the town streets. The rider didn't care about appearances. He put his trust in God to provide for all his earthly needs, including those of his horse. With his unkempt, shoulder-length hair and scraggly beard, he looked a wild man, eyes so full of zeal they seemed able to dig deep into a person's soul. In other rail towns he'd proven a bastion against evil. His fire and brimstone sermons were legendary, and he had a reputation for reaching even the most heinous of sinners, including those acting, in his own words, as consorts of the very devil.

The moment he entered Jacksonville, Preacher Moon felt confident he would leave his mark on the town. From the saddle, he could smell devil opium snaking wafting on the warm, dry, noonday air currents. This was exactly the kind of town that needed him, and he immediately dedicated himself to single-handedly taking on the opium dens, the syndicates supplying the drugs, the brothels, and anyone else attempting to drag Jacksonville down into the murky depths of the abyss. And before the day was out, there was one man in particular he had in his sights: the local gangster-chief of the Green Triad Gang, known to everyone simply as "Gecko." The preacher's first move would be to locate and confront this source of all the evil scourging the town.

Preacher Moon entered the first saloon he came to and made inquires. Moments later, he remounted his feeble horse and headed for the Chinese area on the other side of the half-finished railroad tracks. The saloon-keeper had volunteered that Gecko used Hop Sang's Laundry on St. Louis Street as his headquarters. Preacher Moon had come by the information surprisingly easily, as if the saloon-keeper were curious to see what would happen when the preacher actually confronted Gecko.

As the preacher made his way fearlessly across the tracks, he came upon a melee of drunken men. Two, in the center, were grappling and punching each other in the dusty street. A crowd had assembled about them and was egging on each, without discrimination, to inflict as much physical damage on each other as possible. One of the pugilists had blood seeping from his right ear, undoubtedly the result of a hefty but less than incisive blow.

Preacher Moon pulled his nag to a halt. Despite his inescapable presence, he was hardly afforded a glance. In the end, unwanted and ignored, he concluded that the pain and damage the two were inflicting on each other was most likely merited, and turned his attentions to getting a feel for this part of the town.

Looking about, what disturbed the preacher wasn't really the fight, or, for that matter, the crowd's lack of interest in his presence. It was the sight of a couple in a dark alleyway entwined in an amorous embrace. The woman was wearing a long dress that matched the color of her jet-black hair, giving her exposed skin a deathly white complexion. Her dress and corset were unfastened, and a pale breast was exposed, which the man pressing against her was greedily fondling. The woman was dazedly eyeing a half-empty bottle of whiskey which she was holding in an outstretched hand. The two were completely oblivious of the preacher's disdainful eyes.

Preacher Moon's anger quickly swelled. He dismounted and strode towards the couple, wedging himself between the man and the woman, attempting to separate them.

"Sins of the flesh!" he yelled, his voice booming, his eyes glowing red, as he projected an index finger towards the heavens.

The couple froze, utterly stunned.

The fight in the street stopped in mid-punch.

All eyes turned to him.

"God punishes those who give in to the sins of the flesh! You defile the temple of God, laying on your hands on this woman in such a way," Preacher Moon ranted, ruefully shaking his head, baring yellowed teeth. The damning words, however, seemed without meaning to the dazed couple. They stared at him, pupils dilated, vaguely amused, as if he were a village idiot, then eventually wandered off, giggling together, to continue somewhere else where they'd left off.

Preacher Moon shook his head in disbelief. This didn't portend well. His words, his gestures, even his dispatching of God's wrath hadn't reached them, which infused him with even more fervent desire to break the purported source of this virulent malaise, Gecko himself.

He strode into Hop Sang's Laundry and down the unguarded stairway to the basement. Dismissing all formalities, he smashed open the door with his fist. The scene that greeted him confirmed he had located the source of the town's problem.

Gecko's lair was a dusky, smoky, malodorous room. Crumbling columns with garish, multi-colored dragons sporting ruby-red eyes looked incongruously out-of-place against the peeling ochre walls. The entire cellar appeared as if it might collapse at any moment under the strain of its own load. His eyes latched onto a secluded area, half-hidden by a heavy layer of dense smoke emanating from between two drawn curtains, which he surmised hid an even darker inner sanctum.

The preacher pushed his way past groping couples, dissonant-sounding music and pungent, and sickly, sweet-smelling-smoke to the entrance of the second room. To his surprise, no one bothered to look at or stop him.

The interior of the second room looked like a full scale version of Sodom and Gomorrah. Crumbling silk drapes hung against the walls depicted men and women in all manner of intercourse. Three young, nubile Chinese girls, wearing only a brilliant red midriff sash, their faces painted with colorful pigments, their hair festooned with tawdry trinkets, frolicked from client to client offering lewd suggestive smiles while whispering salaciously into the men's ears. Three disinterested Chinese musicians played intoxicating string music in a distant corner, to which a number of naked men and women on pedestals slithered and gyrated. In the center of the room, an old man stood chanting an what could only be a lascivious poem, encouraging further what was going on all about him.

Everyone else was sitting on the floor, huddled about small low tables. Men with greed in their eyes were gambling away vast sums of money. Winners were delighting loudly their winnings, while the remainder, the losers, quietly cursed their misfortune. Preacher Moon ruefully shook his head, unable to fully comprehend the largesse of the avarice about him corrupting their souls.

When the preacher mentioned the name "Gecko," the nearest denizen gestured languidly towards a beaded curtain, the entrance to yet another room in what was looking to the preacher like an unending labyrinth. Moon picked his way between the tight packed table of undulating bodies, and parted the bead-curtains, entering an even darker room.

"Gecko!" he bawled in a loud, truculent voice, cutting like a knife through a raucous din of incomprehensible Chinese conversation. "The church elders have called me to rid Jacksonville of your foul presence! I warn you, I have bested evil in town after town like this!" he shouted, pointing a bony finger at the center of what appeared to his adjusting eyes to be large table in a lavishly decorated room. "I have come to defeat you and purge your minions of their sins," he continued, his voice, at the end, quavering. "Take heed, as the Lord God is my setter and sword, and I will surely prevail!"

In the relative darkness, the preacher could just make out the low, ornately-carved table in the center of the room with a beautifully decorated cake on it. The cake was surrounded by several dusty bottles of Chinese Maotai liquor and a number of dainty, etched, bone china tea cups. Gecko was reclining behind the table on a very low divan surrounded by bodyguards. He was wearing a finely tailored, white, silk shirt and pants with a grey sharkskin smoking jacket illustrated with gold-embroidered, oriental brocade motifs. To the preacher's surprise, Gecko appeared slender, handsome, and refined with a pleasant, wise-looking face, his sleek black hair pulled back in a braided pig-tail.

"And who might you be?" demanded Gecko, amused at the newcomer's entrance, sensing some fun was about to be had.

"I am God's appointed!" answered Preacher Moon zealously, stiffening his body and extending it to its maximum height to enhance his authority.

"What a privilege," replied Gecko mockingly. As if on command, those about him tittered gently. "You'll have to excuse me, but God's appointed don't often visit my domain," he continued, fingering a heavy gold dragon ring, the sides decorated in green cloissone, that he wore on his index finger, the sign of ultimate authority within the Green Triad.

Preacher Moon instantly disliked everything about Gecko, from his flamboyant appearance and impudent choice of words to the derogatory tone of his voice. His anger in overdrive, Preacher Moon brought the base of the staff he was carrying violently down on the rim of the table, making the teacups tumble and clatter. "You will henceforth stop your activities, or be smitten by the Right Hand of God!"

Gecko considered the threat calmly. "And what form would this punishment likely take?" he asked, as if the preacher's answer might make a difference.

Preacher Moon's features tightened. "You and your family will suffer the heat of Hell's fire throughout all eternity," he clarified, pointing the head of his staff menacingly at Gecko, who remained completely unruffled.

"Belief in a cruel God makes a cruel man," Gecko sighed philosophically. He searched for acknowledgement from his entourage while snapping his fingers. A young girl immediately wafted into the room bearing a bowl of fruit. Her face shone with innocence in the dim light. She was festooned in a long, sumptuous, silk gown, lavishly embroidered with lantern-shaped flowers and vibrant exotic birds with sweeping tail feathers. Pigeon's blood rubies accented fine gold-chains about her neck, waist and wrists. Her winsome eyes locked instantly on Preacher Moon, and her radiant, child-like beauty left its mark on him. The preacher crossed his arms in front of his face as if to protect himself from her image.

Gecko smiled sweetly at the preacher, twiddling the dragon ring on his finger, then glanced at the cake. "Will you not have something to eat with us, Preacher? I was about to cut this cake," he said in a relaxed, convivial way, reaching for a gilded knife placed at its side.

The preacher's face soured. The knife was ornamental and it was clear that Gecko's offer was a gesture of hospitality rather than a threat, and he *was* extremely hungry from the long ride. In truth, he'd lost count of the time since he had last eaten, and then, it had been a handful of grasshoppers he'd come across on his travels. Still, how could he accept food from such a loathsome sinner? "Food from the devil's hand no doubt," he growled in a bitter tone, shaking his head in the negative and averting his eyes from the cake and the exotic fruits the young girl had placed on the table.

"No," contradicted Gecko, "A cake baked by my daughter, here." Gecko beamed proudly.

"Never," replied the preacher, lifting his eyes and staff in the air as if holding up a massive rock and waiting for God to cast it at the tempter before him.

Gecko shook his head. "Isn't it equally sinful to spurn gifts provided by God. Surely this magnificent cake is such a gift. Wouldn't it be wrong *not* to take advantage of an offer of food in order to keep yourself strong in his service? Even Jesus, if I'm not mistaken, indulged in local weddings and feasts." Gecko cut a large slice of cake and as he brought it to his mouth, a look of anticipatory pleasure and contentment swept across his face.

The preacher watched hungrily, searching his estranged mind and soul for guidance.

"Come. Try a bite, Preacher. It would please my daughter who is, as you can see, as sweet as the first apple blossom of spring. Surely you do not want to offend one so young and...innocent?"

Gecko placed the slice on a plate and cut a second, more sizable one, placing it on another. All eyes moved to the preacher, who appeared stuck in quandary.

The young girl took the first plate and offered it Gecko, shyly offering the second to the preacher.

Reluctantly, the intruder laid his staff aside, accepted the plate, took a small bite, sighed, and then literally devoured the remainder, his face broadcasting both unimaginable delight and profound guilt. The cake was delightful, though it had a slightly bitter aftertaste.

"That's better," said Gecko, smiling broadly, having won the first round of brinkmanship.

The noise from the adjoining room abruptly increased. Men were whooping and whistling undoubtedly at a particularly ribald dancer showing off her...the preacher bristled at the thought of what she might be showing. "You offer these poor souls alcohol, drugs and fornication, profaning God's name," he said spreading his arms to encompass all the rooms he'd visited so far. "For this, Jehovah will smite...er...reduce you and your men to...ashes with...ah...fire from the sky!" Preacher Moon tried to regain control, while his stomach rumbled for more of the cake.

"You may be right," conceded Gecko. "However, I prefer to think of what I'm doing as providing these poor wretched souls with some small amount of pleasure and contentment in a world where working people are daily forced to forget the meaning of happiness. What do you provide them with?" he demanded, looking at the preacher through narrowed eyes. "It seems to me that you peddle mainly threats and fear. Your God seems a violent, intolerant, and vengeful one, not unlike these people's masters."

The preacher stiffened, remaining notably silent. Every time he opened his mouth, he seemed to lose a little more ability to think and speak. He'd expected Gecko to be a simple, crude lout, like most of the reprobates he'd felt with before. Though Preacher Moon was clearly not getting anywhere, he still had one more incontrovertible rebuke for Gecko: "I will rest in Paradise while you suffer in hell for your sins," he muttered in his rancor, adding, "'For the wages of sin is death; but the gift of God is eternal life'!"

"Hmm," Gecko said, as if considering the preacher's new warning. "I have a challenge for you." Gecko smiled at Preacher Moon, his daughter, and the others about him in the room. "If you have the power you say, then make the devil appear here in this room, before us all, and make him kneel before you."

The wary preacher knew before Gecko had finished that he was being lured into a trap. He needed to think, but while weighing his options, his normally incisive mind kept drifting. His eyes fixed on a glinting medallion at the base of Gecko's daughter's neck. It seemed to be glowing ever brighter, and he was transfixed. At the same time, he felt himself being drawn into an increasingly serene state the likes of which he'd never experienced before.

When he was again able to focus, he saw to his surprise that Gecko's daughter was no longer clothed: She was standing before him, hands at her sides in resplendent nakedness. A crown of ivy garlanded her head, and a green serpent slithered lazily up her arm. The preacher wanted to warn her, but stopped when he realized she wasn't struggling, but was taking sensual pleasure in the reptile's movement. Her hair was now loose and flowing. Her pupils burned like fiery coals, and she began moving slowly towards the preacher, her body gyrating to the motions of the snake writhing about her. She stopped directly in front of the preacher, grinned, then flicked her tongue at him, a tongue like that of a snake's, narrow and split at the end. The preacher wanted to scream, but all he could think was, *she could catch flies with a tongue like that!*

Preacher Moon tried to reach towards her. He wanted to touch her, but he no matter how much he tried, he could not make contact. He could, however, vaguely make out the sounds of distant voices laughing and mocking him.

His attention shifted to an attendant entering the room, head bowed, carrying a silver platter that was presented to him. The preacher was shocked to see the decapitated head of his horse on the platter, it's eyes wide with supplication, both ears slanted back. Staring at the abomination, the preacher startled when the horse's mouth opened and the head suddenly whinnied plaintively.

The stricken animal's cry jarred him, echoing over and over in his head until the reverend finally spoke: "I…I have somehow raised the devil, and it is in the form of this woman!" No one in the room acknowledged his claim, but no one challenged it, either. Instead, there remained only the irritating background sound of derisive laughter.

Gecko, still stretched out on the divan, was in a state of hysteria. Tears were streaming from his face as the great Preacher Moon slipped into unconsciousness and fell in a heap before him.

When the preacher came around, he was lying outside in the dusty street, shielding his eyes against the harsh glare of the midday sun. An all-Oriental crowd peered down at him like he was some kind of newly discovered bug. Slowly his eyes came into focus.

Gecko was standing above him, his daughter at his side. She was wearing a primrose yellow European frock and bonnet. An ivory lace parasol framed her bewitchingly innocent face. She appeared to be dressed for a special occasion.

It was then the preacher realized his horse was standing quietly next to him. When he tried to sit, he noticed his ankles were bound together and attached by a length of rope to the horn of the horse's saddle.

Gecko calmly raised a hand and abruptly dropping it with a loud shout. The horse bolted, moving quicker than it had done in years, dragging Preacher Moon behind, while the mass of Oriental eyes followed the two, the crowd bemused and sniggering. As the preacher shot out of town, his horse whinnied mightily, sounding like it could go on dragging the preacher for ever and ever throughout eternity.

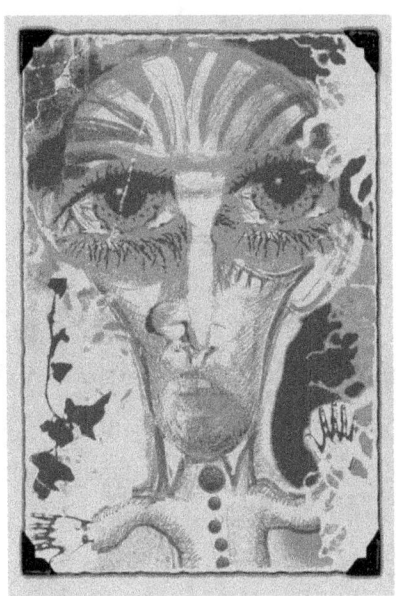

Bug-eyes

Bug-eyes was destined to a life of toil. As his mother, Lady Harriet Lombard, remarked gruffly when holding her swaddled firstborn, "He has disproportionate eyes," adding tersely, "the child's abnormal. Handing the squalling reject back to the doctor, she decreed, "Drop it down the well for all I care."

Dr. Shady, a tall, thin, nervous practitioner from a line of doctors who had served the Lombards for generations, wasn't given to infanticide. After some delicate negotiations with Lord Lombard, the shrieking infant, who should at this point have been profiting from his mother's milk or at least that of a wet nurse, was promptly dispatched to the periphery of the estate where the infant's upbringing became the responsibility of the Lockjaws, who Doctor Shady had known were desperate for a child.

41

Ralston Lockjaw, the Lombard estate gamekeeper, and Hettie, his barren wife, lived in a ramshackle cottage.

The infant was was welcomed heartily by Hettie. Ralston had his reservations, but wisely kept them to himself. A sizable pay increase on the promise of total silence sweetened the pill of having to feed another mouth and tolerate the strange bug-eyed infant. The infant's "death" was officially pronounced by Dr. Shady to all the world, and Lord Lombard determined to keep the child's whereabouts a secret.

Lady Lombard, on the other hand, continued to rue her "cursed luck," blaming the abomination entirely on her husband. In fact, some odd physical defects were known to exist within the aristocratically inbred Lombards. Lady Harriet had hoped for a healthy heir to grace the front cover of many a society magazine, like her society friends and their offspring, not some kind of monstrosity with a grossly conspicuous defect. Over the next several weeks, she took to noting the overly protruding eyes present in the line of Lombard portraits looking contemptuously down at her in the corridors of the huge manor house.

Lady Harriet forgot her displeasure and disappointment when she produced a second male a year later. Thankfully he was far more acceptable-looking. Her husband proudly named him Christopher, and announced his son and heir to the world.

Her third child, Arabella, appeared, at first, a good, balanced edition to the family. However, over time, the girl began to increasingly resemble the couple's supposedly-deceased first infant. The abominable product of her first pregnancy having been theoretically dealt with some years previously and all but forgotten, Lady Harriet felt once again forced to decide the fate of another of "her husband's" offspring. While not entirely untoward, the girl's

42

emerging appearance would, her ladyship concluded, deny her participation in the usual social events; in essence, she would never be fit for "decent" society, let alone secure a suitable husband. One evening, after throwing a postnatal tantrum, Lady Harriet shrieked to the doctor, "Get this baby out of my sight. Dispose of it instantly! Chuck it down the well, like the loathsome firstborn it reminds me of." For the doctor, the Lockjaws once again provided the answer: an additional financial inducement for their silence, and another embarrassing edition to the Lombard family disappeared into their care. After its swift disappearance, Lady Harriet, for her part, announced she was done with child bearing, and that she was turning her attention back to hunting and other "more rewarding pursuits."

Bug-eyes took immediately to his younger sister. In fact he doted on her. With her prominent eyes, she was a child of rare beauty, sporting curly blond locks, skin the color of milk, and lips like ripe pomegranates. Bug-eyes, kept ignorant of his own past, couldn't help but wonder where she'd come from. His sister certainly hadn't been brought into the world by Mumma Lockjaw, that spindly, emaciated woman devoid of child-bearing attributes. Arabella had just arrived one evening, like an unexpected parcel delivery. It was explained to him, rather ambiguously, that the family had acquired the new addition as a "gift from God."

Bug-eye's childhood was a patchwork of restrictions. He was forbidden to leave his parent's sight. A sizable but foreboding fence separated his small world consisting of a dilapidated house, a small garden with cabbages and turnips, and a shed where his father hung wild game, from the rest of the world. Beyond the fence, he could just make out a large stone house on the distant horizon. Who occupied the house, Mumma Lockjaw would never say. She would always respond to his questions with a wry smile, whimsically tut-tutting him while wagging her index finger, like a mother to a child who has just used a wicked swear-word. Despite this, or maybe because of this, his curiosity about the house steadily grew. The place became for him a forbidden fruit, which he was never to eat. With time, he began making up fantastic stories about its purpose and inhabitants. When he shared his visions one evening at the dinner table, his father threatened severe punishment should Bug-eyes ever venture outside his designated area. In truth, the boy was a virtual prisoner, and he felt it increasingly.

When he reached the age where education was supposed to come to the fore, he was marched by Mumma Lockjaw to attend a small local school where he suffered day after day of painful, unrelenting cruelty, mostly consisting of merciless name-calling, usually with reference to various insects with oversized eyes. Gradually, he learned to sit at the back of the class and become invisible. Always the silent outsider, his teacher and the other pupils assumed him to be simple-minded, an assumption he made no effort to challenge, realizing how futile it would be.

But he wasn't as dumb as people made out. He had a faculty for memorizing dates and could easily work out answers to complicated problems. He also had a rampant imagination, and a gift for making up and telling riveting stories.

One day, he had cause to reflect upon his birthright. Arabella had come down with a fever. Mumma Lockjaw had called Doctor Shady, and Bug-eyes had eavesdropped on their conversation. The seedy physician, having consumed a rather large quantity of alcohol at the local pub before proceeding to the Lockjaw home, remarked off-handedly, "The Lombard family, I'm afraid, has always been a sickly bunch."

Bug-eyes' attention latched immediately onto the surname. So his sister wasn't a Lockjaw, and, if true, that would suggest neither was he. Perhaps they were even of the same parentage, given their shared appearance. His curiosity deepened, and he made plans to cross over the fence to find out. Surely the answers lay in the large house on the horizon that was forbidden him, which the doctor had, in his drunken state, called Lombard Hall.

Bug-eyes chose a crisp winter day to carry out his mission. He had, by this time just turned seventeen, and with the onset of young adulthood had come the strongest of inclinations to explore. Ralston Lockjaw had finished checking the waterers and feeders he routinely filled for the kept pheasants, and would be away in the woods, hunting and trapping all the rest of the day. His mother had taken Arabella with her to visit a relative in Whitechapel. Bug-eyes therefore had the day all to himself. He told everyone he was tired and planned to spend it quietly in his room.

As soon as everyone left, he scaled the fence.

At first, it felt strange being on the "other side." Acres of lush park land with copses of small woodland added a splendor to the world extending before him further than his eye could see. Not to be distracted, he carefully maintained his focus on the horizon dominated by the magnificent house which he walked briskly towards. The dwelling kept drawing him closer as if he were being pulled there by some magnetic power. As he approached, he noted the house was constructed in red terra cotta, a fairy-tale mixture of steep-pitched roofs and high towering turrets and dormers, sprawled all over a vast area.

The ground was boggy, making walking laborious, but he made

steady progress. As he drew closer, however, doubts began to enter his mind. Perhaps he was simply overawed by the magnitude of the building. Perhaps there wasn't any benefit to dabbling into something best left alone. Perhaps answers to his questions lay elsewhere, and not in these particular surroundings.

It was at this point he heard the brassy call of a hunting horn, and the eager barks and bays of hounds. From over the brow of a nearby hill, a lone fox shot straight past him, running for its life. Distracted by the intruder between them and the fox, the hounds surrounded Bug-eyes, jostling each other, plumes of breath filling the cold air, saliva dripping from their mouths, their bright eyes searching, their wet noses sniffing him.

Soon a bevy of mounted huntsmen in bright red tunics, pale riding britches, and gleaming black riding boots closed in about him.

It was as if he had exchanged roles with the fox.

A youth, perhaps sixteen years of age, was the first to speak. "Who the hell are you?" he demanded in an aristocratic drawl, adding, "and what are you doing on Lombard land?"

Bug-eyes, having no easy answer to the question, shifted his weight nervously from one foot to the other. "Pardon me, Sir. I don't mean any harm."

The youth looming above him, far from appeased, kneed his horse to get closer and raised his riding crop menacingly. "You realize you are trespassing?" he half-asked, half-stated sternly, "This is private property."

"Um, yes," answered Bug-eyes, trembling as the other young huntsmen reigned in closer.

As the leader peered at Bug-eyes, the situation took a new turn. In the leader's eyes, this was a chance for some fun at the expense of the shaking miscreant before him, a chance to curry favor from his young friends. "My, what vulgar eyes you have," he said, prodding Bug-eyes' face with the tip of his crop. "I don't suppose you need binoculars with eyes like those." The rider turned to his friends and flashed a grin. His friends laughed on cue, several slapping their thighs in feigned hysterics.

Bug-eyes, terrified, stood even more deeply rooted to the spot.

"You're a freak," the youth above him continued. "I'll wager your mother was a praying mantis." Receiving no reply, Bug-eyes tormentor continued. "What's your name? Moth-eyes?"

Bug-eyes had heard every possible insult, so he didn't answer. Instead, he stared into the distance towards the safety of his farmhouse, wishing he'd stayed on the other side of the fence, and that his curiosity hadn't gotten the better of him.

The young aristocrat, put out by Bug-eyes seeming indifference, continued his tirade. "Can you see in the dark without a lantern, Freak?" Again, his friends laughed on cue.

Satisfied he had humiliated Bug-eyes sufficiently to gain all possible additional credence from his group of friends, he took a swig from his riding flask and said, "Normally, I would hand an oik like you over to Police Constable Blackstock, whereupon you would face the local Justice of the Peace, who happens to be a shooting chum of my father, and so tends to hand down the severest of sentences to trespassers and poachers." The young aristocrat straightened in the saddle and lifted his head up in disdain. "But, today, our fox gone, I fancy a bit of different sport," he announced. Taking a gold pocket watch from his trousers, and making a hasty calculation, he continued, "I'll give you three minutes, then I'll blow my horn and set the hounds on you. Maybe, if you're fast…and lucky…you will make it back over that fence. If not, my hounds will make a bloody mess of you, like they were eager to do to the fox."

He turned to his young friends for approval, and together, they lifted their hip flasks and toasted the idea.

"I'd get going if I were you," the leader suggested cheerfully.

Bug-eyes ran like he'd never run before, while the young huntsmen continued to jeer and mock him. The truth was that Bug-eyes had no chance and he knew it. His legs, already heavy from the long walk, the countryside wet and spongy, his pace quickly began to wane, and he began breathing erratically. He simply didn't have the necessary *vitesse* to make it to the fence in time. To his consternation, the three minutes passed all too quickly.

Behind him, the aristocrat blew his horn and the dogs, baying anew, began racing towards him, the huntsmen following at full gallop.

Enlivened by the danger, Bug-eyes renewed his efforts, and calculated that, if he could keep up the pace, he could possibly make it to the fence, though he doubted he would have time to climb over it. As he approached the fence, gulping for air, his heart felt like it was going to burst, and he realized he definitely wasn't going to make it over the fence. Then, out of the corner of one bulging eye, he saw a figure running towards him from the other side, concern for Bug-eyes' peril evident on his face.

Clawing at the fence, Bug-eyes felt the hounds' breath on his ankles. As he tried to clamber over it, he felt the nearest dog sink its teeth into the flesh of a leg.

Suddenly, a shot rang out. The lone figure running towards him had fired a warning shot into the sky. The sound of the report and the collective screams of birds taking flight made the hounds stop in their tracks. The one biting him released his grip and fell, confused, back among the others.

Half-way over the fence, Bug-eyes could see Ralston Lockjaw, reloading his twelve bore shotgun. Two pheasants peeked lifeless heads out of the grimy canvas fowl bag tied to his belt.

The gamekeeper looked enraged. Bug-eyes, despite the pain from the dog bite, rolled over the top of the fence, relieved that his father had appeared in the nick of time.

The young aristocrat rode the rest of the way up to the fence and stared intently at the two on the other side. "Lockjaw, what the hell are you playing at?" he demanded, his face contorted in anger.

"You might have killed the lad," growled Lockjaw, reflecting equal anger back at the young man.

"Killed him?" scoffed his better. "Oh, I doubt that. We were just having some fun."

The other youths nodded in accord. Several sniggered arrogantly.

"Who is he, anyway, and what is he to you?" demanded the young aristocrat, suddenly interested.

Lockjaw paused, prevaricating over whether this was the right moment to make the momentous announcement, then decided. "He's your brother," he blurted out.

"Don't be absurd, man. I don't have a brother. Never have!" With the vehemence of his denial, the young aristocrat's eyes began to bulge, though not quite on a par with Bug-eyes. The familiarity of features between the two young men was obvious to all but the speaker. "I'll have you punished for spreading malicious rumors, Lockjaw," said the rider prodding his horse anxiously with his whip. "My father will see to it."

Lockjaw said nothing and instead, turned and walked Bug-eyes home in silence. That evening Bug-eyes received a severe beating, but he knew it was a lesser punishment than being torn to pieces by the hounds.

A few weeks after the incident, Ralston Lockjaw failed to come home from the woods. It was a particularly cold evening, so much so that no one, left alone, even as well versed a countryman as he, would likely survive the night.

Mumma Lockjaw cried all night, fearing the worst.

The following day Ralston was found frozen solid, his leg caught in one of his own traps. The coroner pronounced his death an "unfortunate accident," but the locals questioned how an experienced gamekeeper with his knowledge of the local countryside and wealth of experience could have gotten caught in one of his own traps. The event spawned a raging, ongoing debate, packed with conjectures, at the local pub.

"He knew every stretch of those woods, he did," one denizen declared.

"He could locate his traps blindfolded," another added.

Back home, Mumma Lockjaw stopped eating, and, dangerously thin already, died after less than a week.

Bug-eyes and Arabella buried her meager bones next to those of her beloved husband in a makeshift grave behind the woodshed.

Shortly afterward, the two remaining Lockjaws were served an eviction notice. Forced to vacate, they decided to head for the city. *Maybe there*, Bug-eyes thought, *our fortunes will change for the better.*

If fact, Arabella's fortune did change and decidedly for the better. As she passed through adolescence, she developed into a stunning woman, her large eyes giving her a hauntingly innocent look. In the city, she was "discovered" by a talent scout. She was mesmerizingly

50

Francis H. Powell

photogenic, he said, and had a charming personality as well.

For her brother, Bug-eyes, fortune was not so kind. He picked up work when and where he could. His sister's fame, in the meantime, continued to rise. Her image soon appeared on the cover of every notable magazine, and she became the talk of the town. She even developed a trademark line of eye makeup, which women everywhere purchased, trying to emulate her large doe-eyes.

One day, Arabella received an invitation to attend the society event of the year, to be held at Lombard Hall in the great room of the very estate where she'd spent her Spartan infancy. Word had it that the manor's young Lord Christopher Lombard, following the sudden death of his father, would be celebrating his newly acquired inheritance and looking for a wife. Excited, Arabella showed her brother the invitation, but instead of sharing her delight and volunteering to escort her, he became insular and pensive. Ignoring his brooding, Arabella ordered a new dress from her designer on Carnaby Street and commandeered a leading male celebrity to escort her. The day of the event, she said a quick goodbye to Bug-eyes, who ignored her, acting totally engrossed in a book with an inverted pentagram on the cover.

Lombard Hall was filled with the glamorous, rich, and beautiful, but young Lord Christopher Lombard had eyes only for one: Arabella. Already fairly drunk from having consumed a large quantity of sherry while hunting during the day, he felt boisterously confident he would bed this new plaything before the night was over. He had only to sit through the staidly formal dinner, organized by his mother, now the Dowager Lady Lombard, and Arabella would be his for the asking.

During pre-dinner socializing, Lady Lombard winced each time she caught sight of the unknown upstart, Arabella, whom she grudgingly admitted resembled herself as a young debutant. As the guests took their seats about the long dinner table, she kept looking askance at the girl, vaguely remembering having disposed of a less-affected female version of the horribly bulbous-eyed first. *What if,* she thought, *that female offspring had somehow survived and turned from an ugly caterpillar into this exquisite butterfly?*

During the protracted appetizer, Lady Lombard noted her young son, Christopher, making increasingly blatant overtures towards Arabella, the young girl seemingly fueling his interest by responding with flirty glances from those big eyes of hers. Recognizing a situation that shouldn't be allowed to get out of hand, Lady Lombard began to veer her son away from the lovely Arabella and direct his interest to other, in her mind, more eligible debs. Christopher's interest in Arabella, however, had reached the point where, to everyone's aghast, the young Lord had the seating placements rearranged to better converse with her.

His mother, as expected, took vocal umbrage to the whole thing, saying it was "bad form and most certainly bad etiquette" to focus his attention on one girl, but her headstrong son got his way in the end. He was now, after all, master of the house, and Lady Lombard had, in the end, to acquiesce.

As a result, his mother spent the first dinner setting sending disapproving glances their way. Yet, she had to be careful. If she antagonized her son too much, he might start questioning why, and this would, of necessity, lead to her having to question Arabella's ancestry. And lurking behind this was an even greater threat: If one of her discarded children was alive, the *second* might also be. And if her Bug-eyed brother surfaced, he could assert his claim as the firstborn male to Lombard Hall. This would bring Lady Lombard's past indiscretions into public light. She shuddered at the thought.

In the middle of the second setting of the celebratory dinner event, Arabella, sitting to Christopher's right, gave the young man opportunity to slide his hand under the table and up her thigh. For her part, she kept blinking her beautiful wide-eyes, conversing politely, occasionally letting out a barely audible squeal when his fingers touched a particularly sensitive spot. In turn, her host's libido began working overtime. He was good looking, and, by her innocent way of thinking, looked uncannily like her bug-eyed brother, whom she worshiped.

Suddenly, the tall doors at the far end of the huge dining hall thundered open, revealing a solitary figure. It was a young man, clearly under-dressed for the occasion, so much so that his appearance made the dinner event and everyone there seem overtly ostentatious. The guests were in the middle of sipping bowls of saffron seafood soup, anticipating the roasted baby pigeons, Baltic herring and beef Wellington, to be washed down with glass after glass of different wines perfectly matched to each. The string quartct serenading the guests stopped playing.

As the mysterious figure approached, there was a collective intake of breath, and everyone prepared for something even more scandalous than the young Lord's behavior towards Arabella.

Arabella immediately recognized her brother and was totally perplexed. He *never* went to parties, and earlier, he'd not shown the slightest interest in this one.

Lady Lombard's face paled.

Lord Christopher was abruptly flooded with vague memories of an incident with a similar appearing youth sometime before. "What the hell are you doing in my house?" he bawled, the emphasized "my" reverberating around the hall. The bug-eyed freak standing before him was developing an unwelcome habit of intruding where he wasn't wanted.

"I've come for what's rightfully mine," said Bug-eyes, locking eyes with the young Lord. He was surprisingly assertive, something no one, including his sister, anticipated.

"It's obvious that nothing here belongs to you," replied his brother sardonically, nodding at Bug-eyes' inappropriate clothes. Though aristocratic faces on either side of the table reflected their accord, a general uneasiness gripped the hall.

Receiving no answer, the young Lord slammed down his soup spoon. "Get out of my sight you vulgar-looking prole!" he yelled, turning to the butler. "Throw this impudent joker out! Set the dogs on him, and make sure he never returns!"

"But he's my brother!" Arabella objected.

Bug-eyes, however, stood his ground. "That's no way to treat your older brother," he said calmly.

The Dowager Lady flinched in horror.

Bug-eyes began to mumble as if placing a curse. Without warning, Lord Christopher began uncontrollably retching until a shiny terrapin slipped out of his mouth and dropped into his soup, followed immediately by another at regular intervals.

Dr. Shady was upstairs deflowering the cook's sixteen-year-old daughter when a servant located and informed him he was needed immediately at the banquet. Reluctantly demounting the young girl, his preliminary diagnosis was, "The seafood must have disagreed with him."

Bug-eyes watched calmly as Lord Christopher, hands about his throat, gurgled, his eyes bulging a little more with each indignity. For his part, Bug-eyes, for the first time in his life, felt quite at home; the many Lombards on the walls peered down at him through their unmistakable bug-eyes as if offering their approval.

Flight of Destiny

Seed

Captain Spender's wife was ovulating, and her husband was, as always, off somewhere on another "top secret military mission," of which, as always, she was neither privy to the location nor its significance. In eight years of marriage, her husband had failed to impregnate her and procure an heir, and Amelia was getting jittery. Her biological clock was beginning to ring its alarm, and refused to be silenced.

Before the captain, she'd twice attempted to enter into a state of matrimony. Both had led proven unsuccessful. Her first fiancé contacted a tropical disease (rumor had it a bout of syphilis) while out on a mission in the colonies, and they never made it as far the alter. The second had died as a result of a swimming accident. The foolhardy man had wagered he could swim, drunk, around a small island off the Italian coast just weeks before the wedding. His naked, battered, decomposing body was discovered swept up on a beach by fishermen the next day.

In truth, Amelia had feared she was cursed until she met and married the solidly dependable Captain Spender, and now she wanted desperately to cement their marriage by producing for him a son. Most of their friends already had two or three babies, a few were even awaiting further additions. What's worse, Amelia, though fond of her handsome husband, was left in his absence surrounded by young virile officers confined to the regimental base, who would gladly provide her with the child she yearned for. The problem was deciding which, in Captain Spender's continued absence, would be the most appropriate choice.

Amelia knew she was attractive. She was tall and lean. She had long dark hair that flowed down to the middle of her back. She had a sweet voice and a seductive laugh. On the other hand, for all of her virtues, she seemed destined to miss out on the joys of childbearing, while her infinitely plainer sister irritatingly boasted five beautiful children, a situation which her indelicate mother was prone to constantly remind her. Furthermore, they were all handsome rambunctious boys. While her mother and her woman-friends genteelly sipped their afternoon tea, her mother would deftly suck up large quantities of gin from a concealed flask, eventually demanding aloud in the most vulgar fashion, "You've popped the cherry with your husband, have you not?" or "Has Mr. Rabbit visited the warren lately?" always ending with, "You *do* know how to please the good Captain, I trust? Getting his todger to stand to attention and..."

"Mother, you are unbearable!" Amelia would retort, her face crimson, her dignity in shreds, tears welling in her crystal-blue eyes.

She wanted to shout to all that it wasn't her fault! It wasn't *her* sexual appetite, prowess or looks, it was her husband's frequent and long absences that were frustrating her, but she couldn't for fear of further humiliation. Nobody ever would lay the blame on her husband, a highly respected officer, naturally deemed red-blooded, virile and fertile. In the end, it was the constant anguish of never getting impregnated and her mother's cruel jibes that tipped her determination to find a suitable seed donor, one with not only a good set of genes not too unlike her Captain, but also with a modicum of discretion.

One particularly hot summer day, she sat on her veranda in a deck chair, a tragic gothic romance in hand, surveying the men as they filed by and doffed their caps. In return, she smiled sweetly at each, exchanging perfunctory greetings. One especially handsome, blue-eyed, auburn-haired, chiseled-faced officer, riding a white Arabian charger and looking particularly attractive in his flashy red and gold field uniform caught her eye. It didn't escaped her for a moment that the young officer could pass as a young version of her husband.

She called out a loud good-day.

His reply was a curt touch of hand to his hat brim and a brief but warm smile. Amelia's wild imagination filled in the rest: Here was a passionate man of few words with all the necessary attributes. And what's more, there was, to her reckoning, an undeniable chemistry apparent between them during the short moment they'd exchanged salutations.

Lieutenant James Rawlston was one of the newer, unmarried, junior officers, and that afforded him an air of intrigue. Gossip had already done the rounds of the post of his alleged sexual prowess, and Rawlston, having just arrived, had, as yet, few friends, giving Amelia a pretext to meet and entangle him in her wiles.

Rationally, brown-haired, brown-eyed Captain Havers would have been a better man for the job, but he already had a wife who was an inveterate do-gooder, whom Amelia ended up having to face regularly, knowing she had led her husband astray. Major Newton, in local circles known as "The Conquistador," had made his availability known, and was her Captain's superior. But the man had a reputation of spreading himself thin, far and wide, and Amelia shuddered at the thought of ending up a another conquest. Besides, he drank, and when he did, he was liable to brag of his "conquests" to the other officers. No, the major would never do, either.

The morning was dwindling when opportunity presented itself. She spotted Rawlston walking her way, slapping his hand with a swagger stick, his riding whip tucked underneath his elbow.

"Ah, lieutenant! Have you come to bring me news of my husband?" Amelia called out matter-of-factly.

Rawlston stopped in mid-stride, turned towards her, tipped his hat, smiling gallantly as he had earlier when riding his horse. "The truth be told," he replied, "I have no idea of his condition or whereabouts, Mrs. Spender."

"Oh-h-h," lamented Amelia in an overly pained voice. "Perhaps, then, you've come to fulfill my as yet unspoken request? I do so need to move some furniture today. It's a task my husband never seems to get around to on account of his regular absences," Amelia said in a hushed, bashful voice.

Rawlston straightened and shifted to show his best profile. He seemed to be considering what she'd said: first, her simple appeal for help, then, with a little skepticism, it's implications. There were, after all, plenty of others in the barracks she could ask who could equally well perform such a menial task.

The two stared at each other, sizing the other up.

"Mrs. Spender," the young buck finally replied. "I need to take a quick wash after exercising; however, afterwards, I should be delighted to help you with any such domestic matters you may require." Rawlston flashed a particularly courteous smile.

Amelia smiled back sweetly, content at having struck accord. "That's most gracious of you, Captain Rawlston," she cooed, feigning shyness.

Rawlston bowed punctiliously, clicked his heels, touched a finger once again to his hat and took his leave, walking away in long, powerful, purposeful strides. Amelia watched him until he disappeared, then busied making herself more attractive, brushing her hair, misting her breasts, wrists and the back of her neck lightly with a particularly sultry perfume. Rawlston, true to his word, returned shortly, looking the true gentleman in a smart blue blazer and white linen slacks.

Inviting him in, Amelia's felt her heart race. The handsome lieutenant sat in an armchair and surveyed her, while Amelia flitted about the room, putting fresh flowers from her garden on the dining table, a gesture she imagined would infuse a touch of femininity into what was quickly becoming the pivotal moment. "You must be tired, after such a vigorous day," she said, looking suggestively over her shoulder and staring deeply into his brilliant blue eyes. "Perhaps you would like a refreshment? I was about to make myself..."

"That would be most pleasant, Mrs. Spender," interrupted Rawlston, imagining a cool drink might flush away some of the awkwardness he was feeling.

Pouring two tall glasses of iced Pimms, Amelia artfully directed the conversation to the lieutenant's previous postings, then to his family. He had three older sisters, all in excellent health, all mothers who'd given birth to sprightly children. His parents he told her were active and both sets of grandparents were still alive and in good health with full mental faculties. In summary, he gave no indication of any illnesses, mental or physical, that might blight a family, alleviating any fears she had regarding some dark idiosyncrasy that might be passed on to the prospective offspring she anticipated they would be shortly creating. She was finding him increasingly pleasant, though somewhat reserved, and try as she might, she couldn't seem to get him to slip him out of formal "military mode." Then again, she reminded herself, it wasn't his mind or personality she was most interested in.

"What about that furniture that needs moving?" inquired Rawlston.

The question demanded an answer, and forced Amelia into an corner, so she decided on a change of approach. Putting on a demure look, she softened and lowered her voice, replying, "That wasn't quite the reason I asked you here, Lieutenant."

"Oh?" the young man replied with a smirk, crossing his legs, concluding the pretense he'd felt she had been maintaining was about to dissipate.

"No," she reaffirmed with a wicked look, observing his reaction, as if testing the water for her next declaration. "I will be direct with you, Lieutenant. I want you to sleep with me," she said, standing and turning her face towards the staircase, as if directing him to follow her up the stairs to the bedroom. Amelia purposefully averted her eyes from the corner credenza that held the family pictures of her much-heralded husband.

Her husband, Richard—she and the few who were closest to him dared called him "Dickie"—wasn't from a big family, less so an aristocratic one. He was, however, from prominent military stock who'd worked their way up into the top ranks. During his frequent absences, she often looked wistfully at the picture of the two of them standing alongside their parents. His parents looked proud. Her parents looked resigned. They had, in the end, approved her engagement to a military man, but with muted enthusiasm.

In truth, the majority of the photos were a shrine to his military prowess more than anything else. One showed him receiving a medal from a stout general with a bushy mustache, another, Dicky's profile, proud and erect, riding a black horse, sword in hand, leading a lavish ceremonial parade. About these two central ones were smaller photos of Captain Spender shaking hands with various dignitaries from around the world. Below them, relegated to the shadows of a second shelf were pictures of their wedding with him in full military regalia and her in a white dupioni dress, a diamond tiara on her head. In avoiding the cabinet, she realized she had inadvertently directed Rawlston's gaze to it.

"I want you to come upstairs with me," Amelia commanded. "Now," she concluded with just enough authority to deflect his gaze from the photos back to her.

"And what of your husband, Mrs. Spender?" questioned Rawlston, taken aback by her forthrightness, the pictures of Captain Spender resonating in his mind. "He's fine military officer, widely regarded as a man of remarkable proficiency and bravery."

"This is not about my husband, Lieutenant. It is you I need and desire right now." Amelia's voice this time carried within it an overture of both excitement and desperation.

An awkward silence ensued, which the lieutenant finally broke. The more he looked at her, the more her beauty, desire and desperation took hold of him. "You are most attractive, Mrs. Spender. I would venture to say exceedingly beautiful. Indeed, exquisitely attractive. All the men on the post talk of your allure," he pronounced, as if she had passed some evaluation going on in his head.

"I am offering myself to you, Lieutenant Rawlston," said Captain Spender's wife, adding with a note of caution, "provided you never reveal our intimacies."

She glided across the room to him and nestled into his lap, brushing her hand down the front of his shirt, sensually stroking the growing bulge between his legs in an attempt to force the issue. By the time they reached the Spender marital bed, both were more than ready to perform the desired act. Once completed, they clung uncomfortably to each other in silence, hardly knowing what to say, both immersed in thought. Amelia imagined the lieutenant feeling regret, even guilt, at having taken a senior officer's wife. But if, in fact, Lieutenant Rawlston did have any such regrets, he certainly didn't show them. After a few minutes, he got up, dressed, neatened himself in front of the mirror and quietly slipped out of bedroom, exiting the house by the back door. For her part, Amelia was glad to hear the door close. They had parted more like strangers than lovers, which fit her original pretense. It was as if he'd finished moving the furniture as promised.

Amelia spent the rest of the day warmed by the fact that she was carrying Lieutenant Rawlston's seed. She didn't catch sight of him later when she returned to sit on the veranda, which was actually a comfort as she didn't really want any true intimacy to develop between them. She preferred to regard him not as a romantic interlude but more as a willing resource necessary to satisfy a need. The day was petering out, the light waning, and she had just retired to her drawing room to finish repairing one of her husband's shirts, when she heard footsteps of a distinctly military bearing on the veranda. Hoping to God it wasn't Lieutenant Rawlston returning for more, she nonetheless smartened her hair and dress. More likely, it would be one of the other officer wives dropping by for some friendly evening repartee.

There was a knock.

Amelia rose, walked across the drawing room and reluctantly opened the door.

There slouched the Reverend Captain Bawdy, the regimental vicar, his distinctive, slicked-back, ginger-colored hair and rakish moustache emphasizing the look of a soldier more than the dowdy appearance of a regimental chaplain. Bawdy took a long pull on a hand-rolled cigarette. "Good evening, Mrs. Spender. May I come in?" he demanded with look of insistence.

Not anticipating company, least of all that of a man of the cloth at such an hour, Amelia felt disinclined to invite the reverend in, but due to the restraints of etiquette, equally compelled to do so. "Certainly, Captain Bawdy," she finally answered disguising her annoyance at the intrusion.

Bawdy looked her up and down as if inspecting one of the troops and smiled, to which she returned a forced smile, before he stumbled his way in. As he passed, she noted the unmistakable smell of alcohol on his breath. His voice was slurred and his normally bright blue eyes appeared red and bleary. Amelia, fooled by guilt into thinking this purported man of God might have caught wind of her shameful tryst, keenly wished the man away. As it was, however, she could hardly get rid of him in such a state without generating gossip and suspicion.

There was never opportunity for small talk with Captain Bawdy. He immediately launched into direct conversation, leaving her feeling even more uncomfortable than usual. "These must be difficult, *lonely* times for you, Mrs. Spender," he mumbled, "what with your husband away so often, and the absence of the patter of little feet."

Amelia was forced to begrudgingly acknowledge his statement, and offered a reluctant smile. "I get by, Captain Bawdy," she said philosophically, "and who knows what's in the offing?" adding unconvincingly, "My husband and I will surely have a family soon. It's just a matter of time."

"Is that so?" asked the vicar, lifting an eyebrow and chortling.

Silence ensued.

"Had a bit of 'how's your father' recently, have you, eh?" he trilled mockingly, craning one bloodshot eye towards her. The word *recently* seemed full of insinuation.

Amelia chose to ignore the remark, more out of fear than indignity. Had the reprobate somehow actually caught wind of her infidelity? Backing away from the man for fear she might still smell of the morning's passionate sex, she silently prayed for her unwanted guest to leave. All such hopes were dashed when the intolerable vicar settled into the seat that was normally occupied by her husband, and more recently by Rawlston. The man was clearly intent on tormenting her.

The reverend had a questionable record surrounding procreation. It was rumored that lurking in various far-off corners of the world were splashes of Bawdy offspring. The man never attempted to deny the scandalous rumors that he had left several African women with more than just the good words of God when the Regiment was on tour there, while leaving Gracie Bawdy, his long-suffering wife, without child. Some said that the chaplain was so busy firing bullets on foreign campaigns, he could fire only blanks at home.

"Perhaps the good Captain isn't cashing in on all his assets," piped up Bawdy. "Army life can be very demanding, leaving neglected wives to pine away at home. The best soldiers are often far from tenderhearted, making them less likely to heed to their wives sensibilities."

Amelia didn't answer, but Bawdy had clearly touched a nerve. When she'd first met her husband, he'd been reasonably attentive, though, as time wore on, he'd become increasingly indifferent towards her. He was so absorbed in his work she felt shut out, and her marriage was not only lacking in ardor, but left her to wonder if he ever pondered on their lack of offspring. It wasn't a topic easily broached, however. With her unfathomable husband, there were many things she had learned to refrain from delving into. Occasionally he would wake up in the middle of the night screaming, having experienced a nightmare. She'd questioned him about these occurrences at first, but he'd always play them down. "Just dreams, my love, nothing more," he would say, wiping the sweat from his brow, but there *was* more to it, she knew. She was certain his brain was reenacting something terrible he'd witnessed in the field. Her husband, she concluded in the end, was a complex and mysterious man. Perhaps he was shielding her from horrors he'd witnessed on his highly confidential missions, and this was affecting his libido.

"Could I trouble you for a drink, Mrs. Spender?" asked the reverend, intruding on her thoughts. "I note you have a bottle of fine brandy sitting on the credenza next to the photos of your gallant husband."

Amelia sighed but acquiesced. As she bent to offer him the drink, the lecherous vicar slipped his hands down her bodice and unabashedly groped her.

The drink crashed to the floor and Amelia took a quick step

backwards, letting out a shrill yelp. The reverend seemed to delight in the offense, as if he were enjoying Amelia's humiliation. "Oops, naughty old me. Do forgive me, Mrs. Spender," he pleaded sardonically. "Do forgive me, Mrs. Spender," he pleaded sardonically. "It's just that temptation sometimes gets the better of me. You understand, don't you?"

"I think you had better leave my house this instant, Captain Bawdy!" Amelia, once over the shock, ordered sternly, her displeasure rising.

"And what about my…refreshment?" protested the reverend. "The good Lord does not look kindly on waste."

"I think you've had quite enough," replied Amelia defiantly. "Will you leave, or will I be forced to call for assistance and report your behavior?"

"Report *my* behavior?" The reverend mumbled, getting awkwardly out of the chair and meandering drunkenly across the room towards the front door. As he stumbled through the doorway and across the veranda, lurching first one way and then the next, she heard another person mount the steps of her house.

Amelia ran to the window and peered out to find, to her horror, it was her husband, Captain Spender, who'd returned from his latest mission. The captain stared at the drunken regimental pastor, surprised to see him departing his house at such an hour.

Captain Bawdy tried, but was too inebriated to fully wipe the look off his face of having accomplished something decidedly wicked; Captain Spender, for his part, observed the reverend's usually neat clothing noticeably askew.

The reverend, only half-sensing his predicament, attempted to offer his fellow officer a compliment; however, the words came out twisted by demon liquor. "Such a lovely wife you have, Captain Spender. A cherry truly worth picking," he muttered.

Captain Spender gave the man a steely look.

Fortunately for the reverend, Captain Spender was equally drunk, though he held his liquor better. Despite his drunkenness though, he could tell he'd stumbled on something he didn't like. He had always resented Bawdy's demeanor, and now, the fact that Bawdy had apparently been milling around his house and wife in his absence. To Amelia's relief, the two men exchanged curt farewells and went separate ways without further incident.

Captain Spender's wife, shocked by the altercation with the vicar and her husband's unanticipated return, visibly paled. Her husband's first words were a further shock.

"What was *he* doing here?" he demanded loudly, his voice tinged with malice.

Amelia was taken aback. Her husband was a man who, as part of his assignments, often confronted grave danger. Though ruthless in war, he was always sweet and gentle at home, never lifting his voice. "He stopped to offer some words of Christian comfort in your absence," she said defensively.

"Christian words...of comfort," scoffed the captain. "You will never let this lout or any other man into this house in my absence," he commanded as if to a military subordinate.

His authoritarian manner frightened her further, and she nodded solemnly. "How about a drink, Dickie, darling?" she offered, hoping to lift the dangerous mood.

Captain Spender, though softening, remained vexed, making a hazy mental note of the change in his wife, a change he couldn't quite put his finger on. Catching the irreverent Captain Bawdy alone with his wife struck him as a kind of violation. Still, he accepted the offer of a drink with a sharp nod of his head.

Amelia, sensing at least a meager opening, poured two drinks, sidled up close to him, and began applying the same sensual tactics she'd used successfully on Lieutenant Rawlston. Her woman's mind told her she urgently needed to entice her husband into making love to her. If she was successfully impregnated by the lieutenant, she would have to make her husband believe the resulting infant was his. Unfortunately, she could see he was fatigued after his mission, and any enthusiasm he might have had was further muted by the quantity of alcohol he had consumed on his return. Their love sessions had, up to now, been confined strictly to the marital bed and were always quite conventional. However, while traveling a few months prior to her recent adultery, she'd picked up a discarded book filled not just with romance but also containing graphic sexual content. The book had opened to her a new world of pleasurable delights. It was, in fact, the very book she had been reading on the veranda when she and the lieutenant first exchanged pleasantries.

In a total break from convention, she doffed her clothes, undressed her husband, and began kissing him tantalizingly all over as the heroine in her book had done. At first it seemed to work; however, to her dismay, in his alcohol-fatigued state, he quickly lost his ardor and slipped into a deep sleep. Amelia therefore extinguished the lights, draped a blanket over his naked body and went to bed. Her attempt at enticing him to take her had failed.

Captain Spender slept long into the next day, and when he woke, was surprised to find himself sitting naked in his favorite chair, draped with a blanket. Amelia was busying herself in other parts of the house, deeming it best to keep a low profile, anticipating he would be moody and prickly.

Over the rest of the week, an awkward *impasse* developed, and before she could break it, he was immersed in preparation for another mission. This one was to last several months.

When he returned home from the mission, she announced she had wonderful news. "Darling, I'm pregnant," she said, studying his face intently.

He took the news the same way he might a change in orders, uttering some nondescript words of acceptance.

Amelia, though disappointed in his spiritless response, consoled herself that there was no way he could know that the baby wasn't his. Her husband soon left on another even longer mission, and she was alone to deal with the pregnancy. In mid-spring, she delivered her dearly coveted baby.

On his return, Captain Spender largely ignored the infant, citing the child's irritating crying and a general lack of attention from his wife. While the infant was, for Amelia, a bundle of joy, to her husband it seemed a tiresome inconvenience.

According to convention, newborns were, without fail, baptized in the regimental chapel with all the regimental officers, wives and children attending. The baptism, of course, would involve Reverend Bawdy, whose duty was to conduct the service.

Amelia chose the name Joshua as the baby's Christian name, claiming that God had, indeed, proved her salvation, providing her with a child in a most "biblical" manner.

From Captain Spender's perspective, the baptism proved painfully humiliating. During his months away, his mind had woven together several dark suspicions. Furthermore, when he bothered to closely look at the infant, other than the child's ears jutting out like his, it didn't seem to have many other of his features. Even more suspicious, the child sported tufts of ginger-colored hair. Nobody in the captain's family had ginger hair. Ever. Still, it was their first, and infants were known to change their hair color as they matured.

To the captain's further despair, the child's eyes seemed to him to be getting bluer rather than browner, in marked contrast to his own dark brown eyes. His fears finally crystallized, when, at the moment of christening, he saw the reverend raise the child in his arms, like a sportsman proudly lifting up a trophy, and noted that the child looked more like the reverend than himself. In fact, the more he thought about it, the more similarities he saw between the infant and the reverend. Far too many to be purely coincidental. The memory of Captain Bawdy sniffing about his house late at night under most dubious circumstances reinforced his suspicions.

Spender found it hard to restrain himself and not challenge those who he now felt certain had deceived him both privately in the past and now publicly before all his fellow officers. While the rigmarole of the baptism proceeded at an infuriatingly lethargic pace, he agonized further, deciding finally to confront his wife here and now. Turning his attention to her, he whispered his anxieties into her ear, pressing her the way he might a prisoner in an interrogation, trying to quietly force a confession. Amelia, horrified, whispered back that his allegations were wild, absurd and ludicrous.

Their back and forth whispering continued, slowly growing louder, until the people around them began hushing and tutting. Distraught, the captain loomed closer to his wife, jabbed a finger at his wife's chest and hollered bitterly, "Did you or did you not have sex with Bawdy?"

The entire congregation hushed, stared at the couple, and held their breath, waiting for Amelia's answer.

Amelia's face flushed, then turned cold and calculating, as she carefully weighed her answer. The reverend froze, a gawky grin emerging on his face, as if flattered to be embroiled in such a scandal. Significantly to everyone present, no words of denial were forthcoming. The tension in the church heightened with each passing second.

"Yes, I did," Amelia finally lied, dropping her head in mock shame, acting out her new deception. While her mind balked at the mere thought of any kind of physical contact with the repulsive reverend, given the circumstances, she thought it better for her, the baby and its real father if the truth remained obscure. It also placed the despicable Reverend Bawdy firmly in the mire. Captain Spender snapped to attention, turned smartly, and left the chapel without another word. The news of the baptism, tainted by scandal, spread like wildfire through the barracks. Amelia took her son home and arranged for her sister to care for him, unsure what her vexed husband might do next.

Later that night, Captain Spender returned home. Amelia watched him cautiously as he strode over to the liquor cabinet and began drinking directly from the bottle. He was a changed man, but overall appeared more appeased than angry, as if a heavy burden had been lifted from his shoulders. Amelia sat across the room silently watching him drink himself into oblivion. Eventually, he finally passed out alone on his chair.

The following day, Gracie, the minister's wife, awoke to find her husband missing, and later, to her utter horror, slumped like an unwanted carcass on the ground by their open garage. He had been viciously beaten. The reverend was taken at speed to the military hospital.

Worse news followed the next day. He had lost an eye, such was the severity of his beating. When later, he was finally able to speak, he related only that he'd been taken by surprise, and had no idea who the perpetrator might be. He spent a long period in hospital before returning to his duties a subdued man.

Several months later, the rumors and speculation having run their course, the barrack gossip turned to Captain Rawlston's announcement of his engagement to Lady Helena Marsdon-Whittle. It was rumored she was with child, and that the marriage had been hastily arranged. A low-key wedding in the regimental chapel was followed a few months later by Lady Helena giving birth to a beautiful blue-eyed, ginger-haired boy. When the Rawlston child was due to be baptized, the ceremony was scheduled with Reverend Bawdy, albeit, with some anxiety, given the tumultuous course of his last baptism. Voice shaky, hands quavering, spirit humbled, the reverend appeared a much preferred shadow of his previous obnoxious self.

Amelia sat in the second row of the chapel, holding little Joshua lovingly in her arms. Her husband, Captain Spender, sat next to her, more interested in the child the vicar was holding than the child's parents or the man's long-winded soliloquy. The infant had, to his surprise, the same notable tufts of ginger hair and sparkling blue eyes as Joshua, who was making gurgling noises while the vicar ranted on.

Captain Spender shook his head to clear his thoughts.

After several furtive glances at Joshua and then at the Rawlston baby, it dawned on him that the two boys were mirror images of each other. They were, he concluded, so alike they could quite easily pass as siblings. *Had the degenerate vicar once again provided the seed?* Captain Spender wondered. He'd thought he'd taught the man a lesson.

Captain Spender shook his head in disbelief. Unable to look at the degenerate reverend, his eyes latched onto Rawlston, who, he noted, was looking neither at the reverend, child nor Lady Helena, but at Amelia, and in a most complicit way. Rawlston and Amelia's shifty glances told him all he needed to know, and his anger abruptly changed direction.

But for the fact that he was in the regimental chapel in the company of fellow officers, he would have gone over and struck Rawlston down. However on reflection, as he looked from one guilty looking officer to another and the many children who bore so little resemblance to their supposed fathers, he concluded his situation was probably no more and no less different from many the other soldiers there with a child procured of another's seed.

Flight of Destiny

Mutant

Louisa Cranston was slowly becoming aware that something wasn't right. First and foremost, she was rocking gently, submerged in saline fluid in some kind of large container, her body awash with strange, unnatural sensations. She had plenty of oxygen to breathe. Attached to her skin were various monitor leads, that she supposed were tracking her heart beat and blood pressure. Beneath the sound of the sloshing water, she could just barely make out the rumble of an engine. From this, she concluded she was being transported in a darkened container to some unknown destination.

Louisa flexed her fingers and used the tips to test the smooth casing surrounding her. Her thoughts were hazy. Her mind kept meandering, suggesting to her that she had been sedated. Worse, as the assumed drugs slowly wore off, she felt the throbbing pain below her waist steadily increase until her lower half felt as though it had been stung by an enormous wasp.

An abrupt thud jolted her further into consciousness, and she recalled being involved in a terrible road accident. The driver had shouted something as the car hurtled off the road. There had been a loud crash. Yes, she remembered that. The car had smashed into a tree, and she had somehow survived, despite her legs being crushed beyond recognition. The driver had not been so lucky and had died. Things were beginning to get clearer. The driver was *not* her husband; he was her illicit lover.

Her husband, Crawford, was a world-renowned surgeon. His second passion was ichthyology, but it was truer perhaps to say he was a man of eclectic and diverse interests.

In his fledgling scientific career, he'd held a defamatory view of art, as it conflicted with his natural predilection towards logic and order. Then one day, he caught sight of a pickled shark in a display cabinet at a business associate's art gallery, awakening within him something new and wondrous. Having acquired a sizable fortune, "investing in art" seemed a reasonable next step for a man of his standing. But it was the unusual and bizarre that attracted his attention, and into which he decided to pour his time and money. This left him less time for his wife, Louisa, who he excluded from his two great passions.

They'd married when she was still a young student. He'd been invited to give a lecture at her medical school, and she had been blinded by the enormity of his intellect and rapidly-growing fame. If indeed she'd ever really loved him, at least her admiration for him had never flagged.

The much-heralded Professor Crawford Cranston made it clear

immediately before their marriage vows that he didn't want any children getting in the way of his career. Apart from being authoritative, her husband proved over time to be intolerably possessive, at the same time showing little interest in fulfilling her physical needs. He'd recently built a research institute, aptly named after himself, on the confines of his estate, and was fast becoming reclusive to the point of maintaining only a small select circle of moneyed friends with similar unusual interests.

Further developments on the estate included building his own personal art gallery in the spacious basement of his mansion, boldly claiming that the works he was collecting would push the boundaries of both art and science further than they had ever gone before.

Louisa, left more and more alone to herself, had fallen for one of Crawford's less acclaimed assistants, who'd taken the time to show her a modicum of attention, something which her cold-fish husband had never done. She and her lover carefully chose the places and times for their trysts, their lovemaking stoked by the ever-present risk of discovery.

Unfortunately for them, on the day of the accident, they'd been careless. Somehow, Crawford had found out, and, filled with jealous rage, had taken action. Tampering with the steering and brakes of her car being beneath him; he paid a lackey to perform the deed. That was probably what her lover had been trying to convey in his last words, she thought. Yes, it was all coming back.

Upon being informed by the local hospital of the accident, as well as the death of the driver and the hopelessness of his wife's injuries, Crawford insisted she be placed under his care. Rather than being mortified by extent of his wife's injuries, an exciting new idea had germinated in his mind. As soon as her condition allowed, he had her transferred to a private hospital in strict seclusion. The moment he felt her able, the surgical wing, operating theater, and passage from her room to the operating theater were cordoned off. Immediately after what proved a lengthy, but apparently successful operation, Louisa, heavily sedated, was prepared for covert transfer elsewhere.

The sound of wheels crunching on gravel distracted her. She seemed to have arrived at wherever they were taking her. She heard vehicle doors open, and the indistinct sound of human voices. Then she felt the container tip slightly and slowly slide out of the vehicle. A moment later she felt the capsule being hoisted, then carried by several men the way the way pall-bearers might carry a coffin. Shortly, her bearers' footsteps stopped crunching on gravel and began clacking on marble. Suddenly, she began to hear familiar sounds.

She could just make out the chime of a grandfather clock, one she knew well. She could even make out the distinctive sounds of two dogs sniffing, panting urgently, following on either side of her container. They were her dogs, Bachus and Griffin, of that she was certain. She was, she concluded, in Cranston Hall.

The tank stopped sloshing. She could hear muffled instructions being given the tank bearers in the brusque manner her husband commonly used when talking to underlings. A moment later the sloshing began again. This time she felt her capsule being carried down stairs. If she was indeed back at Cranston Hall, she couldn't fathom why they, whoever they were, would carry her downstairs to the basement. Her husband had always made a point of keeping her away from the basement. The tank soon leveled out, the entourage came to an abrupt halt, and the container was lowered with a decided "thunk" onto a stone floor.

A black cloth covering the tank was unceremoniously pulled off, the brightness of the light shining in causing her to blink rapidly and look away. When she adjusted to the light, it was to see a circle of men standing about her transparent capsule. Terrified, she followed their collective line of gaze until the full appreciation of her predicament hit her with devastating force.

Her husband, acclaimed by some to be the greatest surgeon of all time, had discarded her pulverized lower limbs and grafted on what looked like the tail of a fish. To emphasize her new condition, he'd preserved the donor fish's decapitated head in a smaller transparent capsule placed on display next to hers for everyone to see. The gruesome head glared through glazed eyes at her and the audience with a fixed, pained expression. The shock was too much for her, and she passed out.

Upon regaining consciousness, she found her husband, Crawford, standing before the capsule, admiring his work, the ultimate synthesis of science and art. He was taking pleasure in pointing out the details of his work to an entourage of men who'd paid generously to be present at the formal unveiling of his newest work. The sick voyeurs, mouths hanging open, eyes agog, nodded perfunctorily as he explained the complex process he'd employed in saving his wife, at the same time, creating an entirely new art form. All peered incredulously at the half-woman, half-fish before them, Crawford's most outlandish accomplishment yet. During the course of their homage, Louisa fainted.

When she woke this time, she found herself in new surroundings: She was encased in a spacious rectangular plexiglass container, her body resting lengthwise on an elevated shelf-like dias with a huge white scalloped shell behind her. Water slowly cascaded mistily from above onto her lower half and, from there, below into a pool just large enough for her to slip into and swim a stroke or two. Whether resting on the ledge above or swimming in the pool below, the enclosure showcased her new body for anyone present to see. Crawford had clearly put much thought into this centerpiece addition to his art collection of the bizarre, as the enclosure was bedecked on the outside with ornamental shells, stones and pieces of coral, creating sea-motif frame with her at the center. At the side of the huge clamshell behind her was a gold-filigreed trident protruding from a fake rock, completing the kitsch mermaid theme. In front of her, on the other side of the glass, her husband stood indulging himself. "A work of art like no other," he kept reiterating as he viewed her from all possible angles, repeating the phrase like a mantra.

Her case was flooded with light, giving her nowhere to hide. *So the price of my infidelity is to be displayed like this, a freak in a lavish aquarium,* she lamented.

Various gadgets were mounted along the sides of the huge tank, which Louise imagined were to maintain her environment and thereby sustain her in her new form for Crawford's clientele to view.

Her deductions were reaffirmed when a group of viewers including a few of her husband's closest friends were ushered in. "She won't be straying again, that's for sure," she heard one say glibly. A ring of laughter accompanied the remark. Louisa, mortified, blushed and tried unsuccessfully to cover her naked breasts with her long yellow hair. Realizing the hopelessness of her situation, she stared back at the circle of gawking men and noticed in the background of the vast room a solitary woman staring at her with a smile on her face. It was Crawford's personal assistant, Aida. *That woman is always lurking somewhere in the background never far from Crawford's side,* thought Louisa, glaring back. Aida returned her glare with a smirk, then she savoring the sight of the men, ogling at the display, clearly relishing Louisa Cranston's anguish. Aida, though slightly older than Louisa, had been, since the first day of her appointment, a shadowy and ubiquitous presence, a subtly intrusive third party interrupting every effort Louisa made to connect with Crawford.

After a time, Louisa discovered she was not alone in the tank. Below her, other marine life shared her compact little pool. She watched a school of timid shoal fish rise to the surface, which, startled by her looming presence, splashed and dashed away. A more adventurous fish brushed against the submerged tip of her tail, causing her tail to reflexively flick the surface of the water. The visitors watching clapped with delight.

Beyond her immediate domain, the gallery was chock full of other of Crawford's tasteless, even profane works of "art." His brilliant scientific mind and new-found artistic creativity appeared to have taken him far beyond the borders of sanity. Grafting an ear from a mouse to its shoulder was one thing, but a fish tail onto a wife, that was pure malevolence.

The men watching her were egged on by Crawford signaling to her to move her long silvery tail. Apparently, they wanted a demonstration, a bit of a show, functional proof of Crawford's genius.

Louisa, angry and defiant, refused to respond. How could they expect her to take on the deportment of a performing fish? Surely even these decadent men could recognize the obscene in-humanness of such an insult? When the invitees' unsatisfied interest waned, Crawford gave her a derisory wave, turned down the basement lights and escorted everyone, including Aida, upstairs from the basement. All Louisa could do was sob bitterly, and wish she were, like her lover, dead. She hated her new existence, but more than that, she hated her husband for what he'd done and was continuing to do to her.

Over the next several weeks, boredom became her greatest enemy. She was left for days between viewings alone with her thoughts and memories, disturbed only by her creepy old toothless keeper, Regan, who, during his brief appearances, would drop some specially concocted "fish-food" through the top hatch of the tank. It took her awhile to lower herself to sliding into the water and touching the slimy finger-food-sized pellets. At first bland and unappetizing, she soon found herself gulping them down hungrily. There was nothing for her to do but rest, swim, eat and contemplate revenge.

Time dragged on until, one day, she noted a red warning light on her chamber support apparatus blinking. Slipping into the water and wiggling closer to it, she noted the water temperature dropping.

Regan arrived shortly, looking as if he'd been awakened from deep sleep. He checked the temperature control console, tapped it several times, and, unsure of the problem, prepared to step into the tank. He normally entered the tank once a week to do some cleaning and check that all the internal sensors were functioning properly. Usually she shriveled into a corner to avoid him and his indecent leers, but this time she swiveled towards him, trying catch his eye with her uncovered breasts.

Regan found it difficult to concentrate on the job at hand, and, after some deliberation, stopped what he was doing, and, eyes wide with excitement, waded over to her. He hadn't had a woman for some time. Of course, her lower body was now a fish, leaving her, in effect, sexless, but this didn't deter an overwhelming desire to touch her.

Louisa licked her lips and cupped her breasts, coaxing him nearer. When at last he reached out for her, she brought a *faux* rock she was holding behind her down on his head, and he fell into the pool, a scarlet river of blood flowing from his scalp into the pool below, agitating the marine life there.

Louisa moved quickly, pulling the gold trident loose, rolling the corpse that a moment ago had been her husband's loathsome assistant in crime face-down into the water. With little effort, she located and detached the bulky set of house keys hanging below him. The open exit immediately above her required her to grasp its lip with both hands and pull herself out, not an easy task even if she had legs. In deference, she tossed the trident out and waited to see if anyone would come when it clattered onto the floor. After a few minutes without any response, she grabbed the rim of the hatch and pulled herself through, slithering her way onto the floor next to the trident.

Louisa next dragged herself and the trident across the stone floor using her her free arm and her powerful tail to move her along. It was arduous work, and soon her arms began to ache. She eventually made it to the stairway. Next to the stairway was a cabinet containing chemicals and medical supplies. Louisa used Regan's keys to open the lower door of the cabinet and procure some chemicals, including a jar of chloroform, then wrestle her way with the chemicals and trident up the formidable stairs and finally into the hallway leading to the main floor reception room.

The clock in the deserted hallway struck two. From the darkness, it was obviously two in the morning, which gave her sufficient time to carry out the next and most taxing part of her plan, requiring her to haul herself and appurtenances up another set of stairs to the second floor.

This final ascent was particularly laborious, the dry rugged texture of the carpet scratching and grazing her. Furthermore, her cumbersome tail was drying out and feeling increasingly uncomfortable. Still, twenty minutes later, she had hauled herself onto the second floor without being discovered. She slithered, concertina fashion, working her way to the master bedroom door. Delicately pushing the door ajar, she worked her way with trident and chemicals in hand, to where Crawford usually slept, only to find, to her limited surprise, not one, but two bodies in the bed.

The room reeked of alcohol.

On the far side of the bed, Louisa could make out Aida's naked form. Louisa felt sickened and angered at seeing Aida in *her* marital bed with *her* husband. Laying down the trident, Louisa wriggled over to the side of the bed where Aida was snoring softly, and doused the woman's night slip which was lying on the floor with chloroform. Reaching up, she placed it over the Aida's mouth and nose and held it there firmly.

Louisa took pleasure in feeling the woman struggle weakly from alcoholic torpor to momentary consciousness then helplessly back into an even deeper unconsciousness. Knowing that Crawford was a heavy sleeper and hearing the depth of his snores, she felt safe in pulling Aida's body from the bed next to her on the floor.

In the morning, when Crawford woke, his head was pounding, presumably from the excessive amount of alcohol he had consumed the night before. He could vaguely recall there being a wild party after his most recent showing of the basement gallery. Eyes tightly closed, one hand meandered to the back of the woman beside him. He stroked her gently, as he liked to do in the morning, slowly sliding his hand further downwards, expecting to feel Aida's slender curved rump. Instead, what he felt was flat, slimy and scaly. He tried to yell, but felt his head felt too queasy, and he directed his hand on another reconnaissance mission, this time to where the cleft between her legs should have been but wasn't. Adding to his confusion, he noticed the crisp morning air had a decidedly fish-like tang to it. Clearly, the body next to him was not Aida's. Forcing open his rheumy sleep-encrusted eyes, he beheld his reconstructed wife.

Sensing something terrible had happened to Aida, Crawford half-rolled, half-arched over the mer-woman next to him and onto the floor. Spread-eagled there lay Aida's lifeless body, the pole of the golden trident visible between the corpse's legs, the other end with its three prongs emanating from her open mouth. Huddling next to the body, Crawford began weeping uncontrollably, babbling, "What have you done?" at the half-woman, half-fish resting it's head on elbowed hands, staring down at him with glee.

"Why, Crawford. I've created another work of 'art' to add to that tasteless gallery of yours," she trilled in a soft, whispery voice, flipping her tail triumphantly.

Flight of Destiny

Maggot

Maggot was enraged and banged his fist on the table! Knives, forks, spoons and plates of food flew into the air. Up to this point, the banquet had been cordial, even good-humored. Necessary pleasantries and toasts had been exchanged. But as soon as serious negotiations had begun, indeed when money was brought into the equation, everything quickly went wrong. Where before congeniality had bound them, blood-lust now welled, taunts were being exchanged and enraged voices were promising vengeance for inexcusable slurs.

Excellency's face reddened and his eyes glistened with anger; his men in unison were grasping the handles of their scimitars.

In response, Maggot's goons eyeballed them angrily, and reached for the lethal weapons they had hidden in strategic places in their clothing, ready to react ferociously at the slightest additional provocation. Maggot's thugs, though severely outnumbered, were prepared to lay down their lives if it meant spilling the blood of their adversaries. A hush fell about the grand hall as Excellency, still seething with anger, slowly and calmly stood, gestured nonchalantly with his bony hand bedecked with expensive rings to his hair-triggered guards, who, in turn, reluctantly let go of the handles of their weapons.

Judd, Maggot's main henchman, playing the diplomatic foil for his master, laughed and tried to play down his master's indiscretion, as if a miscreant joke had gone awry. He reached forward and straightened Excellency's cutlery on the table and smiled sweetly, like a penitent child after a foolish prank.

Maggot, still vexed, snorted, mumbled something inaudible, then wagged a finger at Excellency. Maggot was little more than an overtly maladroit oaf, with a permanent scowl of dissatisfaction fixed upon his overly fleshy face. His baggy clothes, patched and re-patched over the years by his adoring wife, were emblematic of a circus performer who had seen better days. His other standout feature was the trademark medallion that always hung about his neck, which he claimed he'd acquired from a celebrated pirate's plunder. Ever boastful and vulgar, Maggot was a man unlikely to make friends, one who induced mainly fear and loathing in those who came into contact with him. "It's my daughter, Apollonia we're talking about, not a bag of grain or a mule!" he roared, still smarting over Excellency's derogatory offer. "She's my own flesh and blood!"

"Watch what you say and how you say it!" Excellency retorted. "I've had tongues cut out for less!"

Excellency was a more than a capable adversary. No one really knew or dared question his origins or real name for fear of swift retribution. Some said he was raised by vagabonds and horse thieves who taught him unscrupulous ways. Whether true or not, he proved to have great business acumen, had quickly accumulated a huge fortune, and with it, the unconditional respect of everyone. He may have started off as a horse rustler, but he'd worked his way up to buying, selling, and collecting expensive gems. Other rumors of a more fanciful nature circulated, claiming he was the abandoned illegitimate son of a nobleman and a beautiful actress. That rumor, Maggot figured, had probably been spread by Excellency himself, as it allowed him to claim he had noble blood running through his veins. Quite simply, the man was surrounded by mystery, and used it well to elevate himself onto his omnipotent pedestal.

What people did know for sure was that he "acquired" his current palace in a bloody coup. Bandits from the south had overrun the land, expelling the incumbent royalty, who'd fled with little more than their lives. Excellency procured the palace through a combination of bribery and force, and a new dynasty came into being.

Despite his lack of schooling, Excellency, more wily than the likes of Maggot, quickly began holding court, surrounding himself with the finest of legal, military and financial advisers. These days, his deportment had become that of a man of supreme confidence. After all, he'd become accustomed to dining and chatting with princes and all manner of dignitaries.

Maggot, the owner of a once notable circus that in better times had traveled the world, reflected on Excellency's warning and reconsidered his bargaining approach. "Excellency. My show doesn't make much money these days." Maggot's voice lowered and his tone softened. "Families don't visit the circus like they used to." His eyes moistened. "In truth, I'm desperate for funds. The troupe is being pressured to disband. My livelihood is disintegrating even as we speak."

"So you are selling your daughter to save your business?" Excellency scoffed. "Next, you'll be wanting to sell me your soul." Excellency's entourage sniggered sycophantically at the remark. Excellency drew in a sharp breath and shrugged. "Well then, let's get on with it and view the merchandise." His obsequious voice echoed off the massive stone walls of the vast, beautifully decorated hall.

Maggot stood, crossed his arms and stared at the massive wooden doors at the far end of the hall.

A hundred nobles and dignitaries, sitting on either side of the long rectangular table in the center of the room, shifted their attention to the doorway. Even the semi-clad belly dancers, fire eaters, and the animal tamers with their dancing tigers wearing diamond collars, who'd provided the earlier entertainment stood silent and still.

Choosing the moment, Maggot extended an arm aloft and snapped his fingers twice. Two fierce Mongols with shaved heads and leopard skin breech cloths, their brawny, cinnamon-brown bodies glistening with oil, appeared alongside the heavy entrance doors. Everyone in the hall inhaled at the same time, as the two men drew the massive doors open, their loud creaking adding to the sound of fanfare. Four circus strongmen marched into the room, carrying on their shoulders a thinly veiled palanquin with a stunning nubile stretched out on a couch-like seat, the weight of her head resting on a bent elbow. Musicians followed, beating on drums, twanging strings, and piping exotic Eastern tunes.

The young girl behind the veil might have been Cleopatra, except that, but for a fine gold thong, she was entirely naked. Gold coins strung on golden chains hung from all four sides of the palanquin, making chinking sounds with each of the carriers' steps. All this refinery had been gathered together by Maggot's wife, who had purchased, begged or borrowed every ounce of gold she could locate in support of her husband's gambit. Fruit, cherries, strawberries, pineapples, oranges, grapes, and rare exotic flowers, audaciously stolen that morning from Excellency's very own estate, surrounded the nymph. At each corner, burning incense drifted upwards, filling the room with a strong, musk-like aroma.

The girl couldn't have been more than sixteen. Her long black hair flowed over her shoulders down to her waist, barely covering her adolescent breasts. Every male in the room stared greedily, none noticing the smudged makeup highlighting her deep brown eyes, the result of a copious flow of tears at having been coerced into this.

Though her lithe body was perfect in proportion and her beauty stunning, in fact, she was of little use to Maggot due to an unfortunate accident. While standing on the back of a galloping horse while it circled around the ring, the horse, distracted by sudden applause, startled and bolted, throwing her to the ground. Since then, she walked with a limp. Unfortunately, there was no place for a person with an impediment, however slight, in a working circus, and she was instantly relegated from precious daughter to little more than damaged goods. Her younger sister, Candida, had already replaced her as the star of the horse show and the object of her father's love and favor. His redundant daughter was, nonetheless, still a commodity, and, when his coffers ran dry, as they did now, he felt no qualms about exploiting her.

The procession came to a halt in front of Excellency. The music abruptly died, leaving him to stare at the young girl, who looked in every way like a virginal offering in some primitive sacrifice.

Excellency licked his lips.

The tormented young girl flinched and looked away. Unlike her father, Maggot, with his ape-like physique, leathery skin, and pocked face accentuated by bulbous scheming eyes, the man seated before her was neither attractive, nor, for that matter, overtly ugly. His olive-tanned face was punctuated by a pencil thin mustache, and his eyes resembled those of a wildcat. She began imagining with loathing being manhandled by his talon-like hands.

Excellency stood and approached her; several of his courtiers followed, circling and ogling, passing their observations to Excellency. Several women at the table hissed under their breaths.

"Stand before me!" Excellency ordered gruffly.

Reluctantly, she dismounted, cowering before him, pressing her folded arms tightly against her breasts to protect them from his hungry stare. Raising a gilded baton he carried at his side, he prodded her, running it down the contours of her body, noting and analyzing her like a buyer might a new thoroughbred.

"Open your mouth," he commanded.

Apollonia blushed and slowly opened her mouth to reveal a perfect set of radiant white teeth. Excellency circled around, noting the delicate curve of her hips and buttocks. "Is she…pure?" demanded her would-be purchaser, shooting a quick glance in Maggot's direction, as if this would have direct bearing on the "price" of the goods he was considering purchasing.

"Of course, Excellency," said Maggot boldly. "She's never been touched."

Now this was absolutely true. He'd guarded his firstborn with the greatest of care. No man was allowed to speak to her without his approval, and he forbade her to show anyone even the slightest of intimacies. Only last winter, a young Italian knife-thrower went too far for Maggot's liking: With reckless bravado, the young man began following her around like a puppy dog, until he was heard by Maggot to say one day, "*Che bella, donna!*" while offering her a single red rose. That was it for Maggot. He had the young man beaten to a pulp in front of his frightened daughter, then had the mangled body thrown into the river. Nobody ever knew if the young man perished or somehow miraculously survived, but all agreed the incident served a stern warning to every man to keep well away from Maggot's daughter.

Apollonia, having been ordered to climb back onto her throne, eased herself forward to address Maggot in a hushed whisper, pleading, "Father, please. Don't do this to me."

Excellency swiveled on the balls of his feet and waved his baton in the air, as if he were performing a magic trick. "She speaks," he mocked. "And with a dulcet voice!"

Maggot said nothing, but averted his gaze from both his daughter and her future owner. With blatant indifference, he sat down at the table, grabbed a chicken leg from one of the guest's plates and gnawed on it, then guzzled the man's wine.

"Throw in your other daughter, too, and we have a deal," declared Excellency with a mischievous smile on his face.

Maggot's face pinched tightly, and soured dramatically. "Next you'll be wanting my wife and then all the female performers in my troupe," he growled.

Excellency clearly didn't appreciate the circus upstart's rude remark, and began thinking of how to punish the man for his insolence.

Judd, Maggot's second-in-command, looked nervously at both men, fearing this new spat might topple the jittery *ententée cordial* that he had, with the greatest of difficulty, been maintaining on behalf of his master.

Excellency hesitated. Though he felt cheapened by Maggot's insolent remark, he was prepared to overlook it. At the forefront of his mind was the fact that the young girl being offered was clearly unwilling, which made him want her even more. Reluctant types were his favorite. It was the desperate pleas for mercy, the tears, the torment, followed inevitably by submission. Always the proficient negotiator, he frowned and shook his head acknowledging defeat. "All right then," he sighed, "I'll take the other daughter off you the next time you're broke," adding loudly, "assuming, of course, that this one pleases me."

The tension throughout the great hall lightened, many of the guests tittered at his jest.

Gesturing nonchalantly at one of his waiting attendants, Excellency watched the man leave the room and return with a small wooden chest, which he presented, open, to his employer. Excellency reached in, drew out a number of gold coins, and dropped them with disdain into Maggot's open palms.

Maggot fingered the money in his gnarled fingers. His beady eyes drifted from the coins in his hand to the remaining ones flashing and glinting inside the treasury box.

Excellency, seeking to end the negotiation, cleared his throat and ran his spindly fingers through his long hair. "I think I will take advantage of the girl now," he announced with a wicked smile. "Take her to my quarters and have her prepared," he ordered, shooing the palanquin away with a flick of his bejeweled fingers.

The girl's fate decided, the four strong men shouldered the palanquin while Apollonia for a final time searched her father's eyes, beseeching him to change his mind. It was a useless gesture, as

Maggot was busy counting and ogling the gold coins. To his daughter's dismay, he never gave her a second glance, and she was carried, wailing inconsolably, through the massive banquet hall doors, down a short hallway and through another doorway to Excellency's sleeping quarters. The procession stopped in the middle of the room.

Apollonia looked about warily. The quarters were lavish to the point of outright ostentatiousness. The room was paneled in thick slabs of dark teakwood inlaid with mythical, blond, sandalwood figures and bedecked with real jewels. Gold and silver *objects d'art* filled the room, giving it the appearance of Ali Baba's fabled cave. Human-sized alabaster figurines of warring deities in front of fresh six-foot-tall birds-of-paradise flower arrangements in large marble vases decorated each corner.

The centerpiece, the bed, was hand-carved from one enormous piece of mahogany, its cabriole legs and swan-neck posts covered with gold leaf. It was four times the size of any bed Apollonia had ever seen. Four thin mesh tapestries veiled the interior, the one facing her depicting a young maiden caught in the arms of a lascivious pursuer, surrounded by bare-breasted wood nymphs lamenting her impending loss of innocence.

Staring into the face of the inevitable, the girl pushed aside the veil, crawled hesitantly onto the soft bed, and examined a cluster of fresh grapes in an ornate bowl resting on a side table, kept next to the bed in case Excellency required refreshment between his exertions. Apollonia, curled on her side into a fetal position, and, anxious, stared at the grapes and began nervously mouthing a protective incantation she'd heard her Gypsy mother use in a similarly desperate situation.

Excellency arrived a short time later, wearing a light-colored silk tunic embroidered with scorpions. His sick smile suggested that he

97

was planning something cruel. He walked silently to the edge of the bed, parted the veil, scooted next to her and began stroking her silky hair. Swallowing her fears, she assumed a kneeling position and purred, "Excellency, may I first offer you a refreshment?"

Interpreting this as a sign of weakening resolve, he nodded affirmatively and opened his mouth. When he bit into the grape, however, was horribly bitter, and he picked up his baton, arched his arm back and brought it down on her hand. Apollonia shrieked with pain.

"What are you trying to do? Poison me?" he shouted.

Apollonia rubbed her stinging hand, and looked at him with surprising composure. The torment written all over her earlier had lifted completely, which both baffled and troubled Excellency.

Instead of whimpering, the young girl pointed a finger at him and said solemnly, "Everything you smell, see, touch or hear will become bitter, foul and ugly!" Excellency paused, then scoffed as the girl, seemingly satisfied with the effect of her warning, stretched out in front of him like a cat enjoying the heat of the sun. Watching her, he reasoned the threat was little more than a childish ploy to buy time before the inevitable. Still, he'd heard that she came from Gypsy stock, and her mother was said to be well-versed in curses and incantations. A man of his stature, however, couldn't be deterred by impotent threats from a circus owner's daughter or he would lose face. In the end, the threat actually increased his desire, so, despite her warning, he started groping her. Her response was unexpected. She kicked and bit him, and when that didn't work, raked his face with her fingernails and began threatening to scratch out his eyes.

After a while, he simply gave up. In truth, he wasn't feeling his usual self, anyway. His overindulgence at the banquet combined with the horrid-tasting grape and the girl's highly charged resistance, had left him feeling surprisingly lethargic and worse still, impotent. His immediate need was sleep rather than sexual gratification, which he presumed would follow once he'd slept and regained his strength and ardor. Groaning, he rolled off her, and fell instantly asleep.

All night vivid scenes from his morally depraved past occurred interspersed with horrific nightmares, the worst he'd ever experienced, as if the visions had been conjured from hell itself. He awoke next morning to a foul stench. Wrinkling his nose, he attempted to bat it away with a hand, only to realize it was emanating from the palanquin sitting in the middle of the room.

The fruit, which last night had looked so appealing, had turned a sickly brown. Rotten and fetid, white maggots crawled on the fruit, while black clouds of flies hovered and buzzed above it. He felt he was going to vomit. Excellency looked at the young girl sleeping peacefully on the other side of his bed, and vaguely remembered trying to violate her, his failure further embittering him. He surveyed his domain and its treasures for reassurance, but they seemed to have lost their appeal. Everything about him, in fact, had become drab and pedestrian. Excellency sat upright and called loudly for his chamberlain.

The chamberlain appeared instantly, pausing in the doorway to await his master's permission to enter, wondering what the commotion was about. Excellency pointed at the palanquin. "Get this rancid fruit out of here, then throw this damned she-devil out of the castle and have her whipped in the street."

The attendant, wide-eyed and confused, nodded in obedience. The fruit looked fine to him and the girl as lovely as she had looked the previous night. Calling for some guards to carry out his master's unusual instructions, he noted Excellency prodding his chest. From Excellency's perspective, a caustic red rash covered his entire torso, which, when touched, caused him unbearable pain. "And get a doctor!" he bellowed. Thoroughly bewildered, the chamberlain nonetheless did as ordered and called for a doctor.

Four guards entered and carried away the palanquin, munching happily on fruits once outside Excellency's sight. Two guards carrying whips entered next and prepared to drag beautiful girl, now awake and screaming, from the room. To Excellency, her shrill screams were like the discordant cacophony of a hundred out-of-tune violins. The distraught man squeezed the palms of his hands on either side of his head, but the gesture only seemed to amplify the sound and resulting pain.

"Stop, you're infernal screeching, woman!" he bawled, yelling at the guards, "She's a malediction! The woman's possessed! Get her out of her! Now!" The guards rushed to get the girl out of sight and earshot of Excellency, darting her through the palace and promptly throwing her into the street. Normally they would have carried out their orders to whip her, however, fearful, based on what they'd seen, that young girl might be an enchantress and that Excellency's strange behavior was her doing, they ordered some passersby's to spirit her away. *Her* nightmare at least had passed, and she was free of her lecherous tormentor.

Within the half hour, the palace physician arrived and, despite a thorough examination, couldn't find a single physical sign of disease. All the afflictions Excellency was complaining about seemed to be in his imagination. Worse, the innocuous lotions the doctor offered only seemed to make the skin condition, in Excellency's eyes, worse.

Frantic from the irritation of his skin and exasperated with his physician, Excellency decided to try bathing in a herbal solution of chamomile, lavender and lemongrass. He may as well have jumped into a vat of boiling water. Squealing like a pig being boiled alive, he catapulted out and proceeded to run around the room, naked and cursing. All the ugliness Apollonia had threatened him with was happening, and worse, he felt like the experience was driving him on a fast road to insanity.

At the head cook's suggestion, a plate of his favorite foods was prepared: crayfish-and-poached-quail-egg salad with truffle vinaigrette was offered, but to no avail. The mere sight made him queasy. In a last ditch effort, servants encouraged him to down a horn of warm milk with honey to ease his roiling stomach, but he ended up vomiting it out. The fact was, he couldn't face any food or drink; everything looked, smelled and tasted grotesque and uninviting.

That same morning, Maggot received an official looking letter. The circus, it stated, hadn't paid its taxes for years. The anomaly had been brought to light by a rival circus owner formerly in Maggot's employ, who'd held the purse strings for Maggot's circus when it was still lucrative and flourishing. The man had been forced to leave Maggot's circus, it was said, under acrimonious circumstances. On hearing Maggot's audacious plan to sell his daughter to raise funds to reprieve the circus, Maggot's rival had vindictively informed Excellency's exchequer.

Maggot would have to come up with the same amount of money he'd just been paid, or lose the circus, and he couldn't use the money he'd been paid for his daughter as he'd already spent it paying circus members the back salaries due them, as well as splashing out for all those who'd helped him for a celebratory meal. It was time, he decided, to cash in his one remaining asset, his other daughter,

Candida. He'd successfully pulled off the one deal and Excellency by his own word had a weak spot for nubile girls. And, the man had initially offered to buy Candida along with Apollonia. First, however, Maggot needed a plan, and it came to him almost instantly.

He would need to acquire several bottles of the finest wine available. Having already spent all his money, he had to promise sellers double the cost once the business deal was completed. Then he gathered together the most brutal men he could muster to accompany and protect him, just in case things turned sour. Candida, despite the promise of being consort to a man of wealth and a solace to her sister, was vehemently against the idea, but she eventually complied with her father's wishes after he'd menaced her with a whip used to restrain the wild cats in the circus. Maggot's resourceful wife adorned her remaining daughter to look even more desirable than her other. As the party set off for the palace, Candida wept, as bitterly as Apollonia had, en route to the fate that had awaited her. Maggot's wife tried her best to console the young girl, while desperately trying to maintain her appearance.

At the palace, the atmosphere was one of expectant foreboding. With Excellency struck down by an inexplicable malaise that only he could see, doubts had begun floating outside the palace not only about his sanity, but, of greater importance, his ability to maintain law and order. Maggot, desperate to get his hands on the required money, pounded on the palace gates and didn't wait to be acknowledged, demanding to be taken directly to Excellency, threatening to order his armed brutes to slice the ears off any man who stood in the way. Inside, the palace had descended into turmoil. Normally, no one would dare enter Excellency's private quarters without permission; however, with their leader being indisposed, his private secretary, intimidated by the armed visitors, led the party *ex post haste* to where Excellency was currently sequestered. Maggot, brimming with confidence and hopeful expectation, charged directly into the room. Even Excellency's look of outrageous indignation at the intrusion couldn't dampen Maggot's ardor.

"A new proposition!" he said smiling and pointing at Candida, who, standing beside him, did indeed look even more alluring than her sister.

To his consternation, the man who Maggot hoped would be his salvation was in bed, scratching himself raw and howling.

Maggot paused, puzzled by what he was seeing, but continued anyway. "I trust you spent the best of nights with my first daughter, Excellency," said Maggot. "If you found her pleasing, I'm sure you will find her sister even more..."

It was, of course, evident to all in the room that Excellency had not and would not. The man in bed before them seemed a pale shadow of the one who had bargained so adeptly and with such imperiousness for Apollonia. Excellency rolled his bloodshot eyes, and with the all the energy he could rouse, leapt from his bed, grabbed a dagger, and began wildly lashing out at, mostly at thin air, while Maggot looked on, bemused.

Flight of Destiny

Little Mite

Little Mitzi Dashville was desperate to re-win her parent's favor. If only she could get them to laugh at one of her crazy antics, then, maybe, they would melt in adoration, as they had so often in the past, and in the process, rescind the onerous punishment meted to her. Little Mite (she hated that name but had to admit it suited her) was grounded. It wasn't as if she didn't fully merit the punishment. Her unforgivable actions had caused untold physical as well as psychological damage to her victim, little Jed Johnston, as well as dire consequences for her older sister. Still, even long after the event, Little Mite vehemently maintained in her mind that the despicable boy with his sickly sweet nature deserved it.

The Dashvilles, an established family from the upper echelons of high society, traced their roots back countless generations. The

Johnstons, lacking the Nashville's credentials, were considered *nouveau riche*. They lacked the Dashvilles' credentials, but welcomed their fraternity. The Johnsons were rolling in money, while the Dashville fortune was decidedly on the wane, due mainly to Mr. Dashville's lack of business acumen and a streak of ill-advised business ventures.

Dwindling old money met new, and in the process, Little Mite's older sister, Hannah Dashville, became engaged to Jed's older brother, Connor Johnson. The happy couple were filled with expectancy over the wonderful life that lay before them. The whole marriage thing, however, bored Little Mite to death. Furthermore, it incensed her that her parents were directing so much attention at Hannah.

Little Mite's descent into disgrace had begun innocently enough with a formal lunch on the lawn, a sumptuous affair catered by the premiere culinary artist of the region, attended exclusively by the two immediate families. Jed's parents, in hosting the affair, spared no expense. In fact, the chef recommended by the Johnsons had outshone all expectations. Several cases of vintage wines accompanied the *lobster bisque* with *crème fraîche*, the caviar toast, the roast leg of new lamb with Italian stuffing and red wine sauce, the best cheeses France could offer, and handmade ice cream topped with *crème caramel* and rum-soaked raisins. Little Mite had enjoyed the desert. This was followed, for the adults, by rich Jamaican coffee. All in all, both families concluded it a resoundingly successful next step in the long list of social events presaging Conner and Hannah's eventual union.

Aside from the wonderful desert, however, Little Mite was bored and restless. Grownups could be so tedious with their never-ending chatter, particularly this interminable talk about invitations, engagement photos in society magazines, and wedding plans. To help circumvent her boredom, she copied Hannah and Connor, brushing her leg repeatedly against young Jed's, noting with inner glee how his eyes, like Connor's, lit up. Encouraged, she took action into her own hands. She excused herself, got up from the white wrought-iron table, smiled sweetly at Jed, and invited him to wander the grounds with her.

Her parents, as expected, hardly noticed. Waving the two youngsters away, her mother maintained unbroken attention on Mrs. Johnson, who was inquiring about the most fashionable shops for wedding attire, while her father worked hard to hammer out a joint family business relationship with Mr. Johnston. Mr. Johnston, for his part, was nodding politely, acknowledging what Mr. Dashville was saying, while keeping his eyes and ears cocked in the direction of his wife, who he was worried might, in attempting to match Mrs. Dashville in social graces, with another glass of wine or two, might end up letting slip her lower class roots. In fact, Mr. Johnston had met his wife at a meat-packing factory where they were both working at the time. She had undergone a Pygmalion-like transformation since then, but alcohol had a habit of redirecting her comportment back to that of their former days. With his eldest son poised to marry a Dashville, Mr. Johnston wanted to make certain that nothing would interfere with his family reaching, at last, the pinnacle of social respectability.

Little Mite grabbed Jed's hand and led him behind the mansion to the rickety wooden door of her father's workshop. For safety reasons, she was forbidden to enter without an adult present.

Jed, with his impressionably innocent face, blond curly hair and magnetic blue eyes that bore a strong resemblance to those portrayed in paintings of angels, was almost her age. Little Mite tried staring deep into his eyes, like she'd seen Hannah do to Connor, but like the spineless wimp she'd marked him as, Jed averted his gaze and recoiled his hand. He was terribly immature for his age, she concluded, far too sensitive, and too much of a milksop for Little Mite's liking.

Little Mite told Jed she wanted to show him something. "It's going to be fun," she promised, climbing on the bench next to the locked door and reaching for the key she had seen her father place there. Retrieving it, she climbed off the bench and ordered Jed to wait while she unlocked the door.

Jed, unsure whether he should feel happy or not with the unfolding situation, remained torn between following the intriguing little girl and running back to the safety of his parents. He sensed Little Mite was about to do something mischievous, something distinctly wrong, but in the end, his curiosity and daring got the better of him. Little Mite giggled at the boy's naivety.

Inside the workshed, she reached up on tip-toe to a shelf and retrieved a jar of instant adhesive furniture glue, opened and upended it, allowing a sizable dollop to plop onto a rough-hewn coffee table her father had assembled but had not yet finished sanding.

Carpentry was one of her father's secret passions. He loved the feel of the different fine woods, and whenever he got the chance, enjoyed working them into useful furniture, which, when complete, became placed in conspicuous places of honor about the house.

Little Mite called out Jed's name in a luring sing-song voice, and he shuffled nervously closer to her, not knowing what to expect. "Give me your hand," she commanded.

Jed was unsure whether to do so. Still, he'd enjoyed the feel of her soft hand in his while running together from the lawn party to the shed. She was the first girl who had ever really shown interest in him. Though he continued vacillating between obeying this intoxicating girl and returning to his family, he finally gave in to her and bashfully extended his hand.

The moment he did, Little Mite grabbed it and slapped it into the middle of the glue, holding his hand there with all her might.

Jed, shocked by the abruptness and the unexpectedness of the act, stood paralyzed, mouth open, staring at his hand while the glue cured. By the time he'd gathered his wits, protested, and attempted to withdraw his hand, it was too late. After a hopeless struggle, he resigned himself to waiting to see what the little vixen had further in mind.

Little Mite didn't stop there. Once she was sure his hand was firmly stuck onto the table, she grabbed a large rag from her father's workbench and left the shed to search the nearby woods for stinging nettles. Wrapping the bases of the stalks in the cloth, she returned, unceremoniously undid Jed's trousers, pulled them down to his ankles, and shook the bundle of nettles menacingly in front of his face.

Jed was stunned. He did his best to avoid imagining what was about to happen, but was soon shaking his bare flanks and squirming wildly as she whipped his backside and legs mercilessly with the nettles. His first inclination was to endure the humiliation in silence, but the continued lashing and rapidly increasing burning all over the lower half of his body soon left him howling in agony.

It was her initial plan to simply bring the boy to tears, but to Little Mite's surprise, once he broke silence, she couldn't stop. It was as if she had entered an ecstatic trance. After several minutes of exertion, she tossed the nettles aside and left the shed, leaving him sobbing. Equally horrified and excited, she skipped back to the lawn party where the two families were, needless to say, still engaged in conversation about Connor and Hannah's upcoming marriage and the soon-to-be-married couple were equally busy whispering and laughing together. Suddenly realizing the gravity of what she'd done, Little Mite conjured up tears, and in her most theatrical manner bawled, "Mother! Father! There's been a terrible accident!"

The adults stopped chattering and looked at her quizzically. The Johnstons, noting Jed's absence, became all the more concerned. Little Mite, realizing she still hadn't fully captured Connor or her older sister's attention, shrieked, "Didn't you hear me? There's been a terrible accident!"

When she had at last wrestled the smitten couple's attention, she explained between sobs that Jed had, against her better judgment, persuaded her to show him her father's workshop. He had been fooling around with some glue, she said, and had somehow glued himself to the new table her father had made. The glue had brought on an allergy attack and he was now covered in red blotches.

On reflection, it sounded ridiculous, even to a child of her age. Worse, in her excitement, she had failed to make her voice sound entirely convincing; in short, this performance was not one of her better ones. Furthermore, in recounting her version of the event, she had come to regret what she'd done to Jed, fearing her parent's displeasure and the inevitability of a severe punishment, though she continued to take pleasure in remembering young Jed Johnson's squeals of agony, as well as the impact it would have on Hannah, her annoyingly saccharin-sweet older sister.

The Dashvilles and Johnstons marched to the shed where they found young Jed whimpering pitifully, still unable to loosen himself from the table, his backside and legs glowing a brilliant red. An ambulance was hastily called, and Jed and his parents were taken, along with the table, to the nearest hospital.

Little Mite was sent to her room in disgrace.

The Johnstons initially played down the incident, but Hannah nonetheless detected a change in their and Connor's attitude towards her. Connor suddenly became preoccupied with other matters. At first, Connor dismissed her claims of neglect, but it wasn't long before his visits became rarer and his excuses totally unconvincing. Hoping to salvage the engagement, she'd begged him to meet with her to clear the air, the result of which was a vapid and very loud public argument, after which the engagement was formally called off.

Jed, in the meantime, had retrieved his hand, but it had required surgery. The Dashvilles had called in a world-renowned plastic surgeon who had performed a miraculous job disuniting Jed from the table at, of course, the Johnston's expense. However, in the end, the Dashville's olive branch gesture fell short.

Worst of all, at least from Hannah's perspective, Connor was seen the very next day escorting his old flame, Cherry Durmstone, who he'd taken a year earlier to the school Prom, where the two had been crowned Prom King and Queen and, as a result, had become a "couple."

A short while after, however, while Connor was away on a college field trip, Cherry had been invited to a house party, where, after having been liberally plied with alcohol by several football players, she'd ended up doing a solo strip tease. Unfortunately, one of the licentious partygoers had taken photos of the whole affair. She'd stopped short of going the whole way, not so much by choice, but by having collapsed at the critical moment in an undignified drunken heap. The story of this incident spread like wildfire, and, augmented by adolescent fantasy, evolved into an outlandish story of her having been caught *in flagrante delecto* in the embrace of a naked tight-end.

Upon returning from his field trip, Connor, fearful of becoming a laughing stock, decided to break up with the girl, who he'd always dreamed of marrying. This had paved the way for Hannah, who had maintained a watchful eye on Connor throughout their courtship.

Now the pendulum had swung back to Cherry. Connor made no effort to deny that he was once again seeing her, who he now regarded as a more stable prospect than a Dashville. Forgiving Cherry for her past indiscretion, he convinced himself he'd been mislead by the wildly unfounded allegations that had followed.

In the end, Little Mite's prank cost the Dashville family dearly. Hannah had lost a prime marriage prospect, and her father a wealthy potential business partner. What's more, her father had lost the coffee table he'd been laboring over for months, which he'd been intending to give his wife as an anniversary gift. But what pained Little Mite's father most was having to take his belt to his beloved daughter, while his wife, in the next room, wept in anguish over their misfortune, demanding Little Mite be severely punished. The punishment delicately meted, Little Mite's father immediately swept her into his arms, forgiving her and begging her forgiveness, hoping a lesson had been learned.

While Mr. Dashville forgave Little Mite, Hannah vowed to never forgive her sister. Bereft of her lover's affections, Hannah struck out on a mission to convince her father that, as a parent, he was far too liberal with Little Mite, and that this was the very reason why the incident had occurred. She warned that another such incident was bound to happen unless he punished her again, this time more sternly to remind her of the depth of her indiscretion. Eventually, harried and harassed, he condescended. Little Mite claimed the second punishment undeserved, holding to her original story, saying everyone had been hoodwinked by that cute brat, Jed. Barely into the beating, she began shrieking that she would have her father arrested and sue him for every penny he had left, after which she would divorce both her parents. In truth, Mr. Dashville hardly touched her. He made certain each lash directed at her had the same amount of force one might use to swat a niggling fly.

For two hours after the punishment, Little Mite kept up the pretense of having been irrevocably harmed. Little Mite's howling proved so excruciating to her father, he left the house in despair to retire to the quiet of his workshop, where he built a locking cabinet for his glue, and began work on a new coffee table.

Later that year, at Christmas, when the whole event should have finally passed into ignominy, Hannah and parents left for town to do some last-minute shopping, leaving Little Mite, who was still grounded, behind. To Little Mite it all seemed *so* unfair.

The time alone got her to thinking. She went downstairs and opened the family dressing up box, tossing clothes all over the place, until she found a bright and colorful dress from her mother's short-lived hippie days (her father had often ribbed her mother about it, saying it resembled a clown outfit more than a dress). Slipping into it, she looked carefully at herself in the mirror. It made her look totally ridiculous. Her plan wasn't her best or most original, but without a better idea, she decided to hide in her parent's upstairs clothes closet, and, when they came home and couldn't find her, she would jump out and surprise them. They would laugh wildly at her clothing and antics, she felt assured, all would finally be forgiven, and she would regain her lost privileges and favor. Her mother would hug her endearingly; her father would doubtlessly double over with laughter. Hannah would probably never forgive her, but Little Mite would find a way of circumnavigating this problem with time, and, besides, what did she really care about Hannah anyway, so long as her parents loved and adored *her*? If the plan were to work, however, she needed to hide, and hide quickly before they returned.

"Little Mite, we're home," her father and mother yelled as they walked over the threshold, laden with Christmas gifts, their guilt at leaving their youngest alone at home apparent in the worried tone of their voices. There was no sign of Little Mite, but there were clothes scattered everywhere.

"Little Mite, where are you?" her father called with concern.

Little Mite, ensconced upstairs in her parent's clothes closet, rattled some wooden coat hangers and stamped her feet to attract their attention.

Hannah, hearing the commotion upstairs, eyebrows furrowed, said in a low whisper, "Father! I believe there's a burgler upstairs!"

Mr. Dashville looked at his daughter and then back at his wife with grave concern. The two women, lead by Hannah's remark, clearly expected him to act.

Hannah recognized that the situation had all the hallmarks of a Little Mite prank. She was up to one of her antics, another pathetic stunt to win undeserved parental favor. Then Hannah thought of Connor holding Cherry in his arms, and her face twisted with outrage. The situation, she decided, had presented an opportunity to teach her brat of a sister a lesson, and, more poignantly, the perfect chance for *revenge*. Hannah put on a face of fear, tensed her body, made her teeth chatter, and whispered in a quavering voice, "Dad! I'm scared, please, *do* something!"

At first, Mr. Dashville seemed undecided. Then they heard another muffled thump from above.

"I'll get a gun," he replied and crept stealthily across the room to the gun cabinet. Quietly unlocking it, he removed his hunting shotgun, and loaded it. Cradling it in the nook of an arm, he carefully searched the living room, then the dining room and kitchen, and, finding nothing untoward, approached the stairs. At the foot of the stairs he heard another rattle coming, this time he was certain, from his and his wife's bedroom, more precisely the large closet which was full of his wife's clothing and accessories, including her jewelry box laden with the last of the family's heirlooms. With visions in his head of some low-life meddling about in the closet and stealing the last of their most precious possessions, he mounted the stairs.

Hannah and her mother followed Mr. Dashville light-footedly up and into the master bedroom. He was about to demand that the intruder or intruders give themselves up, when the closet door burst open and out sprung a grotesque figure, shrieking and waving it's hands menacingly in the air. Mr. Dashville's trigger finger twitched reflexively. The loud report was followed by a muffled scream and the thump a body flung against the back of the closet.

An anxious silence swallowed the smoke-filled room. Mr. Dashville's wife and daughter peeked from behind, and the three stared with horror at the disfigured, lifeless body of Little Mite. Mr. Dashville dropped the gun, fell to his knees and began sobbing. Mrs. Dashville put her hands to her mouth and wailed uncontrollably. Hannah shrugged nonchalantly while a delicious smile spread across her face. She hadn't felt this happy since Connor had proposed. She could even imagine the possibility of regaining Connor's affections, now that her abominable younger sister was finally out the way.

Flight of Destiny

Gomford

Gomford returned to the village with more than his customary ragged suitcase. Clutched firmly in-hand was a vision of an angel who went by the name of Clarissa Honeychild. A businessman in his thirties, with seemingly all the particulars in dress and deportment, Gomford nonetheless cut a distastefully awkward figure. His face was perpetually bloated, and when he spoke, it was in sniffles and snorts. His eyes resembled those of a crocodile. His thick neck, likened by many to that of a tree trunk, gave him the illusion of massive strength, and left others feeling diminutive and anxious in his presence. Gomford, through no fault of his own, was shunned by his fellow villagers and ostracized by all, to the point that he did all his business elsewhere.

Due to his looks, Gomford had been condemned to a life of celibacy, sharing his bed with only a handful of women, all of whom demanded pre-payment for services rendered. Some outright refused him, despite the fact that he was the most successful businessman the village had ever seen, and, over the years had amassed a considerable fortune, and always paid people well for their services. The idea of this stumpy man smothering them, even for a sizable fee, filled most working girls with aversion. Even Glynnes Trout, the local prostitute responsible for introducing practically every male denizen to sex, an old pro with the willingness to perform even the most depraved of acts with any gender, had disrespectfully declined Glomford, despite his waving in her face a sizable wad of banknotes. The event, told, retold and by now highly embellished, was a favorite topic of late night discussion in the local pub whenever all other conversation ran out.

The fact that he had returned with a woman on his arm, and furthermore, a young woman of such incomparable beauty, sent the village into a frenzy of agitated speculation. When it was further revealed that he had *married* the woman, the whispering campaign hit an unprecedented high, displacing all other gossip. The village women, most with plain prosaic faces and not blessed with even a modicum of Clarissa Honeychild's beauty, felt particularly threatened.

The men, on the other hand, warmly welcomed the pretty newcomer. Their slumbering libidos jolted back to life, they took to whispering lewd comments to one another as she passed on the street. The three village paternal icons, Chadwick, Knoll, and Smerton, all married to loyal, but plain, dumpy, rotund women, could not contain themselves, being swept into thrall by the beguiling newcomer.

Word soon became spread that Gomford would be once again be going away, his business regularly taking him on long trips to distant places. His young bride, of course, would remain behind, and speculation was high as to what she would do to fill in the long periods of time while he was away. A country village had proven more than once to be a lonely place for one so young.

It was Chadwick who paid Clarissa the first visit, the moment he'd spotted Gomford leaving with a hefty suitcase.

Clarissa, sweeping the porch as Chadwick approached, glanced sidelong at him with suspicion. An uncomfortable silence filled the diminishing distance between the two until Chadwick finally spoke. "Good afternoon, ma'am," he ventured with care, doffing his worn, tweed driving cap to reveal a center-bald head. "I...I was wondering if you might need some manly assistance with things, what with your husband gone?"

Clarissa appeared to weigh his offer and intent. "And why would I need help?" she replied, with a curt finality Chadwick hadn't anticipated.

Chadwick was totally lost for an answer, and suddenly felt ridiculous for having started out with such a flimsy line, and worse, one that he felt Clarissa had immediately seen through.

Clarissa broke the silence. Throwing her head back, swishing her long tresses, she sighed, "Well, since you're here and have disturbed me, you may as well come in."

Chadwick had never been in Gomford's house. No one in the village to his knowledge had ever been in Gomford's domicile as he had always guarded his privacy. Chadwick visualized it as an exotic showy abode replete with brightly-colored pillows set on lavishly expensive divans, the room ornamented with objects brought from all manner of exotic lands. In short, the farthest cry possible from his own humble home.

The truth was totally different. The living room into which he was escorted was spotlessly clean but the appurtenances were old and in disrepair. Gomford was apparently not one to spend his hard-earned money on frivolities.

"Take a seat," she said, gesturing at a worn armchair. Several cushion-springs poked out from under the equally worn throw-cover.

Chadwick sat down, clutching his hat in his hand, head bowed, a man drowning in shame, already regretting his initial bravado.

"What is it that you really want?" she demanded, her voice laced with irritation.

Again Chadwick fell well short, being unable to conjure up any remotely satisfactory response. "Um. Well. As I said, ma'am, I just thought...well... with your husband gone, you might need some odd jobs done around the house," he mumbled, with the look of a child waiting to receive a severe and well-deserved punishment.

"What's your name?" she asked.

"Chadwick, ma'am. Lucas Chadwick."

"Well, Mr. Chadwick," she said with a wry smile, "let's dispense with this tiresome pretense, shall we?"

Chadwick wrung his cap tighter in his hands and winced, his pasty complexion paling as he sank further into the uncomfortable chair.

"Be honest, Chadwick. You came here to try your luck while my husband's away. You would, I dare say, like to have your wicked way with me, here and now, if possible, am I right?"

Chadwick was dumbstruck. He couldn't honestly deny what she had so boldly stated, so he just sat there, mawkish-like, looking ever more mournful. When he caught sight of her unbuttoning her blouse, he opened his mouth, but was interrupted before he could say anything.

"So, where do you want to do it?" she demanded in a chillingly flippant voice, catching Chadwick completely off-guard. "In the bed that I share with my husband? Or perhaps on the couch? You're the man. The choice is yours."

"On…on the couch?" he mumbled sheepishly, shocked even further by her brazenness.

"Then on the couch it shall be," she said, like a waitress who'd just taken an order from a customer in some humdrum cafe. The next instant, she was lying on the couch, her clothes in heap on the floor next to her.

"Well, what are you waiting for?" She asked testily, adding, "You came here with a purpose in mind, so get on with it, man."

Chadwick fumbled with his trousers, shuffling toward the couch and Clarissa with them about his ankles, then awkwardly clambered on top of her. A moment later, after his vapid groan, she pushed him off, and each dressed in silence.

Once dressed, she pointed towards the door and shouted viciously, "Now get out and never come back!" The venom in her voice propelled him out the door. On the porch, he looked furtively about while readjusting his rumpled clothes, fearful someone might see him, and make *him* the new subject of unending gossip. It was enough that he now had to face his wife burdened with the guilt of his infidelity.

In truth, he had never in his life even contemplated being unfaithful. He'd gone to visit Clarissa more on a self-dare, to "test the old waters" so to speak, to see if he still had it in him.

Guilt, even heavier than he'd felt when sitting in Gomford's chair staring at Gomford's lovely wife, abruptly seized him. His wife totally trusted him, and more so, had always shown him respect. They had known each other as far back as when they were children and often delighted in the fact that it had seemed ordained from birth that they should marry. Their marriage had, in addition, formally united two prominent village families. They'd each done what was expected and had made everyone about them happy and proud. Only a desperate or daring man like Gomford would think of marrying someone from the "outside," but then again, only a truly depraved husband would muscle in on another's wife as Chadwick just had.

Over the ensuing days, Chadwick fell into a deep, inexplicable melancholy. His friends, Knoll and Smerton probed, but Chadwick would give nothing away. To Chadwick's consternation, his two friends insisted on rambling on about Gomford's wife with suppositions of what she would be like in bed. It was therefore inevitable that one or other would eventually follow in Chadwick's footsteps.

It was Knoll who walked down the path next, stopping one day to knock on the Gomford door. Clarissa opened it with the same probing look she'd afforded Chadwick, and, again, invited the man in with similar indifference. Proving equally inept as Chadwick, Knoll was dispatched with the same speed and brusqueness, and he, too, sank into a similar depression to that consuming Chadwick.

As with Chadwick's wife, Knoll's couldn't understand her husband's sudden shift in mood, as he was usually a happy-go-lucky man, a wise-cracker, a carefree soul, simple in speech and uncomplicated in his needs and desires.

Not long after that, Smerton took his chance. If Chadwick and Knoll had but shared with him the cause of their anguish, Smerton, duly warned, would surely have not of succumbed to the same temptation as they had. Instead, it wasn't long before he found himself in Gomford's house, experiencing the same humiliation with Clarissa, after which she cast him out of her house, leaving him to join his two friends in feeling an abject failure racked with guilt.

It was not long before more village wives noticed a similar change in their men. There was, for example, Dandy Witherbee, the jovial butcher, noted for his charismatic, raucous laugh, and quick wit, who, without fail charmed all who entered his shop. One day his jokes dried up and his normally jocular face was replaced by a haggard hang-dog look. Customers were served in silence, as he lethargically cut and weighed out the bloody chunks of meat. It was as if his life-spirit had been sucked from him, leaving only apathy. The butcher's was no longer a cheerful place to visit; it had become more like a funeral parlor.

This same malaise relentlessly attacked, one-by-one, every male in the village, sparing only the confused women, who observed with mounting concern that many of the younger unmarried men had turned sullen and taken to serious drink. It was, one of the women noted, as if they were drinking to forget. Still, none of the women could pry any information out of their men, or decipher a likely cause for the terrible depression sweeping through the village. There emerged, however, one undeniable fact: The change in the men coincided with the arrival of Gomford's new wife.

Reverend Salmon, whose church in the past had always been full on Sundays, noticed not only dwindling numbers, but also the soulless expressions of his remaining male parishioners. Though invited, encouraged and eventually even threatened to confess whatever singular sin was burdening their collective minds and souls, the reverend hadn't had a single taker. He'd never in his life been uniformly stymied like this when prying into the hearts of men, but, then, the village had always been mostly sin-free, with a dull righteousness generally prevailing.

In actuality, it wasn't just the sullenness of the men that worried the reverend. Procreation, the very essence of family and village life, was being impacted. Since Gomford had returned with his wife, not a single christening had been scheduled. If the situation wasn't addressed soon, it wouldn't be long before the village would disappear altogether.

"Not since the plague has this village encountered such a disaster," he roared in frustration from the pulpit at the rows of empty pews. The reverend, not one for inaction, began spreading fear like thick oil throughout the village until everyone seemed to be drowning in it, creating the desperation he knew was necessary to take the next incisive step: "This village needs to exorcised!" he shouted at last.

A mid-day time was selected. Chadwick was commandeered into carrying a large white-washed wooden cross. The men and women of the village gathered behind him, and the party, with the reverend at its head, went from door to door. Irregardless of the occupants' faith or lack thereof, prayers were said and holy water sprinkled on every lintel. This time-proven remedy for casting out evil would, the reverend assured everyone, work spiritual magic, and the demon or whatever it was that was behind it all, would be cast out, and normality restored. Not a single household dared refuse, though, some of the older women tried desperately to invite the reverend and gathering in for a "cup of tea," which was each time firmly and uniformly declined by the reverend. Such was the seriousness of his crusade.

"Where to next, Reverend?" asked Smee, the village council leader, after they had finished most of the village central.

"That man, Gomford. We haven't done his house yet, have we

councilor?" asked the reverend. Up to now, all the males present had been careful to direct attention away from the Gomford residence. A look of anguish shot through Chadwick's suddenly ashen face and he stumbled, almost dropping the heavy cross.

"Steady, man," the reverend said, casting a critical eye in Chadwick's direction, wondering what could possibly have rattled the man so.

Knoll quickly intervened. "Gomford's not a churchgoer, that's for sure, Reverend, and rather an ugly brute. Besides, he and his wife are not likely to be in. He does a lot of business elsewhere. Wouldn't we do better concentrating our efforts..."

The reverend's face hardened, and he marched his troop down the path to Gomford's, where he banged his fist on the door with deafening thuds.

Silence.

When no one answered, Chadwick, Knoll and Smerton breathed a collective sigh of relief for all the men present.

As Reverend Salmon raised his fist to strike again, the door cracked and a young woman popped her head out. She looked bothered. Knoll squirmed. Chadwick and Smirton sucked in their breath and took a step back as if protecting themselves. The other males in the group shuffled their feet and stared at the ground.

"What the hell do all of you want?" she asked, spitting out the words while fearlessly surveying the reverend and crowd. The eyes of the women narrowed suspiciously; the men further averted theirs for fear the outspoken woman might decide to address one of them.

"I am a man of God. I have come to bless your house, good woman. The devil has attempted to defile our village, and we are here to purge your house of any lingering evil."

"And if I don't want my house blessed by the likes of you?" she demanded.

The reverend opened and closed his mouth like a fish gulping air. "Who are you to resist the word of God?" he finally rasped, pointing a finger skywards while his jaw quivered.

"This is my husband's property," the young beauty stated resolutely.

"And where might he be?" demanded the reverend.

"Not that it's any of your concern, but he's away on business," she replied unabashedly.

The reverend, galled by her resistance and detecting a shift in the group's attention from the issue at hand to what was quickly becoming a test of his power, decided a softer approach was in order.

"Good woman, won't you please permit me to sprinkle some holy water on your door and say a prayer for you and your husband's souls?" he asked in a winsome voice, as if making a humble request for her benefit, which, refused, would make her a *bête noire*.

Receiving no response, the reverend continued his new tactic, gently goading her a step further. "You are the only one in our village to question the word of God."

"Really? God's word or yours, Reverend?" mocked Clarissa, standing firm.

A murmur rustled through the crowd. The reverend's face soured as if he'd bitten into a rotten apple. "God speaks through me," he declared icily.

"Is that so?" queried Clarissa. "And I suppose he likes to go about with a band of hyped up religious fanatics disturbing people who are simply minding their own business?"

The reverend had *never* had his authority questioned like this before. Furthermore, he'd expected a spontaneous show of support from the others, and, as nothing was forthcoming, he hesitated, momentarily incapacitated.

It was clear to the gathered crowd that the young woman wielded considerably more power and authority than the reverend, despite his fiery rhetoric, and to the women present, that Clarissa was quite possibly the miscreant responsible for the change in their men. It stood to reason in their simple minds that she was, in fact, an enchantress, who led good men astray.

Reverend Salmon, having gathered his thoughts, tried one last assault. "Am I, then, to presume that evil lurks within these walls?"

Despite his best efforts, the reverend's eyes slid from the young girl's adamant face to her open blouse and generous breasts, which held such allure, he was unable to mask his feelings.

"You may presume what you like, Reverend," she snapped. "But for now, if you please, take your eyes off my breasts and lead this mob away from my house. I wish to be left in peace. I am bothered too much by the men of this village as it is." Her eyes began searching those of every guilty man who'd crossed her threshold to have his way, her action further intensifying their collective shame. At this point, Chadwick flinched, stepped backwards and in doing so lost control of the cross. As he wrestled to regain control, pandemonium broke out all around him, some scattering, others shouting in fear. At the same time, some adolescents from the city on their way to do fishing, stopped to watch the farce.

The reverend cursed, swiveled around and stomped off, snorting in anger.

"That's a nice bit of skirt you have there, vicar," called out one of the youths. The comment was met with howls of laughter from his friends, followed by a barrage of wolf whistles. The result of all this was that the reverend now felt shamed and humiliated, a sentiment the rest of the men of the village could easily identify with.

Blessings were offered at the rest of the outlying homes, but the reverend and the group quickly lost their zeal in freeing the village of its malediction. When finished, the reverend, back in the sanctuary of his rectory, consumed the better part of a bottle of whisky to dull the memory of a most unsatisfactory day.

In bed that night two questions wedged in his mind: First was how to regain the villagers' respect, and second was how to deal with the young woman who'd not only completely humiliated him, but whose beauty had left him feeling inappropriately infatuated. While most men would venerate such beauty, the reverend felt a growing compulsion to crush and destroy her. The plain-looking women who populated the village were not even remotely tempting. Here, however, was temptation itself, brazenly flouted in public. What could he do to stop the insidious spell she seemed to hold over the village men, him included? The moral fabric of the village was being tested, he decided. He had to act. That would be expected of him. The villagers, for the most part guileless, desperately needed his guidance.

To his surprise, a small delegation of female villagers arrived early the next morning, rousing the hungover reverend and demanding an audience. "We've a Godless woman, likely a harlot, maybe a witch amongst us," Knoll's wife vehemently pronounced, setting the tone.

"We must act, and act now before things get worse," added Cowie, a village Elder, "just as our forefathers would have done." All of the delegation vigorously nodded their assent.

The reverend cracked a smile. He wouldn't need to work them into a retributive frenzy; the villagers were already primed and eager for action. With that weight removed from his shoulders, he need only focus his aching head on what measures would be most appropriate. Being versed in the annals of church history, he was well acquainted with the period when it was common for those deemed guilty of subverting the morals of the community to be taken to a river and given a fatal dunking. A confession of witchcraft would justify the punishment, and, if none were forthcoming it would be a sure sign of guilt. The practice, of course, was archaic, having long since been abandoned by the church, but being short on other strategies, and in need of a way to publicly break the young girl's hold on everyone, it had a uniquely perverse appeal.

Nonetheless, he deemed it important to introduce the idea to the elders circumspectly, fearing there might be some who might react in horror, even report him to the authorities. Choosing his words carefully, he presented the idea as one of *divine* retribution.

As it turned out, the mere hint of a citizen vigilante group dragging the headstrong young woman forcibly from her house to mete out medieval justice seemed to get the villagers' pulses racing. All gave their unconditional approval, the women with sadistic smiles, the men basking in the salaciousness of the idea. The reverend would have to be careful not to attract the suspicion of the local constable, P. C. Cauldfield, a formidable man whose house was located not far from the Gomfords. By the reverend's reckoning, this wouldn't be much of an obstacle. There had never been a crime of consequence in the village, so, for the most part, Cauldfield led a retiring life, never once having been called to action. Done right, the deed could be carried out without rousing the man's suspicions.

A plan quickly emerged. Dr. Musgrove, the village doctor, who had a long history of appearances before the General Medical Council for a succession of serious improprieties and was famous for his reply in his defense, "Well, I didn't kill anyone, did I?" would be employed. With his second, more regular occupation, being that of the town drunk, his inviting Constable Cauldfield to the bar in town for a drink would seem natural. Once there, he would spike Cauldfield's drink. For his part, Musgrove was delighted that, after the years of doubt cast on his capabilities as a doctor, it was he who would play the principal part in the plan, being entrusted to provide a suitable drug to stupefy first Cauldfield, and then the young woman. That left only the matter of getting inside the Gomford house. It was summer. Everyone's ground floor windows, though small, were left open day and night. Chosen for his agility and svelte frame, Cowie's son would climb through an open window, unlock the door, and allow a group to abduct the Gomford woman.

Cauldfield was somewhat surprised that evening when the old doctor, who he'd barely spoken to in years, invited him for a drink at the local pub. The constable, having, as always, nothing better to do, while concerned about the infamous doctor's reputation for not being able to hold his liquor, nonetheless accepted.

While drinking with the dreary policeman proved less than enticing, Musgrove was able to survive Cauldfield's seemingly unending conversation, and also to slip a dose of sleeping potion into the man's drink. The vigilante group in the meantime gathered around Reverend Salmon who marched with them to the Gomford residence (this time, Kroll was made responsible for bearing the cross, Chadwick having been relieved of this duty, after his previous debacle). All waited in silence while Cowie's son slipped with relative ease into the Gomford house.

A minute later, the lad silently opened the front door. Drug in hand, Musgrove and Bland, the village woodcutter and strongest man in the village, stealthily entered the house.

Lang, the village carpenter, and Bland had earlier completed the dunking chair, modeling it on drawings the reverend provided from the church's archives. The finished device had been clandestinely moved to the river and carefully secreted under branches.

After what seemed to all a long and painful wait, Bland emerged carrying a limp body in a white night dress; Musgrove followed with a triumphant smile on his face.

The crowd, transfixed by her beauty and allure even when drugged, let out a collective sigh while the men's tongues hung out of their mouths making them look like famished dogs presented a chunk of raw meat.

The reverend, for his part, was awash with opposing emotions, feeling overall obliged to hustle the crowd towards the river where the incisive part of the plan had yet to be accomplished. "Let's get on with it," he said in a voice tinged with irritation, adding austerely, "We've a heretic to cleanse."

At first the men reacted listlessly as if the drugged woman's presence were exerting a restraining force. Noting the men's languor, the women took to spurring them on.

At the river's edge, the reverend surveyed the dunking contraption Bland had constructed with approving eyes, while the throng assembled around the makeshift seat, watching and waiting, their expectation mounting. The river, swollen but tranquil, would be unbearably cold this time of year. "Place the harlot in the chair, and strip off her robe, so she is naked in the eyes of God. Let the water purify her sin-ridden body," the fervent churchman intoned.

At first, the vigilantes paused, shocked at the extent of the reverend's directive. There was no history of dunking sinners naked, or indeed, any obvious justification for such an extreme action. This, however, didn't stop Bland from brusquely ripping away Clarissa's night robe, and triumphantly casting it aside to the cheers of the once again re-animated mob. Her body was still limp, but the reverend noted the slightest of winces on her delicate face, indicating she was soon to come around.

"Better tie her down," the reverend commanded.

Bland took out some cord and tied Clarissa to the wooden dunking chair, and, as he did, Clarissa groaned, opened her eyes, and, to her horror, found herself surrounded by a crowd intent on doing her harm. Her body stiffened with shock while her innocent eyes widened in terror.

Pointing a bony finger at the center of the terrified girl's face, the reverend solemnly pronounced, "You have been condemned, and are to be punished..."

"Punished for *what* exactly?" she interrupted, struggling helplessly to release herself from the cords that tightly gripped her limbs.

"You have woven some kind of dark magic on this community, and, in the process, have done the devil's work!" the reverend pronounced, his voice cracking on the word "devil."

"Are you crazy?" shrieked Clarissa. "This is absurd! You have no right..." She struggled frantically while searching for words. "You... you will all be locked up for this, you maniacs!"

"Quiet, harlot!" bellowed the reverend. "Repent instead while you still can."

"You're sick! You're all sick," screamed Clarissa, searching the hardened faces staring at her for any sign of compassion. "The whole lot of you!"

The reverend shook his head, closed his eyes, placed the palms of his hands together as if in prayer while the crowd dutifully bowed their heads. The leaves of the trees rustled and a cold night breeze slithered like a serpent through the gathering, making everyone shiver with malevolent delight. The moment of the dunking was at hand. All it would take now would be the slightest gesture from the reverend. Claressa began shaking from the cold and her own abject fear.

"Lord bless this cleansing process," the reverend proclaimed in his most convincing voice, making the sign of the cross and adding while looking up towards the starry heavens, "Deliver us all from the evil that is possessing this woman."

"Damn all you hypocrites to hell!" screeched Clarissa, realizing she was about to become the first woman in over three hundred years to succumb to such a barbaric act, while the truly guilty ones looked on. "You men all know what really went on in this shit-hole of a village!" she yelled.

"Dunk the witch!" bawled Bland, before veering into an uncouth tirade, undermining any semblance of religious ceremony or *faux* propriety.

This time, it was the reverend who was momentarily taken aback. "Hold your tongue, man. We can't have such coarseness tainting a ritual that requires the utmost sanctity."

Bland stopped his unnatural raving while the reverend re-made the sign of the cross, and prosaically decreed, "So let it be done."

Bland carried out the directive without hesitation, not waiting for any further sign. Before she was cognizant of what was happening, Clarissa felt herself lifted high into the air and swung over the river.

From what he'd gleaned from the old records, the first dunking was more a test of the resolve and fortitude of the victim. Some didn't survived the initial shock of the cold water. If this happened, the night would be decidedly flat and would fall well short of his and the villager's expectations.

Elevated over the river, the reverend and crowd watched Clarissa tear desperately at her bonds to free herself from the chair. The crowd, invigorated by her struggling, began chanting, "Dunk her! Dunk her! Dunk her!" Leaving her just barely enough time to catch her breath, the reverend signaled, and Clarissa disappeared into the cold, dark, all-encompassing river.

The crowd held it's collective breath until the reverend raised his hand and stated calmly, "Bring her up."

When the chair reappeared above the water, a dark waterfall cascaded from her gasping body. She was still struggling to break free.

The reverend frowned. "Do you repent your sins?" he demanded.

Clarissa was too breathless to respond.

"I say again: *Do...you...repent...your...sins?*"

Clarissa finally managed to cough up the water she'd swallowed and force out some words. "You men here...all of you who've cheated on your wives...do you not feel the least remorse?" Shocked women stared in disbelief at their husbands and boyfriends. Clarissa's words had scarcely escaped from her mouth, before the reverend gave the signal to dunk her a second time.

Pangs of guilt had begun to surface within the crowd.

"The bitch is lying," muttered one young man weakly, while all eyes fixed on the water swirling about the pole, the only indication of Clarissa's current presence being a stream of bubbles breaking the opaque surface several feet downstream. As long as she remained underwater she was incapable of making any accusations, yet everyone knew she if remained there long, her life would surely ebb away.

"Bring her back up," the reverend said, a flicker of anxiety in his voice.

Bland hesitantly complied.

This time, Clarissa was in a much poorer state, appearing pale white, coughing, then finally wheezing desperately for breath. It was plain to all that this second dunking had taken a serious toll. Looks of apprehension began to appear here and there from within the crowd.

Upon seeing her, however, the reverend's face took on a look of seditious delight. The dunking was proving to be more exhilarating than he'd ever imagined. He couldn't recall when he'd felt so alive.

"So...what you bastards want...is me...dead?" she managed between gasps. Covered with a thin patina of grayish river mud, she began shaking uncontrollably.

The reverend was jolted from his reverie by the unexpected outburst. Clarissa's resistance was surprising. She seemed to possess an unfathomable fortitude. Perhaps she *was* empowered by the devil after all? "Dunk her!" hollered the reverend, forgetting all piety, the transposition from man of God to unabashed torturer abruptly complete.

Bland gleefully obeyed, and the chair with the gasping young woman tied to it disappeared once again into the river.

This time, it seemed an eternity before the reverend ordered her re-surfaced. This time, rising from the swirling river, she appeared in death's grip.

Surveying the girl and the gathering, it dawned on the reverend that an increasing number of spectators were becoming visibly disgusted at the way in which what should have been a rousing event steeped in long-abandoned tradition was developing. Some were whispering that things had gone too far. The crowd had wanted to teach her a lesson, true, but watching the bedraggled young woman cling desperately to life was quickly losing its appeal. There were limits. There had to be. A death on their hands would damn *them* in the eyes of God and, if what they had done ever surfaced, the outside world as well.

"Enough, Reverend!" one man pleaded.

But the reverend was not in a conciliatory mood. "This sinner has yet to confess her sins so they can be washed away. She remains noncompliant. She continues to be a stain on our good community."

"But she'll die," the man's wife protested.

"Are you ready to deliver your men's souls into her hands?" barked the reverend, indignant at the growing show of insubordination. He pointed sternly at the cross being held shakily aloft by Knoll. "Don't forget! He died for your sins! Don't be swayed by this harlot's evil resolve!"

Glacially numbing claws of death drew what little air Clarissa had left from her deflated lungs. With a last semblance of fortitude, she moved her mouth in what the crowd could equally imagine as her final words, a last supplication, a curse or a death reflex. Clarissa was, in fact, desperately trying to gain precious time to recover what strength she could in anticipation of a third dunking, which would likely kill her.

The reverend, sensing the incisiveness of the situation, deemed the dunking would have to continue immediately or this tiresome wave of compassion might take root. "In the name of God, dunk her again! Now, I say!" he yelled, wide-eyed, mouth foaming, beads of sweat flicking from his brow.

While the crowd continued to hesitate, Bland did not.

As the bottom of the chair struck the water, everyone noted the pounding of fast approaching feet. Bright torches abruptly appeared, encircling the riverside gathering and swelling its size. A warning shot sounded and Bland found himself being wrestled to the ground, while other hands raised the chair above the gloomy water and located it back onto solid ground. The ropes about Clarissa were torn from her motionless body, and she was lifted from the seat and placed on the ground. The reverend, abruptly aware of the precariousness of his position, tried to slip away unnoticed, but was quickly apprehended. The villagers, removed from their leader, their disposition fractured, their puissance weakened, fell guiltily silent.

Clarissa coughed, shivered, and coughed again, her indomitable will having prevailed over the brutal ritual.

In the circle of torchlight, it became apparent that, leading the charge had been Constable Cauldfield, who had awakened just in the nick of time with an excruciating headache, incontrovertible evidence foul play. After searching the deserted village, he ran to the first outlying house, ran into Gomford who had returned from his business trip to find the door of his house open and Clarissa gone, the porch muddied with boot prints. Cauldfield and Gomford were approached by an old spinster, Miss Proudfoot, who said she'd seen the villagers carrying a young woman dressed only in night clothes in the direction of the river, confirming Cauldfield and Gomford's worst fears.

Cauldfield alerted the local police, and rustled up the remaining villagers, including a burly ex-military man named John Byfoot. It was Byfoot, who, armed with his old army-issue pistol, had fired the warning shot.

The area police quickly arrived and went efficiently about their business recording names, taking statements and making arrests. As they did, a woman approached Gomford. Everyone instantly recognized her as Glynnes Trout, the long-established village prostitute. After a brief exchange with Gomford, she turned to face the crowd and loudly pronounced, "You are sick, deranged, and wicked!"

The reverend, desperate for any straw, picked up on the word "wicked."

"Wicked?" he repeated. "That's rich, coming from an ugly old hooker like you."

Salmon and Trout locked eyes.

"But I was not always a prostitute, was I, Reverend?" replied Glynnes, pointing an accusatory finger at him.

The reverend choked and sagged, as if being forced to swallow bile, but Glynnes Trout was far from finished. "And I wasn't always ugly, either. I was once a beauty, as you well know, Reverend, until *you* forced yourself on me!"

A hush came over the gathering. All eyes turned to the reverend.

"Till you *impregnated* me!" Glynnes Trout added with loud finality.

The reverend put on the face of a wronged choirboy. "What in the world are you talking about, woman?" he asked, his voice cracking with adolescent-sounding incredulity.

Glynnes Trout gave him a wry smile. "You know very well what I'm talking about. Or have you conveniently forgotten that day when you forced yourself into my house to, as you put it, 'share a spiritual moment'? And have you also conveniently forgotten how I was forced to sell the only thing I had, my body, for a living to provide for *our* baby? *Our* daughter, no less. The one you chose to spurn, because of your shame?"

The reverend's mouth flapped but no words ensued. Glynnes

Trout indicted him beyond denial. He'd lost the trust of the villagers, who now began seeing their reverend, who they previously held beyond reproach, in a different light.

He hadn't *meant* any harm to her, the reverend told himself. He'd simply helped himself to a bit too much altar wine and decided to take a walk, stumbling upon, in his alcoholic daze, a beautiful young parishioner, virginal and innocent, who lived nearby. He'd dropped in on her to uplift his waning spirits.

"You monster! And would you now drown your own flesh and blood," Glynnes yelled, "to erase the evidence of your past wrongdoing to try to unburden on your soul over what you did to me!" Tears were streaming from Glynnes' tortured face.

Gomford placed a hand on her shoulder to comfort her, and as he did, to everyone's, including the reverend's amazement, having at last aired the truth, Glyness Trout began transforming. Her dull eyes brightened with new life. Her stringy grey hair took on hues of gold. The sour face that had accompanied her all the years they'd known her lightened, then disappeared, and she appeared young again. It was as if an old curse had lifted. Simultaneously, Clarissa, who moments ago appeared soiled, sodden and pale from her ordeal, similarly bloomed. In fact, in the glow of the rising moonlight, it was becoming hard to tell Glynnes from Clarissa; in their beatitude, they appeared youthful mother and tender daughter reunified.

The reverend, catching sight of what could only be described as a true miracle, looked at his reflection in a nearby puddle. The man staring back was old, decrepit, washed out, desolate, filled with guilt and shame. As the full weight of his sins descended on him, the dark waters of the nearby river began to call, and he let out a cry like a wounded animal. Lurching towards the river, meaning to drown himself, he was, at the last second, restrained by Cauldfield and Byfoot.

"You've one foot in hell already," offered Glynnes from a distance. "Don't add the other."

Gomford and Glynnes nodded in accord, revealing by their smiles a shared complicity. In fact, they had originally met again by chance in a bar in the city. There they shared over several glasses of wine the pain each carried that had been inflicted on them by others. As they commiserated, each came to realize that the root of their pain emanated from the same source. A plan to take revenge on the entire village, and the unassailable reverend in particular, slowly evolved. In the end, their plan had worked, though it had nearly cost Clarissa her life.

After a long drawn-out trial, Reverend Salmon, due to his continued ranting and raving, was sent to a mental institution, where he spent the remainder of his days talking to himself, reciting incomprehensible religious incantations, their purpose unfathomable to either religious or psychiatric experts.

Others in the village received varying sentences depending on the their involvement and the circumstances. Having paid their debt to society for their crimes, they later returned in shame to the village only to move away. The emptied village left vast swaths of land unoccupied and unclaimed. On the surface, it was dead, its very soul sucked out from it.

Gomford, however, slowly purchased the tracts of land, knocked down the old buildings and houses, and erected new ones in their place. The new apartment houses attracted new families, and the old village transformed into a vibrant new town, filled with attractive young married couples with beautiful children.

Gomford remained in his house, his wealth growing in proportion to the steadily swelling population. He lost weight, his features softened, his snorting laugh was replaced by an endearing chuckle. He was no longer regarded as grotesque, but was held in esteem, finally recognized for what he was: a successful businessman, constantly on the move, always looking for new business opportunities.

The day after giving her statement to the police, Clarissa disappeared, and was never found again. Some said that, plagued by memories of her ordeal and the prospect of public trial, she had gone to live in another country. But, as the years passed, townsfolk noted a new woman living under the Gomford roof. Some said she was the old hooker, Glynnis Trout, who'd miraculously reclaimed her youth and beauty by the river "that night." So much time had passed, that fact and fiction had become impossibly intertwined. Simply put, the new town blossomed, as did Gomford and his wife.

Flight of Destiny

Blind Shot

It was supposed to be the war to end all wars, but it proved to be just another in a long list of bloody transactions by power-hungry politicians, money-grubbing industrialists, and incompetent generals, ending in millions of pointless casualties. He'd barely arrived in the trenches before being ordered by his commanding officer, a man more versed in killing stags on a Scottish heath than military tactics, to send his company of minimally trained adolescents to their deaths. He'd fared luckier than most, or so he was told. The medics found him face down in the mud, barely breathing, and dragged him back to friendly lines. They'd patched up his flesh wounds and applied the usual psychological salve to his fractured mind. The only things they couldn't fix were his eyes. Gas had left him blind.

His unit, due soon to be issued gas masks, had been rushed to the front in a moment of desperation. The general, drawing first from a cigar wedged between his clenched teeth and then from a flask of brandy, had shared with his captain a few words of encouragement before issuing the preposterous order: "They won't need gas masks. The young lads are fit and healthy. If they have their wits about them, they should be able to dodge bullets or whatever is thrown in their direction," adding in a more menacing tone, "and if they don't follow orders and do their duty, they'll all be shot or court-martialed. Better to die an unsung hero than to live out one's life a coward!" he chortled, dismissing the captain.

Captain Farthingale still looked the gallant officer. What had changed was that his eyes no longer served their purpose. He was sentenced to live the rest of his days totally in his head, relying on his inner perception and imagination to "see" the world that carried on normally around him. When he'd gone to the war, he'd left behind a beautiful young wife. When he eventually returned home, he would have only her voice and touch to indulge in. Sightless, he would saddle his family with the burden of an invalid, and grow increasingly bitter, requiring more and more assistance as the years passed. She, on the other hand, could never grow old in his sightless eyes.

Adding to the confusion raging in his head was his love for another woman, the nurse who'd cared for him, who served as his initial "eyes" to the world. He had no concept of how the woman looked, yet his love was all consuming for this compassionate stranger who'd brought him back from the brink of hell and saved what was left of his life.

Her name was Caitlin Brady. She joined the Army Nurse Corps soon after the war began, and the moment she'd glimpsed Captain Farthingale, she'd fallen in love with him. Even with his eyes swathed in bandages, he presented as a rugged, handsome, quiet man, among the thousands of screaming wounded suffering from ghastly wounds or the disfiguring effects of bombs and shrapnel.

The Army doctors had been straight with him, almost brusque: "You will never see again and you should reconcile with this as soon as possible."

Nurse Brady was the only person in his new, limited world who he could turn to. Her voice had a pleasant, melodic, soothing tone. At first he clung to her like an infant to its mother. Equally, like a mother, she quieted his fears and attended to his needs. It wasn't long before he began to pine for her whenever she was off shift. He quickly came to recognize the sound of her footsteps, the rustle of her dress, the sound of her breathing. He could not see her, of course, but he could feel her presence.

One day, she told him he'd received a letter.

What use is a letter to a blind man he thought, but didn't say it.

She offered to read it. It was from his wife.

He nodded his assent, and heard Nurse Brady sit, open the envelope and unfold the letter.

My Dearest Vincent,

The Army has informed me of your condition. What a terrible thing to happen. I can't express how sorry I feel for you. I am staying in the country at Padstow Grange with my family. Despite the tragic news of war, I have some good news: I am with child! Papa took me to Doctor Wilson, who confirmed it. I hope this will bring some joy into your life. No one will tell me when you will be able to come home. Look after yourself, my dearest husband.
Your loving wife,
Camilla

"Great news," said Nurse Brady, without much conviction.

"Yes, I suppose so," he returned, considering the consequences of this new development.

Caitlin Brady had correctly assumed that, based on the handsome captain's polished demeanor and accent, he was from aristocratic stock; the proletariat rarely made their way through the ranks to a captaincy. When she'd taken time to dwell on his circumstances, she'd imagined him unattached, living alone in a huge country manor. A helpless blind man, he would need a practical companion to help manage his vast estate. She was soon dreaming up wild fantasies of the life they would lead together, but now, knowing he was married, and more so, that he was soon to be a father, put a new perspective on things. Or did it really?

Over the next few days, her enthusiasm for the blind captain never once waned, despite the niggling complication of a wife and unborn child. In fact, if anything, it continued mounting. She hadn't known him before he'd lost his sight. She only knew the brave bedridden man who required so much of her. She'd washed him, shaved him, been his mirror to the world, a new world entirely of *their* own. Despite what his wife had said in the letter, she still cherished the idea that he belonged to her and that, in his new sightless state, his wife would never be able to care for him in the way she could. Two questions began to occupy Nurse Brady's mind: *How does one attract a blind man? How would he respond to her advances?*

Captain Farthingale had been lightly dozing, a respite from the monotony of the hospital at night, when he awoke to the familiar sound of Nurse Brady's approaching footsteps. Men about him were sighing and snoring in their sleep. It was unusual for her to visit him at this hour. A moment later, he felt her breath against his cheek.

"Be quiet," she said, touching a finger to his lips.

The captain tried to sit upright, but she curtailed his movement, and instead took his hands in hers and ran them slowly down her face and neck. Her face was…soft. He began actively caressing it, trying to make sense of its shape and contours. His inexperienced touch could not, as yet, tell him if she was beautiful, but his mind had already convinced him she was. He traced the line of her lips while her soft hands caressed his neck and worked their way down his unbuttoned top. He could sense her breathing gaining momentum and her hands warming as they worked their way down his body.

"Your hair, what color is it?" he asked her, between two deep breaths.

"Black," she replied simply.

"And your eyes?"

"Hazel."

His questions were cut short when she kissed him urgently on the mouth.

He'd never kissed anyone other than his wife, who he'd met and married at a tender age. She had been his life joy, yet, now, without his eyes, it was as if nothing existed but Nurse Brady's warm inviting kiss. When he heard the rustle of clothes dropping to the floor, he knew instantly that their kiss was to be the prelude to a far more intimate encounter. What agony that he could not see the body of the woman offering herself unreservedly to him. She drew his hands to her breasts, and let him luxuriate in their softness.

In the distance, he heard new sounds. Another person. An intruder, walking towards them from the next ward. Nurse Brady withdrew, hurriedly slipped back into her clothes and walked briskly away.

He was back in his isolation again. Then he heard Caitlin's voice addressing another nurse, a superior no doubt. "Nurse Peters," he heard her say from some distance away. "I thought I heard someone call out in pain. I've just finished checking the patients and they all seem fine."

"I see," replied Nurse Peters in a voice laced with suspicion. "Then I'd get to bed and get some sleep if I were you," she ordered. "You've a long day ahead."

The sound of the two nurse's footsteps exiting the room was quickly replaced with the murmurs of sleeping men interlaced with the occasional sporadic cry of a man reliving a combat experience.

Nurse Brady by day, Caitlin by night, greeted the captain with more familiarly at each nocturnal visit until they found themselves regularly together in bed, locked in passion, while the other soldiers slept on, oblivious.

Several days later, she said coolly, "Captain Farthingale. I have another letter from your wife. Would you like me to read it to you?"

The captain leaned forward while she fluffed the pillow behind him. "Please do, nurse," he said stiffly, turning his head from side to side as if visually scanning to make certain they were alone. A moment later, Nurse Brady began:

Dear Vincent,
It is with a heavy heart and a great amount of guilt, that I write you this, but it is only proper and right that I do. In my last letter I stated I was with child, leaving you to presume the child was conceived before your departure. In fact, the child was fathered by another, a man with whom you are only vaguely acquainted, and with whom I have been having an affair in your long absence. I can imagine

the terrible hurt and the sense of betrayal you must feel. I can only hope you can find it in your generous heart to forgive me. I know I have done a most terrible thing, and understand if you choose to disown me entirely. I am greatly concerned whether being together again would be in the best interests of you, me, the father and baby.
Your wife,
Camilla

Nurse Brady recited the words tersely, almost mechanically, and when finished, remained silent, wondering how to read a man's thoughts without the benefit of the gateway of his eyes.

The captain said nothing. There were no tears, but then, an officer wouldn't be expected to openly show emotion. His unmoving silence suggested to her that he was in contemplation. She rested a hand on his shoulder, like a mother might do a child who has taken a fall. The captain, however, remained silent, distant, aloof.

"I...had better be going," she said awkwardly, rustling away, leaving Captain Vincent Farthingale to deal with this sudden injection of poison that was even now working its way into both his mind and heart.

In the end, he refused to believe it. The words Nurse Brady had read to him simply couldn't be those of his beautiful young wife. She would never betray him as he had her the last few nights. She would, without a doubt, never even *consider* bearing another man's child.

When Nurse Brady came to his bed that night, he shunned her. He said he felt it inappropriate and wanted to be left alone with his thoughts and torment.

The next day Head Nurse Peters visited him. He pictured her from her voice and her dealings with Nurse Brady as a sturdy, formidable, intimidating matron who tolerated no nonsense.

"You are to be transferred to London, then home," she said in her husky, matter-of-fact voice.

Home, he thought. The shock of hearing the word weighed heavily. *Back to a domicile with a wife who, if the letter were authentic, had betrayed him, and worse still, no longer loved him. What kind of home did he have to go back to?*

The night before his departure for London, he was overcome with anxiety and grief. He was about to be moved from the comforting insular world of the hospital to the far more daunting would outside. He said his few goodbyes, carefully avoiding talking to Nurse Brady. In fact, she barely registered in his thoughts; he was too preoccupied with imagining what his sightless life, plagued by guilt, would be like when he eventually returned "home."

The journey proved arduous. There were the constant forays of new, strange, often frightening sounds to take in: the creaks and groans of the transport truck as it jostled down one after another rutted dirt road; the varied ever-present sounds of war around the next bend; the machine gun like thud of raindrops on the canvas barely covering the mass of injured men as the truck conveyed them back to their country and home. Carrying him back to *his* home, which he would never see again. As the truck rumbled on, he tried to conjure up images of the landscape passing by.

In London, he spent some time in a hospital with a doctor who repeated what the others before him had said: "You are blind. You must learn to deal with it."

In fact, he didn't want to accustom himself to his new sightless existence. He didn't want to return or face his wife. At least, he comforted himself, when the time came, he wouldn't have to look into her eyes. His "condition" would save him that embarrassment. Doubtless, the subject of his time in the field hospital would come up, and his experiences with those who'd cared for him. It was then he realized that, try as he might, he could never forget the nurse who'd shown him true compassion in his moment of need.

He tried over and over to erase Caitlin from his mind. Though their time together had been short, he slowly came to realize that there had been a lot more to their relationship than the physical encounters. In truth, he'd gotten closer to her in a short time than he'd been able to over the years with his wife. Even if he avoided drawing attention to Nurse Brady, his wife would, at some point, undoubtedly sense that his affections had changed, and there would be no disguising that he had betrayed her.

Pronounced fit at last by his London doctor, he was transported by ambulance to his sizable family estate. As the ambulance bounced along the meandering driveway, his anxiety grew exponentially.

The moment the ambulance stopped and the door was opened, he felt flooded by sympathy, first from anxious house staff, then from a distraught Camilla. After an awkward silence, he heard her take a deep breath and venture, "Oh, Vincent, you are back at last! I am so happy to have you home." Her voice seemed full of genuine caring. It wasn't that of an adulterer, but more like that of a lover, delighting in her long-away partner's return. Perhaps he was right about her after all. The thought initially calmed him, but in the next instant frightened him. If he was right about her, then *he* had wronged *her* deeply.

He searched the darkness for her with his hands. She began to cry, extending her hands to him, directing his to the servants.

"Take him inside," she commanded between sobs.

Vincent felt himself being lifted out of the ambulance by

numerous helping hands. Standing shakily on the gravel, wracked with concern over his future and a distinct loathsomeness over both his handicap and his adulterous tryst with Nurse Brady, he grasped tightly onto the hands holding him, and followed, stumbling up the front steps to the door. Inside, he was embraced by the familiar smells of house and home. He was led down the hallway, through a corridor and into the drawing room, all the while memorizing, as he'd been taught in London, the number of steps and the different squeaks of the floorboards.

The house smelled mustier than he remembered. He heard two dogs approach. His dogs. They sniffed his legs, then brushed up close against him, almost causing him to topple. Their master had returned. Being blind he was unable to immediately return their affections. When he began groping towards them, one snarled.

Inside the drawing room, he heard the crackle of the log fire his wife had prepared, its radiant warmth enveloping him in comfort. Suddenly embraced from out of nowhere, he felt tears wet his face, and listened to his wife gently sobbing. The tears, he realized or imagined (it was hard to know which without vision), seemed to him not tears of pity or guilt, but relief. His own face flushed hot, though whether from the fire or his wife's display of affection, he couldn't tell.

When initial emotions finally relented, his wife's mind turned to a matter of importance that was vexing her. "Did you receive all my letters?" she asked softly.

"Letters?" he queried, turning his head toward the sound of her voice, his eyes blank and expressionless. Her manner of asking suggested there had been more than two.

"I sent you many. I wrote to you almost every day."

"I received two," he replied gruffly. "The rest must have been lost."

"Oh," she said, the pain at the thought of so many of her letters not reaching him evident in her tone.

The lost letters disturbed him. He was about to say something when she interrupted.

"I'm feeling quite pregnant," she offered joyfully, taking his hand and placing it on her belly. There was a slight but noticeable bump. This was not the behavior of a woman having another man's child.

Again the captain started to speak, but again she interrupted. "Just think, Vincent. We will soon have a baby to care for. You may even have a son and heir," she said, laughing gently.

All he could do was nod; he felt too overwhelmed to speak.

His thoughts were a whirl of relief and confusion. He'd begun to wonder again if the two letters Nurse Brady had read to him had been concocted, but, denied the ability to look into either woman's eyes, he would never know for sure. It was no longer beyond the bounds of imagination that Nurse Brady had received and read all of his wife's letters, telling him only what she wanted him to hear: maliciously contrived lies concerning his wife, who, based on the evidence of his homecoming, had, it seemed to him, remained faithful. He could, of course, ask his wife outright about whether the child had another father, but that would eventually lead to having to confess his own infidelity.

They nestled in each other's arms that night. At first reticent, he eventually touched her face with his fingertips as he had with Nurse Brady. He was surprised to find that he could call up his wife's face and body along with the passion he'd felt for her prior to his departure for war.

Over the next few weeks, Captain Vincent Farthingale began to adjust to his new life, feeling safer in his increasingly familiar home. He and his wife seemed to have returned to the state they had shared before the war. She had, in fact, become his new eyes, now that Nurse Brady was no longer there to care for him.

He started to teach himself to walk around the house with a cane his wife had presented him, tapping, probing, learning to identify the rooms, hallways and any potential hazards. He even began venturing into the rockery, one of his favorite spots on the estate despite its many and varied obstructions and pitfalls.

His mind was wracked with reflections, including what he would do and say if Nurse Brady ever reappeared. Was she a scheming woman, the type who might attempt to destroy his marriage? He had little on which to base any judgment. Just a blind man's intuition. They'd parted leaving everything unresolved. In his head, he'd taken to imagining her cursing at him in anger for having left her without even saying good-bye.

His fears were further compounded by the fact that, while in the daytime and fully conscious, he could retain his secret, at night, he was prone to mutter about the war and, he suspected, his convalescence in his sleep. Several times, during a particularly restless sleep, his mumbling had stirred his wife from sleep.

Once, after calling out Nurse Brady's name several times in succession, his inquisitive wife repeated for him the name she'd heard him say out loud. He explained she was an infirmary nurse from his public school days, who'd left an impression on him. Camilla didn't pursue the matter. She just muttered, "Oh, I see," then changed the subject. Unable to see her face, he couldn't gauge what her actual thoughts were. She could quite easily telephone his old school and verify whether there had ever been a Nurse by the name of Caitlin employed there.

One spring morning, while opening the drawing room windows, he detected the weather as being particularly clement, and decided to explore the grounds beyond the rockery. His wife had earlier excused herself. He couldn't recall her giving any notable reason, which left him free to wander the house and grounds at his own pace. Outside, he relished the feel of the warm sun on his face. His dogs dutifully followed, romping and barking happily about him. Turning his thoughts to the summerhouse where, before the war, he and his wife had spent many happy hours relaxing and conversing together, he decided to revisit it. It was tucked away on a wilder part of the grounds. The trail there was bordered by brambles. It would be a hazardous walk, but for some reason he felt drawn to do it.

In fact, Camilla had a habit these days of abandoning him from time to time, he assumed to help him build his self-confidence. She was also busy interviewing applicants for the nursemaid position she'd advertised to help with the impending addition to the family. None had piqued her interest until she chanced upon one with a name that seemed to resonate in her mind, a name she'd said had an Irish lilt to it.

Tapping his way along, the path turned steeper than he remembered and twice he stumbled, the second time cutting his leg on some bramble thorns. He was already feeling less sure that he could make it all the way to the summerhouse. Turning back, however, offered the same uncertainty as going forward but without reward, so he plugged on. Several steps more and the tip of his cane tapped what could only be wooden steps. Just as suddenly, he became conscious of other sounds including a falsetto chorus of birds in the distance covering a faint contralto female voice accompanied by a man's baritone. Listening intently, he could just make out what the two were saying, It was immediately evident that he had intruded on a lover's tryst.

The more dominant baritone voice seemed to be doing most of the talking. The tone was playful. He was asking suggestive questions and delighting in the woman's answers. Vincent shuffled closer, trying to place the man's voice. He'd heard it before, but couldn't attach a face to it. While considering one after another of the possible locals, it suddenly came to him: It was young Doctor Donald Wilson! The doctor had shared dinner with them few weeks before Vincent had been called up. His wife had insisted on the dinner, despite the doctor being outside their usual social circle.

At dinner, the doctor had managed to needle Vincent in a multitude of ways. First, there had been the way his piercing eyes were constantly latched on Camilla. Then the ribald stories he'd told of his various exploits, stories which fell well short of the standards a gentleman should have upheld while in the company of a woman at a dinner. The worst, though, had been his outlandish claim of having attained a higher level of consciousness, to which he gave the pretentious name "telekinesis." He'd claimed he could move objects at will, and read and control another's mind if he so wished.

It wasn't long before Camilla demanded an exhibition of his powers. Focusing on the several candles in the center of the table, the doctor had somehow managed to extinguish the flames, pitching the room into darkness. Camilla had applauded eagerly; Vincent reluctantly. For his next trick, the doctor had made the dining room door lock of its own accord. Camilla had expressed further delight; Vincent mumbled his opinion that the doctor would do better to focus on curing the sick, rather than on staging elaborate party tricks.

Just as Vincent identified the man's voice, the whispering fell silent, to be followed by the distinctive sounds of passion. There was a divan in the summer house, Vincent recalled, that he and his wife had put to use in the heady days of their courtship and in the present, Vincent was certain it was once again being audaciously put to use.

Vincent waited for the woman to speak, but it was the doctor who broke the silence. "I assume Vincent knows nothing," the doctor inquired at last.

"How could he?" Camilla's sweet voice replied. "He's blind in more ways than one."

Vincent's heart began to beat like a kettledrum and a wave of nausea swept over him. So Camilla *was* deceiving him. The letters Caitlin had read to him might have been genuine after all! Apparently Camilla was happy to continue being ensconced on his vast estate while enjoying the affections of another man, in fact, the rather lowly and insipid doctor, who had, now that he thought of it, skillfully evaded war duty.

Disgusted, the captain turned, and slowly worked his way back to the main house, his mind in turmoil. Had he been noticed? There was no way he could tell.

Back in the drawing room, Vincent tapped his way to his private desk, located and patted the blotter, raised a corner, and removed a small key. Squatting, he fingered the side of the desk until he located the appropriate drawer and keyhole. Inserting the key, he tried to turn it, but was surprised to find it already unlocked. Reaching inside with both hands, he withdrew his old service revolver and a box of cartridges. To his surprise, he found the weapon already loaded. It was as if he were being invited to use his revolver to take his life or that of another.

Perplexed by these discoveries, he sat silently and waited, cradling the gun in his hands, his mind overflowing with anger and resentment. He'd been a crack marksman prior to being struck blind. Without the use of his sight, he would have to rely on all his other faculties. The exact sound, clarity, direction and speed of approaching footsteps, as well as the timing of the shot, would be his only assist, and even then, luck would still play a major part in hitting his target.

While pondering, he heard two sets of footsteps crunch the driveway gravel, one set lighter, the other slightly heavier. They were drawing quickly closer. He heard soles slap against the weathered stone steps leading up to the house, followed by their click against polished stone as they progressed down the corridor, approaching the drawing room.

Vincent braced the weapon on the desktop, pointing in the direction of the sounds, his index finger curled around the trigger.

"Darling," Vincent heard a woman call out. "A Nurse Brady has come for an interview for the nursemaid position."

The explanation, however, was too late. Galvanized by his wife and her lover's treachery, he'd already squeezed the trigger, aiming just to the right of her voice, in the assumption that the second person would be the doctor. A moment later, he heard the thump of a body falling to the floor.

He'd expected his wife to scream, but that wasn't the case. Instead, a long silence followed, ending with Camilla exclaiming in horror, "My God, Vincent! What have you done?"

Camilla's voice was joined a moment later by the sound of Doctor Wilson's urgent footsteps.

The doctor walked calmly up to Vincent and pried the gun from his hand. Nurse Brady, Vincent now surmised, had been ushered into the room to be interviewed by Camilla, the nurse led like a lamb to the slaughter, in the manner he and the men in his unit had been sent by the bungling General onto the field of battle. Wilson placed the gun on the desk just out of Vincent's immediate reach.

Vincent, feeling utterly crushed, reached for the desk phone to the right of his hand, intending to report the crime and explain that the blame was his wife and the doctor's. He wasn't yet sure how to accomplish this, but he felt certain that given his noble war duty and ensuing blindness, providence would weigh things in his favor, and, once he had explained how the two standing in the room had wronged him, and had, in fact, worked out and executed their own twisted plan, sympathy would fall overwhelmingly on his side whatever his wife and the doctor might say. In the end, it would most likely be Wilson who'd be held to blame. Hadn't he evaded serving in the war? Surely he'd made an ass of himself in front of other pillars of society with his "higher consciousness" act? No judge or jury would look favorably upon such a maverick. In time, the courts would prove his innocence in the inadvertent death of Nurse Brady.

In attempting to dial the operator, Vincent found the line dead. He recalled using the phone earlier, before he'd set out to the summer house, and that there had been no problem reaching his sister, whose husband had recently been reported missing on the field of battle. In his frustration, he held the receiver to his mouth and yelled, "Operator! Operator!" His yells jolting the doctor to action.

"Vincent, Vincent, Vincent," Doctor Wilson tutted. "You won't get anywhere with that telephone. My talent, remember? Indeed, at this moment your situation is most precarious."

Vincent said nothing in reply, so the doctor continued, this time with growing menace, "You've lost your sight, your wife, and now it's time for you to forfeit the remainder of your pitiful life."

Vincent, again, said nothing, but slid his hand searchingly forward on the desktop towards where he'd heard the doctor place the gun, all the while hoping to not attract the doctor's attention. Touching metal, he grasped the weapon, pointed and fired in the direction of the doctor's voice. His ears, ringing loudly from the report, nonetheless detected a faint thunk somewhere within the room, but whether it was the bullet embedding itself in flesh or a distant wall, he couldn't tell.

Had he killed the doctor? He had no immediate way of knowing and the fear of not knowing swept over Vincent, replicating the fear he'd felt in the trenches with his unit the day they'd been massacred and he'd lost his sight.

So, what now? Would the doctor, unscathed, once again wrench the gun from his hand and this time shoot him? Or might the doctor, if only superficially wounded, sneak up and break his neck? Or would it be his wife who would wrench the weapon from his hand and kill him for murdering her lover? Every imaginable scenario passed through Vincent's mind.

After some seconds, he sensed someone moving towards him. The person was repeating his name like the doctor had, but it wasn't Doctor Wilson's baritone, or his wife's contralto. It was the calming voice of Nurse Brady, cutting a divide between his fears, the enveloping madness and cold reality.

Vincent clawed his way to conscious, and smelled the familiar scent of stale urine and disinfectant. Hearing once again the groans and death rattles of men, he realized he was, much to his consternation, back in the military field hospital, in truth, never having left. Somehow, he'd mapped out and lived his likely future in the form of a horribly lucid dream. Worse, the experience offered him no relief. As he regained further consciousness, he reached out desperately to the nurse standing next to him and rested his throbbing head in her arms. Nurse Brady, as ever, soothed and comforted him while he continued to grapple with the reality of his situation.

"Vincent, darling," she whispered in his ear. "Everything is all right. You've passed through a kind of crisis just as you were about to leave for London. It's not uncommon for soldiers who've been through as much as you have. The doctors have been keeping you under sedation."

Vincent didn't reply. Instead, he let himself drift slowly in and out of this new reality, sifting and discarding, one-by-one, the fears that continued haunting him. For a while, he even reflected on whether perhaps it was she, Nurse Brady, who had had him sedated in an attempt to delay his departure, not being able to bear his absence. Obviously, any "memories" he had from his drug-induced dream had been severely warped, some hideously so. For example, he had always harbored a mild dislike for the doctor, but mostly because he was such a frivolous man. Camilla had even remarked to him later that very night, alone, in bed together, that on top of the man's appalling manners, his tricks had proven irritatingly banal. The doctor was unrefined and innocuous. The more Vincent reconsidered it all, the more he was certain the doctor was one of the least likely people Camilla would ever take as a lover.

Over time, Vincent came to increasingly loathe the thought of having to continue to live a life of doubt, paranoia and guilt, and knew he was going to have to decide eventually between the two women, each with a different but equally important claim to his life.

These thoughts led him to a momentous decision. Unless he had another "crisis," he would most likely be leaving the hospital soon. He requested his field uniform, including his belt, holster and revolver, to be brought to his bedside, saying he wanted to leave the hospital feeling that he was "still a man, a military man, a captain who'd served his country and given it his all."

His request was, of course, respected. Holding his field revolver in his hands, he reflected that, as a man who'd endured so much, he had the right to end the hell he was convinced lay before him. He ate what he considered to be his last meal and remained sitting, no doubt feeling the combined effects of the food and his medication, slipped into a deeply troubled sleep. When he awoke, he decided from the snores of the other men, that he still had a chance to take his own life.

Reaching down to his holster, he removed his revolver, snapped open the bullet chamber, and checked its inside with his fingertips.

The chamber was empty.

Running his fingers along the back of the cartridge belt he was wearing, he realized that all the ammunition it normally carried had been removed.

He had not reckoned on the fact that every bullet was precious to the war effort. With no immediate means of committing suicide, he sunk back in despair and resignation.

He awoke the next morning, his head aching, to the tap of a strong finger on his shoulder. "Captain Farthingale, you're to go home at last," Nurse Peters said in her most authoritative voice.

Black Widow

Mercedes Schwartz had just had the most incredible orgasm, but her pleasure was still incomplete. While the man on top of her was still pumping away, she stretched an arm over to her bedside table, grasped the small sharp-pointed pin she kept there, and without hesitating, plunged the pin into his back.

He couldn't have felt much, totally engaged as he was, other than a quick mosquito-like jab, the poison inexorably working its way to his wildly beating heart. When his heart abruptly stopped, she rolled him off with a minimum of bother.

It wasn't as if Mercedes didn't like or appreciate his efforts. At moments like this, she just had this overwhelmingly uncontrollable compulsion to avoid, at all costs, the inevitable "small talk" and hollow professions of love that always seemed to follow. It had happened once before and had left her feeling physically sick. In short, she couldn't stomach any kind of intimacy. It wasn't quite that simple, of course, but to her mind, it had come to make sense to "round things off" in a relationship before she got too entangled.

What had begun as an obsession had evolved into a working plan as to how to deal with it. She traveled to far-off cities to vet her men, placing, when need required, advertisements in high society country life magazines and the classified sections of the best continental newspapers. She promised the reader an "ultimate experience" in a remote country retreat. Her advertisements had the necessary ring of truth, since she could describe her exquisite beauty without embellishment, and, when a client first met her, reality always exceeded even her flattering description. If *they* lived up to *her* expectations, she would wine and dine them before driving them to her vast, isolated estate for the final act. No phones or other means of contact with the outside world were uncompromising requirements to accompany her to her estate.

Of course, when the "act" was done, she was left with the task of disposing of the body, which she went about methodically, but with respectful ceremony. She reasoned that those who'd paid the ultimate price for her pleasure deserved a respectful funeral.

She would wrap the victim's body in a white sheet, truss it with twine, and transport it to a site where she had pre-built a huge pyre. She would then scent the pyre with cinnamon oil to give off a sweet aroma, and dance about it, reciting prayers and incantations to direct the deceased's spirit to its next life. Finally she would shower the pyre with rose petals and touch a flaming brand to it, then watch, mesmerized, as, hissing, crackling and popping, greasy orange flames leaped hight into the sky and the body slowly disappeared. Once the fire died, any bone remnants would be crushed into dust and, along with the ashes, be scattered in the nearest river, the last signs and memories of the deceased quickly slipping beneath the surface and dissolving away.

It hadn't always been like this. Her late husband, considerably older than her, had died not by her hand but of natural causes while making love to her on their wedding night. He'd suffered a massive heart attack at the height of their passion.

Burying her husband less than a week after they'd been married had been difficult, to say the least. The brief marriage, however, had left her with a sizable fortune and a vast country estate. It was probably because of this confluence of events that some regarded her warily, first suspecting, and later stating outright that she had heartlessly planned and executed the whole thing. No one, however, had ever proved the slur.

Her first victim's death hadn't been premeditated, either. It had been a spontaneous killing. She'd become bored, cooped up alone in the huge estate, and decided to go to the city for some excitement.

She had called her friend, Madeleine, who agreed to meet her at a local bar for some definite female, and possibly some added male, conversation. Madeleine, however, had contacted her at the last minute to say she would be unable to join her. Mercedes, in response, went to the bar alone, hoping one of their mutual friends might show up.

While sitting at the bar, sipping a drink and watching passers-by going about their business, she felt a man's eyes surveying her. At first Mercedes felt unsure of how to react to the unexpected attention, but after some discrete glances in his direction to confirm his appearance, she uncrossed her legs and smiled at him.

The man took this as a positive signal, got up, walked over to her, and asked if he could join her. He had a alluring voice and respectfully demure approach. He was slightly taller but of roughly the same age and build as her former husband. Even his mannerisms were mildly reminiscent of him.

With Mercedes' approval, he sat next to her and soon they were engaged in convivial repartee. He was, he said, unmarried, between occupations, traveling alone on a well-deserved vacation.

Mercedes was instantly both drawn to and repulsed by him. Nevertheless, after several drinks and more conversation, she asked him if he would like to drive the two of them in her car to her country estate. He naturally agreed, though a bit too readily for Mercedes' comfort. On the way, she wondered if she was doing the right thing, this unplanned adventure with a total stranger, but, despite lingering doubts, took to rearranging herself to look her best while the man drove on.

The man noticed her preening and briefly scanned her from eyes to thighs, and was more than pleased with what he saw. A confident and self-assured man, after they'd arrived at her estate, he quickly made himself at home. The two retreated to the study where he made a fire and they spent some time on the sofa sipping cocktails. It wasn't long before he openly suggested they should make love. He'd not come such a long way, he assured her, just to admire the countryside.

Mercedes, to her surprise, agreed, but told him she didn't want to make love in her bed, and then fell silent, finding it inappropriate under the circumstances to explain that it was the bed in which her husband had died.

The study, with its luxuriant oriental wool rugs and showpiece Italian-marble fireplace surrounded by several comfortable divans presented a number of intriguing possibilities, and he told her he was amenable to making love *in situ*, if she were also willing. She was, and quickly slipped out her of dress and underwear, stretching out luxuriously on the rug next to the crackling fire. The man, in the meantime, moved between her and the fire and stripped.

From the onset, Mercedes felt a wild, almost forgotten surge of passion. It was only when they'd finished that her mood shifted. He tried to whisper something to her, but she shook her head violently, refusing to hear a word of it. He could have been telling her the secrets of alchemy, but all she felt was the strongest compulsion to carry out an act of which she had never imagined herself capable. It was as if an unknown force took possession of her and drove her to do it. Resisting, she quickly learned, was futile.

The man was still catching his breath while trying to reengage her in conversation, and his incessant muttering left her feeling nauseous. She pushed him off her, and, in one swift action, grabbed the iron fire-plodder and administered a sharp and fatal blow to his head. Completely out of control, she violently thrashed at his face to make sure no more words would pass out of his mouth.

Afterwards, faced with the bloodied, lifeless body, she reassured herself that what she'd done was not "murder." After all, who knows what he might have done to her once his animal lust was satisfied. No, it was more like a ritual cleansing, something that needed doing if she were to resolve things and eventually get on with her life.

The body needed to be disposed, so she rolled it into the carpet on which they'd made love then dragged the roll into the center of the room, where, she recalled, her former husband had lain for his wake. She dressed, then retired, exhausted, to her bedroom.

The next morning she got up early, went to the woodshed, placed some logs in a wheelbarrow, and hauled them to the estate Land Rover, where a short time later, she also placed the rolled carpet containing the body. Then she drove to the most secluded corner the property afforded.

After stacking the wood into a pyre and placing the rug containing the man's body on top, she stopped for a moment's consideration. It seemed derogatory to simply throw petrol and apply a match to the bier. Then she noticed in her coat pocket a bottle of lavender *eau de toilette*, which she poured onto the rug. Taking out a lighter, she lit the wood and watched it blaze, feeling equal parts enthrallment and pleasure as the fire devoured the corpse. As the flames licked higher, she recalled she hadn't caught his name, and, moreover, hadn't bothered to go through his pockets to find out anything about him. He was to her a man who, aside from satisfying her, may as well never have existed.

Later that afternoon, she explained to one of the domestics she'd retained after her husband's death, that because of the house's humidity, the rug had rotted, and she had burned it in anticipation of replacing it with a new one. The housecleaner, who cherished not only the memory of Mercedes' dead husband, but also the contents of the house which she'd continued attending with loving care, flashed her an undisguised look of distrust. Such looks of disapproval, as well the fear that the domestics were whispering nasty things about her, were exactly why she'd cut the staff down to bare minimum and kept those left away when she was in attendance.

The rest of the week, Mercedes' mind was overrun with ideas and plans. Could she lure other men into a similar scenario without being caught? How should she best dispatch them when finished? Using the fire prodder had been invigorating, but had proven messy, so Mercedes began to research better ways to kill a man, and soon came up with poison. After reading about some primitive tribes that killed their prey with a poison dart, she settled to looking into all such poisons for one that was ultra-fast-acting and that would result in the victim experiencing a sudden, massive heart attack. For afterwards, burning had proved a most efficient way of dispatching the body and it had also helped to purge any residual guilt.

It took some time to locate a discreet purveyor of poisons, but she discovered to her delight, that with enough money, securing a lifetime supply was quite easily done. She knew what she was doing was criminal, even monstrous, but she didn't see herself as a criminal or monster like those highlighted in crime shows or who made the headlines in newspapers. Hers technically *wasn't a crime*, she reminded herself. She was compelled to act the way she did by some greater force, and one day, when the time was right, this force would be satisfied, and in doing so, she would find peace.

The month of May brought Mercedes some unwanted news. The irrepressible Manfred Schwartz, was coming to England, and had invited himself to stay at her Huntingdon estate, where he had grown up alongside his elder brother, Mercedes' deceased husband. She desperately wanted to refuse him but felt obliged to acquiesce.

She had met Manfred a few days before her wedding, and had, from that moment, felt awkward in his company. Manfred's life was Africa, where the Schwartz family's fortune had been made in the diamond mines they owned and operated. Manfred had suspicious, doubting eyes, eyes that had latched onto and remained focused on her from the moment they'd first seen each other. She'd mentioned this to her soon-to-be husband, who laughed it off, stating, "Manfred has his own special ways. You'll get used to him soon enough."

Manfred liked to question everything, to test everyone he met, and she'd had the unenviable task of breaking to him the news of his older brother's death. To his incessant questions, she answered that his brother had died of a heart attack, leaving out the circumstances and details. Manfred, unsatisfied, continued probing. "What was he doing at the time?" he asked her gruffly, his voice amplifying in volume.

There had been a poignant silence. She had tried to evade the question, and, in doing so, ended up snapping, "What does it matter? He's dead now, isn't he?" The outburst was sufficient to establish a permanent bond of mutual dislike.

Manfred had sent her disdainful looks throughout the funeral service, and, though they were obliged to stand next to each other at the grave, they refused to acknowledge each other's presence. Now he was paying her a visit, and would, no doubt, stir things up again.

The minute he arrived, her worst suspicions were confirmed. As he stepped through the front door, his eyes darted everywhere, as if searching for any changes to the house. *Like, for example, the new rug by the fireplace in the study?* she wondered. As if reading her mind, he walked directly into the study. She entered the room after him, and the two stared at each other. It was some time before he broke the excruciating silence. "It's been a long time," he said, and began pacing up and down the new rug like a nervous animal.

She forced a pale smile. "Indeed, it has."

"The last time was at my brother's funeral," he said, continuing his interminable pacing.

"You must be busy back in Africa," she replied, wishing him back there.

He stopped abruptly and seized her with his eyes.

"I run quite a sizable concern in Africa," he stated.

Mercedes continued the laborious effort of maintaining the stilted conversation, hoping to keep his attention off the new rug and the death of his brother. She offered him a cigar from the humidor, another diversion, and even paid him a compliment: "You must have great business acumen."

He shrugged his shoulders, as if he'd been told the same thing many times before, then sighed, but said nothing.

He finally turned his attentive gaze from her to several stacks of magazines on the coffee table, remarking, "I didn't know you were a connoisseur of 'Horse and Hounds'." After sifting through the stack he continued. "And 'The Field and Country Life' as well. I'd imagined, being more of a city girl, you'd hate the hunting-shooting-fishing community of which my late brother was so fond.

She tried unsuccessfully to hide her sudden anxiety. The magazines held her most recent advertisement. Manfred's sudden visit was ill-timed in more ways than one.

"I see you've made a few changes," he continued when she didn't reply, his voice assuming an accusatory edge as he lifted a corner of the new study rug with his shoe tip.

"I...I've done a bit of modernization. To make the place a little more comfortable," she stammered, hoping the quality of the new rug would compensate for the absence of the old one.

While circling the new rug, Manfred stopped pacing and looked at her full on. His eyes lit up as if he were about to issue a profound announcement. "My brother," he began, "might be buried a few miles away, but I, for one, still feel his presence here. To me, he never really died, and I would imagine, you might have a similar feeling. It wouldn't surprise me if he was trying to find a way to contact you from whatever place he now inhabits."

"I can't imagine what you mean," she said, startled.

"I don't suppose you had time to get to know my brother that well. I was aware of aspects of him that he would have been loath to reveal. Much of his life was a closed book; I can't imagine he would have opened up to you that quickly."

"I was married to the man," she protested, "even if the marriage didn't last long."

"One night, wasn't it?" Manfred said with a tight smile.

"We knew each other some time before we decided to marry," she said, feeling increasingly puzzled as to where her departed husband's brother was taking the conversation.

"Ah, yes. And one would be inclined to think as such, that you and he had bared your hearts and souls to each other. I have to remind myself that you were his 'private secretary' before you became his fiancé, then wife. You must have thought he was stepwise elevating you to his social and intellectual plane. You may have thought that, but I can tell you with certainty that you were never even close to being an equal match for my rather 'unusual' brother."

Manfred was starting to rile her. "Our contact with one another was brief," she admitted, "but you know nothing of the relationship I had with your brother. You're always so infuriatingly provocative and pedantic."

Manfred seemed unmoved by her accusations. His eyes were fixed on a sizable cobweb attached to a picture, which indicated to him standards in house were being allowed to deteriorate. After a pause, he continued in a sober voice, "My brother was into a number of, shall we say, 'strange practices'. For example, did you know that he dabbled extensively in the occult?"

"What is it that you are implying?" she inquired.

Manfred's deft fingers reached into his shoulder purse, pulled out

172

a clump of herbs and rolled a cigarette. He smiled at Mercedes as he lit it. The cigarette gave off a strong, distinctively repugnant smell. Then he said thoughtfully, "He learned a lot during his albeit short time in Africa. He learned things many Europeans could never understand."

She raised her eyebrows and seated herself gracefully on one of several large divans. "Would you care to be more precise?" she asked, despising the incessant oblique inferences. She was starting to feel like a frog, being pined to a board in preparation for being dissected alive.

"My brother was, shall we say, the 'possessive type'," he said, apparently changing the subject, "even when we were children," adding caustically, "and I would imagine he was the same with his women."

"I wouldn't know," she shrugged. "He didn't appear to be the jealous type."

"I wouldn't be so sure, if I were you," said Manfred, with a snicker. "You see, anyone who tampered with what he deemed was his, always ended up paying a high price."

"Oh, come now, Manfred! Stop your intimidating remarks, won't you? Somehow we must get through this evening together. Let us practice at least a modicum of conviviality. Let's start with why you have come here."

"You are just like my brother said of you Mercedes: You are anything if not direct." Manfred's voice changed into one of mild contriteness. "I suppose I am suffering after a long flight and, well, it is strange being here without my brother. I'd always considered he and I to be close, though most of the time we lived separately, geographically far apart."

"He often spoke of you," she said, acknowledging his remark, "and of how close you were *as children*."

Manfred seemed to thaw a bit, despite her dig at their having been close only as children. "One thing I remember clearly about my brother was that he maintained a fine collection of wines and spirits in the cellar. Does the collection still exist?"

Mercedes shrugged noncommittally. "I would guess so, though I've never really explored the cellars much. Even if it were an exceptional collection, there isn't anyone to share it with."

"I don't suppose you have the chance to socialize much, being stuck in the country like this, so why don't I see if I can bring up one of his finer bottles for us to share in his memory?" Manfred offered.

"If you like," she said, nodding towards the door to the cellar. "While you're gone, I'll freshen up for dinner. I assume you will join me?"

"Of course," he replied, turning, walking up to the door and disappearing down the steps into the cellar.

In fact, he brought up two bottles, a fine wine for dinner, and a sweeter, heavier desert liqueur for afterwards. The first bottle helped substantially towards creating at least a semblance of dinner conversation. Subsequently, the overall demeanor turned less threatening, and Manfred became friendly, then enchanting, and finally quite endearing. In his new state, Mercedes noticed the close resemblance he bore to his brother. In fact, she had to admit that allied to this, he was also the better looking of the two. Over dinner, he told her stories of his life in Africa. Interrestingly, he didn't speak of any women in his life.

Back in the study, flushed with the wine and liquor, Manfred volunteered, "The reason I came here was to see you."

She gave him a look of surprise.

Manfred placed a hand on her knee, and said solemnly, "There are beautiful places in Africa, wondrous sights, but nothing that can compare with your infectious beauty."

Mercedes blushed, then laughed. "You never cease to amaze me, Manfred."

"I've traveled a long way to see you, Mercedes. Surely you're flattered," he said, downing his most recent glass of after-dinner liqueur in a single gulp.

"I had made arrangements for you to sleep in one of the spare bedrooms," she said teasingly, "but perhaps you would prefer to spend the night more comfortably with me?"

"Of course, Mercedes," he replied without hesitation.

"Then please join me in my room in, shall we say, twenty minutes?"

"See you in a while," he said, watching at her as she left.

When he first entered her bedroom, it was too dark to make anything out. Over the years, Mercedes had learned to limit the light. Darkness tended to disorientate her victims.

When his eyes had adjusted, seeing her in bed, he shed his clothes and joined her.

Before his body touched the bed, they began kissing passionately. She quickly determined that he was a better and more assured lover than his older brother, and while they were engaged, the question begged, should he be forced to go the way of the other men before him? The fact that she asked the question rather than acted automatically as she had in the past, suggested to her that Manfred was something new and unusual, someone who, just possibly, might break her compulsion and help her find the peace she sought. She had at hand everything necessary to dispatch him if her compulsion suddenly reared and became overwhelming. He'd disclosed that he lived in a remote part of Africa, and had no wife or family or strong links to anybody. The news of his disappearance would take time to trickle through to foreign authorities, and by then, what could they do, worlds away in Africa?

There were, this time, sentimental constraints, at least in Mercedes swirling mind, and Manfred was continuing to prove the charmer. When, minutes later, they made passionate love, they even crescendoed together. Unfortunately, it was at this crucial point that he made the gravest of errors. The second after they'd finished, he muttered, "I love you."

Something lurking within her took hold, and a hatred far stronger than she'd experienced with any other man engulfed her. She reached over to the nightstand for the poisoned needle and reflexively jabbed it into his back, anticipating she had only to wait a few seconds before he would die. This time, however, was different. His body seized. His heart began to beat faster. He turned red, panting and perspiring like he had a raging fever. But in spite of his dire condition, he showed no sign of dying.

Mercedes screamed when she realized he wasn't going to die. Her mind was in turmoil, half wanting to turn on the light, half hoping to contain whatever was happening in the darkness. As she lay pinned to the bed, the faces of her victims began to flash through her mind. A world traveler, eyes wide and glazed with shock, his paling lips forming the word, "'Why?" An American tourist on an expedition to discover his heritage, an expression of disbelief and sorrow on his face when he realized he would never get to know his past and no longer had a future. Another, a huntsman, who had proved a silent but vigorous lover, his head thrown back, lines of indescribable pain carved into his face as he uttered a final guttural word of pleasure before passing from this world. Then there was the Eastern European on his first visit to the West, who had delighted in the marvelous countryside, unaware that before the next night, his ashes would soon be dispersed about it. The athletically-built Scandinavian, his face fixed in teutonic ecstasy, who had such a peculiar way of pronouncing English words, which she had compassionately corrected after thrusting the needle into the side of his heaving chest. They and many others passed one-by-one through her mind, each's face frozen in its own unique expression of surprise and anguish.

Having pushed Manfred to one side, her pulse racing, her body trembling, Mercedes tried to quell her escalating anxieties. Manfred, in the meantime, gasped, and appeared to be re-animating. *Perhaps I didn't administer enough poison?* a detached part of her brain wondered. *Perhaps he's somehow immune?*

Manfred's eyes opened wide and he lurched forward. Mercedes screamed, expecting to be physically attacked after having tried unsuccessfully to kill him. Manfred, however, seemed unerringly calm and collected as he unraveled himself from the sheets and sat up next to her.

There was a drawn out silence during which he slowly and methodically flexed and extended first his fingers, then his hands, arms, face and chest as if experiencing them for the first time. Satisfied, he turned to her. "You seem to have been busy while I've been away," he said.

It took some time for his words to register between the continued flood of images of the men she'd killed. It took several more seconds for her to realize that Manfred's voice sounded not at all like Manfred, but rather like his older brother, her ex-husband.

Her body shuddered at the thought. "No...no...no!" was all she could manage in reply.

"My dear Mercedes," continued the man sitting next to her in voice of her late husband, "Manfred could never leave well enough alone that which was not his, no matter how many times I admonished him. I may have been the one with the weaker heart, but I was also the one with the sharper intellect and indomitable spirit. So, my dear, I'm back, ready now to finish what was by nature so inappropriately cut short."

The Duke

Montgomery Railton had seen many people hang. In fact, for him a hanging was little more than a routine, like blowing out a candle when leaving a room, except the light being snuffed was someone's life. For years, he'd done his grim and dutiful part as a prison warden, preparing the sentenced for what was to come, often feeling dismayed at the way the condemned wasted away his or her last moments. He'd watched attentively countless times while they picked at their last meal, and wrote their last letters to the few, if any, interested in hearing of their imminent demise. He'd observed their faces, paralyzed with fear, as they were ushered forward on their final walk.

Railton, to put it bluntly, was a dull warden with few other interests. He had a collection of racing pigeons and could be found in the pub drinking half a stout on any Saturday night, but, having never shown the slightest interest in women or having a family, he mostly cut a lonesome figure. He spoke economically, and only on the rarest of occasions would he crack a smile. He was a shadowy figure, always on the periphery, except, of course, when supervising the last moments of the condemned.

A new man had recently been brought in, having been tried, convicted, and delivered by the police. Known simply as "The Duke," he was by appearance and manner of aristocratic stock. He had a distinctive *panache* that was unusual compared to the rest of the wretched souls awaiting death.

Truth be told, Railton felt uncomfortable in the presence of The Duke. He didn't know how to address or treat him. It seemed strange to call a sentenced man "Your grace" and to punctiliously bow to him. The Duke, in turn, didn't dwell on his past like most of the men who passed briefly through the warden's grim world on their way to the hangman's noose. Instead, The Duke retained an unnaturally cheeky disposition and a vision of a rosy future pending his release. Given The Duke's disposition, it could be assumed that his history would bear little resemblance to the others, but it still obviously had, at some point, taken a wrong turn.

The Duke had lived a colorful, and what some, including Railton, might deem a frivolous life. His defense lawyer, a cheery soul with a drinking problem, had proved less than adequate in the courtroom. During the hearing, he'd slurred his words so badly, he might as well have signed The Duke's death warrant. The lawyer, for his part, assumed The Duke had it all in hand, and had given his client free reign. Without guidance, The Duke had rambled on and on about matters that had little to do with the case, while his lawyer dozed off, and disgraced both of them by snorting loudly as The Duke finished his long soliloquy. The courtroom in response burst into laughter. The judge, a straight-laced, God-fearing teetotaler, who eyed both men throughout the hearing with cold contempt, silently concluded that the sozzled defense lawyer and his indecorous client were longtime drinking partners of the devil, and the accused had taken up his ways.

When Railton asked The Duke about his crime, the man talked about the future: namely, how he planned to toast the judge at the St James's Gentlemen's Club when he was freed. He knew people in high places, he said. The Home Secretary, for example, was a personal friend with whom he frequently dined. They played bridge every Thursday. The Home Secretary would never allow his favorite bridge partner to hang. The Duke spoke of his current situation with such levity that it seemed as if it were happening to someone else. It was as if he *enjoyed* flirting with death.

A few days after The Duke had settled into prison, the ravishingly beautiful celebrated socialite, Lady Eleanor Rising-Stanley, visited the prison. After delicately testing the dirtied cobblestones with the tip of her red patent shoe, she gracefully slipped from her liveried carriage. Wearing a crimson frock trimmed with a white ermine shawl, long white silk gloves covered the delicate hand Railton accepted with gravity. She smoked a cigarette poised at the far end of a long holder which she waved in the air like a wand, gesturing that she was ready to be escorted into the prison. Railton, catching her drift, signaled the grizzled entrance guards, who, recognizing her from her many society pictures splashed in newspapers, solicitously opened the rusty prison gates.

Utterly awed, Railton guided her silently down the long stone hallway and through several more gates to the section where The Duke was quartered. There, he left her with two prison guards, glad to escape her company, finding her simply too intimidating. Male prisoners on death row were not allowed to entertain, especially a lady-visitor, alone, in the prisoner's cell, and Railton, who knew every prison regulation to the letter, had initially objected. Such a flagrant break from established protocol was inconceivable to him. Immediately after voicing his concerns, however, he accepted a handwritten order from the Governor, compelling him to escort the prisoner's lady-guest to The Duke's cell and return immediately to the warden office. Railton, of course, complied, though with consternation, and afterwards took to brooding behind his desk about the gossip that would inevitably result from such flagrant rule-breaking.

The two guards posted at entrance to The Duke's prison wing stared transfixed, as Lady Rising-Stanley lifted her skirts and entered the cell-block. Gliding past, she tossed each a flirty smile, trilling a pleasant "Good morning, gentlemen" to each.

The two guards dared not answer, and instead, acknowledged her pleasantry by snapping to rigid attention.

It was some while before Lady Eleanor left The Duke's cell. Both guards smiled inwardly when they noticed that her initially immaculate attire was disheveled, and her carefully coiffed hair noticeably ruffled. For her part, she smiled condescendingly, then winked at the warders as if to purposefully inflame their lascivious imaginings.

Railton, having been tipped off that her Ladyship was on her way out of the prison, noted from his high office window that she had shed some of the poise she'd so effectively displayed on her entry, and could only imagine what had transpired.

Her visit seemed to embolden The Duke. He began ordering his warders about, and complaining vigorously that the food was not to his taste. More palatable food prepared by his own chef began arriving the next day. He soon took to chinking glasses of his private reserve vintage Chardonnay with the guards, sharing with them a bit of caviar or truffled *pâté*. He demanded his sheets be provided by his own household staff and that, like his tablecloth, they be changed every night. The water in his bathtub, which had been installed at his insistence, had to be at exactly the specified temperature. Morton, one of The Duke's two appointed guards, assumed responsibility for placing toothpaste on The Duke's toothbrush, while Smyth took to brushing The Duke's shoes every morning so that they shone bright as a beacon.

One day, a large box arrived for The Duke, which, as prison protocol demanded, he opened in front of his guards. Inside was a new gramophone, a present from Lady Eleanor. Included were select 78s, personally chosen by her for his enjoyment. Placing the player on a stark wooden stool, he wound it up, and Viennese waltzes began wafting through the drab cell block.

While The Duke's situation improved inside prison, outside, the press somehow got wind that he might not be legitimate aristocracy. The Royal College of Arms was consulted and reported that his title, that of the Duke of Grandville, had been unused since the seventeenth century and that anyone claiming it today was no better than a phony. The Duke's lawyer immediately issued a public statement explaining that his client's title had been passed to him from his late father, the reclusive twelfth Duke of Grandville, a little known branch of the family living out in the far reaches of the colonies. The present Duke, the lawyer's statement said, had spent his early life out in the colonies, working alongside his father for the glory of the Empire, unlike his detractors at the Royal College, who'd never done a decent day's toil in their lives. The Royal College, The Duke's lawyer further claimed, were little more than a group of muddled old men, who needed to spend more time searching the archives, and less time downing gin and tonics at their private clubs. The statement ended with a warning that writs would be served if any further defamatory words against the nobility of his client were forthcoming.

In less than a day, The Duke became a national enigma. *Who is The Duke?* was on every newspaper headline and everyone's lips.

The next day, someone leaked a story that The Duke had a young wife, the Duchess of Grandville, as well as a son and heir, young Lord Percival. The Duchess, it was said, was determined to carry on her reclusive life as normal, and felt disinclined to visit her incarcerated husband. She'd been reportedly heard to say that prisons were foul places, unbecoming of persons of her stature. On top of this, young Percival had just started riding lessons, and she was fully involved at the moment watching him attempt to canter his pony.

According to the story, The Duke wasn't only an absent husband, but worse, an absent father who'd gambled away his son's inheritance on a single wager. Somehow, two lines appeared in next edition of the newspaper quoting The Duke as saying in response, "Children are problems that get in the way of more entertaining matters," and "Such trivialities should not be allowed to dampen one's *joie de vivre*." The resulting public outcry cut short any hope of a court appeal.

One evening, the Governor paid The Duke a visit. "Is everything to your liking?" he asked, from outside The Duke's cell.

"The service is good," The Duke replied, smiling and winking at Warden Railton, who stood watching and listening just behind the Governor, having unconditionally refused any further breaches of prison protocol.

"And the company's not bad, either," The Duke added, winking at the two guards, also close at hand.

Railton listened while the Governor reported that the final act of The Duke's sentence had been scheduled for two days hence. The hangman, Rosenthal, and his assistant had arrived earlier on the train South from Barnsley. At this moment, they were busy testing the gallows, trap door and rope. Tomorrow Rosenthal would visit The Duke to check his weight and height. It would be a hanging fit for a Duke, the Governor assured.

The Duke grinned widely, obviously delighting in the thought. "Wonderful," he replied, adding, "it's such glorious fun to be the center of attention."

The Governor, shocked by the man's insouciance concluded The Duke was making mockery of him. The Governor's features hardened, while his voice softened. "Perhaps your Grace would like the prison padre to pay a visit? For a last confession?"

"Good Lord, no, Governor. Why on earth would I want to do that?" The Duke replied with a raucous laugh, apparently finding the thought intoxicatingly funny. "A kind thought, but I plan to enjoy some fine food and delicious wine with jolly old Railton here, perhaps even an after dinner game of poker, as I often hear the guards touting how much they love a game of cards. I wager I'll end up winning considerable money off them tonight."

Railton shuddered at The Duke's compliment while the guards fought to contain their laughter, but The Duke apparently wasn't through. "Besides, priests are such bores, what with all that interminable praying and chanting, compared to these charming fellows, who have seen to it that my stay here has been most pleasant."

The Governor's lips tightened and he started to speak, but The Duke cut him off. "And so, if you don't mind, Governor, I must ask you to take your leave. I've also a race card to study. There's a particular filly I wouldn't mind having a flutter on."

The Governor became incensed. Duke or no Duke, he expected at least a modicum of respect. Condemned prisoners were supposed to plead for their lives, not insult the Governor of one of Her Majesty's prisons. They were supposed to be downcast, at their lowest ebb, and, quite literally, at the end of their rope. Yet here was a man who didn't seem to have a care in the world, who was treating the whole situation like he was on some kind of pleasurable sojourn. As Railton escorted the Governor back to his drab office, he heard behind them *Life is a Song, Let's Sing it Together* by Ruth Etting on The Duke's gramophone.

Railton, while somewhat niggled at The Duke's behavior, had to admit that he retained a certain admiration for the man. Not only had Railton and The Duke formed an unlikely bond, they were of the same height, weight and hair color. Perhaps because of his admiration for The Duke's fearless attitude in the face of adversity, or, perhaps because of their uncanny resemblance, Railton couldn't stop his imagination running wild about The Duke. *Maybe somewhere in the distant past we shared the same parentage*, he wondered, a bizarre thought, but one not entirely out of the question. But for their current situations, their lives could have easily been reversed.

In fact, Railton hadn't known either of his parents. He'd been abandoned immediately after birth and left, wrapped in rags, on the steps of a local church, where he had very nearly fallen victim to a terrible injury, when, next morning, the local parson, having drunk too much port the night before, tripped and accidentally stepped on him.

His sharp incongruous squeal alerted the parson at the last moment that an infant was ensconced within the pile of rags.

As a child, Railton had been shuffled from one orphanage to another until deemed too old to work the public workhouses for parentless children. Service in the prison system had seemed a natural progression. In his formative years, he was the one incarcerated, in prison service he was the one doing the incarcerating. With his dour personality, he proved the perfect candidate for the grim task of preparing the condemned for the gallows. He'd steadily worked his way up to his present position as head warden.

Montgomery Railton paced his office, knowing from prison gossip that The Duke was down to his last card. Sir Anthony, the Home Secretary and alleged bridge-playing "friend" of The Duke, would be loath to send *any* aristocrat to the gallows; however, Sir Anthony hadn't as yet made even the slightest move to stop the execution. As evidence continued to surface that The Duke might, indeed, be a complete fraud, public feelings were running high that the gallows and an undignified death might be the most fitting end to the whole scandal. Just before the Governor had arrived, The Duke had wagered Railton he'd be out before the night was over, Sir Anthony being a "good sport." Railton waited to see if such optimism had any foundation in reality. Late that night, Sir Anthony turned against The Duke, calling him a fraud and, worse than a common criminal, "a stain on polite society."

The next day, Rosanthal, the meticulous hangman, much to the Duke's displeasure, spent time prodding, poking and measuring the condemned, claiming he was only following procedure. Worst of all, the irritating man spoke with a strong vulgar northern accent, chain-smoked cheap shag tobacco, and refused to engage in any semblance of witty *reparte*. *At least they could have chosen a man with a sense of humor and a bearable accent to carry out the onerous task, and not this lifeless soul*, The Duke thought peevishly.

As the evening hour drew closer, The Duke, to everyone's surprise, called for Railton. They spent their time together talking and drinking late into the early morning. The warders were curious, but were able to hear next to nothing of what passed between the two with the gramophone blaring.

In Railton's mind, the two men were doing something he'd never imagined possible: They were bonding, as might two long lost brothers. It was a new experience, one he'd never encountered before. Listening to the cheerful melodies, The Duke poured the last of the last bottle of fine wine into two glasses. On the eve of his execution both were in particularly high spirits. Railton, having been easily enticed into accompanying him on this final drinking spree, was feeling giddy, being a man who normally consumed alcohol in strict moderation.

The Duke, deeming the time ripe, slipped a hand into his smoking jacket and clandestinely withdrew a small packet of powder, which he deftly directed into Railton's glass. Lady Eleanor, it seems, had offered him more than her body: She had also provided him the small pouch of sleeping powder, a vial of opium, powerful enough to render a person delirious, and a hypodermic syringe, all of which she'd hidden on her person, where, in the unlikely event the guards should search her, they would be least inclined to check.

Railton drained the last of his drink with a rousing toast to The Duke and promptly fell face down onto the wooden table between them. The Duke quickly injected the incapacitated man with the opium, then exchanged clothes. Railton, The Duke concluded, looked most fetching, making quite a dapper aristocrat. He applied a dollop of macassar oil to Railton's hair and shaped it into his own distinctive style. Then he sprinkled some of his signature aftershave over Railton. The ruse was complete when he placed his family signet ring on Railton's finger.

Dressed in Railton's drab warden's uniform, which he deemed an unbecoming necessity, The Duke paused before the mirror he had had installed in his cell and admired his work. The switch was complete. All was in order. He was ready to attend his own execution.

Daylight was already peeking through the narrow barred window high above. The time had come, and he hiked Railton up against the wall.

Railton was just conscious enough to appear the broken-in-spirit aristocrat, drunkenly unaware of what was about to happen. The two warders knocked politely, entered the cell and grasped the sad-looking man, shaking their heads in disappointment. At the Warden's signal they dragged the luckless man solemnly down the corridor to the execution area. The Duke offered none of his usual jokes or banter, but just mumbled incomprehensibly, occasionally moaning while reaching up and placing a hand on his temple. The man half-standing, half being held upright on the gallows wasn't the self-assured man with whom they had become so familiar, the man they had wagered would face his death as he'd lived his life.

The prison padre, dressed in simple black vestments, clutched his worn Bible tightly in his hands and gasped at the sight of the broken man who, earlier, had vehemently refused last rights. The Governor, sitting on a dias across the room, had a glib look on his face.

On either side of The Duke stood the humorless Rosanthal and the prison doctor. Behind stood Rosenthal's assistant, eyes sunken like death itself, holding the noose in his hands. Rosenthal seemed to be itching to pull the lever and get it over. Anticipation gripped the dreary chamber, imbuing it a palpable sense of gruesome urgency.

Outside the prison, the crowds and the press gathered like jackals eager for their share of the kill, while Lady Eleanor, largely ignored, sat hidden from sight in her carriage on the distant periphery of the crowd, waiting sedately.

"Do you have any last words?" demanded the Governor.

The condemned man, the noose snugged tightly about his neck, looked at the Governor like a dumb mule, lolled his head briefly forward towards the "Railton" standing behind the Governor and mouthed something that sounded vaguely like "not me." The Governor seemed confused at first, but signaled with a disinterested wave of his hand for the execution to proceed.

The perfunctory black hood was slipped over the condemned man's head.

The padre opened his Bible and started reciting.

The Governor locked eyes with Rosenthal and nodded.

Everyone in the room sucked in a breath.

The padre continued droning on hypnotically, but no one paid him any attention. Everyone's attention was focused on the emasculated figure on the stand. The trap door abruptly opened, the condemned man fell a short distance, jerked, then began to swing gently in a tight circle.

It was over.

After a suitable time, assured by the doctor that the prisoner had truly met his end, the undertaker lurking in the wings began going about his business. The Duke was to be buried in the prison cemetery in an unmarked grave—poetic justice many would later remark. The crowds outside the prison silently dissolved. In the end, no one really cared about the man who had successfully played them for fools and had, in the end, met his death so ignominiously.

Ten minutes later, the Governor was pouring himself a stiff whiskey from a pocket flask and peering out of the window of his carriage, watching a man walk officiously towards Lady Eleanor's carriage. He could see it was Railton, undoubtedly doing his duty, perhaps following up on a last request by passing a final letter to her. There was, though, something odd about the way Railton walked. It seemed almost akin to The Duke's cocky swagger. As Railton approached the carriage, the door opened, he climbed in, and, to the Governor's surprise, before the door was shut, the driver cracked his whip and the carriage rolled ahead, tapering quickly into the distance. At the same moment, dark clouds began to form in the Governor's mind. *What if...?*

Flight of Destiny

Bitch

There was going to be a dogfight. Two snarling savage beasts were scheduled to tear into each other, and the crowd, composed mainly of dockers and members of the local waterfront criminal fraternity, would shortly be gathered in an abandoned warehouse, screaming for blood. The stakes had never been higher, but as yet, McFadden, the bookie, ringleader and perpetrator of all that happened on the docks that was illegal, as indecent and debauched a man as ever could be, was nowhere to be found.

McFadden's "boys" were perplexed but continued doing their part to maintain the fevered excitement. Each had done his assigned part to build up the fight and drive the attendees into a betting frenzy, cajoling the reticent few, and threatening the rest with bodily harm if they didn't attend and place bets.

McFadden, the burly, forty-five-year-old, six-foot-eight docker with a granite face, steel-cold eyes, and a voice as rough as splintered wood, had, as ever, set it all in motion. The unspoken godfather of the neighborhood, McFadden commanded enormous respect from everyone on the waterfront through a combination of extortion, blackmail, fear, and brutal intimidation. To his inner-circle he was known as "Jip."

Despite his intimidating size and demeanor, he rarely had to use his steel-hard knuckles; McFadden had chewed "backy" for so many years, he merely had to breathe on a person to render him incapable of resistance.

McFadden was nominally married to Shirley, a squirrelish, childless woman of thirty-five who looked as though she'd weathered twice as many years of adversity and woe. McFadden boasted an assortment of children by various other women, some close acquaintances of Shirley. In fact, McFadden had "stolen" Shirley from his one-time school friend, "Squeamish" Jack Harmeson, through a combination of deceit and terrorization. To Shirley's dismay, Harmeson hadn't even tried to stave off McFadden's advances. Afterwards it became obvious to all that McFadden had no feelings for Shirley; it was the vanquishing of Harmeson's love for the woman that had spurred him on.

In fact, had Harmeson attempted to defy McFadden, it's likely Harmeson would have been discovered floating the next day under the docks minus essential body parts. Since then, Shirley lost her desire to live, her will broken by her bullying "husband," being further diminished by her periodic attempts to drink herself into oblivion.

Gnasher, Sam "The Hammer" Royston's legendary black male pit bull, was set against "Squeamish" Jack Harmeson's terrier, Puck. The

Hammer was McFaddens' number one henchman, and Gnasher, the terror of the docks. Puck, Harmeson's pet terrier, couldn't fight her way out of a wet paper bag even if she tried. Puck was the one of the few dogs local children felt at ease to pet, or, in contrast, to insult, often calling her "Puke." Puck was Harmeson's last remaining pleasure in his otherwise devoid life, and it pained him to think another precious companion would soon be taken from him.

All in all, Puck wouldn't have a chance. Several of the aging dog's muzzle-hairs had recently whitened. Maybe, Harmeson half-heartedly reasoned, by agreeing to fight Puck, he was saving her from the inevitable indignation of old age. Puck was a docile, some might say completely placid mutt, and, out of conscience, the moment Harmeson reluctantly agreed to the fight, he began to train Puck as best he could, hoping to provide her some dignity in death. In truth, it hurt his heart to have to bait and anger her.

His most ardent efforts failed to inspire the dog. The sanguine animal was interested in just two things: food and sleep, and Harmeson eventually realized that training Puck to defend herself was a lost cause. Keen to make a few bob, McFadden had spread the word that Puck, when it came to fights, transformed into a vicious fighting machine. In reality, he'd set up the fight for his own cruel pleasure, calculating it would send Squeamish Harmeson spiraling over the edge and leave him a totally broken man. If she somehow survived, she'd be bloodied and maimed, and McFadden would have the pleasure of seeing Harmeson walking the streets with his butchered dog, guilt and pain etched permanently on his face.

Several days before, McFadden had sent The Hammer and Gnasher, accompanied by two of his biggest brutes, to corner Squeamish in the Red Rooster, a local dive close to the docks where everyone liked to hang out.

"McFadden's got a proposition for you," said the The Hammer, chuckling, grabbing Squeamish Harmeson's threadbare duffle coat, and pushing him into a chair.

A 'proposition?' thought Harmeson. *With McFadden, it will undoubtedly be something depraved.*

McFadden's two goons spread out, causing Harmeson's fear to transform into abject terror. Squeamish released himself from The Hammer's clutches, called for a pint and distanced himself as far as possible from the three. Puck followed, positioning herself around her master's feet and began gently snoring.

The Hammer jumped onto the nearest table, a malevolent smile on his lips, and pointed a threatening finger at Puck. "That dog of yours looks menacingly dangerous," he said loudly, chortling at his own wit. Everyone in the bar sniggered, ready to pander to whatever McFadden's second-in-command had in mind.

Harmeson reflected on his antagonist's sudden outburst and instinctively reached for his pint of bitter for some much needed fortitude, unsure where the conversation was leading. Sam "The Hammer" Royston climbed off the table to stand directly in front of Harmeson. Leaning his bulk forward, he nodded his head at Puck.

"I've been told that inside that mild exterior is an invincible fighting dog" he said, tapping his fingers on the tabletop as if to perk up the sedate dog snoring loudly at Harmeson's feet. Royston and the circle of bar denizens gathering about Harmeson and Puck burst out in hysterical laughter.

"If you say so," Harmeson cautiously replied, looking nervously from Royston to his two men and then at Gnasher, growling in the distance. Harmeson was trying his best to appear detached, hoping The

Hammer would move on to someone or something more interesting.

Royston, however, persisted in staring him down. "Hows about we set up a fight? Your terrifyingly ferocious Puck, with her famous jaws of steel, against my pathetic excuse of a dog over there."

Gnasher, Royston's trained assassin-dog, a mass of muscle, equipped with notoriously razor sharp teeth, bristled with ferociously, as if his canine brain comprehended the slur just made against his fighting prowess. Royston jerked Gnasher's chain to quiet him.

Everyone in the tavern had by now stopped what they were doing to see where this would go. It was obvious to all that this was a blatant attempt to lure Harmeson into a dog fight which could only result in Puck's annihilation.

The Hammer continued. "Just so you and everyone here knows me and McFadden are good sports, my boss will offer thousand to one odds to anyone willing to bet on your secret brute of a dog there." He pulled out a huge roll of bills and shook it tantalizingly in the air. Royston's eyes bored into one after another man staring hungrily at the wad, daring them to bet. Harmeson sat silent, the full extent of his terror only evident in his fully dilated pupils. Puck suddenly awakened, looked up at her master, snorted and fell quickly back asleep.

Sam wasn't finished yet. He'd managed the first part: terrorizing Harmeson, calling him out and capturing everyone's interest. For the finale, he spat into Harmeson's pint and tossed it on Puck.

Puck accepted the humiliation without resisting. Harmeson, though further embittered, did nothing. The crowd, on the other hand, circled closer about him and laughed until they were hoarse.

Harmeson reluctantly stood and coaxed his drenched canine towards the pub door. It didn't matter if he accepted Royston and

McFadden's challenge or not, the results would be the same. As Harmeson skulked out the door, Royston gleefully accepted on both Puck and Gnasher's behalf, ordering a free round of drinks. Glasses were lifted, shouting erupted, and bets began appearing, sealing the contest.

At the designated time, the warehouse had quickly filled, and was soon bustling with excitement, except for one notable absentee: There was no sign of McFadden. It was most uncharacteristic. Normally, the man would be "larging it up with the boys" and his criminal friends. His voice would be voluminous, his presence so apparent that he would seem omnipresent. Instead, the fight had to be put on temporary hold and search parties sent out to locate the missing man. It was, after all, a fight set up by McFadden and McFadden had to be there to give the event credence.

Royston was frowning ominously. Gnasher, tied to a post, was baring teeth and snarling, lunging on its chain at Puck.

Squeamish Harmeson, standing across the ring at the opposite post, looked remarkably cool, as if he and Puck had gone for an afternoon walk and stepped into the ring to take a rest. Unchained, waddling in an ever-tightening circle about her master, Puck finally flopped down and began snoring.

Royston, on a hunch, had dispatched some dockers to a fish storage locker not far away. It was a place McFadden favored when concluding illicit deals, or when meting out punishment to unfortunates who ruffled him. It was a place where screams, muted by the thick metal walls, couldn't be heard outside.

When the dockers arrived, they found the thick metal door ajar and heard moaning from within. Someone was behind the door, and from the grating sound of metal against metal emanating from inside, that person was secured to the inside, quite probably with metal cuffs or chains. Fearful of intruding on one of McFadden's "punishments," the dockers pushed open the door the slightest of fractions, just enough to see what appeared to be a burly man dressed in gaudy pink women's clothes. The freak was lying in a heap, his hairy arms handcuffed above his head to the inside door handle. A trickle of blood was seeping from a pair of deep puncture wounds on one of the cross-dresser's lower legs.

Exercising more curiosity than caution, one of the men chanced a look at the victim's face. It was heavily made up, the cheeks caked with rouge, lips coated with bright pink lipstick, all of which had obviously been applied in haste.

The front docker whispered to the two behind him outside the door, "God's trousers! It's friggin' Jip McFadden! An' he looks right like a Nancy boy."

The two dockers behind him stared at each other in stark disbelief, fearful the man who'd spoken was making a tasteless joke that could have terrible repercussions. The idea of McFadden dressed like a tart on the day of the big dog fight didn't even deserve thinking about, and yet, impulsively they passed the untoward message on to the others standing behind them. Whispers soon turned to shouts to open the door further, and, acquiescing to the crowd's growing demand, the first docker opened the door the rest of the way.

It was McFadden, eyes glazed, head lolling from side to side, drool dripping from the corner of his mouth, incapable of speaking coherently.

The first docker, seeing the full absurdity of it all, couldn't contain himself any longer and broke out into laughter so contagious that his other two friends and subsequently the entire crowd quickly joined. They'd never seen or imagined such a pathetic sight. While they laughed and guffawed, one of group broke away to inform Royston of their discovery.

In minutes, everyone who'd come to attend the dog fight had taken his turn peeking into the locker, exploding into laughter, pointing at McFadden and making snide remarks before rejoining the crowd outside. It was a spectacle, a freak show that topped even the promised dog fight.

McFadden, finally roused from his torpor, turned livid with rage, and began yanking against the cuffs with all his strength. The cuffs, however, remained firm. In the process, his short pink skirt rode up. Without thinking, he began wiggling madly trying to force it back down, his efforts only succeeding in adding to the comic spectacle. One docker remarked through tears of laughter that it was rather like watching a snake shedding its skin. McFadden mumbled some loose threats, but quickly realized the hopeless of his situation. He'd lost all possible dignity. No docker would ever be able to forget this image of him.

What had happened to him, McFadden wondered. Who was behind it? Was it Shirley, wanting revenge for the years of maltreatment and his cheating on her? It seemed improbable, as he'd slapped any form of dissent out of her years ago. Was it possibly Sam "The Hammer" Royston's way of usurping him? Or had he pushed one of the Nancy-boys he so liked to torment too far?

The crowd began murmuring, having come to its own conclusion. Malice hung heavily in the air. Rough hands one-by-one reached into the shadows for pieces of wood and old pipes. Tough guy Jip McFadden had apparently, over the years, been nursing some secret urges, and he'd gotten caught in the act, they concluded. There was nowhere for a man like that on the docks.

In the end, only one thing could be ascertained for sure: Harmeson's sudden evolution. Had any one of the crowd remained behind in the ring, he would have seen Squeamish Harmeson smirking from ear to ear, happily taking in the pandemonium before leaving the ring, Puck trotting behind him with extra spring in her step.

Flight of Destiny

Slashed

It was two o'clock in the morning, and Constanzi was totally, completely drunk. A lanky, awkward man in his early forties, he had aged prematurely, bearing the marks of a man who'd suffered and experienced far too much disappointment in his lifetime. Constanzi's long unkempt hair was matted with sweat, his eyes, normally the color of blue granite, were deeply bloodshot. A morning stubble had begun sprouting from his lower jaw. Constanzi weaved his way down a narrow alley to the door of an imposing building and awkwardly levered it open with a metal bar.

The door creaked, moaned, then gave way with a thud. Constanzi stumbled in, grinning, eyes blazing, a look of conquest plastered on his face. Casually tossing aside the metal bar, hands shaking, he lit several candles, and looked about in awe. Canvases, some finished, others still in progress, decorated every available space of the high stone walls. Even drunk and in the gloomy light, the works looked magnificent, even more so than the few who'd seen them claimed.

Swaying back and forth, he marveled at the way hundreds of jars of pigment were meticulously laid out on a narrow table, each according to hue. In front of the jars were rows and rows of brushes arranged in descending thickness. Unlike his, this studio was impeccably organized. He mumbled something unintelligible, and listened to it echo throughout the room. The space felt more like a mausoleum, or, at the least, a sacred space, leaving him feeling small and unimportant. *Unimportant? I'll show everyone how far I am from being unimportant*, his inebriated mind screamed. *Which painting should I damage first?* He pondered for a moment with the relish of a child surveying a pile of unopened gifts. The first to catch his discerning eye was a work-in-progress. It was a sizable piece, standing impressively on a large easel, worked on so recently he could smell the odor of fresh oil paint.

He reached for a jar marked "Cadmium Orange" and with a palette knife conveniently lying nearby, scooped out a large dollop of the handmade oil paint and smeared it crudely over the face of a cherubic looking angel staring upwards at a sky of luminous clouds. *Not so cherubic now,* he thought.

Next to this picture was a completed rendition of the infant St. John, holding a cross in hand, staring with apparent horror at the desecrated picture next to him. Constanzi splattered titanium white across it, then ran his hands over the canvas in violent sweeping motions until the infant vanished. The three wise men's noble heads fared similarly when splattered liberally with dollops of yellow ochre.

Constanzi lurched towards the next painting, his mind calculating how much damage he could inflict using new colors and techniques. This time he chose burnt umber. Scooping a fistful into his right hand, he shakily climbed a stepladder next to another painting, barely managing not to fall, successfully smearing the contents of his hand over the middle third of the huge painting. Carefully descending the ladder, he noticed a bucket and mop. Maestro's apprentices were required to mop the floor every morning before he arrived (Maestro's studio had to be spotless to match the perfection of the paintings). Constanzi poured a bottle of walnut oil into the bucket, slapped the mop in, swirled it about, clambered back up the ladder, and, like a workman cleaning a wall, began obliterating the top portions the large painting, covering the sky with a crude veil that reminded him of excrement. As the fluid trickled down the canvas, it began obscuring all of the fine detail work Maestro had painstakingly put in the painting.

Grabbing a handful of aquamarine, the original color of the now-obscured sky, he completely eliminated the central figure, a heavenly depiction of the current Pope, poised as if about to join the saints in heaven. In one motion, he'd reduced the pontiff to little more than a crude blue stripe. Satisfied, he took another pull from his shoulder wineskin and cackled devilishly.

The next picture was a nativity scene with the Madonna depicted as chillingly radiant, in the way only a master painter could. She looked like beauty and perfection incarnate, with her liquid eyes and delicate white skin, her gentle hands cradling a supine baby Jesus. Constanzi slipped a hand behind his back, drew out his hunting knife, positioned it above his head like a person might do if he were about to stab someone in the heart, and slashed the Madonna's face again and again until the canvas drooped in limp shreds. *Weeks of meticulous work ruined*, Constanzi thought with a twisted smile. Then, just for good measure, he spat some of the wine he been swigging onto the picture and watched it trickle down the shredded canvas onto the floor. Good work, he told himself, but he still didn't feel satisfied.

Opening a bottle of turpentine, he hurled it across the room at the canvas. It deflected off, but its contents splattered everywhere, creating rivers of bleeding colors on the masterpiece as well as the ones next to it. The effect gave Constanzi an idea. He'd noticed a painting in a corner covered by a cloth. It was obviously a painting that meant something special to his brother, Maestro, but wasn't meant to be part of the impending exhibition for which these pictures had been chosen. It was likely he'd painted it for his own personal gratification. Constanzi ripped off the cloth that shrouded the painting and placed the work flat on the floor. It was a painting of the martyrdom of St. Sebastian, depicting a thin but muscular young man pinioned to a tree with arrows piercing his body at multiple angles. Constanzi recognized the model. It was Jacomo Visconti, Maestro's youngest apprentice, who some said Maestro treated like a surrogate son, his own son having died in a freak accident, trampled to death by horses while attempting to cross a street. Regarding the piece, Constanzi wondered whether Maestro held more than just fatherly love for the youth. St. Sebastian looked mildly erotic, as if the work were more of an adulation of the boy's flesh than his fealty.

Constanzi grabbed two sizable jars, one of midnight black and another of titanium white, added some walnut oil to make each color more fluid, dipped in an exceptionally large brush, and began splattering the painting with black drops. Onto this, he spattered a layer of titanium white drops. It took some time to completely obliterate the image on the canvas. The new abstract image he'd conjured reminded him of a constellation of moving fish seen at a distance from above. It suddenly occurred to him that out of the destruction, he was subtly redefining painting techniques, inventing new forms of expression, *espressionismo astratto*. He, Constanzi, he assured himself, was way ahead of his time, though, of course, Maestro could never understand such a novel concept.

His eyes darted about the room and seized on some drawings. They were great works, in charcoal, that showed the meticulous attention to detail, form, contour and perspective for which his brother was known.

Looking at them, Constanzi shivered. Dawn was approaching and the studio had become icy cold. In a fit of pure malice, he ripped the drawings to shreds, tossed them in the fireplace, retrieved some matches from his pocket, and threw the lit match into the hearth. The drawings whooshed into flames, and Constanzi watched contentedly as they darken, shriveled and turned to black ash. After warming himself, he returned his attention to the few remaining canvasses.

It was but a few days before the works were to be transported to Rome for exhibition. Every art patron in Italy planned to be present at the show. There was even talk of royalty from Portugal, France and Spain attending. Of course, a representative of the Vatican would be there, maybe even Pope Julius himself. There would also be some notable absentees: Maestro's wife and their children, including his favorite, Faustina, who not only had developed a passion for painting, but whose ability dangerously challenged her father's. To protect her daughter from her husband's vagarities, her mother had poisoned the girl's mind, turning her against her father. There was no way Maestro could give his benediction to her precocious talent, along with any abounding ambitions, anyway. There was no way Maestro could allow her precocious talent to challenge his.

Constanzi rushed from remaining painting to painting, venomously slashing and defacing them, hardly pausing for breath inbetween. His limbs soon ached from the effort, and he sat down, panting, to take in all he'd done, trying, at the same time, to picture Maestro's face as when he took in the carnage. Constanzi imagined tears trickling down his brother's face, the man's mind swallowed up in unimaginable pain. The exhibition, of course, would have to canceled, a bitter blow, given that his brother's career was poised to elevated to the highest plateau. Perhaps he wouldn't be able to recover from such a severe blow. He'd put his life and soul into this exhibition, as if it were his epitaph, and it took the man forever to complete a painting.

Compared to Maestro's works, Constanzi's were deemed by most art affectionados as crude at best. But he, at least, didn't paint religious scenes for rich and influential patrons like his obsequious brother did. Unlike his brother, Constanzi refused to bow to the establishment. He had principles. What he didn't possess was his brother's connections and, admittedly, to some small extent, his brother's deft mastery of the brush.

Despite this, Constanzi had managed to persuade a couple gallery owners to exhibit his works, mostly on his brother's name and reputation. He always invited his brother, but Maestro never came. That was to be expected. Maestro constantly cast a vast shadow over all of Constanzi's creative endeavors. It was that issue which Constanzi was addressing now.

But his brother had done worse than best him as a painter. He'd long ago taken from Constanzi the one light in his otherwise miserable life, the enchanting Martinella, Constanzi's first and only love. They'd met at the Marquis de Fonaine's annual masked ball to which he'd been invited, his acclaimed brother being unavailable.

She was a ravishing beauty, well formed, a delightful conversationalist. He could still vividly recall what she'd worn that night: a rose-tinted silk dress with balloon sleeves and expanded ruffs at the wrists. A white circular lace collar showed off her long neck. Her hair was arranged in golden ringlets. The instant their eyes met, he fell in love with her, and it seemed to him that she reciprocated *in toto*. Her wealthy merchant family, of course, disapproved of the relationship, but this had only made the bond between them stronger.

Then he made the mistake of introducing her to his brother. Maestro, married with five children and another on the way, flagrantly pursued her in front of everyone, including his pregnant wife. Vicious gossip began circulating, but a public figure like his brother could get away with such things. Finally, even Maestro's most vociferous detractors gave up stating their disapproval, and the ensuing scandal ended up simply adding to his legend.

Maestro stole Martinella's heart by claiming she was the elusive woman who'd always escaped him, but whom, found at last, he would immortalize in his next painting. She paid constant visits to pose in his studio, providing ample opportunities for Maestro to corrupt her. Martinella soon began shunning Constanzi, and on the odd occasion when she chose to speak to him, the conversation centered exclusively around his brother. That was proof enough for Constanzi that a sordid affair was taking place between the two. Unfortunately, he couldn't compete with Maestro. Maestro always took whatever he wanted, as he'd done since they were children. Constanzi's loss of Martinella was another twist of his brother's knife, the incisive one that sent him on tonight's downward spiral of drunkenness, to numb the hurt as well as the rage that had been growing inside him ever since.

Maestro sold his first painting, "Saint Peter at the Gates of Heaven," at the age of sixteen to a friend of his uncle who was well connected in the church, and Maestro was instantly lauded as a prodigy who would influence the art world for generations to come. At eighteen, he commanded a seat at the first table at the best banquets in Rome. Influential merchants, royalty along with their courtesans, and the highest-ranking members of the Church flocked to see and be seen with him. He even dined privately with the Pope on occasion.

Constanzi consumed the remainder of his wine in one long gulp and still craved more. Surely his brother, the connoisseur, had some tucked away. He weaved his way to some cabinets, drawn as much by intrigue as his thirst for more alcohol. They were locked, but easy to break into, revealing dusty bottles of the finest vintages lined up in rows like soldiers ready for battle. Constanzi grabbed the first, smashed its neck against the cabinet, located an empty paint jar and poured the wine into it.

While doing that, he noted a bundle of letters tucked in a corner. Recognizing the handwriting on the outside envelope—it was unmistakably Martinella's—he tore the bundle apart and began reading it. It was addressed, "Mi amore, Maestro."

"Your tender kiss…with passion's heat…our bodies pressed together…you, dear Maestro, own my heart, my soul, my body…I am yours to take..." Constanzi couldn't read further. Each sentence was a stab to the heart. She'd told Constanzi she was a virgin, saving herself for her wedding night, though obviously for Maestro, thought Constanzi bitterly, this sweet notion didn't apply.

He downed the entire next bottle of wine in one gulp, then retched. The letters had opened old wounds and, with them, new, even stronger anguish he hadn't realized existed within him. The letters were an insult to the memory of his love for her. Then Constanzi noticed a letter in the bundle in another's handwriting.

Why was he surprised? Martinella wasn't the only mistress Maestro kept.

This letter was written by the Pope's niece, Catherine Santa Maria di Sala, another "model" lured to his brother's couch. The thought that Maestro had callously taken from him his Martinella while at the same time pursuing another, pushed him into an even greater rage of vandalism. Exhausted, he daubed crude black vitriol on another of his brother's paintings, a scene of the last supper, another fine example of linear perspective, adding in ugly graffiti, "*bastardo truffante.*"

Exhausted, he stood back to admire his work, allowing his fevered mind to turn to lighter thoughts from earlier in the evening. He had been drinking with some of his debauched artist friends, making up lurid tales about any woman hapless enough to enter the tavern, shouting the tales aloud, at the top of their voices. One of his friends had had his face slapped after having concocted and broadcast a particularly indecent tale a little too effectively. The gesture, far from stopping the antics, roused the mavericks to increasingly banal *repartee.*

Leaving the tavern, Constanzi eventually found himself meandering his way home, by chance passing his brother's studio. He had never been invited in, and, being thoroughly inebriated, the temptation of breaking and entering proved too great.

Now, head swirling, too drunk and fatigued after his rampage in the studio to find his way home, he decided to rest a moment on Maestro's infamous couch, the very couch where, no doubt, Martinella had lain, opening her legs to his brother. A little rest, he reasoned, would do no harm. It was still dark and there was plenty of time before

Maestro or his apprentices would arrive. Before he rested, he shed his outer garments that were splattered wet with noxious smelling paint, to put on Maestro's favorite, luxuriant, silver fox fur coat, a gift from a nobleman whose wife Maestro had undoubtedly painted and tainted. The beautiful foxes had been slain, skinned and stitched together in Maestro's honor. For good measure, Constanzi placed one of Maestro's trademark hats on his head, and, thus warmly attired, fell onto the couch and was quickly snoring away, his "brief rest" transforming into unanticipated deep slumber.

In the meantime, Peruzzi, Maestro's lawyer and the manager of Maestro's business affairs, a man of sixty years with a constant stoop and metal frame eyeglasses perched on a beak-like nose, woke up early and was in the middle of a light breakfast of poached quails' eggs, fresh brioche and Parma ham when a loud rap on the door broke his tranquility. A young apprentice with whom he was only vaguely acquainted burst into the room, out of breath, his strained face drenched in tears. The bearer of cataclysmic news, he talked hurriedly of a brawl in a tavern the night before, a stabbing and a fatality. He hadn't actually witnessed the fight, but this morning, on his way to Maestro's studio, he overheard two people in the market talking of a fight between a nobleman and the "world's greatest living painter" which ended with the painter fatally wounded, his dying moments being spent on the cold stone steps of a monastery close to the tavern. While trying to gather more information, he'd lost the two men in the growing crowd. The monastery bells had begun tolling a death knell even as he rushed to tell Peruzzi.

Troubled, Peruzzi commanded the boy to sit, catch his breath and recount once again, slower and in careful detail everything he'd seen and heard. After composing himself, the young apprentice recounted that the night before, the young apprentice had observed an embittered nobleman, the Duke de Modina, at the tavern, sunk in his chair, picking at his food and supping his drink, eye-balling Maestro with malicious intent, while Maestro recited before those at his table a litany of insults aimed at the Duke, each of which was met with ripples of laughter from Maestro's drunken entourage. It was plain the nobleman had come to the tavern to settle a score. Maestro would have been better off trying to appease rather than bait him. Young though he was, the apprentice was savvy enough to realize Maestro was in grave danger, but when he'd tried to reason with his master, he'd been chastised for interfering and told to go home. As Maestro's apprentice prepared to leave, the nobleman was joined by several rough-looking combatants.

At the heart of the dispute between Maestro and the nobleman was a woman, one who Maestro had taken on as a student for a huge payment, which the Duke now proved reluctant to pay. The Duke's exquisite sixteen-year-old daughter, Serafina, a beautiful waif with an elfin face, long flowing hair and a sweet childlike voice, in many ways resembled Maestro's youngest and favorite daughter, Faustina.

Serefina's initial drawings of a still-life set up by Maestro had been promising. The young girl clearly had a sharp eye and a propensity for depicting form. Maestro encouraged her to work on a larger version, thinking it would yield similar results. The "larger" work she later presented him looked to Maestro as if she'd been possessed by the spirit of the devil, or perhaps, somebody from the future. When Maestro questioned her about the work, it became clear that her strange notions of art challenged all the classical rules he cherished. Serefina ended with the blatant statement that truly great artists didn't simply imitate nature, they saw within it and judiciously recorded the geometric patterns upon which nature was based.

Maestro, taken aback, tried to curb her exuberance, at one point declaring, "artists are given their talent by God to glorify his divinity," and that she seemed more "infused with the devil's spirit." Being a strong believer in her convictions in art as well as in religion, following his cruel jibe, she began crying profusely. He feigned attempts to console her, saying he'd spoken out of turn, but had the perfect consolation for both of them in the form of a glass of wine from a bottle which he claimed had been presented to him as a gift by no less than the King of France.

Head lowered, she at first declined, saying, "Father doesn't allow me to drink alcohol."

Maestro, however, was unmoved. Parroting back her words, he laughed and added, "But father's not here, is he? Besides, who but a fool would decline a glass of wine of such exalted provenance, one that would doubtlessly prove equally resplendent in flavor. The King of France doesn't bestow his finest wine on lesser mortals, he explained, looking at her with a beaming smile.

The young girl, overwhelmed by the famous painter's *largesse*, considered why her scrupulous father would eulogize the sanctity of the cheap communion wine but deny her even the slightest taste of a truly fine secular one. Also, Serefina's sweetheart and intended, Jean Louis, had spent much time talking of the vineyards on his father's estate that he would someday inherit, and boasted of having a sophisticated palate. Suddenly, wanting all that had been forbidden her, she accepted a half glass, though being nervous in Maestro's company, she ended up accepting more and more until she started to feel light-headed and giddy.

It was at this point, when Maestro sensed the girl's resistance weakening, that he chose her to be the next in his long line of conquests, and cleverly applied another of his ruses, piling log after log in the fireplace to augment the heat in the studio, suggesting as he did that should she feel warm, she might loosen the first fasteners of her dress. Serefina was at first shocked at the suggestion and blushed terribly, not knowing what to say or do. Still, it was true that in her heavy clothes she felt hot, awkward and restricted. After another glass of wine, which by now tasted better than she'd ever imagined, she hesitantly agreed. It wasn't long before he was persuading her to unfasten another layer, then another, until the bodice of her lavishly embroidered dress was fully open. Shamelessly naming one after another a long line of female dignitaries who'd passed through his studio, he furtively moved closer to her, until, at last, he reached inside her dress and began caressing her petite breasts. Again she initially resisted but quickly succumbed to combined effects of the wine, heat and Maestro's deft touch which were collectively inducing tingles of pleasure throughout her body that she had never experienced before.

Soon both were *sans guarde robe,* her "teacher" above her, her virtue lost in a single sweeping moment of passion. The Duke, in the meantime, arrived early to collect his daughter, and wasn't at all prepared for what his eyes took in upon walking into the room without knocking.

In a state of shock, the Duke averted his eyes and mumbled something about daughter's progress. This was followed by an awkward pause during which time Maestro struggled to stand and tidy himself up while the young girl furtively redid up her dress. Maestro, in answer, began flippantly pouring scorn on his pupil's artistic talent, saying even he "couldn't turn tatty rags into silk garments." An argument ensued, in which the Duke, affronted by Maestro's taunt and *indiscretion*, declared haughtily that the artistic floodgates would none-too-soon open for a new set of more analytic and less indulgent painters. Painters like Alfonso Pandeli, under whose tutelage his eldest daughter had excelled. Maestro would, he concluded, soon find himself forgotten in Pandeli's wake. Maestro, hating having his work compared to anyone, especially a mediocre still life painter like Pandeli, made the point by giving the Duke an emphatic one finger salute.

In his rage, the Duke's eyes latched onto Maestro's painting of the martyrdom of St. Sebastian. Rising to his full height, the Duke expressed shock at the decidedly secular manner with which Maestro had depicted St. Sebastian. "You seem to have a talent, *signore*, for making the virtuous appear perverted and debauched. Rather than venerating God, your work desecrates all that is sacrosanct. In essence, it is little more than a wanton display of overindulgence!"

To hear words like these coming from a short plump philistine like the Duke made Maestro seethe. The Duke, for his part, was equally enraged by his daughter's giggles and uncharacteristic air of frivolity.

A few months later, Serafina, for undisclosed reasons, was sent to a distant nunnery. Word spread that she had brought shame on the family, and that a single visit to Maestro's studio had impregnated her with more than just wisdom of art. To this, most people chortled and simply shrugged their shoulders, pointing out that Maestro had more illegitimate children than he had completed paintings.

Galvanized by events and intent on revenge, the Duke ordered one of his men to shadow Maestro to determine where he spent his evenings. Once briefed on Maestro's after-hours movements, plans were put in place for the Duke's long overdue revenge.

It took Peruzzi some time to fully take in the news of his client's demise and the enormity of its consequences. Stuffing some papers into a satchel, he dragged the apprentice out the door and on to Maestro's studio. If what he'd heard were true, there were formalities he would need to immediately address in order to make certain the Maestro's legacy was secure. On their arrival at his studio they found the door ajar.

Peruzzi's suspicions aroused, he pushed the apprentice aside, instinctively drew his dagger, and slipped silently in. Peruzzi scanned the area, still dark in the early dawn. As he entered, he heard the crunch of broken glass beneath his feet. Something was clearly amiss.

Easing his way carefully to Maestro's preeminent painting of the Nativity, he stood in shock, mouth open, eyes locked onto the Madonna's shredded face and the deluge of colors randomly smeared over the painting. Maestro's centerpiece for the upcoming exhibition was utterly profaned. Peruzzi continued to scan the studio while resisting what his eyes were taking in. All the exhibition paintings had been equally savaged. He winced at the sight of the master's partially burnt sketches and drawings strewn across the floor, priceless pigments overturned onto them, the whole studio floor streaked with colored footprints. Paint brushes, handmade at enormous expense from the finest sable hair, were snapped in half and scattered about. The smell of stale wine hung in the air.

It was then Peruzzi caught sight of a figure, attired in the fur coat and hat Maestro adored, lying motionless on the couch. The figure, by all appearances the dead Maestro, snorted and moved.

Peruzzi and the young apprentice jumped back as if they'd witnessed the dead come alive. The apprentice stood frozen, leaving Peruzzi to make sense of the macabre scene. Holding his dagger at the ready, Peruzzi inched forward and kicked the specter.

It groaned and immediately began muttering profanities. The man's breath slapped Peruzzi in the face, like a towel soaked in cat urine. It also stank of alcohol.

Peruzzi flinched, retreated, then flung open the shutters in a bid to stir the man. When daybreak's light hit the man's face, Peruzzi gasped in further disbelief. It was Maestro's brother, the freeloading reprobate who was constantly demanding that Maestro sponsor an exhibition of his own works or loan him money to support his drinking habit. It had been Peruzzi's distasteful responsibility to politely but firmly refuse him, as his employer's credibility would have been undermined if the great Maestro were associated in any way with the work of such a crude amateur.

"What do you want?" moaned Constanzi, wincing and staring at Peruzzi through swollen eyes.

"Maestro's dead," said Peruzzi, tears suddenly welling. "I came to the studio and, seeing you on dressed like him, lying on his couch, thought for a fleeting moment that you were he, that maybe this young man had not seen what he related. Instead, I find you here amidst this carnage. The paintings! My God, the paintings! What have you done?"

Peruzzi's voice grated painfully on Constanzi's ears, but the news of his brother's death reinvigorated him. The weight of his brother fame incessantly oppressing him lifted.

Peruzzi opened his satchel, took out a sheaf of papers, and shook them in Constanzi's face. The distraught lawyer tried again and again, but could find no words. Constanzi, awakened from his stupor, his interest ignited by the papers, stood shakily and grabbed them from Peruzzi's hands. They were written in Maestro's hand. They were his last will and testament.

"There are…legal ramifications…to consider," said Peruzzi, pulling himself together at last, trying to act the part of a custodian of the law and Maestro's earthly representative.

Constanzi, hardly in the mood for observing protocol, did a quick read.

Peruzzi's jaw quavered and he shook his head ruefully. "Your brother was killed in the early hours, and you do not display even the slightest of sadness or least modicum of respect," Peruzzi said, *au fait* with the gist of the testament. Looking Constanzi square in the face, he lamented, "As you can see, your brother entrusted all his major works to you. A misplaced trust, I would say, given that you have destroyed them all." Why all these works had been left to Maestro's brother, Constanzi, Peruzzi could only guess. The destruction Constanzi had caused, however, was not entirely without positive effect, Peruzzi mused. Constanzi would doubtless have claimed that at least some of the works in the studio were by his hand. Not now! Peruzzi tore the papers from Constanzi's hands and turned on his heels to leave.

Maestro's ignominious brother would undoubtedly end up in a lunatic asylum, given the style and extent of his destruction of the national icon's work. Peruzzi, on the other hand, had long ago, in return for his services, been bequeathed some of Maestro's "earlier, less refined paintings." Admittedly not Maestro's finest, they would nonetheless soar in value providing Peruzzi with a comfortable retirement. Gathering up Maestro's bedraggled apprentice, Peruzzi took a last look over his shoulder at a destitute Constanzi, hands clasped over his heart as if wounded yet again by his cursed brother.

Flight of Destiny

Visitors

"Are you finished, yet, Mother?" asked the young boy in a desperate voice. The boy posing the question, Marcus Pring, backed away from the sliver of open door, knowing his plea wouldn't likely register with his mother immediately, preoccupied as she was in the next room with the naked man heaving up and down above her and panting urgently.

The plucky six-year-old sighed, and returned his attention to the toys spread out on the living room floor while his mother finished with this night's "activity." Marcus was used to unknown visitors paying his mother such visits throughout the day and evening, and sometimes, like today, late at night.

He'd seen the present visitor before, but the man had never said a word to him, merely nodding solicitously whenever he noticed

Marcus, which was rarely. Given the frequency of his visits, Marcus had wondered if he might possibly be his father. Marcus, in fact, had no inkling of who this man or even who his father was. His world revolved around his mother. When questioned by other children about his father, he would evade the subject, or, when pressed, make up some ill-conceived story, most often that his father was a war hero, though he was hard pressed when questioned about specifics, living as he did in a country that had been at peace for the last twenty years, a fact which the other children of his age didn't hesitate to remind him.

The groaning sounds in his mother's room got louder, then abruptly stopped. A moment later, Marcus heard the bed-springs squeak loudly, indicating that the visitor had climbed off the bed. Marcus huddled as far away from his mother's bedroom door as possible and made a wish.

His wish, modest as it was, came immediately true: His mother appeared in the doorway. She stood, one arm extended above her, the side of her body pressed against the doorway. She was wearing a long, see-through dressing gown, its floral print barely perceptible from constant heavy wear. Noting her son, she walked to him, grasped his hand, and directed him to the nearest chair. After taking a moment to compose her disheveled hair, she looked down at him and smiled warmly.

A visible combination of awkwardness and relief rushed though Marcus, and he blushed.

"There, there, darling," she started to say to the boy, her voice as sweet in his ears as her face was beautiful in his adoring eyes.

The man appeared in the doorway, dressed in a grey pin-stripe suit, trilby hat in hand. An ornate gold tiepin held down his salmon pink tie. Draped out of one of his pockets was a polka dot gentleman's silk handkerchief. His attire alone singled him out from the other visitors, and, for that matter, anyone living in the neighborhood. The man casually drew out his leather wallet, pulled out some crisp-looking notes, and, with a vague smile, handed them to the little boy's mother, whose eyes sparkled as if she'd been gifted with far more than anticipated. No words were needed; the exchange that occurred was a mere formality. The man made his own way to the door, not turning or even saying good-bye. As the front door closed behind him, order was restored once again to Marcus' life.

Marcus' mother stretched out her hand and waved the bills. "I can buy you some new toys now," she said cheerfully. "You'll like that."

Marcus had long ago intuited that the visits, if nothing else, meant that he and his mother, at least for a while, wouldn't have to go without necessities. In fact, he'd had plenty of opportunities to see the practical benefits of the "gifts" these men bestowed upon his mother. No visitors meant he and his mother would scrimp on food. Seven visitors a week meant his mother could provide the daily basics and a special treat for Sunday lunch. More, and this man in particular, meant luxuries like tasty jams, a joint of lamb, even a new toy or two. On particularly good weeks, the two of them had even been known to buy things that their neighbors couldn't afford like a radio and phonograph. There were even occasional trips to the seaside, short holidays, just the two of them. Last week, after counting the money she had stashed in the old coffee tin for the umpteenth time, his mother mentioned that one day soon they would move to a bigger apartment in a better part of the town.

While his mother occupied herself in the bathroom, the little boy pulled a chair beneath the window to get a better view of this night's departing visitor. A man in a grey uniform doffed his hat and opened the door of a fine car for the man. Marcus' mother reappeared while Marcus was still taking in the scene.

"Come away from the window, darling," she said tetchily. "It's rude to watch people like that."

Marcus shrugged but didn't move, continuing to stare out the window. The man holding the car door open closed it after the evening's visitor got inside, then walked stiffly around to the driver's door.

"How about a game?" his mother asked enthusiastically. "Or, perhaps you're hungry?"

The ploy worked. The little boy climbed down and settled for a game. While they played, he seized every opportunity to center her attention on him, as if trying to absorb all her energy.

Sometimes their games would be interrupted by the doorbell. When that happened, his mother would carefully compose herself, open the front door a crack and exchange a few hushed words with the visitor before offering a quick apology to her son. That was the signal, Marcus knew, that he would be left to play the remainder of the game by himself. The visitor and his mother would quickly disappear into her bedroom, the man following close behind her. It was always the same routine.

Only when the men left could Marcus repossess his mother. During the course of these "visits" Marcus felt jealous, even bitter towards the men-visitors, though the feelings were ones he couldn't yet identify, being so young. His conflicting feelings, nonetheless, became embedded within his youthful psyche.

Mother had firmly instructed him not to talk to anyone about their "visitors." Mother had firmly instructed him not to talk to anyone about the "visitors." His curiosity remained, but Mother was Mother, and he obeyed her without question.

One rainy afternoon, Marcus was staring out the window, trying to see between distorting rivulets running down the glass. He liked to watch the rain splatter on the pavement, and the people, umbrellas up, dodging one another.

Mother was occupied once again with the smartly dressed man in the grey pin stripe suit. They were busy in her room making the sounds to which the little boy had become so well accustomed, when the doorbell rang.

Marcus didn't know what to do. His mother had instructed him never to answer, especially when she was busy in her bedroom with someone. But the doorbell kept ringing and ringing, followed by the sound of a fist banging urgently on the door and finally the calling out of his mother's name. It was a voice he wasn't familiar with. Mother came out of the bedroom, flustered, rearranging her nightgown, and casually cracked open the front door.

A man was standing there, soaking wet, with an anxious look on his face.

"My God, Hugo, what are you doing here?" she asked in utter surprise, inspecting the bedraggled man as if to make sure he was real flesh and blood.

"Got lucky and escaped. I've little time. The police are on my tail," the man panted coarsely, a mix of rain and sweat running down his face.

"Then you'd better come in," she said, looking quickly up and down the street after he'd entered. The man with whom she'd been previously occupied in the bedroom suddenly appeared, not yet fully dressed.

The little boy was stunned. Except for their clothes, the two men looked exactly alike. He'd seen twins. There were a pair at his school, but none as perfect a reflection of each other. Then things began happening. In the distance, police sirens sounded, slowly becoming louder and louder.

The newer visitor eyed his look-alike with suspicion bordering on disdain, but such was the peril of his situation he said nothing, being entirely at everyone's mercy.

The man in the grey pin stripes spoke first: "Quick! Dry off and get into my clothes. I keep a spare suit here. My driver is waiting in the car. Tell him to take you to the nearest coastal town. From there you can slip out of the country under an assumed name. Stay away at least until the furor dies down." The speaker reached into a pocket and pulled out a wallet stuffed with money. "Take this," he added, offering the man standing in front of him more than half. All the while the second visitor was changing his clothes. After expressing hasty gratitude to his benefactor and a quick goodbye to Marcus' mother, he headed for the front door. There, he paused to look over his shoulder at little Marcus, and, for an instant, it seemed as if his eyes wanted to devour the child.

Marcus, feeling ill at east, lowered his eyes and crossed his legs nervously, perplexed. The boy's gesture proved just enough to break the newer visitor's gaze, and he exited. Marcus looked up at his mother. She was not her usual self. She looked dazed, almost tearful.

Marcus pressed his face against the window and tried to follow the man's retreat, while his double, standing behind his mother, whispered soothing words to her.

It wasn't long before a new set of visitors arrived: the police. A large portly man in a nondescript tan trench coat broke the temporary tranquility by banging on the door. When Marcus' mother cracked the door, he introduced himself. "Inspector Crankie, at your service. This is Sergeant Spade." The inspector flashed a badge while pointing to the gruff, half-shaven reptile of a man standing next to him.

The Inspector looked with annoyance at his silent partner staring open mouthed at the barely clad woman on the other side of the door clearly disinclined to let them into her abode. Crankie elbowed Spade, who closed his mouth and stopped staring. "We're searching for Hugo Earnshaw, an escaped convict," croaked Spade.

Mother shuddered, then frowned.

"Don't mind the sergeant, madam," replied the Inspector, elbowing Spade again. "We've been advised of a possible sighting in this immediate vicinity within the last twenty minutes or so."

Mother bowed her head, volunteering nothing.

Crankie began eyeballing what little of the room he could see through the crack. "We need to check the premises and ask you a few questions," he said, pointing with his chin towards the interior.

"Surely that won't be necessary," said a baritone voice from behind the woman.

Crankie cocked his head, noting the man who had just stepped behind the scantily clad woman. "And who might you be, sir?" he demanded, leaning forward, trying unsuccessfully to push his way in.

"Lord Crawford Earnshaw, if you must know," said the man in a composed Etonian accent, adding, "You won't find my brother here if that's for whom you're looking. Even he's not so foolish to return to a place known to the police."

Crankie's demeanor abruptly changed. "And what might you be doing here, your Lordship, Sir?" he asked, bowing slightly.

"My brother is, how shall I put it, the black sheep of the family, who strayed and admittedly did some very shameful things for which he is now serving time in prison. I am visiting Eleanor, his sweetheart," he said, turning towards Marcus' mother, "to make certain she is adequately looked after in his absence."

Crankie nodded in silence, assimilating the information, and, far from convinced, turned his attention back to the escapee's paramour. Her attention, in turn, was fixed on the man standing next to her for advice as to what to say and do. At Lord Earnshaw's signal, she dispatched Marcus to her bedroom with a wave of her hand, opened the front door, and admitted Inspector Crankie and his assistant. She was subsequently questioned at length. The Inspector seemed to derive pleasure from her uneasiness.

"And what do you do for a...living, madam?" he demanded, eyeing her form beneath her floral see-through dressing gown, thinking to himself, *strange attire for a visit from a Lord of the realm.*

"This and that," replied the woman obtusely. "Whatever is necessary for me and my child to survive."

The Inspector walked about the living room, noting the radio and phonograph. This woman, the wife of a felon, was, he reckoned, living beyond her likely means. Crankie was a most perceptive police officer. Nothing, it was said, slipped by him.

Spade, in the meantime, continued searching and sniffing about the apartment. When finished, he nodded in the negative to his superior.

In truth, neither was getting anywhere, and Crankie was starting to feel frustrated. The woman hadn't offered anything he didn't already know, and her answers were mostly prosaic. The escapee was still at large. His time was being wasted. Then it occurred to him that, perhaps this was all a ploy to give the fugitive more time to get away. Deciding that the situation required a new strategy, he called for the little boy, who was, he'd noted, peeking around bedroom door, watching and listening to all that was transpiring. This, by Crankie's reckoning, was a likely sign of complicity.

Marcus came and stood meekly beside his mother while Crankie bore into the boy with his eyes. The boy shifted his weight nervously from one leg to the other and, throughout the subsequent interview, kept looking up at his mother for cues as to what to say. Each time, both Mother and Lord Earnshaw would look edgily back at him and then each other. A smile began unfolding on Crankie's lips. *Yes*, he thought, *the boy is the key*.

"You look like a smart young chappy," said Crankie with mock enthusiasm. "I suppose you like sweeties," he continued, increasing his smile. "Me, I like sweeties. Always have. I like to carry some with me. Would you like one?" he asked, pulling a toffee from his coat pocket.

The little boy nodded affirmatively, but hesitated to take it.

Crankie placed it in the little boy's hand. Slowly and methodically Marcus unwrapped the gift.

When he raised it into his mouth, his mother interrupted, "Marcus, darling, you know to never accept sweets from a stranger." The candy stopped dead just before before entering her son's mouth and was dejectedly offered back to the Inspector.

"Please keep it. I have more," interjected Crankie, rustling them about in his pocket. "I'm a police inspector, son, and I need your help. Me and Sergeant Spade here."

Spade nodded in accord.

"We need to know," the Inspector continued, "if anyone, besides your mother's friend here has been in this apartment in the last couple hours. An unfamiliar man, perhaps?"

The boy nestled closer to his mother, who placed a hand

delicately on his shoulder.

"Answer me, boy," demanded Crankie, his eyes suddenly blazing like embers.

The little boy cowered.

"Perhaps another sweetie?" ventured Cranky in a softer voice.

The little boy shook his head negatively. He hadn't eaten the first one. What good were all the toffees in the world if he couldn't eat them? Crankie noted that the sweeties weren't working.

"Perhaps if I was to offer you a more substantial reward," said Crankie, his eyebrows rising, his face looking more conspiratorial. The Inspector reached into an inside coat pocket, drew out his wallet, and waved some crisp notes in front of little boy's eyes. "Imagine all the sweeties you could buy with these, laddie," he said in his most tempting voice, adding cheerfully, "You could even buy your mother something…"

Lord Earnshaw coughed. "Really, Crankie. Bribing a child? This is highly irregular."

"Let the boy speak," ordered Crankie, concluding from Lord Earnshaw's interruption that some progress was at last being made. He had only to break the boy's last bit of resistance.

Turning back to Marcus, Inspector Crankie said, "Now, be a good boy, and just answer this one question: Has another man been in this apartment recently? If you do, this money is yours, and you will have helped the police and that's a very fine thing to do."

Recalling his mother's contented face when "visitors" gave her money, Marcus imagined the thankful smile he would receive when he turned the Inspector's money over to her. Clearly, money made her happy. Marcus finally spoke. "Yes. There was another man here recently."

Crankie lapped up every word with delight. "Yes, yes, yes! You're being a very good boy," he said, handing the boy the notes and signaling to the sergeant to search the apartment a second time. Offering the bank notes to his mother, Marcus was surprised to see Mother and Lord Earnshaw's faces looking pained rather than pleased. Marcus shrunk deeper into his mother's embrace. Crankie, in the meantime, pressed forward. "Now, see? I've given you all that money, just as I promised. It's only right that you should tell me more." The Inspector loomed larger, and raised his voice: "Where is the man now? Is he hiding in the vicinity or did he leave? Perhaps you spotted in which direction?"

The little boy exchanged a fearful glance with his paling mother. Seeing her reaction, the Inspector ushered Marcus to the window.

"He went that way," Marcus replied in a barely audible voice, pointing with his finger to the end of the street. "In a big car."

An enormous smile stretched across Crankie's face. "Now we're getting somewhere," he proclaimed, glancing sternly at the pair of adults he planned to re-interrogate. Turning to Lord Earnshaw, he said, "I don't suppose the car belonged to you, Lord Earnshaw?" Technically, Crankie didn't need the toff's answer. By now he had worked out a likely scenario; it would help, however, if he could get someone to confirm it.

Lord Earnshaw straightened to his full height and stared down at the Inspector with indignation as if an intolerable breech of conduct had just occurred. "See here, Inspector. I went along with your bribing the boy, but you're going too far with this new accusation," he said in his most demeaning upper class drawl.

Crankie snorted and retorted sarcastically, "You needn't answer, your Lordship. It is, after all, quite unlikely that anyone living in *this* neighborhood would even *have* a car. I'll wager your younger brother stopped by and is using your car this very minute to try to get away. It all makes perfect sense to me."

Lord Earnshaw seemed thoroughly disinterested. "It may *look* that way to you, Inspector, but all you've presented thus far is conjecture..."

"I am sure having a twin for a brother, you two would have strong ties of loyalty. Isn't that right, Lord Earnshaw?" the Inspector interrupted.

Lord Earnshaw ran his hand through his hair, sighed, and answered obliquely. "What exactly are you getting at, Inspector?"

"It's only logical that you would feel obliged to help your *twin* brother. No one would suspect that someone like you, given your position and reputation, would break the law by aiding and abetting a fleeing criminal." Receiving no reply from the aristocrat, Crankie continued: "I seem to recall that your brother's arrest caused quite a stir. 'Lord of the Realm's Brother sent to Prison,' wasn't that the newspaper headline? That must have proven difficult for you. You wouldn't want to tarnish your reputation further now by *interfering* with the law, would you, your Lordship?" The Inspectors face twisted into one of menace.

"Exactly what do you want from me, Inspector?" demanded Lord Earnshaw.

"What I want from you, your Lordship, Sir, is confirmation of what this nice little boy just told us. Details about the vehicle and its final destination would be especially helpful."

Both Crankie and Spade stared intently at Lord Earnshaw, who recoiled, but said nothing.

"Well, your Lordship, I think we had better be on our way," said the Inspector. "We need to send out the word and 'gather in the net' so to speak. Given the circumstances, I'm afraid I must insist you come with us."

"Really, Inspector. I am very busy man," Lord Earnshaw snapped.

"Obviously," said Crankie winking sarcastically at the woman. "Now if you will please come with me. Our time, too, is precious."

Lord Earnshaw removed his wallet. "Since you've been so kind as to give the child some financial inducements, I would like to gift you these," he said placing a sizable sheaf of notes in the Inspector's hand. "You, the sergeant and your wives could have a nice long holiday on this. And, if this isn't enough, I have more in my briefcase," Lord Earnshaw added, looking about the room for it.

Crankie shook his head and tutted. "For one thing, your *Lordship, Sir*, I'm not married. Police work and marriage don't mix well. And second, it would be breaking the law for either of us to accept your 'gift'. As I am sure you well know, bribing a police officer is a serious offense, and I think enough offenses have already been committed under this roof for one day."

The sergeant stared wide-eyed and open-mouthed at the quantity of notes the Inspector handed back to Lord Earnshaw.

"Come now," Lord Earnshaw said, adding another similar-sized sheaf of bills from his briefcase to those in his hand. "Inspector, Sergeant, I'm not in any way offering a bribe. Think of this as a private charitable donation to your paltry police pensions. Everyone knows police pensions are barely enough to live on these days, and I would imagine both of yours are not too far off."

Crankie's waspish face indicated Lord Earnshaw had said the wrong thing. "Retirement" was a word Crankie detested. He refused to envision himself retired. Police work was his life. "Spade," ordered

Crankie, "Arrest Lord Earnshaw for interfering with the course of an investigation and if he resists, add to that resisting arrest and attempted bribery."

Marcus' mother looked forlornly at her benefactor, who said to her only, "I'll be back soon. They can't hold me. Inspector Crankie knows this. He's bluffing. Everything will work out in the end."

After the crowd had left the house, an awkward silence descended. Marcus was at last alone with his mother, but something felt terribly amiss. The little boy had offered the money the Inspector had given him to his mother, but she hadn't appear pleased. There were questions he desperately needed answered.

"Mother, who is the man the police are trying to catch?"

Mother blanched, though she continued to seethe with a mixture of grief and anger. "They're after your father, boy," she said at last, dabbing at a tear.

"What will happen to him when they find him?" Marcus inquired innocently.

"This time, I fear he will hang," said Mother, placing her hands on either side of her face and sobbing hysterically.

Marcus watched his mother, not knowing what to do, then began to cry in sympathy with her, letting the money the Inspector had given him fall to the floor and scatter about like litter. Money apparently wasn't as important as he'd been lead to believe.

His mother kept crying.

If Mother was not going to comfort him, he reasoned, he might as well look out the window and satisfy his ever-present curiosity. He walked over to the window, pressed his face once again against the glass, and caught sight of the Inspector walking down the street followed two steps behind by the sergeant and Lord Earnshaw. What he saw next both thrilled and mortified him: In one deft movement, the sergeant lunged at the Inspector and shoved him in front of a fast moving truck.

Too late, the truck screeched to a standstill and the driver got out, racked with guilt, pleading his innocence at having run over a policeman who he insisted had "jumped out in front of him as if from nowhere."

Marcus continued watching.

Sergeant Spade was soon directing an ambulance crew to take away the mangled body, while the truck driver, continuing to proclaim his innocence, was loaded into a police car and taken away. After a few minutes, the sergeant was rejoined by Lord Earnshaw, who had made himself scarce while the remaining officers finished their work. Towards the end, a discussion took place, during which Lord Earnshaw passed each officer including Spade a fat wad of money. Spade took his, but looked unimpressed, at which Lord Earnshaw passed Sergeant Spade another wad. The two men shook hands and walked off in opposite directions.

It took some time for Marcus' young mind to absorb what he'd observed. In the course of a few hours, he'd seen money given for service, money offered as a bribe, money scorned, and money given in exchange for a man's life. With money, Marcus reappraised, people could do *anything*. He climbed down from the window, and carefully picked up the money the Inspector had given him, arranging it into a neat stack and slipped it into his pocket. Yes, with money one could do anything.

Flight of Destiny

The Pact

Jarret Lamb, an unassuming, middle-aged businessman sporting a well-groomed beard with the first flecks of gray on his fleshy face, hated hospitals. First, there was the stench: that unavoidable whiff upon entering of alcohol, ether, and iodine. Then there were the endless waits for the doctors to say anything pertinent, and the interminable anxiety as to what the white-coated demi-gods were secretly plotting to do next. Another thing he strongly disliked was the artificial smiles of the bone-weary yet perfectly attired nurses who walked the long dreary corridors in silent white shoes and blindingly white aprons, their hair tied back in tight buns. And if all of this wasn't enough, the walls displayed detestable pictures of seedy holiday destinations that seemed to Jarret to be screaming, "*If* you get out of this hospital, you could visit such a place," though, in fact, no one who hadn't just escaped death would ever want to go there. They were like phony rays of sunshine in an environment where death stalked the halls waiting for any possible opportunity to wreak its havoc.

Unfortunately, he was, this very moment, caught in the clutches of just such a nightmare. His wife, Jessie, due to give birth to their first child, had needed to be rushed to the nearest hospital instead of giving birth at home in the tranquil manner they had envisaged. Due to "complications," both she and the baby were facing a grave, life threatening situation, which the doctors and nurses assured him they were battling to stabilize.

It was supposed to have been a happy event, he reminded himself. Jarret, preoccupied with advancing his career, was an unlikely romantic who'd resigned himself to a life of bachelorhood, only to fall in love with his future wife the moment he set eyes on her. They'd been inseparable ever since. It was as if their souls had been welded together by some unseen all-powerful force. The rest of the world could be discounted, as long as they were together. They'd had their share of arguments, like any couple, but, in the end, it always came down to the simple fact that they loved each other dearly and were indefatigably committed to each other.

The young doctor assigned to the case, with his off-putting squint and excruciatingly monotonic voice, was, in Jarret's opinion, far too young to be charged with such responsibility. Each plodding sentence he offered seemed like another knife thrust into Jarret's heart, while each carefully hedged prognostication delivered another blow to his delicately thin hopes. Furthermore, behind all the jargon, he sensed that mother and baby had little hope, given the desperateness of the situation.

Jarret wrung his hands. What could he do? Should he pray?

Where would that get him? Standing by her bedside, it was all he could do to just to take everything in. He stared dumbly at Jessie's pale, nearly lifeless face. His love for her poured out until he began to sob, something he had rarely done as an adult and never openly in public.

According to the young doctor, her life was ebbing. She was heavily sedated and about to be taken to a special surgical area where, deep in the bowels of the hospital, last ditch efforts would be taken to save her and the entombed baby.

Despite his love, Jarret, though invited to be at his wife's side during the surgery, declined. Apart from his avid hatred of hospitals, he could not bear the thought of watching his wife breathe her last breath while being sliced open. Preoccupied with dark thoughts, he left the hospital in search of a tobacconist to help blunt the pain and the excruciating wait. He walked and walked, losing track of time and direction—was he subconsciously distancing himself from it all?—he eventually stumbling down a dark shadowy street strewn with discarded prams, punctured footballs, and smashed bottles. Suffused with the odor of rancid food, stale urine and old feces, the street reeked of danger. He never would have walked down such a street in normal circumstances. Then, suddenly, he became aware his was not alone. A well-dressed man with shiny patent leather shoes was walking purposefully towards him, as if he had something important to say.

"Jarret Lamb?" the dapper man asked in a sweetly scintillating voice, pausing before the distraught Jarret.

Jarret froze, astonishment momentarily replacing his pain.

"I can see you've a lot on your mind just now," the man said calmly, examining Jarret minutely.

Jarret eyed him back with suspicion, not knowing what to say.

"It's your wife and child, isn't it? They're in mortal danger," declared the man.

"And how could you possibly know that?" demanded a stunned Jarret.

"I just know," the man replied matter-of-factly. "And, what's more, I can help." As they locked stares, Jarret notice that the man's eyes had a peculiarly hypnotic draw, as did the mesmeric tone of his voice. His clothes, posture and demeanor echoed confidence. He also emitted an enchanting aroma, rather like an orchard of ripe fruit trees.

"H...how?" faltered Jarret.

"Your wife and child will survive," avowed the man, resting a hand gently on Jarret's shoulder, like a father might when consoling a penitent son. Then his voice dropped and took on a more cautionary tone. "But only if you do something for me in return."

"And what exactly might that be?" asked Jarret, confused, but desperate for any shred of hope upon which to cling.

"You need only shake my hand and everything will be righted. A few days thence you will receive a letter with instructions. In exchange for your wife and child's lives, you must carry out the instructions exactly as written." The man's voice lowered further to a rasping whisper. "You have no alternative, really."

"I see," replied Jarret. Though trembling, his heart racing, he couldn't help but think, *What do I have to lose? The man is probably just a lunatic, but regardless, he seems more purposeful and sincere than the doctors, who've thus far offered no more concrete a solution or hope. Crazy or not, he* is *all I have.* With that, Jarret shrugged his shoulders and offered the man his hand. As they touched, Jarret felt an icy-cold electric spark jump from the man to him.

"There. Done and agreed," said the man. "Now return to your

wife and child."

The next moment, Jarret felt as if he had awakened from a dream. He was no longer in the filthy alleyway, but standing, dazed, on the street just outside the hospital. He shook his head in disbelief, concluding that the stress of his situation had finally got to him, and continued his search for a tobacconist, troubled now not only by his wife and child's condition and but also by what he had, in his state of hyper-anxiety, just hallucinated.

He located a shop, bought a pack of cigarettes and, hands shaking uncontrollably, quickly lit up. His jangled nerves temporarily dampened by the rush of nicotine, his mind raced back to Jessie and the baby. He couldn't live without her. His life would be empty. His job, which he'd worked so hard for and which provided them a reasonable standard of living, would be of little value without her to share it with. After several more puffs, he walked back to the hospital to wait for whatever news the infernal doctors could provide.

As he entered the waiting room, the young doctor he so disliked approached him. The young man's face didn't seem to carry the same weight of gloom it had before, though it was still etched with concern. For the first time, he offered Jarret a morsel of hope: "Your wife is alive, and the baby has been saved. Your wife is a fighter, Mr. Jarret." The surgeon, the doctor explained, had excelled at his task. "I'm cautiously optimistic that, if your wife continues to improve overnight, she might just pull through."

Jarret felt as if a crushing weight had been lifted from him. The young doctor reluctantly agreed, after considerable badgering, to allow Jarret to visit Jessie. A moment later, gowned in surgical robe, hat and shoe covers, Jarret was standing by her bed in the recovery room, gently holding her hand.

Jessie was still unconscious from the surgery. Nonetheless, he felt compelled to kiss her gently on her cheek. The baby, swaddled tightly and sleeping in a special cot at the other side of his wife's bed, looked pathetically small. So tiny. so vulnerable. But *alive*.

After several hours, Jarret, exhaused, returned home to his empty house. It felt horribly vacant. He mindlessly watched some television, falling asleep on the sofa in his clothes just before dawn.

His dreams were restless and disturbing. An unknown woman, head bowed, a black veil hiding her face, pushed an empty pram mechanically ahead of her through the deserted streets of a crumbling city. An ominous, dense, ashen-gray haze loomed everywhere above. Ravens, watching from the roofs of houses, cawed, and stray dogs bared their teeth and snarled as she passed.

Jarret awoke to the sound of the refuse collectors shouting at one another. After washing, he downed a cup of instant coffee and made his way groggily back to the hospital.

His wife, he learned from the nurses, had had a difficult night, but the doctor assured him, "She's now stable, able to sit and feed the baby. You can speak with her if you like. But remember: She needs quiet and rest."

Jarret, usually composed, tossed up his arms in wild joy, unable to contain the shriek of elation that burst out from him. In the hospital room, Jessie offered him a faint but hopeful smile in recognition of their change in fortune. She looked weak, but intensely happy to have her child and husband at her side. Jarret expressed his profound relief that she'd pulled through, sobbing tears of gratitude that both wife and child had been saved.

She and the baby, who they named Agnes, after spending several more days in hospital, were released. With her and the baby back home, normality was restored and their home came alive with joy and hope.

Agnes added substantially to their shared bliss. Jarret went to work in the morning and came home at night filled with the pleasure of being a husband *and* father. Nothing could shake their new state of joy, a state they fully deserved, being good hard-working people struggling together to provide a decent home for their new arrival.

A letter arrived in the middle of the week.

Jarret found it resting on the doormat as he opened the front door on his way to work. His name was embossed on the front like one might see on an invitation to a lavish formal event. The letter inside was succinct, as if drafted by a lawyer, with careful attention given to every detail.

A timetable, it stated, had been set in motion and had to be punctiliously observed. Two keys fell out of the envelope as he was reading the letter. The smaller was to a luggage locker at a nearby bus terminal. In the locker, he would find an unaddressed parcel containing a pistol and silencer. The larger was to the back door of a Mr. Walter Pandini's house. The man, he was assured in the letter, would be at home alone today at noon. He was to be eliminated. Shot dead. No other outcome would do. There was no explanation offered as to *why* Jarret was to eliminate Pandini, just that he was to do it as previously agreed without hesitation.

Jarret gasped, carefully avoiding the word "murder" that was struggling to form in his brain. He had always been a man untouched by evil thoughts or temptations. He and Jessie both shared strong moral values. He even worked for a business that was ethically sound. Now he was being asked—no, ordered—to take a life.

While he didn't personally know Pandini, he knew of him,

through the newspapers. Pandini was a notorious mobster turned local politician. The man publicly claimed he had "seen the light" and wanted to atone for his past mistakes by making life better for those less fortunate. He was married to an ex-porn star recently turned socialite who was constantly featured in newspapers, radio and television for her charitable works, all financed by Pandini's huge and dubiously acquired fortune. While she did good works, Pandini was busy laundering his ill-gotten fortune and exploiting the charitable organizations with which his wife was associated. Jarret felt nothing towards the man, certainly no admiration or any of the usual emotions commonly associated with killing.

As if anticipating Jarret's initial inclination to simply ignore the letter, it ended with a curt warning: "Should you chose not to follow these instructions, Mr. Lamb, your wife and child will find themselves once again in mortal danger, this time without reprieve." The letter was unsigned and after a few moments, crumbled into dust in his hands.

Jarret felt as though he were suddenly back in the despicable alleyway the night of his wife's surgery. According to what the man had said, both orally and now in writing, he was duty-bound to perform the act or face unthinkable consequences. Dwelling momentarily on the life of bliss that had been his the last week, he went to work, explained to his boss that he needed to see a doctor as he wasn't feeling well, and took a taxi to the aforementioned bus terminal, where he used the first key to collect the paper-wrapped package. It seemed weighty, so he moved discretely into a bus station toilet cubicle to open it. Inside, as promised, was a tube silencer which attached with ease to an accompanying pistol.

The long-barreled weapon felt cold and unnatural, almost alien, in his hands. Still, he had everything required: the silenced pistol, the house key, and the necessary details to complete the required act.

He stuffed the gun down the front of his trousers, flushed the brown paper packaging down the toilet, and hailed a taxi, instructing the driver to drop him off about a mile from the address in the letter to deceive the taxi-driver of his final destination. It wouldn't do if the driver could connect him directly to the site of the killing. Once there, a couple of shots, his debt paid, the slate wiped clean, he would walk a mile in the opposite direction, catch a bus back to work, and explain to his boss that it had turned out to be a minor ailment. All would be done, his obligation fulfilled.

Pandini, it turned out, lived in an exclusive estate in an area populated by the *nouveau riche*. Each mock-Tudor house with its perfectly cut grass and hedges had a spacious hot tub, Olympic-sized swimming pool, private tennis court, and copies of Greek and Roman statues scattered about. As critic's of the area were inclined to point out, it was where opulence met kitsch.

Jarret paid the cab driver and drifted, unnoticed, towards Pandini's house. As he approached, he noticed dark clouds gathering, placing the house and surrounding area of his intended victim in shadow. A single black Rolls Royce limousine was parked in the driveway, an ostentatious statement of Pandini's wealth and power. Jarret fumbled with the key, finally getting it into the slot. Slowly, silently unlocking the door, he slipped in, and pulled the weapon from his trousers. It felt totally beyond conceivability being in another's house, lethal weapon in hand.

Pandini was in the adjoining living room, apparently watching a sitcom replete with canned laughter and applause, eating his lunch off a TV-tray.

The man froze the moment he caught sight of the intruder. "Who the hell are you?" he wheezed, a barely eaten sandwich falling from his hand, scattering it's contents across the white carpet. "And what do you want?" he added with his next breath.

Jarret said nothing, directing the nozzle of the gun at the center of Pandini's sweating head. He had expected Pandini to react more violently, either physically or verbally. Surely that was what a gangster would do. Perhaps Pandini had a weapon of his own secreted somewhere on his person or nearby for situations like the one in which he now found himself.

Jarret's concerns, however, proved unfounded. Pandini was, quite simply, paralyzed with fear. The man's composure had collapsed, as if acknowledging his death. Perhaps Jarret, through some unimaginable coincidence, looked to Pandini like a notorious assassin from his past? Whatever the reason, Pandini stared at Jarret as if he were staring at the angel of death.

"T…Take whatever you want," he stammered, trembling, the tone of his voice a plead for mercy, as if he'd experienced this same situation before, but at the other end of the weapon.

Jarret said nothing, though he, too, began trembling.

There were, it seems, two cowards in the room. The question was, which would do something definitive first.

A roll of thunder sounded outside. This was the perfect time, Jarret told himself, trying but unable to squeeze the trigger.

It was a simple enough act, a little more pressure on the trigger and the act would be done, but from the start, he'd had grave doubts as to whether he was capable of actually carrying out the deed. At first, he considered just wounding his victim, a kind of partial payback, but the shadowy man in the alley with whom he'd had made the promise seemed both resolute and omniscient. Surely he'd know whether Jarret completed the job, and the consequences for Jarret's family could be fatal.

The pistol with its silencer suddenly weighted heavily in his hand, and Jarret's arm began twitching. With so much movement, he knew he there was no way he could fire accurately. Miss by a fraction of an inch and the man would scream out for help, meaning he'd then have to fire again and maybe even another time. He'd seen enough films and news reports of heinous crimes to realize that murder was an ugly, messy business. Beads of sweat began appearing on his face.

While these thoughts tormented Jarret, Pandini, who was now babbling like a baby, suddenly clutched at his chest, his face twisting in agony. His body shook, he turned ghostly white, and he collapsed. The man, Jarret concluded, had become so frightened that he had a heart attack and died without a shot ever being fired.

Jarred looked down at the gun shaking wildly in his hand, and suddenly felt jubilant. He'd completed his mission without having to kill anyone. Gone in a flash was the guilt that would have shadowed him for the rest of his life. He'd accomplished that which had been asked of him. He could look his wife and child in the eye. If he'd felt deserted by God before, he now felt God was good, fair, just, and on *his* side at last.

Jarret slipped the gun back into his trousers and left, leaving Pandini's lifeless body sprawled on the carpet. After half a mile, he crossed a bridge, and, making sure he wasn't watched, tossed the pistol and silencer into the river. The moment they struck the water, they sank out of sight, and Jarret felt a huge burden lifted from his shoulders. He changed his mind about taking a bus and took another taxi back to work instead. At day's end, he drove home, his life solidly back to normal.

Flight of Destiny

As he turned the corner to his apartment, he noticed a fire engine and an ambulance, lights flashing, parked in front of his house. A woman was being carried out of his house on a stretcher, her face covered by a sheet. Spotting Jarret, a busybody neighbor, Mrs. O'Mara, waddled up to him, wailing, "What a tragedy! You poor, poor man!" Jarred looked vacantly at her and started to say something, only to be interrupted by another outburst. "To lose your wife and the baby as well!" she cried.

Flawless

Sirius Piecroft's face appeared like a brightly-colored field of fungus. Yellow protrusions, the size of giant peas studded his care-worn face, imparting a sickly distinctive gloss, its slickness even more pronounced when touched by sunlight. As tropical diseases went, medical practitioners ranked this affliction as one of the oddest and severest ever seen.

He hadn't always looked like this.

Sirius was known as a soft-spoken academic type who spent every moment of his free time devouring the works of the classical Greek writers such as Pythagoras, Hippocrates, Plato and Aristotle. Living in the heady world of existential humanism, he had little interest in setting foot outside his home in England. Indeed, apart from his three years at university, he'd hardly left where he'd been born and bred, consequently he was hard-pressed to account for the origin of his affliction. The only coincidence he could think of was that it had emerged at the same time his made his offer of marriage to Juliana Stanford, a beautiful young girl of fine aristocratic pedigree who had, at the time, a horde of suitors chasing after her.

On that fateful day, he had dressed, despite the strong sunshine, in his best long lovat-green tailcoat. Though flushing like a sailor in the boiler room of a ship sailing the tropics, he adjudged such a momentous event demanded the most refined in clothing, and his beloved lovat-green tailcoat was just that. In a secluded corner of the vast palatial gardens of Juliana's family estate, he broached the subject with utmost delicacy, only to have his confidence dashed when a colorful insect flew into his mouth with sniper-like accuracy during the second syllable of the word "marry." He'd had to fight to get to the word "me" between vain attempts to spit it out. In the end, he was forced to swallow it in order to finish the proposal. This totally ruined what should have been the happiest and most important moment of his life. Juliana's concern over the predicament was far less than his. Despite the fractured sentence, she replied in the affirmative, and plans for a lavish wedding immediately began germinating in her mind.

Later that day, Juliana's father, an ebullient rotund man with a bushy mustache and high blood pressure, when approached with Sirius' request for his daughter's hand in marriage, responded in a booming, "Splendid! Splendid!"

The requisite sit-down inquisition followed. As to how the academician planned to maintain Rafferty Stanford's daughter in the affluent lifestyle to which she was accustomed, Sirius stated honestly and forrightly, "As best I can." He sailed through the rest of the interview with equal ease, the old man parroting back each of Sirius' answers with a beneficent nod of approval: "Five hundred and fifty pounds a year. I see. From your parent's estate. Yes. A sufficient annual allowance, I agree. And an offer to teach at university. Good future prospects." Each echo and nod was marked with a larger smile.

Sirius' credentials having been duly scrutinized and approved, the only matter left was that of the wedding date. A six-month engagement period, though it seemed long to Sirius, was duly agreed upon, and the two men shook hands.

A party was arranged to formally introduce Sirius' fiancé to his family, as well as prominent family friends. At the party, the groom-to-be introduced his betrothed to his two younger brothers, including one Jonas Piecroft, the black sheep of the family, having redeemed himself with stories of numerous laudatory, though admittedly unsubstantiated wartime heroics. According to Jonas, during his final stretch overseas "empire building," he'd been instrumental in holding off an attack by countless savages armed with clubs, spears and a singular wish to wipe every last colonizing soldier from the face of their land. It was his bravado, and his alone, that had saved a substantial number of men and officers in his brigade from brutal slaughter. At least, that was the way he told it to the family and to a captivated Juliana. In short, the party was a complete success, and Sirius' family and friends welcomed Juliana into the Piecroft family with open hearts and arms. It was around this time that the first blemishes appeared on Sirius' face.

At first he thought it to be a bad case of shingles, but concern mounted following innumerable visits to baffled medical practitioners, and following that, a legion of quacks, whom he was forced to turn to, when conventional remedies failed. After a long list of medications, lotions and painful remedies including leechings, blisterings, and bloodlettings, he came to the stark realization that the disease, whatever it was, wasn't going to subside. In fact, over this time, his face continued growing progressively more disfigured, and Juliana, not surprisingly, ever more distant. At first, she visited Sirius' home, diligently inquiring every day after her husband-to-be's health. Later, however, she began presenting increasingly *effete* excuses that kept her away for ever longer periods of time.

Sirius soon felt not only her physical absence, but more profoundly, her absence of heart. He was at the point of confronting her directly, when, sitting face-to-face in the sanctity of his favorite room, the family library, when he was dealt two savage blows, one immediately after the other:

"Sirius, I can't marry you," Juliana boldly declared that day, her face devoid of emotion. Then before he could respond, she trilled, "Your brother, Jonas, has just asked father for my hand in marriage and father has approved."

Sirius remained silent, trying to take in the enormity of her declarations while the mantlepiece clock ticked the seconds away in the otherwise silent room. Unable to summon words, he stood, then walked abruptly out of the room and house. He wandered aimlessly around the estate for hours, his mind charged with equal measures of pain, anger and betrayal.

During the days that followed, Sirius melted into the periphery, into a world of his own, avoiding anyone who attempted to reach out to him. He eventually locked himself in his room in the secluded west wing of the house and began taking his meals alone, speaking only from behind his closed door. He adamantly refused speak to Jonas, who tried repeatedly to justify what happened in the form of numerous soliloquies outside Sirius' door. Finally, one day, Jonas wrote a crudely drafted letter to his brother, stating he was only doing what any dutiful brother would do—interceding on behalf of his incapacitated brother —and shoved it under Sirius' door.

Over the next several days, Sirius began ordering the servants to bring him a bottle of wine, first with his meals, progressing later to bottles of gin without any food at all. Drinking, he discovered, blunted his feelings, freeing his mind to wallow in painless indifference. In the meantime, arrangements for Jonas and Juliana's wedding proceeded.

Sirius had no intention of attending the wedding. It was apparent to him even in his foggy state of mind that his presence would not be welcome, and his absence not missed. The wedding was the crystallization of all his anguish, and ideas started popping into his mind, at the forefront, the idea of revenge. His hatred for his brother soon reached such intensity that there was only one way to appease the demon that was slowly taking him over and that was murder. For poetic justice, he reasoned, it would have to happen at the altar, just before Jonas and Juliana spoke their final vows.

There remained only the teasing problem of how to enact the murder. The idea of using an axe, dispatching his brother with savage blows to his head, came to him as he watched a woodsman chop up a disease-ravaged tree through a window. Each blow, he imagined, would dilute his pain. In truth, he had never handled an axe, and to his mind it seemed a clumsy instrument. A knife in the heart would be more appropriate, but Jonas had always been the stronger of the two. A shot to the head would be faster, easier, and almost as symbolic, but being severely near-sighted from all his reading, and having, in the past, proved an abject failure with firearms, in the end, it left the axe his weapon of choice.

Donning the tailcoat in which he'd proposed to Juliana, the wedding bells calling, he hefted the woodsman's axe, slumping it over his shoulder, and headed in the direction of the church where the marriage service had already begun.

The entrance to the church building was decked with flowers and bright ribbons. Sirius had to shield his eyes from the happiness they represented, and slithered inside keeping to the shadows. The congregation was too engrossed in the ceremony to notice him. His eyes followed theirs and latched immediately onto Juliana and Jonas at the altar. To his horror, the bride and groom looked the picture-perfect couple, Juliana appearing even more beautiful in her long flowing dress than he'd ever seen her before. His brother was dressed in full formal military uniform, bedecked in spurious medals. Sirius shook his head in disbelief at the depths to which his brother had gone to take his betrothed from him. He knew from their many childhood experiences, his brother was a liar, cheat and coward of the highest order

With the priest's words, "If anyone present knows a reason why these two persons should not marry, let him speak now or forever hold his peace," Sirius burst from the shadows and ran, screaming, down the aisle waving the axe above his head.

Heads turned sharply.

People gasped, recoiled, then screamed and hid as best they could.

"Jonas! Jonas! Jonas! Jonas!" Sirius shrieked like a wounded animal as he staggered onto the altar where Jonas and Juliana were cowering. He immediately swung the axe in a wide arc with the most menacing of intent, but as it neared the crown of his brother's head, Sirius was suddenly engulfed in a violent coughing fit, and the axe missed its mark. Instead of Jonah's head, it lodged into the alter with a loud thud.

Sirius clutched at his throat and fell on the floor, his body seizing in a violent fit. The next instant, a beautiful, brightly-colored insect flew out of his gaping mouth and wafted away.

Sirius' face instantly began transforming. The ugly protrusions disappeared, leaving him pale but without disfigurement. His face was as it had been just before he had proposed to Juliana: flawless.

Juliana, still in a state of shock, looked from one brother to the other. In Sirius, she saw a man deeply wronged. In Jonas' she saw for the first time a deceiver. His charm, his tales, the uniform he was wearing, suddenly seemed as false as his unsubstantiated claims of valour and bravery. It was plain to everyone watching that the pendulum of her love and affection had swung back in Sirius' favor. Juliana gently stroked Sirius' face, as if in reaffirmation that it had, indeed, genuinely transformed back to its original perfect state. The gesture, however, proved too much for Sirius' brother, and Jonas lunged for the axe, yanking it out of the altar.

"Jonas! No!" Juliana screamed, placing herself in front of Sirius. Shielding him, she ended up taking the brunt of Jonas blow on the side of her face. Jonas was forcefully grappled to the ground, and, in a fit of rage, began ranting wildly at his brother, while Juliana collapsed in a heap.

Her father insisted she be taken forthwith to see the local doctor, where, in truth, the cut was found to be not as grave as it looked, in the end requiring simple cleaning and a few small well-placed stitches. In Juliana's mind, however, it was a particularly conspicuous wound.

Meanwhile the two belligerent brothers, Jonas and Sirius, were escorted to the local police station, where Sirius explained to the bemused officer that he had been being held a prisoner in the clutches of an inexplicable malady that had not only blemished his body but had warped his mind as well. He couldn't explain the madness that had possessed him and driven him to arrive at the church, axe in hand, and pleaded that the officer could ask anyone, and they'd all say he was simply not a violent person before his illness. The investigating officer took a long, hard look at him. Despite the bizarreness of his story, the young man appeared otherwise rational, and was certainly no longer a threat to anybody. After a stern warning, Sirius was freed. His nightmare over, he was now at liberty to recommence his life.

His brother's fate was far less redeeming. Jonah, for his part, left an extremely bad impression on the officer. For a start he was uncooperative and offensive. Added to that was the testimony by countless attendees that they saw him try to kill his bride, a very public act of a violently depraved lunatic. The constable, familiar with the Piecroft family who were otherwise well respected in the neighborhood, deemed it best to keep the ranting young man under lock and key until such time as he regained his composure. Two days later General William Piecroft arrived to collect his son and announced that he had volunteered his son's services to the Reverend Dorian Piecroft's church mission for lepers in Africa. Jonas was booked on a ship for Africa the following day. Under the threat of disinheritance, he set off disconsolately to join his pious uncle and dedicate the next five years of his life to serving those suffering from the worst skin disfigurement imaginable. Upon his departure, the general reminded his son that only completion of his commitment to his uncle would regain the family's favor.

Time passed.

Juliana, her still face wrapped in bandages, began to nurture the hope that Sirius would forgive her, and they would find reconciliation. He would, of course, have to see beyond the scar that would disfigure *her* once alluringly flawless face, something she hadn't afforded him when *his* affliction had developed. Still, her hopes rested with the fact that he was by nature a truly kind man, unlike his lying brother. Surely, she thought, he would find it within his heart to love her as before. Before, she'd been so young, so fickle and immature, but she'd grown within immeasurably during her medical convalescence. Surely Sirius could see this and forgive her. When at last her bandages were removed, Juliana grabbed for a mirror only to have her hopes dashed. No words of comfort could disguise the slight but still ugly, blemish on her face. She could hardly bare to look at herself.

Juliana spent the remainder of her convalescence cocooned in her room, spurning all social contact, wishing beyond hope that the scar would vanish. It never did. Worse, nothing she did could completely cover it up. Caking her face with makeup only made her look more grotesque.

Juliana, imagining how Sirius had felt when he'd taken to sequestering himself, slowly become delusional, blurring reality with colorful fictions of how she wished her life to be. She complained constantly of pain on the side of her face, so a doctor was called. He saw no reason she should be in pain as the wound had healed, but she insisted she was suffering immeasurably, so reluctantly he prescribed small doses of morphine, in reality prescribing it more to sooth her anguished mind.

One day, after a markedly strong dose of the prescribed medication, her attention was drawn to the sound of voices outside her door, especially one particular voice that she recognized to be that of Sirius. The voices on the other side of her door sounded animated and happy, and a sudden surge of hope gripped her. Sirius had come to ask for her hand once again in marriage. Despite her misgivings at the thought of him seeing her scarred face, she began calling his name, each time with increasing fervor.

The voices on the other side of the door abruptly paused.

The latch clicked metallically.

The door opened.

Sirius stood before her.

It was as if her prayers had been answered.

He didn't seem abhorred by the scar, at least, it didn't show in his face. Indeed, he was smiling. Then she noticed he was wearing the long lovat-green tailcoat he had first proposed to her in, and her hopes turned to ecstasy. As he got closer to her, however, a specter from the past, Sabina, Juliana's younger sister, appeared beside him.

Sabina had always floated about the periphery of the family, like an unremarkable book consigned to the bottom shelf in a library. She'd been sickly as a child, and had been sent away by her father to be brought up by nuns in a sanatorium in the south of France, where the climate was more agreeable. Her name never warranted mention, and Juliana, over time, forgot about her. Perhaps, she assumed, she had simply passed away, her demise remaining a closely held secret.

To Juliana's current displeasure, her obscure little sister had blossomed into a woman of tremendous beauty, in fact, a mirror image of Juliana down to the last detail before the axe had blighted her face. To her further consternation, Sabina was wearing a dress almost exactly like the one Juliana had worn the day Sirius had proposed. Her sister had even put her hair up the same way, and she was using Juliana's fragrance.

When Sirius turned his eyes to Sabina, Juliana's fears transformed into cold reality. Sabina had stolen more than her looks. She had stolen Sirius' heart, and he had fallen in love with a flawless version of Juliana. It was too much for Juliana to bear. Putting a hand on either side of her horrified face, she screamed like someone falling into the depths of hell. It was a scream so loud, so distraught, that not only shocked Sirius and Sabina, but caused the birds outside to take flight forming one black ribbon across the sky.

Sirius, shocked by Juliana's behavior, tried to reason with her, console her, explain the purpose of his visit, but his words were drowned by the ferocity of her anguish Then suddenly she stopped screaming and her body seized violently, after which she fell limp and unbreathing into Sirius' arms.

To everyone's surprise, the family chapel bell, which had been silent since Juliana's curtailed wedding, tolled plaintively.

Outside, overhead, the dark raucous ribbon of birds coalesced and cast a night-like shadow across the family estate. Suddenly, a particularly ugly raven swooped onto the window ledge, surveyed the scene with its jet black eyes, screeched, and flew away, its cry and form dissolving into the engulfing darkness.

Flight of Destiny

Two Sides of the Truth

Part One - A Man Dies

Demetrius Monk's life had been cut cruelly short by a quirk of misfortune: During a short sojourn in Paris, he was pushed onto the Metro track by a man recently released from a mental hospital. Terrified onlookers gasped in horror as the demented man let out a shrill laugh and Demetrius was divided into thirds by the advancing train. The day before, Monk's assailant, who'd not spoken for twenty years, inexplicably started speaking and his frustrated psychologist, who'd experienced a long list of treatment failures, had happily reported the success and promptly released him.

Following an hour of pandemonium, the mental patient, still

screaming hysterically, was hauled off in a straight-jacket. The area was cordoned off with yellow "Police - Do Not Cross" tape, and the appropriate authorities informed so they could go about their somber duties investigating the incident and cleaning up the mess.

Demetrius' wife was informed of her husband's fate. An awkward phone call followed from Demetrius' wife to his mother, who, as a result of the ravages of senility, didn't react to the tragic news or its implications as might be expected. In all fairness, the Monk family was littered with males named Demetrius, so, perhaps, his wife mused, the old woman thought that some more distant relative had died. In fact, Demetrius' mother was simply more concerned with other matters. While receiving the call, she was repeatedly pushing on the lever of her malfunctioning toaster, wondering when her son would next visit her and fix the wayward appliance.

Demetrius' wife, the beautiful Giselle, finished the call and struggled with her own mixed feelings about the death of her husband. She was, at the time, emotionally embroiled with a waiter, whom she had befriended and bedded while Demetrius was elsewhere. She and Demetrius had had another of their stormy spats earlier in the evening, and she'd left the hotel furious to go to a nearby café to buy a cup of coffee. In the process she encountered a waiter just off duty who, noting her distress, persuaded her to have a stiff drink instead and offered her a sympathetic ear.

The waiter, Rémi Boucher, who was well-versed in providing an empathic ear to beautiful, rich, lost-looking foreign women, charmed Giselle into a rendezvous in his small apartment conveniently located just above the café. The man exuded sympathy, pointing out that her husband had abandoned her in a city where love and romance abounded, and, at the least, needed to be taught a lesson. A woman's feelings should *never* be taken lightly, he offered. "We French know how to treat women," he exclaimed proudly, looking deeply into her eyes.

Giselle tearfully accepted the used Metro ticket on the back of which Rémi had added his phone number, complete with door number and entry code to the upstairs portion of the building. Giselle nodded forlornly, fully aware that in her condition such an encounter would most likely end up leading to one and only one thing: adultery. She smiled weakly at the waiter's expectant continence, thinking that it would, at least, be more satisfying than the lousy sex, she and Demetrius had been having recently, and pocketed the ticket. The waiter followed her with his eyes, as she walked out of the café and across the road back to her hotel.

Giselle returned to the hotel room and smoked a cigarette, convincing herself that there was no way she would ever be foolish enough to enter into a rendezvous with French waiter, only to find that Demetrius had, as was his way after an argument, left their hotel room during her absence to take a walk to "cool down." Often as not these cooling down excursions led to steamy hot encounters with the first woman who caught his attention and who, in turn, succumbed to his considerable looks and charm.

Feeling hurt as well as a well as petulant, though she still loved Demetrius, Giselle dialed the number scribbled on the back of the metro ticket. Having informed the waiter, she slipped away from her lonely hotel room to join him.

His studio apartment was not only minuscule, but offered an array of odors, being littered with empty wine bottles which the waiter had pilfered full from the restaurant. Nicotine-stained wallpaper was peeling from the wall. In one corner brightly colored mushrooms sprouted from a patch of bare damp plaster. Ashtrays, placed liberally about the room, were overflowing with partially-smoked cigarette butts. Plates of unfinished food were stacked high in the kitchen sink and left to fester. Dirty waiter uniforms were distributed randomly about the threadbare carpet. Rémi had few possessions, and what he had, were covered by a layer of dust and ash.

Giselle, in her melancholia, showed little resistance when Rémi pushed her onto her back on the couch, causing a plume of dust to rise into the heavy atmosphere. Several frenzied kisses, a short spate of meandering hands and exotic sexual positions later, and Giselle's passion for the humble waiter, and his for her, peaked. Rémi, it seems, truly *was* far more adept a lover than Demetrius.

Returning back to the empty hotel room, the afterglow of her illicit affair was shattered by the fateful phone call. Still breathless from the tryst, she had to force herself to play the part of the grieving widow. Everything after that seemed a dizzy confused whirlwind.

Several days after her husband's death, upon returning home, she received a call from Rémi. His final words, accentuated with a forced sigh were, "If only I could be there to comfort you, *cherie,*" the sounds of several females giggling in the background. When he tried to flatter her by saying she would look fetching in black, she cursed her naivety and hung up on him.

The next week past slowly, driving the grist of her combined sadness and guilt deeper and deeper into her soul. It was only after Demetrius was finally buried that the first positive ray of light appeared: Demetrius had left everything to her. She'd always known he was rich and successful, but in all their years together they had never discussed finances. He was a man of hidden thoughts, unlike Rémi, who'd talked constantly about himself even during their lovemaking.

At the reading of the will, Demetrius' mother voiced her concern about not having her toaster fixed as well as some other menial tasks she needed done about her house by her son. In the end, the maligned body and soul of Demetrius was left to rest, a life incomplete, cut short by tragic circumstances.

Part Two - The Real Truth, or at Least, An Alternative Version

You are at liberty, of course, to believe what is written above. It is an account...but with some vital flaws. This I know, for I am Demetrius Monk. A skeptic might, at this point, ask why I didn't immediately contest the above version of events. The reason is simple: I have been confined these past twenty-odd years in a mental hospital, spending most of that time in complete seclusion.

It all began one night on a combination business and pleasure trip to Paris with my wife. I was given the news by a couple *gendarmes* that she had been pushed under a speeding train by a crazed Parisian waiter named Rémi Boucher. I tried, but simply couldn't come to terms with my sweet Giselle lying on the tracks, sliced into thirds. My grief was so strong, so intense, so unyielding, I was judged unstable and incarcerated in a lunatic asylum on the hope that, one day, I might be let back into the very society that had stolen from me the one person I held most dear, the beacon of my life, my loving, sweet wife, my dearest Giselle.

The initial shock of her death, as bad as it was, proved less debilitating than the guilt that followed. *If only*, I kept thinking while locked in my asylum room. *If only*, I tortured myself over and over again.

She wanted us to be together every minute. Paris was to be our second honeymoon. However, when I told her I needed to briefly stop at my company's Parisian office, a needless argument broke out. I promised her that by the time she'd taken the short metro journey to the Louvre, viewed some outstanding paintings and sculpture and returned, I would be waiting, and the rest of the vacation would be ours and ours alone.

What made my guilt even worse was the fact that I never actually went to work. Instead, on a whim, I ended up walking the streets, looking in shop windows with the ridiculous notion of surprising her with a special gift, partly to appease her and partly as compensation for all my previous neglects. Alongside this was I was on a mission to buy a toaster for my mother, who'd long complained there was a fault with the one my father had brought back from Paris years before. If only I hadn't given her the idea of taking the metro to the Louvre, as it was at this station that Rémi Boucher pushed her beneath an oncoming train.

An eye witness to the tragedy claimed the well-known womanizer and rake, a lowly waiter, had crudely propositioned Giselle, who vociferously rejected both his invitations and increasingly public advances. In response, the unbalanced lout had reacted in the most horrific way conceivable, pushing Giselle beneath the oncoming train.

Even during the early days of our relationship, my friends told me I was blessed to have met a woman not only as beautiful but as totally devoted to me. Even though we would on occasion exchange harsh words, as all couples occasionally do, our love and passion for each other always shined through. Year after year in the asylum, I wallowed in grief and guilt, while psychologists, one after another tried to break through my despair.

In truth, I let myself fall into madness. Such was my love for Giselle. I am, it seems, about to go back into the "normal" world now. I have only one final meeting with a panel of psychiatrists of the sanitarium, and I feel confident now that I will, at last, be pronounced sane. I have been much maligned these past years, and I implore you, my judge and jury, to believe my version, because all the other versions, which are numerous, have been circulated by misguided newspapers and rumormongers, and are, quite simply, inaccurate and untrue.

Body Parts

"He's coming, Professor Banshaw," said Janus, a tall gaunt laboratory technician of decidedly nervous disposition who had worked with Banshaw for many years. The eminent scientist, Professor Roderick Harvey Banshaw, a short stocky man with thick rimmed glasses, a bush of wild white hair, constantly shifting calculating eyes, and a soft-measured soothing voice, followed Janus' eyes anxiously to the doorway.

The bulky figure of multimillionaire Dalton Kane strode imperiously into the vast showroom that was stocked up with what looked like perfectly shaped prosthetic limbs, torsos and heads—row upon row of tall glass cases displaying body parts. The room had a dead, sterile ambience, like that of a deserted airport terminal at three o'clock in the morning. "Banshaw," Kane said, glaring purposefully at

269

the Einstein look-alike staring at him. Expecting to see some return for all the money he'd paid, Kane continued, "What have you got for me?"

"Shall we start with legs, Mr. Kane?"

Kane nodded, waving his hand dismissively.

Professor Banshaw signaled, and Janus led Kane solicitously to the first of a long row of transparent display cases, each with a unique serial number and different pairs of shapely legs. On the walls behind the cases were posters of women in various poses. Beneath each was a slogan: *"The Exact Fit," "Perfect Women Never Grow Old," "No More Quarrels: Only Smiles," "A Perfect Partner for the Perfect Marriage."* A new photo of a boy and a girl playing had just been added with the slogan, *"Coming Soon: Perfect Smiling Children."* Above the line of posters, a long banner read, *"The Happy Face of the Next Human Race."* The banner and each poster bore the trade name "Foch Robotics."

It had all started with the production of female androids for use in the airline industry. Indistinguishable externally from humans, these indefatigable unsalaried check-in clerks and flight attendants proved a huge financial success. In a world saturated with "smart" objects, most passengers accepted these new additions to the workforce as a natural transition. Even staunch feminists shrugged their shoulders, saying the world had always treated women as objects and their sex as advertising platforms, so a talking, moving Barbie doll at a check in was no real surprise.

A few, however, were outraged. Religious leaders of all faiths called it a blatant defamation of the human race, and the soulless robots a personal insult to God. Their anger relented, however, when places of worship became flooded with devout women automatons in perfect attire, who listened, prayed, sang and tithed most ardently.

After the service, outside places of worship, the spiritually-charged androids could be found among the "natural" worshipers talking of plane delays, safety procedures, and baggage restrictions, hinting at a possible limitation in their understanding of spiritual matters. But, who cared, really?

Despite their limited socialization skills, they became so well integrated into society that people, especially men, who, forgetting altogether that they were automatons, began attempting to get their telephone numbers and invite them out. This opened up an entirely new side-business: android companions, custom made for rich men. This new application required Foch Robotics to make a number of updates to their initial line. Their new versions had to be able to do more than give out airport or travel information while maintaining a sweet smile. They had to be made considerably more human and, most important, totally compliant to their owner's proclivities.

As chief scientist, Banshaw had worked night and day on this new line. He had to produce a new version that could respond to the widest range and newest trends in owner needs, while successfully addressing their specific owner's quirks and foibles. Banshaw introduced novel software programs with incredibly complicated algorithms, and added long-lasting motion-recharging batteries. Improving their limited vision had proven challenging, but all new models were equipped with a pair of video cameras built into remarkably human-looking eyes. A new Foch laboratory had been tasked to develop a synthetic human-like skin the alluring texture of soft baby skin, but both water- and tear-proof.

These new models, fondly called "wifelets," had no sweat glands and therefore could easily be programmed to clean and maintain themselves as needed. In parallel with the laboratory's success in skin production came similar strides in hair production, resulting in always-perfect, self-regulating hair. They were also given realistic external and internal organs, though, of course, conception was not possible. As they couldn't actually enjoy sexual interaction, they were programmed to pant, squeal and say, "Oh, darling, you're so *amazing*," while always displaying the trademark Foch airline attendant smile of satisfaction. In short, Banshaw designed and programmed them to give their male owners not only a social companion but one that could provide the owner a massive coital ego boost.

Interestingly, Banshaw had never had much intimate contact with women. Discounting a short-lived dalliance while at university, he was otherwise a man difficult to communicate with, except in scientific matters. He'd never understood women or their needs, nor really wanted to for that matter, and had come to accept, even relish, a celibate life. This meant Banshaw had to engage outside expertise, namely survey panels of rich men with sophisticated sexual tastes, to guide him in developing the new line. Banshaw, at their recommendation made the new models meeker and more subservient than airline attendants, while at the same time, equipping them with a broader enough knowledge to please their most educated human counterparts. But most importantly, he built in the ability to adapt to their owner's needs, wants and desires. Prototypes were extensively evaluated, the final test, on his insistence, being administered by the President of the Foch Robotics, Sir Findlay Foch himself.

It began when Banshaw reported his early successes to the president, and Foch hinted he'd like to test one of the new models. for That day, he made sure his wife was away, claiming unconvincingly, "It's a good opportunity to try out its cooking skills." Banshaw, despite his desire to see the project come to successful completion, was loath to let one of his new creations out of the laboratory. Also, he suspected Sir Findlay had plans to test more than just the unit's culinary skills. On the other hand, strictly speaking, what he suspected the man had really planned could never *technically* be adultery. In fact, what was really bothering Banshaw was that he felt strongly protective of his creations. It was as if each were a diamond-in-the-rough, which he felt compelled to polish and maybe continue polishing all by himself.

Sir Findlay, however, was not a man to whom he could say no. Sir Findlay's chauffeur called ahead and appeared at exactly the stated time to collect the merchandise, leaving Banshaw to spend the weekend agonizing about what might be happening, like a father might over his adolescent daughter on her first weekend away from home with an eager over-sexed teen-ager. The unit was returned promptly Monday morning, its clothes and hair disheveled. It still had its trademark smile, but it appeared somewhat confused for several hours; Banshaw had had to do some reprogramming before it entirely regained its natural equilibrium. Sir Findlay, in the meantime, walked about the complex with an even bigger *Foch* smile than usual, and, on passing Banshaw in the hallway, had remarked, "Good work, Banshaw. Extremely good work."

As with sex, the new wifelets couldn't enjoy the taste of food, despite being programmed to be perfect cooks. The wifelets were nonetheless programmed to *comment* about the food they cooked. While "eating" with their owner, they would occasionally pause and say reflectively, "Perhaps I should have put in a bit more salt," or, " I might have overdone the potatoes just a little." Of course this was never true, but it added to the authenticity of a meal. They might even say at the dinner table, "I think I'm putting on a little weight." This, of course, could never be the case, though their form could be adjusted over time to fit their client's changing desires.

Banshaw beckoned Kane over to the first display case. Kane loomed over it, analyzing the legs with a critical eye, and shook his head in the negative. "Too sturdy," he declared, moving on the next display, adding caustically, "It's not like I'm buying a horse, man." It went like this until at the third to the last display, he cocked his head to the side, made a more stringent inspection, put a finger to his nose and sighed, as if coming to the only decision possible, "These will be acceptible." Janus noted the serial number.

"Shall we do feet, arms and hands also today?" asked Banshaw, ushering Kane to a different row of display cases.

The distinguished Mr. Kane found the process of choosing appendages laborious, so after twenty minutes of additional consideration, he directed Banshaw to choose for him whichever feet and arms he deemed most appropriate as long as the result was "graceful." The hands, Kane pointed out, needed to be the "hands of a pianist." *The man must really love music*, thought Banshaw with a shrug, directing his client to the final row of display cabinets.

"That leaves only the head and torso," Banshaw stated softly.

Kane ended up prevaricating over the head. "Wide eyes, youthful cheeks, petite nose, full lips, blonde hair," he said, as if reading from a mental list based on an image that only he could see.

As they began moving from display case to display case, Banshaw became progressively more forlorn, as Kane dismissed one after another for a variety of disparaging reasons. Mr. Kane, however, finally made his choice. "That one, over there," he stated with finality, pointing to the last cabinet, one that had been created the day before, and was modeled after a nineteen sixties French film star: delicate nose, succulent pout, long tousled blonde locks, unnaturally big eyes,

274

producing an almost cat-like appearance. Banshaw and Janus breathed sighs of relief. Each head had to be unique, ensuring that no two clients would encounter similar-looking companions. This was, of course, to also avoid any embarrassing social situations or gossip.

For the torso, Kane quickly chose the "slender one with ample breasts and athletic hips," then, checking his watch, he took his leave, barking out an order as he would in his own factory: "Have her assembled and ready in two days."

After Kane left, Banshaw let out the remainder of his breath and turned to his assistant. "Thank God that's over. We've never had such a difficult client. The man's nearly impossible..."

Janus gulped, nodded his silent accord, and the two began assembling the various parts and testing them for integrity.

Exactly two days later, Mr. Kane swooped back into the room like a swan landing on a placid lake. "Is she ready?" he half-asked, half-demanded.

"Yes, of course, Mr. Kane," replied Banshaw, looking edgily at the white-curtained screen in the corner of the room, then back at Janus. Janus smiled weakly, shrugged and nodded his reassurance.

"Well, bring her here, man!" bawled Kane. "Let me see her!"

"She's behind the screen," replied Banshaw, gesturing to Janus, who walked over to the screen and slowly pulled it aside.

"Mind you, she's still integrating," Banshaw added nervously.

The assemblage process had gone perfectly. She seemed to be asleep, but when approached, she opened her eyes and moved effortlessly towards the three men.

Kane's eyes narrowed. Banshaw, noticing his reaction, took off his laboratory coat and draped it over her. She hesitated, looked questioningly at Banshaw, then stepped in front of Kane and looked him over.

Banshaw watched the couple, noting with relief the look of approval spreading across Kane's face.

"I assume you haven't named her," Mr. Kane said, as if the privilege, like naming a dog he'd just purchased, was his and only his.

"Not as such," said Banshaw. "At the moment, she is simply referred to as Fem7602. However, she is programmed to imprint on whatever you choose to call her."

"I think Electra will do nicely," said Kane, a man used to making executive decisions. "Your...name...is...Electra," he said to the woman standing before him, like a manager giving a new employee the simplest of instructions.

The assembled woman said nothing.

"I hope you've not provided me with a simpleton, Banshaw," said Kane with an air of aloof menace.

"Of course not," said Banshaw, aggravated by the slur. "We've done the most extensive testing. As I said, she is still integrating..."

Kane ignored the professor, and addressed the woman directly in a louder voice, as if talking to a child: "My...name...is...Dalton... Kane. I am to be your...husband," he said in his clearest, most businesslike way. "Your name will be Electra. Me, Dalton. You, Electra," he said, pointing from his chest to hers. "You will live with me on my sizable estate, and do whatever I tell you. Have I made myself clear?"

"I see," she finally replied, much to everyone's relief. She seemed to Banshaw to be functioning the usual way all the others had when after first being introduced to their client.

"You've given her a nice voice," Kane said aside to Banshaw, obviously delighted, "and I like her brevity of word," he added in

276

additional praise.

"Yes, sir. We offer only the best, Mr. Kane," reminded Banshaw. Janus nodded in silent but strong agreement.

"The last Mrs. Kane had a voice like a strident owl, and would drone on and on. It ended up driving me mad," said Kane with a sour face.

"Don't worry," reassured Banshaw. "Mrs. Kane, that is, Electra, will give you no such trouble. She has a sweet voice *and* demeanor. Just what you need after a hard day of work." Banshaw said, winking.

Kane stiffened, then prepared to give his wife-to-be additional instructions. "Now, woman," he said seriously, "I like my house run neatly and efficiently. I like my women easy to manage. You must follow my instructions to the letter. To the letter, do you understand? "As to my sexual requirements," he paused, continuing with particular gravity, "I prefer once a week, sometimes twice, depending on my inclination. I generally like 'missionary position,' but I am not impartial to others for variety."

Electra stared at him, as if processing his demands.

"You will be a *compliant* hostess," Kane continued, "politely socializing with my business acquaintances, both male and female, but you must never be flirtatious. I won't stand for that."

Electra continued to stare fixedly at him, finally blinking in what Kane took to be a signal that she'd assimilated what he'd said and was ready for more core instruction.

"I expect perfect manners. You will be civil and accommodating to me at all times." Kane turned to Banshaw, "This isn't too sudden or difficult for her, is it Banshaw?"

"Not at all, Mr. Kane," replied Banshaw adding dutifully, "our products are one hundred percent reliable and carry a lifetime guarantee. Should you experience anything you don't like, you need only…"

The vacant expression on Electra's face abruptly vanished and her eyes seemed to light up. "And what of my needs?" she asked. "Do I get a say in all of this?"

Banshaw's face blanched. Had he gone too far with her artificial intelligence? Had she somehow acquired human level reasoning or petulance?

"*Your* needs?" spluttered Kane with a gasp.

"*My* needs," reiterated Electra. "I am, after all, about to become your wife."

Kane looked angrily from the woman standing before him with her hands on her hips to Banshaw, then Janus. Banshaw, totally flummoxed, bowed his head in shame, while Janus just looked confused, wondering how a software mistake of this proportion could have occurred.

Turning back to his wife-to-be, Kane growled, "That's as may be. Listen you little minx: I paid good money for your assemblage, but I'll be damned if I will tolerate any insubordination, especially from a glorified talking machine!"

"Well, most sorry, Mr. Kane," said Electra sarcastically, "but part of that assemblage included a *mind* in addition to a body. I'll be damned if I am going to let you and all that bulk violate me unless you also address *my* desires."

Kane's face reddened. Nobody but *nobody* ever spoke to him in such a manner, and worse, she had alluded to him having a "weight problem," an issue about which he was highly sensitive. The first Mrs. Kane had used his ample weight as a stick with which to beat him into submission, causing him much anguish.

"Now listen here!" he snapped. "If I wasn't in the company of others, I would give you a firm hiding, right here and now!"

"Am I to assume, then, that you are a violent man, Mr. Kane?" responded Electra. "Is it because you have difficulty expressing yourself verbally, and therefore feel compelled to resort to violence?"

"Don't push me, woman," roared Kane menacingly, lurching forward as if he intended to tear her apart component by component.

Kane's threat, however, didn't deter Electra in the least. Instead, she continued, "You must remember that I've only been in existence for the shortest of times, and the only experience I can draw from is my brief association with the Professor, his assistant and now you. The professor is interested only in science. His assistant, unremarkable as a man, is nonetheless totally dedicated to his work with the professor. But if you, Mr. Kane, are representative of most other men, I would prefer to be dissembled and returned to the storage cabinets I came from, rather than live a life of repression with you. What kind of existence would that be?"

"But I have *money,* woman. More than you can imagine," boasted Kane, holding his head high, adding philosophically, "Most women I've known couldn't wait to get their hands on so much money."

Electra, who had been programmed with only a limited notion of money apart from the good household budgeting skills she would need to run Mr. Kane's household, held her head up equally proudly and smiled. "Well, not this one."

Kane turned to Banshaw, anger blazing in his eyes, fists clenched, shaking with rage. "What in God's name have you created, Banshaw? A *creature*, no matter how attractive, who thinks and answers back...I mean..."

"I am truly sorry, Mr. Kane. You must remember that she was

programmed just for you based on the answers you provided to our psychological section. She is totally and uniquely designed for you. Surely this isn't anything more than a corrupted subfile. Nothing we can't fix..."

"Well, I won't have it, Banshaw," said Kane shaking his head. "I want a full refund! Now! A temporarily malfunctioning arm or leg I could live with, but a..." Kane stopped and resurveyed the otherwise perfect creature standing before him, "...woman *who thinks for herself?* No!" He'd hesitated at first, thinking that this new wife would be quite economical compared to the first Mrs. Kane, who he'd had to constantly lavish with expensive jewelry to incur her favor.

"But...but Mr. Kane..." protested Banshaw.

"There should be legislation against people like you," interrupted Kane, jabbing Bradshaw in the chest with a fleshy finger. "You should be shut down for creating such an abomination."

"But, Mr. Kane," said Banshaw repeated in desperatation, "I'm certain I can fix this unfortunate glitch. We can have it sorted out and fixed by tomorrow."

Kane hesitated. He'd built his wealth and his reputation on reliable products and service, and that made him think. He wouldn't be standing here today if he hadn't been invited by another heavy-weight industrial tycoon, Gordon Lockman, to meet the new Mrs. Lockman. Kane had accepted the man's invitation with reluctance. If she was anything like Lockman's previous wives, she would be flighty, course, uncouth or worse, completely unhinged, as the man had simply the most terrible taste in women. She had proved quite the opposite. She was not only surprisingly attractive, but her manners and demeanor were excellent. She was like the women Kane had seen in old films, standing quietly in the background behind their husbands, ready to serve tea anytime of day or night with a warm rapturous smile. Nothing like the women of today, who are never content, sponging money off their husbands, demanding attention but never satisfied, always complicating a man's life. After an outstanding meal, cooked and served not by professional staff but by the new Mrs. Lockman, Kane left feeling truly envious of his friend's wife. That night, he couldn't get her out of his mind. She was everything he desired in a woman, reminding him vaguely of the new airport workers, who he found so polite and delightful.

The following day he'd probed his friend about where the man had met such a woman, saying, "I didn't realize such women existed in this day and age."

Lockman had been reticent at first, but when Kane hinted he must have found her via the internet, or paid an agency to somehow locate the perfect wife, Lockman succumbed. "She's not human," he said at last in a hushed voice.

Kane had laughed heartily at what he perceived to be a rare Lockman joke. It took some time and effort on Lockman's part to convince Kane otherwise. When Kane's finally "got it," his initial surprise quickly turned from disbelief to wonder, and he inquired, "What do you mean she's not human? She seems perfectly human to me," breaking out in barrage of nervous laughter.

Lockman quietly explained. "In truth, she was designed both physically and mentally to fit my needs, wants and desires. We've never had single argument."

Kane laughed again, but this time it was more like a curious chuckle. After thinking a moment, Kane admitted, "I wouldn't mind one having one like that for myself. Can you provide me a contact number, so I can acquire something similar?"

Lockman passed on the details, imagining Kane would benefit as he had, though he explained that, at this early stage of development, each "companion" was a one-of-a-kind creation rather than a particular established product line. Kane had attended the required preliminary meeting with Dr. Banshaw, who reiterated basically the same. Kane had subsequently given Banshaw and Janus a detailed outline of his expectations, but now...

"I'm leaving!" yelled Kane, shifting back to the present, his face redder than ever as he charged out of the room.

"And to think," Branshaw said, shaking his head, "You could have been the second Mrs. Kane."

Shrugging in a most human way, Electra replied, "I *could* have, but it would clearly have led to an unprecedented and acrimonious divorce.

Branded

Branning had been running, his long legs helping him gain an extra boost of momentum in the dwindling light. He was late for an evening business meeting, had lost his bearings, taken a wrong turn, and was now trying to compensate for his lateness by running as fast as he could. Turning a corner, he ran straight into an old woman. The old lady fell backwards and as her body hit the pavement, he heard an excruciating crack.

The frail old lady's shopping bag, laden with provisions, had flown out of her hands as if in slow motion, creating a picture of carnage all about her. Hitting the ground, a bottle of milk exploded, adding to the mayhem, while three ripe apples careened wildly in different directions along the pavement. Seconds later, a red rivulet appeared from beneath her head and began coalescing.

A crowd of curious bystanders gathered, forming a circle about the scene. Branning, sitting upright on the pavement, legs splayed outwards, braced himself and shook his head as if trying to awaken from a nightmare. It took him a moment to realize he hadn't suffered any serious injury. The old lady had apparently taken the full force of the collision.

He stared blankly before him, his heart beating violently, his chest heaving, and gasped for breath. When he finally regained a semblance of composure, he blurted out, "The old woman, is she all right?"

It was a futile question, and no one responded. He was the perpetrator. It was clear to everyone in the growing crowd that he'd knocked over and killed the old woman.

Branning struggled to his feet, and, assessing the situation with slightly more detachment, realized his only reasonable action was to get the woman immediate medical treatment. He reached into his pocket, pulled out his cellular and called emergency services. It wasn't long before he heard the welcome sounds of an ambulance siren.

Two medics entered the circle carrying a stretcher onto which they placed the woman's limp body. Branning was asked some details by the medics, but could only tell them one basic fact: He'd run straight into her. She was whisked away at speed, and he followed in a taxi. His hope was that some brilliant young doctor would work a miracle and resuscitate her.

At the hospital, Branning was pushed aside into the waiting room. There, he phoned his assistant, explained his absence, and told her to offer his sincerest apologies to everyone at the meeting. Then he called his wife, knowing she wouldn't yet be home from her work, and left a vague message about having had an accident, admonishing her "not to worry. "

A half-hour later, he was joined by a white-coated doctor, who, shrugged his shoulders and said, "We did everything we could. Technically, she was dead on arrival. The injury she sustained to her head, was accompanied by both a stroke and a heart attack." The doctor excused himself when a plainclothes policeman appeared, explaining there were procedures to be followed in cases like this. Branning was ushered into an office, where he gave his statement. There wasn't much to say. It was an unfortunate accident, pure and simple.

Still, Branning felt absolutely disconsolate, haunted already by what had happened. He learned from the policeman that the old lady's name was Margaret Ottman. She was ninety-two. The doctor had emphasized that, given her frail condition, she hadn't long to live anyway, having such a poor heart. She might have lasted, at best, another month or two, not that Branning drew much comfort from this.

Branning went home and collapsed into his concerned wife's arms, weeping uncontrollably as he told her between sobs of the singular chain of events that had led to the old woman's death. For her part, his wife had never seen him in such a state, and tried her best to console him with what words of comfort she could educe, but whatever she said, it always returned back to the fact that he'd killed an old woman.

The nagging guilt refused to leave, and his wife's attempts at solace only seemed to increase it. Branning kept imagining the old lady's family and friends at the funeral, going through the equally great pain of saying goodbye to a dearly loved one. He wanted to be there, to tell them how sorry he felt, but his wife and friends counseled otherwise. It was better, they said, to let the family grieve, and allow things to run their course. How would her family react to having the man who had cut short her life at her funeral service?

Time passed. He noted her obituary in the local paper. The family requested no flowers, suggesting instead a donation to the hospital in the deceased's name. He sent a sizable sum of money, a form of indirect compensation, and felt slightly better for it.

The obituary listed her principal surviving family member as one Malaika Ottman, which struck him as an unusual name. Calling the funeral home, he duplicitously identified himself as a distant relative who'd lost touch over the years with the family, and wanted very much to reconnect. The director was pleased to help, and Branning discovered to his surprise that the survivor with the exotic name lived relatively close by. He wrote a contrite letter filled with expressions of remorse for his part in what had happened. Writing the letter proved cathartic, further lessening his guilt and self-recrimination, but when, after several weeks, he didn't receive a reply, he began to wonder if he'd somehow offended her, and his guilt returned.

Finally, a letter arrived, addressed to him in a bold, flamboyant hand. He opened the envelope, held it before him in his shaking hands, and read:

Dear Mr. Branning,

Thank you for your kind letter. I was deeply saddened by my mother's death, but she lived a long and fruitful life. At the time of her death, her eyes and mind had deteriorated; she probably wasn't fully aware of where she was going. With solid assurance that I'm fine, I thank you again for your kind thoughts. Of course, you can't be held in any way responsible. I am not a great one for writing, preferring instead to talk face-to-face. Perhaps we can

meet sometime, and I can show you that I bear you no ill feelings.
Yours sincerely,
Malaika Ottman

The letter went a considerable way towards easing his mental pain. The next evening, he decided to leave work early and, feeling an urge to visit the woman and explain things in a more personal way, he headed towards the address, hoping to bring closure to all that had happened.

As he stood on her doorstep, his hands began shaking and lines of sweat appeared on his face. Though tempted to walk away, he forced his hand to ring the doorbell. What was he thinking disturbing this woman, he wondered?

"Coming," a husky voice called out from behind the closed door, above the sound of a washing machine juddering away. The moment she opened the door and their eyes met, a brief but poignant silence ensued. Malaika was tall, almost statuesque, with long braided hair held back by an ornate scarf of African design. She peered at him with her big brown eyes, making him feel even more on edge. She had dark brown skin and gave off an aroma that hinted of cedar wood. Tattoos of written characters ran the length of her arms up to her bare shoulders. The old lady had been Caucasian white. There was no way the woman standing before him could be her biological daughter. That meant Malaika was most probably adopted. If this was the case, she would likely have less of a bond to her deceased mother. This revelation eased his guilt a little more.

He was the first to speak. "Ah…my name is Michael Branning. I wrote to you about your mother."

The Amazon-like woman before him eyed him suspiciously,

hesitated momentarily, then showed him into a disheveled living room cluttered with exotic African artifacts. Sitting on a cane chair on an hand-painted African batik cushion cover, he proceeded to talk through that terrible day and how it had all seemed to come about because of a small, unintentional mistake on his part: turning left instead of right.

Malaika silently took in what he was telling her, a thin but compassionate smile spreading slowly across her face. After a few minutes, she interrupted. "Please, Mr. Branning, you needn't be so hard on yourself," she said, the washing machine in the background changing from rumbling to whirring.

Branning, who'd got the feeling he'd been rambling, stopped talking and listened while Malaika explained how her adoptive mother had been a fountain of wisdom to her. Everything she knew about life she had learned from her. Sadly, after her early twenties up to quite recently, they had become estranged. Malaika, against her mother's wishes had married a brash young man she barely knew. The marriage lasted only a month, but was enough to create a permanent rift between the two women.

Her adoptive mother, Malaika said, had always been wary of close relationships. Her adoptive mother, Malaika said, had always been wary of close relationships like marriage, having been abandoned by her biological parents; she was brought up by a British couple living in Africa. The couple already had five children of their own, but wanted to adopt an "unfortunate underprivileged child." The family moved back to Britain when Malaika's adoptive mother Margaret, was in her late teens. Margaret had married a British war veteran, knowing from his injuries that he could not provide her with children. She never remotely loved him, but the marriage facilitated adoption and Margaret, with a respectable husband in tow, was able to prove to the adoption board she could provide a stable family structure and home for an adopted African baby, specifically, Malaika. As soon as Malaika settled in, the war veteran had served his purpose and was swiftly evicted, leaving Margaret to bring up her new daughter as she pleased using the money her foster parents had passed to her.

Malaika was an unusual woman, and, as she talked of her life, Branning's initial curiosity turned into admiration, and admiration to physical attraction. Surprised at his carnal interest, he forced himself to break eye contact, and perused the room and its artifacts more closely.

Branning and Malaika soon discovered they had a common interest: calligraphy. She had piles of books on the subject stacked everywhere, as well as individual characters from many different languages beautifully penned and framed all over the walls of her house. Her adoptive mother, Margaret, had nurtured this interest, encouraging Malaika to attend a British university to study art history, a course which included calligraphy. Due to her outstanding academic skills, she won a scholarship, which had delighted her foster mother, though her sojourn at university proved brief. Malaika came to hate the pompous students that typified the university, and began to mix with the local dissident crowd. Skipping classes, and acquiring a reputation for drug and alcohol abuse along with numerous tatoos left the Dean of the university feeling that he had no choice but to expel her. He'd always hated students with tattoos, anyway.

Malaika's mother had been deeply disappointed. Malaika had shown such promise, her teacher's having prognosticated early on that if she studied hard, she would go far academically. In the course of a single semester, however, Malaika had thrown it all away, and set her life on a downward spiral.

Branning, in return, shared with her that he'd never really wanted

289

to be a businessman. His parents had told him to forget about art, literature, history and every other humanity, explaining there was no future in such. He was better off studying business. With a solid business background, he would always have steady work and an income. He subsequently became a mediocre businessman, able to hold his own, but never excelling.

Talking with Malaika, he felt he was in the company of someone who understood him. Apart from the tattoos on her arms, which, he reasoned, aptly reflected her bohemian past, he perceived her as having attained a solid air of middle class respectability. She could, he felt, fit easily within his social circle.

The truth was vastly different.

The woman before him was intentionally mimicking her adopted mother's phrases and tone of voice. Malice felt compelled to carry off the pretense, one for which Branning was clearly falling.

The two paused, as if catching their breath in preparation for another round of shared discoveries, and in those moments, Branning had time to consider more carefully what he'd seen in the room in which they were sitting. Resting on the mantelpiece, was a pristine white human skull.

The room had a museum quality about it, crammed as it was full of things Malaika and her adoptive mother had acquired, all of which he sensed held deep personal value. Resting on the mantelpiece was a pristine white human skull. With shimmies of light constantly darting off its shiny surface, it caught the eye and instantly directed it to a meandering crack running across it. Malaika had surrounded it with marigolds, as if it were a shrine. His eye next caught a chalice, neighboring a candelabra decked with small ceremonial candles on a table in the adjoining dining room. The dining room and table, like the living room, were cluttered with what appeared to be even more exotic artifacts and *objects d'arts*.

Malaika began talking about a book of autographs of historical value, which she and her mother particularly cherished. Her mother had purchased book at a private auction many years before. Unfortunately, the book was, at that moment, at the bookbinders, being restored. "You must come again another time and see it," she insisted. "It contains samples of autographs of many leading politicians, literary figures and artists, dating back to the nineteenth century. It's priceless."

Branning hesitated.

"Why don't you come next week?" she said, her voice conveying loneliness. "It should be back by then, and we can look at it together." She ran her hand through her long hair and smiled seductively. His head nodded in agreement without his conscious consent. In truth, he'd never met anyone as totally enthralling. Stronger, more primal feelings were stirring inside.

The washing machine shuddered to a halt.

After a quick glance at his watch, he made his excuses and parted, reaffirming his promise to call on her the following week. His wife would be conveniently occupied with her evening pottery class. A week later, he found himself once again on her doorstep.

This time when the door opened, Malaika was wearing a short skirt, which directed his attention to her slender shapely legs, and he found himself, as he had at the beginning of his first visit, momentarily speechless. She waited, as if milking the moment, then invited him in.

Once Branning was installed in a seat, she asked, "A cocktail perhaps? I could make a couple of chilled African Amarula Creams."

Branning accepted, definitely feeling the need for a drink.

Malaika disappeared into the kitchen, returning with two glasses containing what looked like frothy milk. Drink in hand, Branning sank deeper into his seat while Malaika took her place on the sofa on the other side of the coffee table. Leaning forward she lit the candelabra, which had been moved during his absence from the adjacent room to the coffee table. Circled about the base of the candelabra like an unearthly wreath was a collection of feathers, bones, amulets and what appeared to be tiny, ancient, carved African female fetishes.

Malaika crossed her long legs, locked onto his eyes, and raised her glass in a toast.

Whatever self-control Branning had quickly disappeared in the overpowering seductiveness of the moment, leaving him feeling awkward and ill at ease. In defense, he tipped his glass and gulped at his cocktail. "Ah, what about the book?" he ventured, trying to resurrect the conversation they'd begun during their previous encounter.

"Oh, that. Yes. Frankly, I forgot all about it. I was supposed to call the bookbinder yesterday." The book, Michael concluded, had obviously not been of real importance to her, serving more as a pretense for securing his return. Malaika twiddled a ring on her finger and stared intently at him.

Branning tried again to strike up a conversation, but Malaika's piercing stare kept curtailing any manner of speech. While trying to think of something to say, he felt a stab of excruciating pain in his head, followed immediately after by a pounding headache. The headache was so bad he could hardly focus his tear-wetted eyes on the woman sitting across from him. It felt like he'd been tossed backwards onto hard ground and banged his head to the point that everything was now whirling around him. He sincerely hoped it would pass, but it didn't, leaving him feeling obliged to seek some respite. "I'm sorry,

Malaika, but I seem to have a sudden blinding headache," he stammered.

Malaika's stare turned to concern. "Oh, I've the perfect remedy right here," she said, refilling his glass. "This will ease your pain."

Branning drank deeply, while Malaika resumed staring intently at him. It wouldn't have taken any coaxing on her part to get him to drink. The pain in his head was now such that he'd do anything to make it go away. After several deep draughts of the unusual cocktail, the headache, as promised, eased off. Branning seized the moment to suggest that he should leave, but when he tried to stand, he felt so relaxed and weak, he felt compelled instead to lie down.

"Are you all right, Michael?" Malaika asked. "Perhaps you need to rest. Let's go upstairs..." she offered, adding, when he politely declined, "It's not a problem. Really. I'm just concerned for you."

Branning thought further about the offer. Being married, he knew in his mind he should remain adamant; however, whereas before his head was pounding, the world now seemed to be increasingly spinning about him as if he had somehow become caught in a mental vortex. Being clearly unable to walk home, he acceded to her invitation. In fact, the more he thought of it, the more the idea of going with her upstairs to her bedroom became singularly enticing. With Malaika's assistance, the two worked their way laboriously up the stairs. Opening the door to her bedroom, she said softly, "The best thing for you right now is to lie flat and close your eyes."

Despite his dizziness, he noticed before closing his eyes that it was a spacious bedroom. It had an odd, musty smell, and there was a dusty picture of Mother, surrounded by a crowd of smiling faces, at the bedside.

"Lie down and relax," she suggested, adding, "I need to freshen up. I won't be a moment." He did as told, and listened to her rummaging in the adjoining bathroom. The musty smell was replaced by that of aromatic cedar laced with a sharp chemical that, although familiar, he couldn't quite identify. She was soon beside him on the bed. Though fully clothed, she had loosened the buttons on her blouse, and he could vaguely make out a well-filled, purple colored silk bra.

"Now," she said in that mesmeric husky voice of hers, and he felt the gentle exhale of her breath on his cheek. They were about to kiss—it seemed like the natural order of things to Branning—but before he could indulge, a new spate of dizziness overcame him, his vision dimmed, and he blanked out.

It all had been carefully pre-orchestrated. Malaika had recognized his vulnerability the moment she'd set eyes on him. She'd had plenty of time to plan.

For her initial attack, the headache, she'd used one of her mother's techniques to send negative energy. But to truly incapacitate him, she'd needed a more modern, more clinical method. She'd carefully avoided divulging the fact that her ex-husband had been sent to prison for several years for selling illicit drugs, and that, since his recent release, he'd opened a tattoo parlor which provided the perfect cover for his resurrected drug business. Through him she acquired a drug that perfectly fitted her needs.

She'd told Branning only part of the truth concerning her relationship with her foster mother. They'd indeed become estranged, but had recently reconciled, and Malaika had found herself in a tight corner, possibly facing a stretch in prison, charged by the police for aiding and abetting a known criminal. Her ex, meanwhile, had distanced himself from her after whittling away her savings.

In the end, it was Mother who'd proved Malaika's salvation. A stint in prison, no matter how short, would have broken her. Mother not only put up the bail, she paid for one of the best lawyers in the city to defend her, though she never acknowledged this to Malaika who, in turn, surmised there was nobody else in her life of such means. Thanks to the adroit skills of the lawyer, Malaika was found not guilty.

Released from custody, she was free but alone with nowhere to go and no resources, and decided to visit her mother. She'd not seen Margaret for quite a while, and was shocked when she saw her at how much the woman had aged. Her mother, despite looking horribly frail, hugged her warmly and once again opened her heart and home to her. Malaika, in response, resolved to care for her mother to atone for her earlier indiscretions.

The day of the accident, a friend who had just had a baby had called for Malaika, the father having absconded. It was a mission of mercy. Her friend begged her to stay overnight, as she desperately needed somebody to talk to after all she'd been through. Malaika prepared everything so her mother wouldn't need to leave the house, but soon after Malaika left, Mother had set off for the store, even though she had no immediate need for milk or any other provisions. It was an automatic, almost reflexive, act. Perhaps she imagined Malaika, as usual, walking beside her. In truth, she simply couldn't break the pattern of their nightly walk together, since their reconciliation.

On Malaika's return, she had found the house empty and immediately called the police, who said an officer was already on his way to see her. When the patrol car arrived, not one but two somber looking police officers came to her door. "There's been an accident. I'm sorry to have to inform you that your mother is dead," the older of the two officers said respectfully.

After a period of anguish, her mourning gave way to the first inklings of anger, and its close cousin, revenge. The two women had been in the process of rediscovering themselves and their relationship as mother and daughter. Whoever had caused the accident had shattered the healing process, leaving it forever incomplete. The two police had provided only essential details, stressing it was an accident, reiterating several times that no one had been charged as, technically, no crime had been committed.

Clearly, there would be no justice from the police, Malaika concluded.

The story of the unusual "accident" worked its way through the community until it reached Tommy Ingle, the local convenience store owner. Tommy bore a natural hatred towards anyone not "local," and being an outspoken Communist, he had a particular hatred for capitalistic businessmen. In his store, alongside the rows of products he was selling (admittedly produced by the capitalist system he so reviled) were posters denouncing the bourgeois and hailing the virtuousness of proletariat. When he'd heard that a callous businessman from outside the neighborhood had mowed down poor old Margaret Ottman, it filled him further with hatred.

When Malaika visited his shop shortly after the death of her mother, Tommy "the Commie" Ingle met her with lowered eyes. Jaw thrust forward, his brawny hands clenched, he said, "I've heard on good authority that the clumsy bastard who killed your mother was more concerned with dusting himself off and getting on his way to some business appointment than for the condition of your dear mother. Some say they hear him curse her for getting in his way and delaying him. When the ambulance came, having been 'inconvenienced' enough," Tommy continued, "the man sped off in a taxi, doubtlessly to spend the time after his business meeting drinking cocktails, carousing and laughing with some freeloading capitalist friends and their whores about what happened to your mother." Unclenching his fists and looking Malaika in the eyes, he sighed a long sigh. "The police never do anything. They're under the control of the middle and upper classes. These so called 'respectable' businessmen are always above the law, while our prisons are crammed full of downtrodden, hard-working victims of the system like you and me." Tommy having vented his anger, Malaika left with a refrain replaying in her head: "No justice, no peace!" Perhaps they were the last words her dearly departed mother had thought. They certainly seemed apt.

When Branning's letter arrived, Malaika had initially dismissed it as patronizing and inadequate. On reconsideration, however, it opened up some possibilities. She had recently tried unsuccessfully to communicate through a medium with her mother's spirit and obtain more details of what had happened. Unfortunately the only spirits the medium seemed capable of getting in contact with was the bottle of gin Malaika had given her in prepayment.

As Malaika walked home from the failed séance, she noticed a piece of paper on the ground. Curious, she bent down and picked it up. It had one word written in what she could swear was her mother's handwriting. As she held the paper closer, a gust of wind released some raindrops clinging a sycamore tree high above her, which fell and soaked the paper, obscuring the word and whatever message it might have represented. When Malaika got home, she examined the sodden piece of paper, and eventually convinced herself of two things: First, the writing had definitely been in her mother's style, and second, whatever had been written on it had to have been the word *revenge*.

Branning awoke, reclined and naked on the bed, his chest stinging, his head once again throbbing, he could hear Malaika washing her hands in the bathroom. His mind was still fuzzy and he felt disorientated. He was having an acute problem remembering how exactly he'd come to be where he was, when Malaika walked in, and with a look in her eyes that completely unnerved him, commanded him to stand. He complied groggily, his legs barely able to support his weight.

"Now, get out of my house!" she yelled as loudly as she could.

"But my clothes..." he protested, desperately searching the room for them without avail.

"I burnt them," she hissed. "Leave! Now! Before..." she screamed, pointing an extended finger towards the door.

He was so shocked he couldn't move, so she pushed him roughly down the stairs and out the front door.

The cold evening air slapped him rudely back into full consciousness.

"Get hell out of here!" she shrieked. "And don't ever come back!"

Branning clamored down the front steps and started to run down the street in the general direction of his house. Pedestrians on both sides of the street eyed him incredulously as he streaked by.

At home, his wife had just returned from her pottery class, placed her latest creation on the table, and begun admiring the work, thinking what a nice surprise gift it would be for her husband, the front door bell rang, to be replaced a second later by urgent banging. As she placed her hand on the doorknob, she heard a loud groan, and opened the door.

Her naked husband stood there in the doorway, panting, fighting for breath, his face filled with pain and shame. In the center of his bare heaving chest was a massive tattoo which said, "*Murderer*" in delicate, expressive Gothic calligraphy. Below it was inscribed the date he'd knocked over and killed the old lady

Flight of Destiny

Fire and Brimstone

Rufus Symes woke in the middle of the night, eyes irritated and stinging, mouth dry and parched. Still in a semi-dreamlike state, he reached for a bedside lamp, switched it on, and clasped a glass of water. A mound of rolling naked female flesh by the name of Helga stirred on the other side of the bed. With the room illuminated, he noticed wisps of smoke seeping into the room from under the closed door. He mumbled several profanities, and forced himself to awaken while the acuteness of the situation slowly solidified in his muddled mind. Clambering out of bed, he yanked on some dirty clothes scattered on the floor. Stuffing his wallet, car keys, and mobile phone into a grubby bag, he yelled to Helga, "The place is on fire; it's going to go up like a tinder box," while double-checking to make certain he hadn't forgotten anything.

"Ze boys!" Helga said urgently, having failed to master the "th" sound in the English language. "We must set off ze alarm! We must save zem!"

"Do what you like," Symes replied callously, "but I'm getting the hell out of here!" Symes was the night warden, and, having been temporarily diverted by other matters, had failed to do his required late night rounds. He was now in the process of further shirking his duties, deserting his post, leaving the denizens of St. Benedict's Correctional School for Boys to the mercy of the fire. Hand on the doorknob, he turned to Helga and flashed a toothy grin. Helga, a young Danish Bible Society volunteer sent to the school to help redeem the many strayed souls, was sitting on the side of the bed, hauling her sizable underwear up trunk-like legs.

"See you, girl," Symes mumbled, slipping out the door, having wrapped his face in a dirty undershirt as a shield against the smoke. He ran down the hallway for the nearest building side exit.

Helga's mind was a confusion of hurt, fear, anger and bitterness. She'd arrived several months ago, and, thus far, had been unsuccessful in both her mission to save the dark souls of the wayward boys and her every attempt at improving her English.

Rufus Symes, a small ugly man with oily skin and a distinctive limp, which he used to his advantage whenever he wanted to extract sympathy, had instantly latched onto her, deeming her the only potential conquest in a remote country area with a dearth of female flesh, something which she had in abundance.

At first she resisted Symes' overtures. But he began filling her head with pitiful stories of his childhood, the difficulties of being shunted from one foster family to another, the incessant years of cruel bullying he had sustained because of his handicap. She listened, wide-eyed, her face wetting with tears. He plied her with story after story of rejection, ending with his being cast out and forced to fend for himself as a teenager alone in the back alleys of the nearest city. Coming from a sheltered background, Helga was eminently susceptible to such heart-wrenching stories, especially so, given she was suffering from acute homesickness. Symes knew exactly how to manipulate her, ending his sad tale shivering like a boy just pulled from an icy sea.

Helga wrapped her bulky arms around him like a protective mother trying to sooth a sorrowful child. Rufus, seizing the opportunity, started to gently caress then kiss her bare neck. The kisses, a new experience for the young woman of God, sent flutters of ecstasy coursing through her. All the stern warnings about the ways of men she had received in Denmark were forgotten in the explosion of passion Rufus' kisses unleashed, and, amply seduced, she slowly allowed herself to proceed further down the path leading to the sins of the flesh.

Once he had her hooked, he got her to drink some homemade hooch he kept stashed away for just such occasions. That night, giddy and carefree, caught up in the moment, a whole new world opened to Helga when she opened herself to Rufus. He did things to her that night she'd never imagined. She sensed that he hadn't the remotest love for her, but, helplessly swept along by the unforeseen wave of passion, she simply didn't want to stop, despite abhorring herself at the same time for what she knew she was doing. Later, around midnight, while Rufus slept the sleep of a man fulfilled, the stern eyes of the members of the Danish Bible Society appeared to poor Helga on the ceiling, staring down in anger and disgust at her. By two o'clock in the morning, she was wracked with uncontrollable guilt, though by the next night, she was starving for more and before long became a regular visitor to his bed.

When she managed to locate and put on the rest of her clothes, she rushed out of the warden's apartment, and shrieked up the stairs, "Fire! Fire!" Eyes burning, coughing uncontrollably, clutching the front of her dress to her nose, she headed towards the fire alarm, hastily read and reread the English instructions, then in frustration tried everything she could think of, finally activating it. It instantly began clanging so loud she had to put her hands to her ears and moved away

Dribs and drabs of boys began to appear at the upstairs landing, choking, cursing, and flaying the air to fight away billows of acrid smoke.

Reverend Doubty, the principal of the school, lived in a separate house along the driveway. The moment he heard the alarm, he slipped on his fisherman's sweater, some worn corduroy trousers, a pair of gumboots, and ran up the drive towards the school, which appeared to have sprouted two devilish smoky horns. As he barked out orders, the front door to the boy's domicile burst open and the house spewed out a pile of boys followed by a thick column of smoke, flashes of flame licking ominously within.

Several boys ran past him, crazed with fear, screaming wildly. The reverend, hearing one of the boys cursing hysterically, shouted above the melee, "Damn you, Heany, stop swearing! You know better than to take the Lord's name in vain," while he continued his approach to the building, now enveloped in flames.

Helga appeared in front of him, panting, her minimal nightclothes and hair disheveled, stinking of smoke, her face slick with smoke-blackened perspiration. The reverend stopped and stared, considering whether or not to ask for an explanation, ruing he'd come upon the one person who, due to her limited linguistic skills, was least likely to provide him much insight into what was happening. In deference to the situation, Reverend Doubty asked simply, "Have...you...seen... Symes?" adding parenthetically to himself, "The beastly man is supposed to be our fire officer."

Helga looked up at him blankly for a moment, then answered in the same sing-song manner the reverend had asked the question: "I... don't...know...Reverend Doubty," between breaths.

Furious, the reverend growled back, "Damn that man!" and made an urgent decision. Irrespective of where Symes was, someone needed to take matters in hand. He turned to the other members of staff gathering about him. "Matron," he said to an elderly lady in shawl and nightclothes holding a flame lamp in a shaking hand, "you set up a first aid area and care for the injured." Turning to the gardener, he ordered, "You, Hardgraves! Call the fire brigade. I will do a roll call and see to the boys."

While everyone sprang to their duties, flames began licking brightly at the outside of the building. An upstairs window exploded, belching out a dark plume of smoke. Several of the younger boys, spluttering and shivering in the cold night air, started sobbing. A few were crying in pain, some having sustained injuries from the fire, others terrified by the ensuing rout. Turning to those nearest him, the principal bawled out in booming voice, "Stop your blubbering and listen for your name!" Clipboard underarm, he marched officiously up and down the graveled road, yelling out names in alphabetical order: "Heany, Hudson, Jonstone, Krull, Maudlin, Noteworthy... Noteworthy?" Receiving no answer, he screamed louder, "NOTEWORTHY!" Jonathon Noteworthy was notably absent, perhaps a victim of the fire, but then again, just as likely the cause, given his history.

The boy had been sent to St. Benedict's following "a fire incident." He'd come home early from school one day and noticed a distinct smell of old fish. Looking about, he noticed a bloodstained striped apron, a white hat, an oiled sweater, a pair of heavy woolen trousers and two rubber boots scattered about the living room. Upstairs, he heard a repetitive thumping coming from his mother's bedroom. Running up the stairs three at a time, he burst into her bedroom, thinking somebody was attacking her. His eyes caught sight of Mr. Lucius Pike, the fishmonger, his thin sallow face with two tiny polka dot eyes, naked on top of his mother.

Mother and Pike looked at him with a mixture of surprise and guilt. His mother quickly pulled the bed sheets close about her, hoping for a modicum of modesty, which both she and Pike were unfortunately denied. Mrs. Noteworthy was a pretty widow, respected and desired by the men of the community, even occasionally courted by one. He was commonly known as "Fishface."

Pike climbed off of the bed, stood, pulled the tattered bed cover around his skinny body and backed away, while Noteworthy's mother hastily slipped a robe about her and tried to placate her son's obvious disgust. "Jonathon. Darling," she said in an awkward, apologetic voice. "Dearest…"

Pike offered a gawky smile.

Jonathon Noteworthy didn't say anything. His mind was working overtime. No wonder the family had had copious quantities of fish of late. He ran downstairs and burst into tears, reflecting on the treachery of what he'd just witnessed, while Pike stumbled down the stairs, slipped into his trousers, sweater and boots, and draped the bloody apron over his arm. "See you, Jonathon," he muttered, as he fled for the door.

Noteworthy ignored him. Though Pike quickly left, the stench of raw fish remained. At first Jonathon attributed the smell to Pike, but following his nose, he walked into the kitchen and discovered a newspaper bundle. Picking it up, a couple of pungent herrings fell out, no doubt, thought Jonathon, payment for the fishmonger having had his way with mother.

Staring at the fish, an idea suddenly came to him: Pike needed punishing. In kind.

Retribution came exactly two nights later, when Noteworthy broke into Pike's store and filled a large sack with every kind of pungent fish he could lay his hands on. Bass, eel, haddock, mackerel, mullet, sturgeon, turbot, it didn't matter. He dragged the sack to Pike's house and peeked into the man's living room window.

Pike was curled up asleep in his favorite chair pulled close to the hearth for warmth, a woolen blanket draped over his skinny legs, snoring loudly, while a television in the room announced the latest fishing news.

Noteworthy rummaged about outside, located a ladder left by some workmen, and climbed it, carrying the stuffed sack over his shoulder like a coal miner might carry a sack of coal onto Pike's roof, and then began dropping the fish, one by one, down the chimney. As the fish landed on the fire, the living room filled with acrid smoke and the mixed smell of raw and charred fish. Pike awoke when the sizzling fire made a loud pop and a glowing coal or piece of fish, it was difficult to tell which, leaped from the hearth onto the man's blanket. Several more pops and Pike's living room burst into flames.

A neighbor, awakened by the shrieks, noted a boy on Pike's roof trying desperately to stuff a huge halibut into the chimney. Twenty minutes later, Noteworthy was escorted off the roof by the fire brigade and dragged away by the police, while Pike was taken to the nearest hospital.

Though Pike was basically uninjured, the judge, who was a keen fisherman, sentenced the hapless boy to time in an "approved school," and St. Benedicts, known to accept the most unmanageable youths and make their lives hell, was chosen specifically for this reason.

The incident with the fish notwithstanding, Noteworthy was a sensitive boy of calm unassuming nature, who, as his mother had predicted in tears before the court, found it impossible to settle into his new surroundings.

The night of the school fire, he hadn't slept. He was feeling bitterly lonely, and undertook to visit the night warden to see if the man, who he'd as yet only seen from a distance, might show him some much needed sympathy. Noteworthy knocked nervously on the night warden's door, and, hearing inside a familiar thumping, vague groans, and distant cursing, jerked his hand back from the door.

Symes, commonly called "Slimes" or "Slimebag" by the inhabitants, eventually thrust open the door. "And what are you doing up at this hour, boy?" he asked, angry to have his tryst with Helga interrupted.

"Please, sir, I need to talk. I'm miserable lonely, sir. I miss my home and mother terribly," Jonathan said in his gentle voice, his eyes moist and desperate. Symes, carefully blocking any view the boy might have of the interior, cruelly aped Noteworthy's words in a blatantly sarcastic tone, while looking as if he'd swallowed a sour lemon. Then, in a sudden burst of action, Symes dashed at Noteworthy from behind the door like a tiger released from a trap, heaved the boy up by his pajama collar, and pinned him against the hallway wall.

Noteworthy flinched and turned his head away, his nose assaulted by the smell of stale liquor and unbrushed teeth.

"Let me down!" he squealed, trying desperately to shake loose from Symes' vice-like grip.

Symes dropped him to the ground, and limped back towards his apartment door. "Go back to bed, scum, and let that be a lesson," he muttered. "I don't take to sniveling wimps or prying eyes," he growled, slamming the door behind him, leaving Noteworthy in a heap on the floor.

Noteworthy started to cry, his tears slapping the wooden floorboards as he lumbered back to his room along the long drafty corridor in even more distress than before.

Later that night, Symes, having escaped the mayhem, drove up the hill and parked his car in a secluded place surrounded by trees. He opened the window and smoked a roll-up while savoring the sight of the school burning. He had little more than bitter hatred for the school and those incarcerated in it. In fact, he had pretty much equal hatred for the boys as they had for him. His anger had turned to outright rage when the inmates took to taunting him about his limp, the result of a case of mild childhood polio, the situation rekindling painful memories from his past.

At the foot of the hill, Reverend Doubty had begun chatting with the members of the fire brigade now that the fire was in the last moments of burning the building to the ground. He'd been appointed principal just last month of what was about to become little more than a pile of ashes and rubble, and worried about his future as he thought angrily of Symes.

He could vividly recall the day he hired the derelict. Despite the man's endeavors to appear zealous by memorizing, reciting and referencing passages of the old testament, Symes had failed to convince the scrupulous principal, who had felt reticent to hire the man in the first place. But, given the fact there were scarce takers for a night warden job in a school for delinquents, and that it would have been unchristian to not give a man with a limp a job, the principal had acquiesced.

Symes, still perched on the top of the hill, was finishing his cheroot when he heard some twigs snap, and saw a figure approach. He took a long draw and disdainfully flicked the ashes out the window.

It was Noteworthy.

"Oh, it's you," Symes said, yawning with relief.

"I did a terrible thing," Noteworthy blurted out, his face ashen white, his eyes looking fearfully to the heavens. "I…I set fire to the school!"

"That's a terrible thing, indeed, lad," said Symes, sarcastically, "though in my book, it might not be as bad as all that. Quite the contrary. There was nothing but scum in there. Scum like you." He flicked the stub of his cigarette out of the window at the boy. The stub bounced off the wretched boy, and Noteworthy lowered his head and hunched his shoulders, as if waiting for Symes to pass sentence.

"What will happen to me, do you think?" asked Noteworthy.

Symes replied with sadistic pleasure, "What will happen to you? You'll most likely either get sent to prison, or you'll spend the rest of your life in some mad house, I suspect. Either way, they'll likely throw away the key," he pronounced, chuckling.

But Noteworthy was not the hapless little boy he wished Symes to believe him to be. Indeed, he had a plan: He wouldn't have felt the need to torch the school if Symes hadn't been pounding a woman that night, which triggered the whole pyromaniacal incident. There were no fish at hand, so Noteworthy had had to be more prosaic this time. Recalling that the laundry chute ended just two doors down from Symes' room, he snuck into the kitchen and found not only matches, but a can of cooking oil. He poured the oil down the laundry shoot then set fire to a rag, which he calmly added.

"Now, if you've got any sense, boy, you'll take your scummy ass and run as far away from here as possible," Symes concluded, assuming that with this final exchange, he would see the last of all the reprobate boys.

Noteworthy, as predicted, trudged guiltily off into the darkness.

Symes took a swig from his pocket flask. Symes took a swig from his pocket flask. Soused by the alcohol, tired by his exertions, and envisaging a long journey yet before him in order to distance himself sufficiently from the school, he decided to take a short nap.

Noteworthy walked quickly and purposefully back to towards the school, his youthful mind re-tuning his vindictive plan. There would be questions to answer, and given his history, he would need a hard and fast alibi. He was mulling over the latter when spotted by the principal, Reverend Doubty, who was moving his conversation from the firemen to some waiting policemen.

The cleric called Jonathan over gruffly. "Noteworthy, where the hell have you been?"

Noteworthy, who had always felt intimidated by the reverend, succeeded with effort to remain calm and put on a not overdramatic performance that, in the end, proved quite convincing. He began by staring the reverend and policeman full in the eyes to fend off any thoughts they might be harboring about him having started the fire. "Sorry, sir. I had to escape. It was Mr. Symes. I saw him set fire to the building and feared for my life. He was like a mad man."

"Symes?" repeated the principal. The policemen narrowed their eyes and leaned closer to the boy, to take in what he was saying. "Where is Symes?" asked the principal and policemen in the same breath.

"Hiding in the woods, sir," answered Noteworthy, relishing the situation and deciding now was the time to push Symes further into the mire. "He's in his car on up on the hill. He was planning on leaving, but I think his drinking got the better of him."

The most senior of the policeman ordered several officers to apprehend Symes and bring the man to him for questioning.

When they returned with the man, the school was smoldering, the garish flames replaced by a forest of flashing police, fire and ambulance lights. People were talking into walkie-talkies and angry boys were casting accusatory remarks at each other while emergency medical staff tended to their injuries.

The school master, seeing Symes approach, yelled out the man's name, and the two policemen slipped their arms out from under the man's armpits. Symes teetered, shifting awkwardly from one leg to the other while offering the principal a ridiculous grin.

He was, as both the reverend and police duly noted, very, very drunk.

"Evening, Reverend Doubty," he slurred, the stench of alcohol on his fetid breath slamming into the principal the minute Sykes opened his mouth. "Th' Lord works in mysterious ways, don' yer think? It wouldn't surprise me if a few sinners burnt tonight," he chortled, winking at the reverend.

The rector grabbed the drunken man by the arm and said accusingly, "This boy says he saw you set fire to St. Benedict's."

Noteworthy added his accord by way of a nod.

Symes lurched forward as if to grab the youth, but stumbled and ended up laughing as if he were horsing around. Directing his bloodshot eyes in the general direction of the reverend's voice, he replied, "Surely, sir, you wouldn't believe this…this *juvenile delin… delin…delinquent's* word over mine?" His head lolled towards Noteworthy as he jabbed an accusatory finger. "This…this…bleeding arsonist was sent here because he…"

The principal stared strongly into Symes' eyes and demanded fiercely, "Where were *you* earlier tonight?"

Symes sighed, and a mischievous look crept over his face. "There's a simple explanation to that. Oh, yes, there is. I spent the evening in…*Bible* study…with the delightful Miss Helga Larson." Symes directed his eyes humbly downwards and stared at the gravel, his voice diminishing to that of a hushed whisper. "And there, I am ashamed to admit, she…she seduced me. Yes, Reverend, she did. The horny woman seduced me!" Symes lifted his mournful eyes to appraise the result of his "confession."

The reverend looked confused. He could picture Helga Larson smothering a man under her great weight, or baffling him with her lamentable English, but not seducing a runt of a weasel like Symes. The schoolmaster was nonetheless duty-bound to try to make sense of the muddled explanation, and cleared his throat. "Right. Yes. I shall speak to Miss Larson at once," he said, and he left Symes to hunt down the woman.

Symes was counting on the fact that Noteworthy's accusations would, in the end, be dismissed out-of-hand. Who would accept the word of a delinquent with a past history of arson? Helga would have to back him up, as an up-to-recently pure young girl, sent by a Bible Society and weighted down with guilt would feel obligated to do. He was also counting on her having felt a certain love for him, her "first," though, of course, it wouldn't ever be reciprocated. In short, he was fully convinced she would exonerate him. Still, he felt a bit twitchy, watching the schoolmaster march away engrossed in a deep conversation with two policemen. Two other policeman remained, one on each side of Symes, alert and watchful.

Helga was attending to a boy's wounds when the reverend and policemen approached. "I'm sorry, miss, but we've a few questions we need to ask you," the first police officer said.

"Yes?" she answered hesitantly, shooing the bandaged boy off with a cherubic smile.

The other policeman pointed at Symes in the distance. "I presume you know this man? The night warden, Mr. Symes?"

Helga looked nervously from one policeman to the other, her eyes finally settling on the stern-looking rector.

"Have you had carnal intercourse with him? Were you with him tonight?" the principal asked, not mincing words.

An awkward silence followed during which Helga gave her secular and spiritual superior a deeply wounded look, as if in answering his question, her honor would be severely damaged. "Meester who?" she asked sweetly, a lost look on her face.

"Meester...I mean Mister Symes," repeated the reverend irritably.

Helga seemed to be thinking, then slowly shook her head in the negative. "I know *of* him, ov course, but 'ave no eenterest in 'knowing' zee man further," she said, glancing a second time at the man standing in the distance. "'Ee appears a most ungodly creature," she added sanctimoniously.

"Of course, of course. It is as we all thought," the leader of the school said to the two policemen. "My sincerest apologies for having to ask so indelicate a question." Finished, he led the threesome back to where Symes was waiting. Noteworthy, in the meantime, joined Helga, a self-satisfied smile appearing on both's lips as they watched the two policemen escort Symes towards the waiting police van.

Cast from Hell

Part 1 - Descent into Hell

There it was: I was to be banished from hell.

There had been little reason given for this action. Indeed those in authority hadn't gone into any detail. Maybe I was too good for hell; it was inconceivable I was too bad. In the end, I was simply to be cast out, and there was nothing I could do.

They had a plan, of course. They were going to exchange my soul for another person's. I couldn't return to my old body. It was totally destroyed. A particularly unpleasant car crash had seen to that, and what few remains were left were long buried in the cold ground. My soul, I discovered, was to enter the body of a woman who, at this moment, was in a coma. It was their general policy to handle returns this way.

I wasn't sure how I felt about being re-integrated into the world, but the idea of being a woman had a certain appeal. Ripples of anticipation kept running through my re-energized soul. I was put through some kind of "re-entry" training, mostly involving learning how to be Miranda Styles. I wasn't sure I liked the name, but, again, I had no choice in the matter.

I had died a man of forty-five and was returning in the body of a twenty-five-year-old female. What's more, she had quite a pleasing body, and a pretty face that had, no doubt, turned a few men's heads. Of course, in the hospital where she was now resting with tubes threaded into and wires attached to her defunct body, she didn't look it. In fact, she looked grotesquely sub-human and would remain so until my arrival.

As I scanned her life-file, I noted she hadn't had many lovers. She'd been prudent to the point of being "almost" virginal. This would, of course, have to change. I was on a remit from hell. Once solidly in her body, she/I would come out of the coma, and I would implement some drastic changes, promiscuity definitely being one of them.

Her wardrobe was also going to have to change; I planned to make her a heart-breaker. I would have to shorten her skirts. And all that adolescent horseback riding stuff about which she seemed obsessed, an obvious diversion from her lack of sexual activity, would have to change. I've always despised the hefty four-legged animals. Thankfully, there wasn't any indication of a current boyfriend to complicate matters. In summary, all the signs looked promising, and once the denizens of Hell judged me up to the mission, I would be ensconced in my new body and could immediately go about creating merry pandemonium. Life would be one big kamikaze dive for Miss Styles.

Studying further her habits and demeanor, Miranda appeared to me to be a little too demure, some might go so far as to say as dry as dust. I would make her more care-free, almost shallow. Oh, and when I took over, she would develop more of an interest in alcohol. I couldn't bear to go through another life being abstemious like she was. It would be too dull. Party, party, party! That would be the new order of things, and I would make certain she was introduced to the pleasures of drugs to help perk things up even more.

It was going to be fun shocking her parents. Watching them fuss over her comatose body every day was lamentable, given that throughout her life they'd clearly cramped her style. They'd sucked the spontaneity from her like energy-parasites. With my plans for their daughter, they would be in for a wild ride. Of course, they would put this marked change down to the riding accident or the coma or both, when, in fact, it would be me, sent up from Hell, pulling her strings. I delighted at the thought.

My adventure rejoining the human race was temporarily put on hold while a few medical and logistical problems were addressed. While the sudden wait was infuriating, it provided me time to further consider my new, upcoming physical existence. For example, where would I reside? Dreary Miranda had lived in a sleepy town in the country. By my reckoning, it was time for her to move to a big city, maybe even the capital. There would be more men to prey on and unlimited opportunities to distance myself from her staid parents. Her life, or rather my life, was going to be spiced up beyond recognition.

I would, of course, have to bide my time through the obligate period of "rehabilitation." No one wakes from a coma, gets up and begins living a libertine life. I would have to visit doctors and neuro-psychologists. It would take some time before I could let completely loose, weave my evil magic and wreak hell back among the living.

Existing in hell amidst the fallen angels, some of the sickest souls who ever existed in Christendom, had been grueling, to say the least. Lucifer, the so-called Prince of Darkness, for example, proved to be a total letdown. The centuries had worn him down, and he had an irritating habit of droning on and on about the "good old days." He didn't possess the charm I had anticipated, or command the fear for which he was notorious. Okay, he was still trying to mess up the world to get back at God, but he had become bereft of ideas as to how to accomplish this, to the point of lacking any originality. Lucifer's mind dwelled constantly on religious wars. He was still pinning his hopes on igniting religious hatred, polarizing nations, waiting to the perfect moment when total chaos would reign and he could   step in. I had imagined him in strict control of all his minions, sending them about on virulently destructive missions, infiltrating them into positions of power and influence as heads of huge multi-national corporations, for example, but, no, he'd given up on this strategy. He just couldn't be bothered.

In the Middle Ages he'd been at his peak, his heyday, slugging it out with God for souls. In those days he warranted respect. He was feared. He kept society in check. He actually served a function. You couldn't afford to be sent to that correctional place known as "Hell" because you'd pay for your sins with eternal damnation in a pit of fire and brimstone, left there to agonize through endless inventive tortures. These days, the world's leaders had usurped his job with their ineptness, lies, greed and monetarily-advantageous wars. This, allied with natural disasters, hurricanes, earthquakes, food shortages and environmental degradation resulted in increasingly destructive world epidemics that were recreating Hell on earth. Lucifer didn't have to do anything anymore and had grown lazy in his ways. He'd become insipid. He no longer had to conjure up evil, that task being performed daily for him by literally millions of mortals. The world, at the same time, had become more informed, more educated, more pragmatic. There were so many disgruntled disbelievers, some even dared to call him and the Great One a sham, and Heaven and Hell just another cock-and-bull story.

Hell's merchandise still went up for sale every year around the thirty-first of October, but Satan himself had been trivialized, cheapened, and was no longer taken seriously. Even the churches were detaching themselves from him. Whereas in the past, he'd been used as a rod to beat people back into their places, now he was largely ignored. As you can tell, my expectations of hell were quickly dashed when I arrived there. It was far removed from William Blake's famed illustrations of *Dante's Inferno*, and it didn't even remotely resemble a Brueghel painting.

To my surprise, there was no evidence in Hell of people being grievously punished. The slothful were not being goaded with burning coals. The gluttons were not being tormented with thirst and hunger. There were no hedonists being bathed in burning pitch and stinking brimstone, or envious individuals howling with grief over that which they could never possess. The proud were not being brought down. The covetous were not being denied. In fact, the damned seemed to be living in a modicum of comfort. I never detected any weeping, wailing or gnashing of teeth. The place, called by some *gehenna*, the bottomless pit, was admittedly no holiday camp, but things there had grown shoddy and dysfunctional. It would require major rehabilitation to scare even a child. Being lodged with fellow rejects was sobering experience, not unlike being in a holding center for suspected criminals, refugees or illegal immigrants. And despite all this, the sad truth was that *I hadn't made the grade.* I was one of the unwanted, a fence sitter, existing nowhere between two divides.

To be sure, there were others in a similar situation. The Savage brothers, for example: Delinquents from the moment the twins were born. Expelled from schools, abhorred by society, generally hated and feared. Thinking with their fists, addicted to violence, bad-mouthing judges, they never had any respect for authority. Portrayed as antisocial monsters, they were really little more than petty thieves, abusers of alcohol and drugs, cruel womanizers, modern-day Neanderthals.

In their forties, the two actually started to mellow out, seeing their lives in a different light. Both started doing charity work, lecturing *pro bono* at youth clubs on weekday nights about the perils of drugs, teaching kids to recognize right from wrong and not to go down the route to perdition. In the end, they didn't live up to their name, and, falling well short of Hell's minimum requirements, they became, like me, part of the rejected. Placed alongside Nazi war criminals or tainted Cardinals, they were light weights, almost squeaky clean.

I'd tried to put forward my case before the hierarchy of hell, mostly for my own self-esteem, not that I really wanted to hang around, the tedium was getting to me. As it turned out, I simply wasn't sufficiently evil in their minds to warrant consideration. I had been a bit unruly in my youth, sampling drugs, partying and drinking to excess, but I'd never done anyone other than myself much harm. If anything, I'd let the people around me down. I cheated on a wife or two, but in these modern times, who doesn't? Cheating in marriage was half-expected. I learned to feed off people, trick them out of their savings, but that was because of my job, working for an insurance firm. What I did may have been bad, but it wasn't sufficiently illegal or immoral. Quite simply Hell didn't want me.

Part 2 - Descent from Hell

My wait was finally up; a minor minion visited and instructed me to make my final preparations to return to humanity in the form of Miranda Styles. Shortly afterwards, I was placed in Charon's hands. It was his responsibility to counsel arriving and departing souls.

Charon, an irascible old timer with snow white hair and fiery eyes, advised that it might take some time for me to get used to being human again. He warned that initially I was likely to experience strange physical and psychological sensations.

"Yes," I replied, fidgeting with excitement, my head at this point overcharged with short skirts, rampant sex, and a life full of indulgence, all of which I could barely wait to initiate. Charon looked at me irately, indignant that I wasn't taking heed of his guidance the way he would have liked. After he had finished the briefing, never fond of loiterers, he gruffly bade me farewell. At last it was time to go.

It looked like a vast airport terminal: vacuous, tedious, humdrum. By contrast, I have often tried to imagine Heaven. To me it would be one long party in a great vivant night club, not unlike the second life to which I was now looking forward. At Charon's command, I closed my inner eye as instructed and waited while he transported me to earth's dimension.

Though I'd prepared extensively for the moment, it felt...odd...

entering my new body. The female body lying on the bed felt light, airy, invigorating. I felt a heart beating, pumping life throughout me. I touched my thigh. It was softer than I imagined, and as I did, I became conscious of a man dozing in a chair across the room. Initially I thought it might be an overly dedicated doctor, or perhaps a male nurse, catching a moment of unauthorized sleep. Then it occurred to me this was my/her father.

Through my grogginess, I made out another figure, a skinny-looking woman leaning over the bed rail, staring at me through thick, heavy-rimmed glasses that made her eyes appear large and frog-like. Her skin was pale. Her face, caked in makeup, was smudged and blighted by tears. Doubtlessly the strain of my condition had taken its toll on this woman. My immediate impression was that she resembled a gaudy, bedraggled drag queen. Her trembling lips were overly red and fixed in a quixotic smile in celebration of the miracle that was happening before her eyes: Her precious daughter was returning to consciousness. I opened my eyes slightly wider, and, looking down at the bed, tried to make more sense of the body I had inherited. I could see two generous peaks, gently rising and falling in cadence to my breathing. Then I caught a side glimpse of myself in the room mirror. I was beautiful, even in my sickly state.

"Miranda! Miranda!" my new mother called out in a shrill hysterical voice. "You've come back to us! Harry! Wake up! Our daughter's returned!" My new father snorted and awakened with a jolt. They'd spent monotonous hours staring at their near-lifeless daughter, and now…

A doctor immediately appeared in a pristine white coat, and gently pushed my mother aside. Flashing a light first in one, then another of my eyes, he declared soothingly, "She's going to pull through after all!"

My future life beckoned, but, as ordered, I showed restraint. I still had to blend into Miranda Styles. Given her personality, there *had* to be a gentle evolution or people would question her return, and this might present problems. I blinked my eyes and gave a quick glance at the three faces beaming down at me. Having made certain that they fully believed I had come out of my coma, I re-closed my eyes and slept. After that, refreshed in mind and spirit, I stayed awake for longer and longer periods, during which I was careful to respond, Miranda-style, to the doctors, nurses and my parents. After a time, I decided to start using my voice. I was well versed in the phrases Miranda commonly used. It would only be fair to say that I had direct access to her personality in our shared mind, a personality that I would soon discard.

When my condition had been deemed by the doctors as "much improved," I knuckled down to fully ensconcing myself into my new body, attentively working the escalating rehabilitation program, enjoying watching everyone rejoice in each and every one of my successes. A handsome young physical therapist, fresh out of school, said my recovery was "remarkable." In fact, I was looking forward expectantly to the day when I could leave the hospital. In the meantime, I needed to continue re-experiencing the world through my "new" senses. Soon I would be "well enough" to walk about entirely on my own. The thought occurred to me that at that point, I should exchange my simple hospital gown for more sophisticated women's clothes. I would also have to deal with other impending womanly things, like the powerful mood swings that seemed to sweep over me, and, of course, my period. I would have to shield my thoughts from others more carefully than I had before, and learn to employ new, more "feminine" communication strategies. In short, I would need to learn how to lure the right men to me while discouraging undesirables. Hopefully these "adjustments" would continue to be instinctive and run smoothly. The moment I started to walk on my own, at first with an admittedly labored shuffle, I noticed men's heads begin following me. They seemed to be watching me with hungry, feral looks, grinning and whispering under their breath in a conspiratorial manner.

While in the hospital, I developed a flirtatious relationship with a porter, a good-looking cocky youth with peroxide blond hair. He had a girlfriend, also a hospital employee. The resulting gossip caused a highly charged shiver to run through the otherwise sterile hospital. When the youth told me he'd split up with his girlfriend on account of me, I rejoiced at how effortlessly I'd ruptured their relationship. I hoped it would take the broken-hearted girl as long a time to recover as it had me when, in my previous existence, my first love broke up with me.

When it was time for me to leave the hospital, the porter scribbled his number on a cigarette packet and snuck it into my hand. Would I *please* call him, he urgently implored. I said I would, of course, and flashed him the sweetest of smiles, but in reality he didn't have a chance in Hell. Everything thus far was a learning game for me to test my powers and enjoy a bit of mischievous fun.

Back "home," my mind was operating in full force, though my body was still struggling with the changeover. After a brief time, however, I was able to delight in the feline way I could move and learned how to best exploit my lithe body. I spent time dancing by myself in front of a mirror. Miranda's taste in music was ghastly conservative, but I found one track I could gyrate to while running my hands up and down my upper torso, continuing to explore my feminine facets while allowing my masculine aspects to be ebbed away. After spending hours of mind-numbing remedial therapy with one after another therapist, as well as countless tedious weekends with my parents, who were constantly fretting over me, I was judged sufficiently fit to return to the boring job Miranda had had before the accident. I worked diligently for several weeks waiting for the right moment, then quietly handed in my notice and made hasty preparations to leave the nest and head *post haste* to the capital.

My parents protested vehemently. They talked endlessly of the dangers of the big city with all its temptations and pitfalls, but that, of course, only spurred me on. I was young and innocent their eyes, and they were cautious conservative people, who'd lived ordinary, uneventful lives and were satisfied with their meager existence. That definitely wasn't on the cards for the "new" Miranda.

Though Miranda's work qualifications and prosaic resume fell well short of what most employers considered "minimum," I applied to join a major law firm as a personal assistant. To address my shortcomings, for my interview, I chose the shortest figure-hugging skirt I could purchase, and used all of my newly acquired feminine charms to their full effect on the male interviewer. He was surprisingly easily manipulated and even more eager than me for me to start. Working as a legal secretary made my life much easier. I immediately upgraded my confined studio apartment to a more spacious one with a view of the city and all its bright lights.

On my first actual day of work, my interviewer introduced me to the newest member of the law firm, the lawyer who I would be working under. As I entered his office, he was arranging his desk. I noted immediately the photo in a sterling silver frame on his desk of a young woman, her eyes looking adoringly at him while she proudly held a cherubic looking daughter in her arms. While describing to me my secretarial duties, I took in his attractive face, cultivated voice, and confident demeanor. Looking again at the photograph on his desk, the temptation to test his fidelity was simply too hard to resist.

In fact, everything about my new job proved temptingly exciting. I had my own desk and work area just outside his office, and the kind of work he and the company were involved in was promising. As he explained, "Our company services important clients: writers, film stars, celebrated musicians. At times, I'll expect you to entertain them while I attend to their legal needs. You know, bring them drinks, snacks…make them feel comfortable." I felt confident that I could do this well, and, further, that he and I would work well together. I had finally arrived in the glamorous world I craved, a world in which the previous Miranda would surely have been completely out of her depth.

To further augment my financial situation, I took on a flat mate, a party animal who was constantly inviting me to join her. I uniformly declined, however, devoting all my attention to securing my job by seducing my boss. That is, until she began inviting me to embassy parties and fashion launches. Such functions well fitted my desired life style. I also learned from accompanying her, that women often hunted in packs. It gave them more options.

At my second diplomatic function, I spotted a young French business student visiting on an internship either shamelessly networking, flirting or both. I watched him chatting with a better-than-average-looking American girl who was going to great lengths to keep his attention. The moment he noticed me, he stopped conversing with her, excused himself, and headed directly towards me.

We established an immediate rapport, much to the consternation of the American woman I'd diverted his attention from. I could see in

Francis H. Powell

his eyes that my Gaelic admirer had me down as fresh meat, far more promising than the crestfallen American he'd abandoned. Our repartee flowed as freely as the unending cocktails, and in the shortest of time we were well on the way to getting both well acquainted and extremely drunk. During the course of the evening, I casually made it known how I wanted the night to end. I'd chosen him to be my first lover. He was witty, cordial, fresh-faced, and a few years younger than me. He hailed from a rich family with connections, hence his invitation to this lavish event.

We left together in a taxi to his house in an exclusive neighborhood. Our drunken sex proved disappointingly mechanical, but, at the same time, it was sex as I'd never experienced it before: sex from an entirely different perspective, namely that of a woman. As a man, I'd often wondered what it was like for a woman, but was totally unprepared for the reality.

The morning after was awkward. We were both suffering from our night of alcoholic and physical overindulgence. Neither of us had much to say to the other, him due to his youthfulness, and me because I was still getting acquainted with all that my new gender role involved. I unenthusiastically logged his number into my mobile phone, at the same time noting that I'd received fifteen messages, twelve from my fussing parents, who had called hourly throughout the evening, night and early morning, no doubt wracked with worry for my nocturnal welfare, heightened further by my not answering their calls. The calls started to niggle me. What were my parents to me, really? Despite their kind ministrations, we had had time to develop only the most tenuous of bonds: They had provided me with a body, but for all intensive purposes their real daughter had exited the moment my soul replaced hers. The rest of my messages were from my roommate, presumably curious about what had happened to me, as I had slipped away from the party without saying farewell.

As I exited my conquest's house and closed the door behind me, I felt a mixture of relief and...hollowness. Relief because I'd accomplished my first sexual experience as a woman, hollowness because something within me felt incomplete. That something nagged at the back of my mind while I caught a taxi and headed back to my flat. Whatever it was, it was of an urgent nature. Later, at home, it came to me. Not wanting to countenance a *petit bébé*, I apprehensively asked my flatmate if she happened to have a spare "morning-after pill." This was new territory for me, but, I realized, a necessary part of being the kind of woman I wanted to be. She immediately reached into her handbag, withdrew her personal "emergency pill" and handed it to me. My mind now at rest, we sat together at the foot of her bed recounting each's last-night experience, talking, laughing, and giggling frivolously until we both became light-headed.

As we talked, inhibitions loosened, and my roommate beckoned me to join her under the *duvet*. As she was in her bra and knickers, it seemed logical for me to take off yesterday's party clothes, leaving us nearly naked together. We both, I think, felt a rapidly growing empathy. Her bra, I noted, was gossamer thin and transparent, displaying angular sharpish breasts. Her nipples were the color of dark cherries, and unnaturally prominent like the rubber teat of a modern baby bottle. At various times while we gossiped, they became alert and fulsome. Though she wasn't stunningly beautiful, she had a pleasantly open personality, and her pert body glowed with youthful vibrancy. Her scent was that of lilies and almonds. Her skin was as white as marble; in fact, she could have passed for a living statue. Her bellybutton was neat and compact. When she innocently rested a hand on my thigh, a shudder of excitement ran though me, something far stronger than I had experienced during the previous night with my French youth who I had already relegated to the back of my mind. Parts of the old me and the new me began wrestling in my head. The old masculine me would have unreservedly leapt on her. The new feminine me held back. I was no less desirous of her, but my desire was more reflective and no longer driven by male testosterone. Instead of acting, I reflected on how she would react to a kiss from me. Her liquid eyes suggested favorably, despite all the parties and her constantly saying how she was "on the prowl" for another male intrigue. A single kiss with her would have carried more weight than all the meaningless ones I'd shared with the French youth. Confused, I excused myself and slipped out her room.

That night, after careful reflection, I concluded this wasn't the time in my life to explore further the intricacies of what could only lead to same-sex love. Too complicated, I told myself. Besides, my thoughts of her were soon overshadowed by stronger ones concerning my new boss, thoughts that had been lurking in the back of my mind ever since I met him. Now *here* was a highly desirable forbidden fruit I could wrap myself around. After little more than a week together, he'd begun working me harder, more like an associate than an assistant. In between the long hours of work, there were moments when I noticed his eyes surreptitiously taking in my physique. In such moments, I was certain his mind was filled with wanton lust, kept barely in tow by his dedication to wife and family and his professional code of conduct. When important clients were present, he seemed to like showing me off, as if proud of me, like he might a gilded trophy or award, often displaying the behavior a man might adopt when introducing his fiancé. At the same time, I sensed he was pleased with my work. In return, I made myself always "at his disposal," putting in many extra hours. It was one thing being his loyal assistant, and quite another moving things further along in terms of a physical relationship.

I found my mind slowly becoming dominated by the sexual tensions created by our constant proximity and increasingly close interactions. We both knew we were waiting for the inevitable, punishing ourselves in the meantime by not acting on our constantly building desires. Whenever the situation got the better of me, I would call the young Frenchman, and re-engage him in order to exorcise my sexual frustrations.

In the meantime, to make matters even more complicated, my feelings for my flatmate continued to grow. When alone together, which seemed to happen increasingly often, we would fall into talking about anything and everything. We discovered we shared a similar philosophy of life, combined with a matching wry sense of humor. We both held the attitude men were to be used and abused. We "connected" emotionally and came to relish one another's company. We were also both unashamedly tactile. However, soon, not only our relationship but also that with my Frenchman would be swept into further confusion by an unanticipated turn of events.

Late one afternoon, word began circulating that the legal firm was planning a surprise party for their newly invested partner, my boss, to celebrate his elevated position. The remainder of the afternoon, champagne flowed and fancy *hors d'oeuvres* circulated around our section on silver platters held by dapper young waiters in sleek formal attire. The mood was celebratory and relaxed. At five o'clock the party was still going strong and my boss called me aside. He told me he needed to meet with me in his office, offering no reason. Due to a heady consumption of alcohol, nobody really noticed when we slipped away from the party, he first, with me following several minutes later.

I was curious. There was no work I knew of, no pending business that we needed to discuss, and technically the working day was over, which opened up an intriguing possibility. On my way to his office I stopped at the nearest woman's room, made a few adjustments to my appearance, and sprayed a bit of perfume on my neck and wrists, then quietly joined him.

He was sitting in his leather chair behind his desk attending to some papers, but his tie was loosened. It was obvious to me that he was not focused on any work, he was simply waiting for me.

He looked up from the papers and stared at me while I stood in the doorway. He put down his pen and walked over to me, extending a hand to direct me across the office, not to the secretarial seat next to his desk that I was accustomed to occupying, but to a black leather sofa he used when entertaining clients. I glanced around the office, and noticed an important idiosyncrasy: the photo of his wife and child, usually the centerpiece of his desk, was lying face downwards. He stood in front of me, and tugged at his tie, which I proceeded to free from his shirt. No words were needed or spoken. He began unbuttoning his shirt almost casually. I finished unbuttoning him, and in the next moment, our bodies were entwined. We somehow ended up on the carpet, such was the power of our lovemaking. Outside the office, sounds of laughter and party chatter slowly grew as one after another champagne bottle popped. Muffled peals of laughter soon mixed with the surreal sound of unanswered telephones ringing in the background.

After the tornado-like whirlwind of physical activity had passed, I was again left feeling disappointed. At the bare minimum, I'd expected a flow of post-coital chatter, not necessarily professing exclusive undying love for me, not yet anyway, but at least voicing some reassuring compliments on my physique, or a bit of tenderness, and to be held in his arms for a few precious moments. None were forthcoming. Instead, he quickly dislodged himself from me, as if he'd completed another work task rather than an act of love.

We dressed in silence, each putting on our own clothes as might two people after a workout in a pool or gym. Finished, he tightened and straightened his tie, then walked across the office room to return to the party, curtly wishing me on his way out a terse goodnight. It didn't matter. We both knew our relationship had changed.

I, for one, was going to use it to my advantage. I would make certain he would never forget this moment. I would milk it, develop it, even flaunt it if necessary to make certain he wouldn't be able to explain it away later as a "momentary indiscretion," like my roommate said married men often did. Moreover, I was not just going to hold him accountable for what had happened, but was determined to derive yet more benefit and pleasure from it.

The next workday began like every other. After calling me into his private office, he systematically reeled off the various day's tasks he wanted me to do. At first, I felt flustered, even annoyed, that he hadn't once commented on last night's liaison. Instead, he acted as if nothing had happened. I left his office bitter and angry, but once back at the safety of my desk, I decided to seize the moment and remind him.

I walked directly back into his office, leaving the door slightly ajar, making the danger of anyone outside seeing or overhearing what was going on the spark for what was to come. He was on the phone, reviewing the details of a contract with a client, and was, I felt, purposefully ignoring me; I could hear large sums of money being bandied about.

I moved to the center of his inner sanctum and started gyrating as if dancing to some inaudible music. The moment his eyes shifted towards me, I locked mine onto his and smiled. His first reaction was shock, but I could already see his interest shifting from the phone call to me. He squirmed awkwardly in his chair, then tried unsuccessfully to re-establish his composure. My actions were having their desired effect.

While he continued talking distractedly to his client, I peeled off my tight sweater, displaying my newly acquired transparent bra. If anyone had walked into his office now, he would have been in a most compromising position. My job would also be on the line, but that was of no matter to me at this moment. My clothes fell onto the carpeted floor in one after another dramatic flourish. He began stuttering as I began revealing bare flesh.

"Ah...something's come up. I'll call you back later," he said to his client, then slammed down the phone and raced to the door, closing and locking it with urgency. No one outside his office had been party to my thrill-seeking game, but my gamble had paid off, as, in an instant, we were once again writhing on the floor in a repeat of the evening before. I knew that moment I had taken full possession of my new power, and he was mine to toy with.

In my capacity as his personal secretary, I was responsible for answering all his incoming calls. His wife called, without fail, every day, and she and I became familiar with each other's voice. That evening they had made arrangements to go to dinner together, just the two of them, and he was running late, so I did my duty and entertained her while he finished his work.

Flight of Destiny

She wasn't really anything special as far as looks were concerned. In fact, she had an overlong face, with a prominent jaw, gawking eyes and a full mane of blond hair. From just a short conversation with her, I ascertained she was the kind of wife any sensible man would choose: reliable, organized, and assured. Indeed, just the sort of wife who could be counted on to accompany her husband to dinner parties and events frequented by people of influence. Her look was that of sensible cardigans, flowery patterned skirts, all well below the knee, a silk scarf around her neck, a liberal spray of Channel perfume. She was the type of mother who would delight in watching her child put her mount through it's paces at her first equestrian *gymkhana*. Her laugh annoyed me no end. It had a shrill edge to it and sounded forced rather than natural. Even my boss, her husband, winced ever so slightly whenever she laughed. Understandably, this evening, he appeared edgy.

I was careful to speak and act within the strict boundaries of an office secretary, but in my mind I was replaying the lurid encounter I'd had earlier that day with her husband in the very room in which we three now stood. I couldn't see how he could actually desire this plain Jane, this horsy-looking country type, and it seemed little wonder to me now that he'd so willingly engaged in an affair with me, if nothing else, to add spice to what must be an otherwise dull life.

My eyes darted expectantly from her to him and back to her as I listened to them converse in the abbreviated, somewhat stilted fashion typical of married couples. I tried, but couldn't imagine them engaged in sex; they were too incongruous. She looked much more glamorous in the photograph on his desk. No doubt she'd had her hair and makeup done specially for the photo, and chosen a photographer who excelled in conjuring up a flattering but misleading portrait, I thought venomously. His unsuspecting wife to me was not a rival, but more of a lame competitor.

I wished them good night, adding something trivial and banal like, "Have a nice evening," in a sickly-sweet voice of which I had never imagined myself capable.

She, in turn, acknowledged me as an aside, and, when they'd left the room, I immediately called my French lover from my desk phone. We hadn't met for a while, but I ventured he and I would have a far more rousing evening than my boss would have dining with his inert wife. My Frenchman was in and available, but, he said, it had to be at my flat. No problem. When we'd finished our very noisy lovemaking and I'd seen him on his way, I shifted my attentions to least partially compensating my inconvenienced flatmate by walking into her room and nestling platonically up to her. Such tenderness had become an nighttime ritual. We no longer reveled just in repartee; we each found a special kind of solace curled against the other's warm body. It wasn't uncommon for us to drift off to sleep in each other's arms.

I awoke the next morning in her embrace after a particularly satisfying sleep, and remained there, suffused with contentment, until she woke. She smiled warmly at me, then got up and made breakfast, saying over coffee, "I don't like that French friend. I'd rather you didn't invite him to come by again."

"Why? What's wrong with him?" I asked, taken aback.

"I don't think it's good for you to keep seeing him," was all she would venture, remaining evasive. We had become close friends, almost a couple, and I sensed in her words an air of possessiveness, making such behavior by my Gaelic charmer, *mon loup,* a nuisance, perhaps even an irritant to her. Taking her evasion as an invitation to share more, I filled her in about my affair with my boss. To my surprise, she seemed to find what I told her first distasteful and later excruciatingly painful.

From that day on, a growing tension began to permeate our apartment, punctuated by waves of despondency which manifested in her aloofness each time I went out. At the same time, she was becoming the only person in the world I had genuine feelings towards. Everyone else, including my boss, seemed superficial. Despite our problems, I still relished sharing our day's adventures and experiences in one another's bed at night. A perfect evening was talking together while sharing a bottle of wine, listening to music, and drifting off into sleep in each's embrace.

Several days later, my boss called me into his office. He looked apprehensive. I had a feeling he was harboring an important announcement, and sensed it wasn't going to be something I would like. He told me that last night he'd had a talk with his wife "about us." I had come to suspect that he was the type that might crack under the weight of an affair. He had too soft an underbelly. I'd seen him once sobbing after his mother called to say that his old nanny, who no doubt had pampered him during his halcyonic childhood, had passed away. He couldn't, he said, continue our affair. He called it "deceitful" and "sordid," words which I assumed had come directly from his wife's mouth. This from the man who I had witnessed joining the firm and slowly becoming a willing party to its corruption. I was fully aware that he had, on several occasions, not only prompted his rich and celebrated clients to fabricate evidence, but also pocketed some of the money for himself, strictly off the books, when deals were completed. So rather than deal with his guilt, he'd decided to play the "good husband," even though it was obvious that the man no longer had a single moral bone in his body!

I assumed he'd likely next fabricate a reason to terminate my employment; however, to my surprise, he called me into his office the next day and told me he needed an anniversary present for his wife and would I go and purchase one for him to give her. Apparently, he'd relegated yesterday's admission and me to history, and now wanted me to serve as a co-conspirator to help him save his marital face. He gave me the address of an expensive jeweler and told me to buy the most lavish bracelet I could find, then purchase a suitable card and bottle of champagne. He gave me an indecent amount of money, saying collusively that I should keep whatever money was left over. The request gave me an idea.

I set off to fulfill his demand but instead of going to the jeweler he mentioned, I went to a department store and bought a cheap, "on sale" bracelet which would give away its value to any observant woman on close examination. I had it lavishly wrapped, then bought a prosaic card and a reasonably priced bottle of champagne, and with the rest of the money, plane tickets for myself and my flatmate to Amsterdam, planning for our first ever cocaine binge. My boss never once brought up the cheap gifts I'd bought and more significantly the fact that I had pocketed most of the money.

Now that I felt avenged, my thoughts were that I should do my part to, as he suggested, "let things simmer," at least for the present. This wasn't the time, I concluded, to pull any more stunts. Head down, I concentrated on my office work.

It turned out to be the right choice. There was considerable further mileage yet to be gained from our "relationship," including a substantial pay raise, meant, I assumed, to help me keep my mouth shut.

When I complained to my flatmate about my "man" problems, she seemed loathe to listen, interrupting me to announce that she'd lost interest in men. Conceivably, this meant she was attracted to women, and, given that she had hardly any close female friends other than me, that she was declaring a monogamous interest in me.

The next evening, already tiring of the intense, almost claustrophobic nature of our increasingly fraught relationship, I felt the need to get away from everything for a while. My flatmate, who'd been drinking, told me she was depressed, and had taken a sleeping pill. We curled up under her duvet and she quickly fell asleep in my arms. I delicately extracted myself from her embrace, walked into the living room, and called my French lover.

He answered the phone, and half an hour later he reluctantly let me into his flat while talking on his cell phone. He conducted me into his bedroom, then turned his back on me and continued talking, the phone conversation obviously outweighing me in importance.

Feeling aggrieved, I busied myself looking about the room, my eyes settling on an open letter on his dressing table. Bored, I picked it up and read it. Even with my rudimentary knowledge of French, I could decipher its overtly romantic tone. It was clearly written by his fiancé, whom he'd failed to mention. Apparently, he'd come to England for *two* reasons, one of which he had also carefully avoided talking with me about: The first was to improve his business prospects. The second, however, was to garner enough money for their wedding. So, the deceitful bastard had been using me all along, just as I had been using him!

The envelope was scented and had a reddish impression of her lips on the back. A photo of her fell from an inner fold of the letter; in it, she was smiling happily, as if infused with all the joys of the world. Next to her was my duplicitous Frenchman, arm about her waist, in a typical lover's pose. She *was* beautiful, I had to admit. Unquestionably so. And her love for him was evident. I crumpled the letter and tore the photograph in eighths. According to the letter, she was to arrive tomorrow.

My two-timing lover continued talking on his phone in the next room, I assumed totally immersed in conversation with her, so I slipped off my slinky underwear, carefully rubbed on my scent, and tucked them in his top drawer among his things. Being a man, he wouldn't notice what any woman in love would spot immediately.

Rejoining him in the living room, I discretely dropped a tube of my lipstick under his sofa cushion and one earring under the sofa. Having completed *my* preparations, I waited until he finished his call. The moment he put down the phone, I attacked. I sensed resistance, but I didn't care. I tore off his shirt, making the buttons fly into the air, knowing that not only was it his favorite shirt, but also the one in the photograph, most likely a present from her. We had a what turned out to be a somewhat vacuous lovemaking session, which didn't, in my opinion, amount to much of a swan song. When it was time to part, he told me he didn't want to see me again. I gave the impression I was shocked and deeply hurt. Then began to work on his guilt, throwing a tantrum, saying I was so devastated I felt suicidal. In actuality, at this point, all I felt was relief. The end of this relationship was long overdue. As he escorted me out the door, I felt sure he was glad to see me gone, no doubt regretting we'd ever met. For me, I'd messed with his head and hoped I had left a sufficient stain on his relationship with this other woman that he'd never be able to get over me.

On my way back to my flat, I decided I needed a weekend in the quiet of the countryside to gain perspective on my seemingly out-of-control life. A weekend with my parents. It would no doubt prove dull but they were always supportive, and that was exactly what I needed, having left a trail of destruction in my wake, and feeling battered and bruised emotionally.

When I informed Angelica, my flatmate, she rounded on me about betraying her when I slipped out the night before. It was true that what I'd done had been despicable, but our conversation reinforced my feeling that she was trying to shackle me. She had so many parties she could go to, and yet she mourned our parting for even a couple of days.

Later that day, she seemed resigned as she watched me fold my clothes and arrange them in my case. Several times she tried to initiate intimate physical contact, but each time I maintained my resolve and pulled away. Eventually her self-restraint broke altogether and she clasped my hands with desperation. She tried to kiss me, but embarrassed, I spurned her intimacy, laughing instead to ease the tension, in the end, making cruel light of something I knew was terribly important to her, and just maybe to me. Stretched to my limit, I couldn't constrain myself from making several more insensitive retributory remarks. I told her she was being ridiculous, that she needed to sort her life out, that I was a free spirit, answerable to no one, and that I resented her clinging to me as if I was somehow beholden to her. If she wanted some lesbian action, she should seek out a lesbian bar. My intentionally hurtful words, cast her into the depths of depression. After several moments of tense silence, her face and shoulders drooped. She was no longer the powerful Grecian sculpture of a woman I'd first met. She looked pathetic. I remember, thinking back on this moment, that I'd destroyed her.

When I dislodged my hands from hers, she retired to her room, where it sounded as if she were pacing up and down. As I left the flat, I heard muffled sobbing, then a hysterical scream followed by the sound of china smashing against a wall. I could have easily changed my mind and returned, if only to sooth her, but I didn't. Instead, I walked callously away.

On the way to the train station, I called my parents and told them I was coming. Naturally, they were delighted. I was evasive about which train I would catch. I didn't want two overprotective parents waiting at the station to smother me. I wanted to appear a successful, independent, self-assured woman, totally unlike their pre-coma daughter. I can't deny that the thought of being pampered by them had appeal, but what I really needed were some long walks in the country to sort out my feelings and re-establish the agenda I'd committed to prior to leaving Hell.

The train arrived at my destination late in the evening. The platform was dark and deserted, and I felt truly alone. I breathed a sigh and began dragging my case down the dark cobbled road to my parents' house. As I trudged along, wisps of night fog began creeping about me, obscuring the stars, then the moon, and finally the scenery. A few moments later, it began to drizzle.

It was then I heard a twig break behind me, followed by the click of heels on stone. I didn't panic, but I recall feeling distinctly uneasy. I picked up my pace, only to hear the footsteps behind do the same and slowly get closer rather than more distant. I turned abruptly in an attempt to see my stalker, but the combination of darkness, fog and drizzle made it impossible to see anything more than a foot away.

I turned and further upped my pace, my effort being frustrated by having to drag the case across cobblestones. The dense fog abruptly parted, and, in that moment, I turned and caught the outline of a person not far behind me. The fog immediately re-engulfed the elusive figure.

My sense of dignity hindered me from calling out for help, but I nonetheless discarded my luggage and began running, hampered now by the high heels I was wearing. I couldn't shake my pursuer. To my horror, I could hear labored breathing directly behind me.

I froze when a hand grasped my shoulder and turned to face the specter in what seemed like slow motion. As I did, I felt a watery splash on my face followed by excruciating pain. I closed my eyes and began to scream at the sound of my flesh sizzling. Trickles of the liquid ran from my face into my hands, which began sizzling, adding further to my horror and pain. My legs buckled and I fell to the ground. Writhing in agony, I screamed until my voice went hoarse. My assailant, whoever it was, hovered over me for some time, no doubt to witness my agony and relish the results of the effort.

In my half-conscious state, I thought about all the relationships I'd destroyed, any one I could imagine sufficient for the victim to enact this outrageously savage revenge on me. I finally passed out, but not before I heard my assailant trudge away. When I awoke, I was back in Hell, this time with no further level to descend.

About the Author

Born in 1961, in Reading, England **Francis Powell** attended Art Schools, receiving a degree in painting and an MA in printmaking. In 1995, Powell moved to Austria, teaching English as a foreign language while pursuing his varied artistic interests adding music and writing. He currently lives in Paris, songwriting, doing concerts, writing both prose and poetry. Powell has published short stories in the magazine, *Rat Mort* and other works on the internet site "Multi-dimensions."

Other Works by This Publisher

If you enjoyed *Flight of Destiny* consider these other fine works from Savant Books and Publications:

Essay, Essay, Essay by Yasuo Kobachi
Aloha from Coffee Island by Walter Miyanari
Footprints, Smiles and Little White Lies by Daniel S. Janik
The Illustrated Middle Earth by Daniel S. Janik
Last and Final Harvest by Daniel S. Janik
A Whale's Tale by Daniel S. Janik
Tropic of California by R. Page Kaufman
Tropic of California (the companion music CD) by R. Page Kaufman
The Village Curtain by Tony Tame
Dare to Love in Oz by William Maltese
The Interzone by Tatsuyuki Kobayashi
Today I Am a Man by Larry Rodness
The Bahrain Conspiracy by Bentley Gates
Called Home by Gloria Schumann
Kanaka Blues by Mike Farris
First Breath edited by Z. M. Oliver
Poor Rich by Jean Blasiar
Ammon's Horn by Guerrino Amati
The Jumper Chronicles by W. C. Peever
William Maltese's Flicker by William Maltese
My Unborn Child by Orest Stocco
Last Song of the Whales by Four Arrows
Perilous Panacea by Ronald Klueh
Falling but Fulfilled by Zachary M. Oliver
Mythical Voyage by Robin Ymer
Hello, Norma Jean by Sue Dolleris
Richer by Jean Blasiar
Manifest Intent by Mike Farris
Charlie No Face by David B. Seaburn
Number One Bestseller by Brian Morley
My Two Wives and Three Husbands by S. Stanley Gordon
In Dire Straits by Jim Currie
Wretched Land by Mila Komarnisky
Chan Kim by Ilan Herman
Who's Killing All the Lawyers? by A. G. Hayes
Ammon's Horn by G. Amati

346

Wavelengths edited by Zachary M. Oliver
Almost Paradise by Laurie Hanan
Communion by Jean Blasiar and Jonathan Marcantoni
The Oil Man by Leon Puissegur
Random Views of Asia from the Mid-Pacific by William E. Sharp
The Isla Vista Crucible by Reilly Ridgell
Blood Money by Scott Mastro
In the Himalayan Nights by Anoop Chandola
On My Behalf by Helen Doan
Traveler's Rest by Jonathan Marcantoni
Keys in the River by Tendai Mwanaka
Chimney Bluffs by David B. Seaburn
The Loons by Sue Dolleris
Light Surfer by David Allan Williams
The Judas List by A. G. Hayes
Path of the Templar - Book 2 of The Jumper Chronicles by W. C. Peever
The Desperate Cycle by Tony Tame
Shutterbug by Buz Sawyer
Blessed are the Peacekeepers by Tom Donnelly/Mike Munger
Purple Haze by George B. Hudson
The Turtle Dances by Daniel S. Janik
The Lazarus Conspiracies by Richard Rose
Imminent Danger by A. G. Hayes
Lullaby Moon by Malia Elliott of Leon & Malia
Volutions edited by Suzanne Langford
In the Eyes of the Son by Hans Brinckmann
The Hanging of Dr. Hanson by Bentley Gates
Written in the Stars - An Anthology edited by Sabrina Favors

Coming Works
Elaine of Corbenic by Tima Z. Newman
Ballerina Birdies by Marina Yamamoto
All Things Await by Seth Clabough
Crazy Like Me by Erin Lee
More, More Time by David Seaburn

http://www.savantbooksandpublications.com

www.ingramcontent.com/pod-product-compliance
Lightning Source LLC
Chambersburg PA
CBHW051228260626
47162CB00002B/325